WHEN WILLA JO TEMPLE IS FOUND STABBED THROUGH THE HEART ON THE FLOOR OF HER BEAUTY SHOP, THE GOOD FOLK OF SUMMERSET, NC ARE SENT INTO A TIZZY.

It's up to her ex-husband, Sheriff Tal Hicks, to investigate. Evidence points to four possible suspects: Willa Jo's business partner; a town socialite; a preacher's wife; and Willa Jo's live-in lover.

Willa Jo kept a notebook containing all the secrets she's learned while doing hair. Rumor has it Willa Jo is going to write a book, exposing everything. But now, Willa Jo is dead and the incriminating notebook is missing, leaving the sheriff with very little to go on. As he interrogates the suspects, he finds himself attracted to newcomer, Clarissa Myers. He delves into her past only to discover she has deeper ties to Summerset than anyone imagined. Before the sheriff can complete his interrogations, however, another suspect, Avenelle Young, confesses.

The sheriff is skeptical about Avenelle Young's guilt because she refuses to discuss what happened with Willa Jo. Her statement is a terse declaration of guilt, with neither motive nor method explained. The sheriff has no choice but to incarcerate Mrs. Young.

During the investigations, as the secrets of Summerset are slowly revealed, each family touched by Willa Jo's death must come to terms with the new information being unearthed. The repercussions are far-reaching, and forgiveness hard to come by. However, at the heart of the book is the possibility of reconciliation among the town folk as they learn the real 'truth' about one another.

"Anne Clinard Barnhill's first book came from her heart. Her second two historical novels were masterfully researched and her most recent book, *The Beautician's Notebook,* is just a lot of fun. The story centers around the tragic and suspicious death of the popular local beautician at The Sassy Lady, Willa Jo Temple. Willa Jo is so popular, as a matter of fact, that she has a string of husbands and boyfriends and, for the price of a haircut, she'll entertain clients with tidbits of her outlandish behavior. As Willa Jo shares her scandalous life, others reveal bits and pieces of their own past indiscretions. As Willa Jo says, 'You'd be amazed at what people will tell you while they're getting a pedicure.' What only a few people know is that Willa Jo is taking notes and some say she plans to write a tell-all book one day. Upon her death, the notebook goes missing and when it's found, suddenly there are quite a number of suspects. This is a great 'who-done-it' that will keep you reading until the very last page."—*Brenda Bevan Remmes, author of The Quaker Cafe and Home to Cedar Branch.*

"What a treat! Anne Clinard Barnhill has penned a mystery with heart and soul. Her characters are so likeable — even lovable — that I hated to think of any of them guilty of a heinous crime . . . despite their many motives. An intriguing and heartwarming novel."—*Diane Chamberlain, NYT bestselling author of The Silent Sister.*

"More red herrings than in a fishmonger's wheelbarrow."—*Molly Weston, Mystery Writers of America Raven Award Winner.*

THE BEAUTICIAN'S NOTEBOOK

Anne Clinard Barnhill

Moonshine Cove Publishing, LLC
Abbeville, South Carolina U.S.A.

FIRST MOONSHINE COVE EDITION APRIL 2017

ISBN: 978-1-945181-11-5
Library of Congress Control Number: 2017937786

Cover image by Orville Hengen, Marie-Pierre Fletcher, Maxine McCullar and Jason Smith; cover design by Moonshine Cove staff.

For all mothers and daughters

Acknowledgment

First, I'd like to thank Gene Robinson and the folks at Moonshine Cove Publishing, LLC for taking a chance on *The Beautician's Notebook.* This book took over my life while I was in the middle of an entirely different novel, thanks to my own beautician, the inimitable DeLana Holden, owner/operator of A Cut Above Beauty Salon in Shallotte, NC. She inspired me with her stories of funny things people said while getting their hair done and she told me she'd kept a notebook of these tales. From that point, Willa Jo Temple was born and the entire, fictitious town of Summerset, NC came to life.

I'd also like to thank Lisa Anderson, owner/operator of The Spa at Anaya Salon, and her staff, for technical advice.

Another expert who advised me, kindly giving me a tour of the local jail and government offices as well as explaining procedure and North Carolina law, was Det. E. H. Carter, Jr. He doesn't know it, but he became my inspiration for Sheriff Tal Hicks. Please note that any technical errors are mine and mine alone.

Another thanks goes to my friends, Marie-Pierre and John Fletcher, whose beach house provided much-needed experience about what it's like to live at the shore.

I'd like to thank my early reader and fellow-writer, Kathryn Lovatt, for her always right-on comments, and to Jean Newland, another early reader, for her encouragement. To my parents, who have provided me with good examples of how to live fully and well. And finally, I'd like to thank my husband, Frank, my first reader always, for his honesty, his insight into what makes a good story and for his unwavering faith in my work.

About The Author

Anne Clinard Barnhill is an award-winning writer who has published two, acclaimed historical novels *(At the Mercy of the Queen* and *Queen Elizabeth's Daughter),* one short story collection *(What You*

Long For), one memoir *(At Home in the Land of Oz)* and one poetry chapbook *(Coal, Baby).* Her memoir was used as text in a college course and a short story has been staged.

Anne Clinard Barnhill lives on the coast of North Carolina in a garage apartment next door to her parents. During basketball season, Anne, her husband, Frank, and her parents enjoy watching the Tar Heels. The mother of three sons, Anne enjoys visits from her boys and their families, playing charades, bridge and ping-pong. She also sings in the church choir and fiddles with the piano. She is currently at work on two novels set in West Virginia where she grew up.

https://www.amazon.com/Anne-Clinard-Barnhill/e/B001JP7XSC/ref=sr_tc_2_0?qid=1485271047&sr=1-2-ent

Other Works

Novel:

Queen Elizabeth's Daughter
At the Mercy of the Queen

Short Story Collection:

What You Long For

Memoir:

At Home in the Land of Oz

Poetry:

Coal, Baby

The Beautician's Notebook

Chapter One

"Sharing a tale always eases the burden of carrying it around."

~The Beautician's Notebook

Early May

Sheriff Tal Hicks worried about his daughter, Annie Jo. He hadn't been able to find her to give her the bad news. He'd tried her cell — she didn't have a land line — he'd sent an email, messaged her on Facebook: "please call me we need 2 talk" She hadn't responded. No surprise there. How long had it been since he'd spoken to her? Six months? Seven? Now, he was on his way to her trailer.

He dreaded seeing her. He was nervous about being around his two-year-old grandson, Lawson. Even for a short time. The boy made him uneasy, reminded him of all the ways he'd failed his daughter. Annie Jo was estranged from Tal, but kept a tenuous relationship going with her mother — *used* her mother, the way Tal saw it. Willa Jo sometimes babysat their grandson. Probably gave Annie Jo a little cash once in a while; hell, probably every week. Willa Jo wouldn't want Lawson to go hungry.

Where had it all gone wrong with Annie Jo?

She'd been in and out of trouble since middle school. First, it had been cheating on tests. Then, shoplifting fingernail polish at the local Walmart. Good God, nail polish? In high school, she'd come home drunk or high and Willa Jo would call him, all teary, asking him what to do. They'd tried everything — counseling, tough-love, kicking her out — nothing seemed to deter her from her downward spiral. Tal knew she slept around a lot — you hear things in a small town like Summerset. But when she got pregnant and decided to keep the baby, he and Willa Jo had hoped she would grow up, become responsible. Had she?

How the hell would he know *what* she was doing? Maybe she *had* matured; after all, she'd stayed out of trouble with the law for two years. Tal figured little Lawson kept her busy. Plus, she'd picked up a few shifts waitressing at The Porky Pig when she could get Willa Jo to babysit. He hoped the news he was about to give her wouldn't send her into a tailspin.

He pulled into the yard where the dilapidated trailer stood. The grass was tall with a few dandelions dotting the lawn. A little plastic wagon half-filled with dirty water lay on one side of the porch step and a tricycle was turned upside down nearby. A couple of pieces of paper —from old McDonald's 'happy meals' it looked like —littered the porch itself. Hicks shook his head as he stepped on the stoop and banged on the metal door.

He heard the baby cry and Annie Jo swearing under her breath.

"Who is it?" she yelled.

"It's me —Daddy," Tal said.

He thought he heard her say, "Oh shit," but he couldn't be sure. Maybe it was the wind or the baby babbling. She opened the door, little Lawson on her hip. Tal hadn't seen her in such a long time. All he wanted to do was hug her, tell her everything would be okay. But he knew she'd never allow it.

She looked rough, dark hair hanging all stringy around her face, her eyes puffy. She mirrored her mother, but she wasn't as pretty, not as striking. Lawson seemed healthy with chubby cheeks and a head of curly black hair capping his head. His big brown eyes looked up at Tal as if looking at a stranger. Of course, he *was* a stranger to the child.

It was Tal's fault the boy didn't know him. Tal had stayed away, afraid of making things worse with Annie Jo. She'd told him she would never welcome him back into her life--- she'd made that damn clear. And he had acquiesced. Coward.

Plus, if he found the punk who'd done this to Annie Jo, he knew he'd beat the shit out of the boy. So, he steered clear of his daughter and her friends. And his only grandchild.

Tal looked at his brown-skinned grandson and gave the kid a smile. The boy smiled back tentatively.

"What do you want?" Annie Jo said. She didn't even invite him in.

"I have something to tell you," he said quietly. She must have sensed something in his tone, because she immediately opened the screen and nodded for him to take a seat.

The trailer was a mess — toys and clothes strewn everywhere, sippy-cups on the sofa and floor —Hicks shook his head. How had it come to this?

"So, what's so important you have to drive all the way out here to tell me," Annie Jo said.

"I called, left messages. I emailed. I even used Facebook," he said. "You didn't respond."

"Didn't get em. I'm a little busy here," she said, nodding to her son. "So why are you here, Daddy?"

"It's about your mother....we got a call early this morning from Trudy. Annie, honey, there's no easy way for me to say this....Trudy found your mother dead on the beauty parlor floor when she came in for work...I'm so sorry," he said. Never get *that* picture out of his head — Willa Jo, splayed out on the floor, blood pooled beneath her. He'd seen bad stuff before. Hell, he was a professional. But the vic had never been his ex-wife, the mother of his only child.

He shuddered.

"Dead? Mom? Bullshit! This is just another scheme. Ya'll trying to shock me into getting my life together — going to community college? Moving back in with Mom?" Annie Jo said, her voice full of bitterness. She grabbed a pencil out of Lawson's hand and handed him a stuffed kitten. "What's really going on, Dad?"

"I wish it *were* some crazy scheme — your mama sure did pull a few, didn't she?" A slight smile played over his mouth as he thought of Willa Jo and all her finagling. "But no, Annie Jo — the sad truth is, your mama's dead."

Lawson started to fuss. Not a loud squall, like when a baby was hungry. Just a soft little whimper, as if he could sense something was very wrong. Annie Jo sat down hard on the sofa; her knees had given out. The jolt made Lawson cry louder.

"What...what happened? Mom's only forty-three. Was it a heart attack? A stroke?" she patted Lawson's back absent-mindedly, the way all mothers do.

"I...I'm not quite sure. She was stabbed in the chest with her scissors...she might have fallen or ...well, we just don't know yet...there could be someone else involved."

"Do you mean she might have been....*murdered*? Who in the world would want to kill Mom? Did they rob the place? I know she sometimes kept right much cash in the drawer — I've taken a few bills myself — but she never kept enough to get killed over," said Annie Jo, her voice rising, her words tumbling out. "Mom would have given a robber whatever he wanted — she told me that a zillion times."

"We're just not sure yet, honey. I've got my deputies scouring the place now and I'm talking to folks —delivering the news." He rubbed his temples. He'd delivered this kind of news many times, thought he'd hardened himself to it. But to his baby girl? He was at a loss.

"But you're sure Mom is....dead, right? Oh, my God! Oh, my God!" she said, her face pale. Her mind couldn't grasp the news — Tal knew that familiar response — denial. She held Lawson tight against her. No tears. They would come later. Now, she would try to make sense of everything. Tal had seen just about every kind of reaction when someone learned of the passing of a dear one. He prepared himself for *anything* with Annie Jo.

"How come the Summerset police aren't taking care of things — look Daddy, I know you still love her. Hell, everybody knows it. Aren't you too close to the case?"

He hadn't expected *that.*

"Well, it's in Chadwick County jurisdiction — she lived outside the city limits. And my Major Crimes detective is out on maternity leave. So, reckon it's up to me." He stood to leave; there was so much left to do.

"But Daddy, who will make all the arrangements? What should I do?"

"Baby, I just don't know right now. Reckon you and your granddaddy will have to get together and plan things out. In a day or so. Why don't you call Kayla? You need your friends right now."

Suddenly, Annie Jo hugged him, Lawson still in the crook of her elbow. He slowly wrapped his arms around them both. They stood there, touching, for longer than he could have ever dreamed. Maybe there was hope for them, somehow. Maybe Willa Jo hadn't taken their chance for reconciliation with her. After a few minutes, he broke the family hug and took his leave, reminding her again to call her best friend, telling her to call him day or night if she needed anything, anything at all.

He knew she didn't wanted him to go, not yet. But he had no choice. He had a job to do. As he walked to the car, he could hear things crashing in the house and Lawson crying. Annie Jo....his poor baby.

Chapter Two

"Now don't you tell me anything you don't want me to put in my little notebook."

~The Beautician's Notebook

Early May

Tal Hicks never got over Willa Jo. Never married again. Oh, he dated around — a few schoolteachers and one gal who taught a kick-boxing class. He got laid as much as he wanted — women seemed to like him, called him good-looking. For the last six months or so, he'd been carrying on with two women, one in Wilmington and one in Myrtle Beach — he didn't want his private life to be the talk of Chadwick County. He kept himself in shape, both for the job and for the women. But no woman he'd met so far had interested him enough to think in terms of the 'forever' love you saw in the movies — the kind he'd found with Willa Jo. He figured once a man had been married to a woman like Willa Jo, well, every other woman seemed to pale by comparison.

Tal and Willa Jo had grown up together, from first grade on. They were in the smart kids' classes, though neither of them ever made it to college. But they'd done okay for themselves. The Sassy Lady brought in a pretty penny for Willa Jo and her partner, Trudy. And, though a sheriff's salary wasn't much, the pension was awesome — that was why Tal had stayed in law enforcement so long. That, plus the fact he'd always wanted to be a hero. Always wanted to help people and save the day, if he could.

Did a piss-poor job saving Willa Jo.

She'd been a beauty, even as a child. That long, dark hair — you don't see many little kids with black hair. Most of them have various shades of blond and brown. It marked her, that hair. Made her different. Willa Jo's mama, Miss Bessie, used to fix Willa Jo's hair in all kinds of ways. Sometimes, she came to school looking like she was going to a Miss America contest. Other times, her hair would be in two pigtails. When she wore her hair *that* way, Tal knew they were in for some fun, like stealing apples from old man Ballard's tree.

Back then, Willa Jo was fearless. And a tomboy. One time —they couldn't have been older than nine —they'd gone to church camp up in the mountains. On the third day of camp, Willa Jo talked Tal into hiking up to the rock quarry. Years ago, some company had mined gravel and left behind a big lake of fresh, blue water. The campers told stories about the 'Ghost of the Quarry,' supposedly a girl who had thrown herself onto the rocks because of a lost love. Willa Jo wanted to see the place for herself. The quarry was forbidden to campers because of the danger. The camp counselors had told the kids several teenagers had drowned there, and if Tal's mama had known he was going, she'd have tanned his hide with a leather strap. But his mama didn't know. She far away, back home in Summerset.

The morning was fine, though hot. It was early June, right after school had let out for the summer. Willa Jo and Tal met at the outdoor amphitheater where the campers had their nightly bonfires. She grabbed his hand and led the way. By the time they'd walked all the way to the quarry, sweat rolled down Tal's face and he could see Willa Jo was struggling with the heat, too. Willa Jo had packed a lunch and Tal couldn't wait to drink cold water from his thermos.

Finally, they arrived and Tal watched as Willa Jo slipped her dress over her head, revealing a green bathing suit —Tal was struck at how it matched her eyes. Willa Jo climbed down the rocks to a boulder that jutted out over the water.

"You gonna jump from here? Or you too scared of the 'ghost girl?'" Tal said.

"Ghost girl don't scare me. You comin?" she said.

"Er...ain't it awful high?" he said.

"High enough. I can feel the wind — it's cold! Come on!" she yelled as she dove into the water below. It must have been twenty, thirty feet or so. Tal was scared to death Willa Jo would hit a rock as she went down or smash her head on one after she'd broken the smooth surface. That was what had happened to 'ghost girl.'

They'd been told the quarry had one safe place to land and if you missed it, well, you were out of luck. So the camp counselors said.

One. Safe. Place.

Willa Jo didn't miss. She was bobbing around in the water, waving her arms for Tal to join her. He didn't want her to think he was chicken-shit, so he said a quick prayer and did a cannonball into the coldest water he'd ever felt. Willa Jo was there, treading water, waiting for him.

"You're awesome, Tal! The best!" she said, hugging him.

Tal felt as if he'd grown a couple of inches. The rest of the day, they sunned on the rocks, eating cheese crackers, playing games, diving into the water again and again. They saw no sign of the 'ghost girl.'

And now, Willa Jo was gone. The love of his life lay in her own shop, her hair-cutting scissors stuck in her chest. What happened, Wil? What the hell happened? That look on Annie Jo's face, the few tears he'd seen her brush away as he left her —her pain added to the hurt he already felt. His sorrow gurgled up, threatening.

Hell, he was a professional. He didn't have time for tears. Something suspicious had happened to his ex-wife and it was his job to find out what it was.

Chapter Three

"A woman's hair is her crowning glory but I've lost my crown — can you help me?"

~The Beautician's Notebook

Early May

"Mad Dog" Tommy McGee panicked when he saw flashing blue lights reflected on his bedroom ceiling. He had some weed stashed in Willa Jo's walk-in closet and he just knew the sheriff was coming to arrest him. Almost 10:30 in the morning, and Mad Dog wasn't even dressed yet. He'd had a late night, drinking and making love to Willa Jo — whew, that woman could go all night long. She was already downstairs at work. When she'd first suggested he move in with her, he hadn't liked the idea. Customers coming and going all day, the fumes of the beauty parlor wafting through the house. But doing hair and earning money made Willa Jo happy and when she was happy, Mad Dog was, too. She made her dreams come true and Mad Dog had a dream of his own. Willa Jo said she could help him, but he knew he had to keep her satisfied to be certain she would carry through with everything she'd promised.

Racing cars, the faster, the better. That was Mad Dog's dream. And he was getting close, all because of Willa Jo.

Richard 'Rock' Bonner, Willa Jo's daddy, from over at Bonner's Chevrolet, backed Mad Dog for a year, but, sadly, he'd lost every damn race. None of it was his fault! He'd had a string of bad luck — broken axel, blown transmission, a couple of flats. Bonner'd withdrawn his measly support after that. But Mad Dog was coming back! He was a damn good driver, and the best there was at weaseling extra horse power out of any engine, in spite of his lousy luck. Willa Jo had promised to sponsor him herself, her and some of her rich friends — he thought she'd said something about her best friend, Clarissa Myers, coming in on the deal, but he wasn't sure. Clarissa meant *money*, lots of it.

He heard the Sheriff knocking on the door, hard.

Oh, hell. He grabbed his jeans from the floor, brushed his fingers through his hair, getting his hands caught in the wind chimes Willa Jo had hanging everywhere. Why the hell did they have to have chimes every-damn-where? He took out his ear plugs and put them in the box on the sink. He'd worn them since he'd moved in with Willa Jo — those damn chimes. And the yakkity women getting their hair done. He stumbled out of the bedroom and headed toward the relentless banging on the front door.

"Morning, Sheriff. What can I do for you?" Mad Dog said through the screen.

"Mind if I come in, Mr. McGee? I'm afraid I have some bad news."

Shit. The weed. Mad Dog scratched his head, trying to figure out how to keep the sheriff from finding it. Good thing he hadn't brought one of those sniffing dogs. He opened the door and led the sheriff into the living room and indicated for him to sit down. Then, Mad Dog sat down across from him on the sofa. The chimes on the windows outside were tinkling and ringing. The noise was getting on his nerves.

"There's no easy way to say this, so I'll just come out with it. Willa Jo's dead. Found this morning downstairs in the shop."

Mad Dog sank back as if he'd been punched in the gut. He couldn't breathe. His head swam and he thought he might pass out. He'd just made love to her twelve hours ago —how could she be dead, right in his own —well, her own —house? How could he not know?

"W-w-what…I d-d-don't believe it…h-how?" Mad Dog's stuttering came back, just the way it always did when he was stressed.

"Trudy found her this morning when she came in to work…lying on the floor. She called 911 —didn't you hear the ambulance?"

"N-naw. I-I used ear p-p-plugs — the damn chimes," said Mad Dog.

"I see," said the sheriff, looking around at the wind chimes all around.

"So, what could have happened? Was it a robbery gone bad? What the hell happened?"

"That's what I'm trying to determine, Mr. McGee. I have to ask you some questions," said the sheriff.

"Sure…whatever you need."

"Are you okay? You look sorta pale."

Mad Dog shook his head as if that would change things. His heart thumped against his ribs and he felt as if everything were under water.

"No...no, I ain't okay. What do you want to know?" Mad Dog regretted the couple of bottles of wine he and Willa Jo had polished off that night. He couldn't seem to understand what was happening. Willa Jo? Dead?

"Did you see or hear anything? I mean, it happened right here. You must have at least heard something." The sheriff was eyeing him funny, like he thought Mad Dog was guilty of something.

"No sir. Crazy as it sounds, I didn't hear nothing. I wear ear plugs — damn chimes," said Mad Dog, gesturing to the chimes hanging both inside and out.

"I see what you mean —her collection seems a little over the top," said the sheriff.

"Well, that was Willa Jo, wasn't it? Hell, she's even got em in the bedroom."

"Did you notice or see anything — anything at all?"

"Didn't see nothing, either. We drank some wine —the ear plugs. Willa Jo plum wore my ass out...you know...How...how could such a thing happen?"

"Think, man! A car engine? A creaky floor? Anything? I cannot believe you were right here and heard *nothing*!"

"You calling me a liar, Sheriff?" Mad Dog couldn't think straight. He knew the sheriff suspected him — how could he *not*?

"How you and Willa Jo been getting along lately?"

"Great! Things were great between us. We spent most of last night...you know...basically screwing each other's eyeballs out — that's why I'm still half-asleep."

The sheriff looked perturbed when Mad Dog said that about screwing Willa Jo. Hell, he wouldn't like the idea of his ex-wife and Mad Dog getting it on. Willa Jo'd told him Tal Hicks was still in love with her. Everybody knew it.

"Sorry...I meant we were 'making love,' " said Mad Dog.

"Can you think of anyone who would want to harm Willa Jo?"

"No. From what I saw, everybody loved her,"

The sheriff gave him a hard stare. Oh shit. The sheriff thought *he'd* done it, killed Willa Jo. Everybody would think it was him. All the TV programs showed the husband as the guilty party. Or the boyfriend. Mad Dog was Willa Jo's live-in lover. They'd been living together for three years — best years of his life. Willa Jo'd been married three times already — that was enough for her. Said she didn't believe in the 'holy institution of marriage.' Called it a penal institution —he joked and said it was more like a 'penile institution.' That made her laugh. Lord, how Mad Dog loved Willa Jo's laugh. Big and loud, her mouth open and her eyes crinkling —Mad Dog thought she was the most beautiful woman he'd ever seen, even though she was forty-three. Ten years older, but that didn't matter. Hell, she was a wild woman in bed and, though he was younger, Mad Dog had a hard time keeping up with her. Thinking about her made him feel empty and sort of sick at his stomach.

"That part's true —at least, that's what I thought, too. Believe me, Mr. McGee, I'm as shocked as you are," the sheriff said.

"I'll bet. ...Look, I know you were her first husband...she told me about all her husbands."

"Yeah. I reckon I was first in a long line of fools for Willa Jo. She had something special, didn't she?"

"Hell yeah."Mad Dog could feel tears at his eyes. Dammit, he didn't want to cry in front of the sheriff.

"If you think of anything, anything at all that might help, give me a call."

"I will. I will."

Mad Dog sat back on the couch after he'd walked the sheriff to the front door. He could tell the sheriff thought he was crazy or lily-livered to allow the woman he loved to be murdered in the basement of their house while he slept above, slept blissfully the way you do after you've exhausted yourself in the sack.

Mad Dog reached for his cell phone and swiped to his address book, called his boss over at Woodridge's Garage where he was a mechanic. He told old man Woodridge he wouldn't be coming in today. All he could think about was Willa Jo. She was gone and now, his racing dream was gone, too.

Oh Willa Jo! What happened? What the hell happened? Mad Dog thought Sheriff Hicks had seemed pretty torn up himself. He wondered if her second husband, Ricky Temple, knew yet. Temple was part of the Temple family who had owned most of Temple Beach, one of the islands about fifteen miles from Summerset. Willa Jo had kept the Temple name (and half the Temple money) even after she'd married husband number three —Judge Luffy. Luffy turned out to be a wife-beater and that marriage didn't last six months. Mad Dog couldn't believe he knew all the stuff he knew about Willa Jo's husbands. Oh, Willa Jo...what was he gonna do now? So many thoughts, jumbled like fish in a net, swam around in Mad Dog's head.

He thought back to when he'd first met Willa Jo down at the Paradise Café on Temple Beach. He was knocking back a few beers after working in the shop all day.

That night, Willa Jo had walked up to him, pretty as you please, holding a fresh drink.

"Would you like some Sex-On-The-Beach?" she said, her full lips in a smile he could have died for right then and there. She was the sexiest woman he'd ever seen.

"What?" he stammered like a school boy.

"It's my favorite drink — can I get you one?" she said.

All Mad Dog could do was nod. He wasn't used to women coming up and buying him drinks. Not that he hadn't had his share of the ladies — but he usually had to make the first move. Willa Jo handed him *her* drink, then stepped up beside him at the bar. She crooked her finger at the bartender and he seemed to know exactly what she wanted. Another drink appeared in front of her in a matter of seconds.

To Mad Dog, Willa Jo was a force of nature. Once she set her eyes on a man, he didn't stand a chance. He could never understand why she picked him — he wasn't Hollywood handsome. He wasn't ugly either —just sort of so-so. At least, that was how he saw himself. But in Willa Jo's eyes, he was something else. She was always talking about his smile and the way the hair curled on his chest — red ringlets, she'd called it. She took him home with her that night and wouldn't let him leave. Within two weeks, he'd cancelled the lease on his apartment (Willa Jo had paid the fine) and moved all his stuff into her house.

Mad Dog was proud that she was his woman, even though she refused to marry him. He knew every man this side of the Mississippi would have crawled through broken glass to have a chance with her. Her dark hair was almost black and thick and wavy. And long. Halfway down her back when she didn't pin it up. When she danced, her hair moved, too, and all Mad Dog could think about that first night at the Paradise was how her hair would look all splayed out on a pillow, Willa Jo staring at Mad Dog with those big green eyes while he pumped himself into her. That was just the effect she had — you couldn't look at Willa Jo without thinking of getting her in bed.

She had one of those great little bodies, compact and tight-looking. Nothing sagged or jiggled. She was in shape, but she still had great curves. Lots of beauticians wore gobs of make-up, but not Willa Jo. She knew she was pretty enough without that gunk. Red lipstick and a little something around her eyes — and White Shoulders cologne — that was Willa Jo.

Thinking about her had made Mad Dog start to get hard. But she was dead. Dammit! Dead. How was he going to go on without her? Oh, Willa Jo, what have you done?

Chapter Four

"You'd be amazed at what people will tell you while they're getting a pedicure."

~The Beautician's Notebook

Early May

Temple Beach is a sliver of land, one in a chain of slim islets off the coast of North Carolina — the Chadwick Island Beaches, they call them. About a dozen miles long, Temple Beach is shaped like a golf club with a putter on the eastern end and a wood on the western. Scattered across the sand like shells are beach houses, colorful pastels for the most part: yellow, pink, aqua, lavender. But every once in a while, a bright red or blue one will appear, announcing itself loudly among the more muted shades.

In a wise decision made years ago, the Powers-That-Be ordained that no structure could be built higher than three stories on the island. Hence, you won't find tourists stacked like sardines in high-rises, the way they are in nearby Myrtle Beach, S.C., just an hour away. There, the hotels are crammed together —barnacles clinging to the shore. A vacationer could hear an argument two or three hotels away —that's how close they are.

Not so, here. At Temple Beach, the tides lap the sands, peacefully undisturbed for approximately seven months out of the year. From November to March, you can walk down the beach and see nothing but an occasional dolphin or a V of pelicans. Even on the Fourth of July, when the island is at its most crowded, you can still find a spot on the beach to stake out as your own, smooth your towel and plant your umbrella. And you won't have to rub shoulders with anyone.

And that privacy is exactly why Clarrisa Myers convinced her husband, Ralph, to move to Temple Beach Island. Clarissa's favorite time was when the coast was deserted completely and she could pretend she owned the whole island. She loved the roar of the ocean and the occasional cries of the gulls. Most of all, she enjoyed the constant changes of the sky and sea, the way the waves made her feel small and fragile, yet their sound was comforting, like a mother's heartbeat.

White sand contrasted with emerald green water. On cloudy days, sand the color of sludge pushed itself against a black sea covered by pewter clouds, hanging low and heavy. Or, on windy days, the water turned olive green capped with white foam, the sky a clean, clear blue dotted by puffy clouds scudding by. The shifting of the elements, shuffling and reshuffling themselves every moment, the glorious sunrises and sunsets — Clarissa loved it all.

Each morning, Clarissa and her husband, Ralph, walked along the beach with their little dog, Mitzy. Mitzy was a bichon, white and fluffy with button eyes. She seemed to love the island as much as Clarissa and Ralph did. Clarissa thought Mitzy looked like a fat sea biscuit on the sand.

Ralph and Clarissa had lived on the island for fifteen years, moving down from New Jersey, Mahwah to be exact. Ralph wanted to retire to a warmer place and Clarissa always did whatever Ralph wanted. She figured that was the best way to stay married to a rich man, a man thirty years her senior.

But it had been Clarissa who found Temple Beach. She couldn't explain why she was drawn to this particular place, as opposed to any of the other Chadwick County islands. After all, each had its charms. But the minute she set foot on Temple Beach, she felt a stir of something, as if the Universe had said — *This is it, Clarissa, the deep desire of your heart: home.* She didn't think; she didn't question. She simply told Ralph this was the place for them, and, for once, she'd been able to sweet-talk Ralph into doing something *her* way — it hadn't hurt that Ralph, too, loved the water.

Ralph was a millionaire. How many millions, Clarissa didn't know. All she knew was anything she wanted, she got. Ralph didn't blink when she wanted to redecorate the house every other year — new furniture, flooring, paint, the whole nine yards. She liked that. She liked it very much. She was happy to play Eliza Doolittle to his Henry Higgins. After all, he'd spent a small fortune creating her — a nose job, a college education, charm school to learn proper manners — who knew such places still existed, but they did. Ralph found one. And then, he draped her in silks and designer everything. She had enough rings to wear diamonds on her toes. The only thing Clarissa had to do to receive this bounty was to be charming and agreeable. She could do that.

After all, Ralph had saved her and she would do anything to keep him happy.

"So, what are you going to do this fine Mayday, my sweet?" Ralph said, stopping to pick up what looked like a complete whelk shell. He threw it back into the water when he discovered the bottom side was broken.

"Ooh, I'm getting a mani-pedi at The Sassy Lady," Clarissa said.

"Humph." Ralph walked a little ahead of her now.

Clarissa knew Ralph didn't like her going to The Sassy Lady because her best friend, Willa Jo Temple, ran the place. Ralph didn't approve of Willa Jo.

Clarissa would never forget the first time she met Willa Jo. She and Ralph had recently moved to the island —it had taken them weeks to unpack and get everything organized. They'd had to pick furniture and curtains, re-do the front deck and replace the kitchen cabinets and appliances. Before she knew it, Clarissa's roots had grown out to almost two inches. Not a good look for a forty-year-old brunette who had gone blond to suit her husband.

But Clarissa was very picky about who did her hair. One day, she was at the local Piggly-Wiggly (Clarissa *loved* the names of Southern stores —Piggly-Wiggly, Food Lion, Publix, Lowe's) when she saw a woman standing by the ice cream section, mesmerized. The woman had a precision cut in a rich brown color with golden highlights.

"I couldn't help noticing your haircut —very chic. Where do you get it done?" Clarissa said. She realized she must have sounded odd, so she tried to explain. "I'm new around here."

"Oh, honey, you don't have to tell me you're new —you don't talk like folks from around here. The best place for hair is The Sassy Lady. It's in Summerset —just about a fifteen-minute drive. Go all the way down Main Street, past the DMV and you'll find it. It's in a house, but you'll see the sign. Just go right in. Be sure to ask for Willa Jo," the lady said. She turned to leave, then leaned back around and whispered, "Believe me, you don't want Trudy."

Clarissa followed the woman's instructions that very afternoon, and made her way to The Sassy Lady. She felt odd parking in someone's driveway, but there were a couple of other cars there and the sign did say 'The Sassy Lady.' Clarissa tiptoed up to the door, knocked lightly and then pushed the door open. A thousand chimes announced her. She gave a little jump in surprise.

Inside, everything was silver and mirrors and black —except for the chairs, which were lipstick red. Sort of like a disco from the 70s, yet Clarissa thought it all worked. Somehow, the décor seemed stylish, cutting-edge.

Two beauticians clipped and snipped, one white and the other, black. Clarissa was surprised because she was in the South, and she had not expected to find an integrated salon, even in 2017. She felt her phone buzz and saw a text from Ralph —'when r u coming home' — she texted him back –'soon.'

The white beautician stopped cutting hair and looked at her.

"Can I help you?" said the woman, laughing. "Sure looks like I can!"

Clarissa blushed. "Well, as you can see, I'm in need of a color and cut —as soon as possible."

"Well, I'm all booked up for the next two weeks. How about end of May?" the woman said.

"Are you Willa Jo?" Clarissa asked. She remembered the warning about the other beautician.

"Sure am. And this is my partner, Trudy," she said, nodding at the black woman.

"Nice to meet you both," Clarissa said. She really didn't want to wait three weeks to get her hair done. She wasn't used to being told 'no.'

"Is there any way I can get in earlier?"

Willa Jo stared hard at Clarissa for what seemed like a very long time.

"I can tell by your accent you ain't from around here —so tell you what I'll do. Be here at 7:00 this evening and I'll fix you up right."

And that was it —the beginning of an abiding friendship. Clarissa knew Willa Jo was something special from the moment she first laid eyes on her; she knew Willa Jo was somebody different, somebody full of piss and vinegar. Willa Jo looked about the same age as Clarissa, with long, almost black hair; Clarissa could tell the color was natural. That hair reminded Clarissa of her own, back before she'd gone blond for Ralph.

That night, Willa Jo welcomed Clarissa with a mani-pedi, a saucy new cut that was perfect for her and a dye-job that took out the brass from Clarissa's hair and made it look soft, like Clarissa had been born blond.

Over the next few months, Clarissa came to adore Willa Jo —not in any sort of weird way —she wasn't a 'lezzie,' as Willa Jo called it. But there was something about Willa Jo that sang out to her and let her know she'd found a soul-mate, someone she could literally let her hair down around.

That's just the kind of thing Willa Jo would say —funny stuff and silly. Sometimes, when Clarissa got her hair done, she'd spend the whole day at the salon. She and Willa Jo would talk and laugh; Willa Jo always had champagne chilled and ready. And chocolate covered cherries! Both women loved them — one more thing they had in common.

But Ralph didn't care for Willa Jo —said she was loud and trashy. Definitely not the kind of woman he wanted Clarissa to cultivate as a friend. He'd told her over and over to make friends with the other women who lived on the island —women of her station, women with rich, powerful husbands Ralph might connect with for business. Ralph wanted her to go out to lunch, shop and be ready to cook up a party on the spur of the moment. But Clarissa didn't find those women of interest. First, they were much older than she. At forty, she wasn't interested in talking about grandchildren, or seeing cruise pictures. Don't misunderstand —Clarissa loved the charmed life she lived with Ralph. It was so much better than anything she'd known before he saw her waiting tables at Jersey Girl's Pizza Parlor and scooped her up, changing almost everything about her.

But after a few years of doing nothing but going to aerobics and hitting the mall, all those things she'd dreamed about doing as a kid, grew a little boring. There was nothing for Clarissa to sharpen herself against; everything flattened out into a pleasant life with few worries and even fewer surprises. She knew how damn lucky she was, being rescued by Ralph. But the other women seemed to expect it, as if they were somehow entitled to live such a life. Clarissa had noticed that when hard times hit —cancer, a car accident, a broken child —the women often didn't have what it took to survive. They hadn't had much practice with problems. Clarissa? She *knew* she could survive. If Ralph took every penny away from her, she could make it on her own. She'd done it all through her childhood and she knew, deep in her bones, beneath that 'dumb blond' hair beat a stout heart.

And that's one of the reasons she loved Willa Jo. Willa Jo had been through some stuff, too. She was tough and sassy, just like the name of her salon. And she was anything but boring.

That first meeting years ago had been a blessing in Clarissa's life, one for which she continued to be grateful. Life was good, especially with a friend like Willa Jo.

***

Clarissa was driving her new, sunburst yellow Corvette convertible when she heard her phone blare out "Light My Fire."

Ralph.

Why would he be calling her? He knew she was heading to Willa Jo's.

"What's up?" she said, slowing down on the two-lane road.

"Baby, I got some bad news...I'm so sorry. You need to come home."

"What's wrong? I've got my mani-pedi ..."

"Just come home, honey."

"Okay. I'll call Willa Jo and tell her I'm not going to make it. I'll pull over, don't worry."

"You don't have to call Willa Jo —I...I don't quite know how to tell you...I sure as hell didn't want to tell you over the phone...."

"You're scaring me...what on earth is wrong? Are you okay?"

"Honey —are you off the road?"

"I'm pulling over now —Okay, I'm completely stopped. What is it?" Clarissa's breath was coming fast.

"Sweetheart.... Willa Jo is dead. Now, come on home."

"Dead? But I just talked to her last night. How can she be dead? What happened?"

"I don't have all the details. But the sheriff's office just called — they were calling all her appointments for today. I'm so sorry. Do you want me to come get you?"

Clarissa sat in the driver's seat. She couldn't move. Willa Jo...dead?

"I...I'll be okay. I'm on my way."

Clarissa couldn't believe it. Willa Jo — dead. It didn't seem possible. Just last week they'd driven up to Wilmington to visit a psychic, The Crystal Chick. Willa Jo swore the Chick was the real deal. They'd each gotten a reading, but The Crystal Chick said not a word about Willa Jo being dead in a week.

Not the real deal, after all.

Clarissa didn't seem able to take it in. Willa Jo, gone, just like that. She didn't know what she was going to do now. Without Willa Jo to steady her, she feared she might go painfully astray.

Chapter Five

"You can tell a lot about a person from their toes."

~The Beautician's Notebook

Early May

Avenelle Young was typing up her husband, The Reverend Rory Young's, sermon for this coming Sunday. That's how she thought of Rory these days —not as her spouse or friend, but as The Reverend, the very arm of God, reaching out to judge and condemn her and anyone else with whom he disagreed. Like Abel, their younger son. He'd disinherited Abel just because the boy wanted to be a musician. Sure, Abel walked on the wild side —The Reverend didn't know it, but that unconventional streak must have come from Avenelle herself. Oh yes, meek wife. Avenelle.

The Reverend reminded her of the God of the Old Testament: angry and looking for vengeance and blood. If he'd known half of what was in Avenelle's heart, he might have fainted.

Her fingers trembled as they flew over the familiar keys. She felt cold and wondered if she was coming down with something. She'd had a difficult morning. To say the least.

The title of the sermon was "Secrets and Sin" and Avenelle felt a shudder in her belly as she began her weekly task. Could The Reverend know about her? Could he have stumbled on her deepest, darkest secret?

No, that was impossible. Avenelle's hidden past was safe; she was just being silly. Ever since the menopause hit her a couple of years back, Avenelle had not been her old self. She didn't smell right. She felt like a dried up locust, a shell of her former self. She missed her estrogen, even missed the messiness of her periods. Oddly, she yearned for the cramping that hit her every month. Those painful cramps had given her a couple days' respite, a time to shut herself away from Rory (he'd been plain Rory back then, back before he'd shown how cruel he could be) and their sons, Adam and Abel. She could escape into the coolness of the guest bedroom with its lilac walls and flowered bedspread. The boys knew not to disturb her during these times and even Rory stayed away. Now, there was nothing to break the constant work that seemed to seek her out. Nothing to save her from The Reverend's ever-growing needs.

She stared again at the computer screen, silently cursing herself for ever learning to do word processing in the first place. It had been The Reverend's idea, during the last recession, to let Mrs. Keene, secretary for almost thirty years, go. He replaced Mrs. Keene with Avenelle. For the last seven years, Avenelle fulfilled all the secretarial duties, including typing up these ridiculous sermons.

Oh, she shouldn't have called The Reverend's sermons ridiculous. She was unsettled this morning. She felt a case of 'the crazies' coming on. She'd had 'the crazies' since childhood. The first time 'the crazies' hit her was in seventh grade. She'd been late to class and the teacher angrily sent her to the principal's office. She'd been scared out of her wits — it was the first time she'd ever been sent to the principal. When he asked for her name, for some bizarre reason, she'd answered, "Algebra." She must have thought he'd wanted to know the class for which she'd been tardy. Or something. At any rate, she'd started laughing and laughing. He had to send her to the nurse's office to get her calmed down.

For the last few decades, she'd been able to fend off 'the crazies.' Usually, they showed up when she was under a lot of stress. She'd been calm for the most part, but not this morning. And she knew when 'the crazies' attacked, they attacked with a vengeance. They made her say and do things that were, well, crazy. Like considering The Reverend's sermons silly and pretentious. Another black mark in her book. Who was she to criticize The Reverend? Even if she thought his sermons didn't have much substance — no help people could use in real life. Nothing to tell you what to do with a broken heart and nothing to help you figure out the meaning of it all.

At fifty-six, Avenelle would be surprised if she got any answers about life's deep questions. So, she made the best of things — she enjoyed her grandson, Kevin, her older son, Adam's boy — and she worked in The Reverend's garden. Working in the sandy soil among the green plants and the multi-colored flowers soothed her more than any sermon she'd ever heard.

She jumped when her phone blared out "Amazing Grace" and quickly answered.

"I'm typing up your sermon right this minute," Avenelle said.

"Glad to hear it — listen, Nelle, I've got some bad news. Willa Jo Temple's dead. The sheriff found her body on the floor of The Sassy Lady — hair-cutting scissors straight through her heart — at least, that's what I heard from old Mrs. Croner." The Reverend's voice dropped to a whisper. "I'm afraid we are in for some hard times in Summerset — everybody's saying it might be murder."

"Oh my word — murder. Here? In Summerset? I don't remember there ever being a murder here. And Willa Jo! Of all people. What should I do?" Avenelle could feel her stomach twist.

"Well, go ahead and finish with that sermon, but I'll have to come up with another one for the funeral — it's set for Sunday afternoon. I'll have to comfort and calm folks. Right now, why don't you make up a casserole and take it over to Rock Bonner. I know he and Willa Jo weren't close, but he *is* her daddy," said the Reverend. Avenelle could hear him twisting his collar around—he always did that when he had to deal with a death.

"And make a little something for that young man she was living with — that washed up racecar driver. I think his name is McBee or McKay or something like that. I'll be home at suppertime." The Reverend sighed.

Avenelle almost panicked at the mention of Willa Jo's father, Rock Bonner, but she forced herself to remain calm. She had nothing to fear. Nothing.

"I'll make something good, but you'll have to deliver it. I feel a migraine coming on," Avenelle said as she ended the call. She didn't want to face Rock Bonner, not today.

She leaned back in her chair and took a sip of iced tea, something she kept at her desk when she worked on The Reverend's sermons. Her hands were shaking. It was real — Willa Jo — dead. Murdered. Avenelle couldn't stop imagining Willa Jo splayed out on the floor, blood oozing everywhere. Willa Jo would not have liked that, not one bit — she was a nut for cleanliness, always sweeping and mopping the shop. Avenelle tried to concentrate on her typing, but her mind kept wandering back to Willa Jo.

Avenelle had known Willa Jo since she was a little thing, no bigger than a minute. Willa Jo's mother, Bessie Jo, had done Avenelle's hair for years and she could remember little Willa Jo playing around the shop. Back then, it was Bessie's Beauty Parlor, plain and simple, like Bessie Jo herself. Bessie Jo had done a good enough job on Avenelle's hair, though sometimes she got too much red in the strawberry blond — but Willa Jo — well, she was a hair wizard.

She *shoulda* been good, after she threw a fit to attend that fancy cosmetology school up in Raleigh the minute she graduated high school. But that was Willa Jo — always wanted the best things in life and had a hissy fit if she didn't get them. Avenelle blamed Bessie for that. Bessie could not tell her only child 'No! ' It just wasn't in her.

Bessie was a little ahead of Avenelle in high school. Avenelle would always remember how Bessie had become pregnant right after her junior year. She and Rock Bonner — that was Richard Bonner these days, of Bonner's Chevrolet — had gone steady all during sophomore year. When Bessie found out she was pregnant, Rock did the right thing and married her. That was probably the only time in his life Rock Bonner had ever done the right thing, Avenelle figured. They had a big wedding up at Sabbath Home Church and Willa Jo was born six months later. The Reverend performed the ceremony, though he told Avenelle later he counseled them extensively about the nature of their sin and told them they could make things right by bringing up the baby in the house of the Lord. *That's my Reverend. Always on the side of the righteous.* The Reverend was about ten years older than Avenelle and always extolled the pleasures of purity to her right up until their wedding night. Avenelle tried not to think of *that*; instead, she turned her mind again to Bessie and Willa Jo.

Bessie was forced to quit school because back then, they didn't allow pregnant girls to continue their education. But a baby didn't stop Bessie. She went on to Chadwick County Community College and became a beautician. She stayed close to home, like a person with good sense. Not like that daughter of hers. Going to Raleigh is what ruined Willa Jo — that's what Avenelle thought anyway. No, that wasn't quite fair. It was Bessie that ruined Willa Jo, Bessie who gave that child everything she ever wanted. Willa Jo was ruined long before she went to Raleigh.

Avenelle tried once more to type up the Reverend's sermon. She wasn't in such a rush now, since he'd have to write a new one and she'd be required to type that one up, too. If she didn't get this current one finished today, well, the Reverend could kiss her foot. Avenelle poured herself another glass of iced tea and carried it outside. 'The crazies' were beginning to make their appearance known in the usual way — her big toe throbbed. She knew she needed to 'chill out,' as Abel called it. Her younger son was an expert at taking life easy.

She sat in her favorite wicker chair on the back porch. There was a cool breeze and her flowers looked so pretty. She sipped the tea and thought about Willa Jo and Bessie and Rock and sex and death.

After Willa Jo came back from Raleigh, she shocked the whole town by setting up her own beauty shop. Everyone had figured she'd join Bessie Jo, a mother-daughter team to keep the women of Summerset looking their best. But no, Willa Jo started The Sassy Lady, located in a pretty new mall right next to Belk's. The site was perfect. She must have borrowed money from somebody — everyone figured the money came from Judge Luffy — he never could turn down a pretty face. And off she went — in direct competition with her mama, mind you — and opened up her own shop. Before you could say 'dip-squat,' all the younger crowd headed to The Sassy Lady; Bessie was left with the old-timers, like Avenelle.

At first, Bessie was furious. She called Avenelle and asked to meet her at Duffer's Bar and Grill. Why, Bessie should have *known* Avenelle could not meet at such a place, being engaged to The Reverend by then. But she went anyway; she even drank a beer, after she'd asked the waitress to pour it carefully into an iced tea glass.

"My own daughter," Bessie said, as she slugged back a huge gulp of Budweiser.

"I'm so sorry, Bessie — I know how that must hurt," Avenelle said.

"But why? Why would she do such a thing? She knew she could come in with me — it would save her a lot of money. Why?"

"I don't know — sometimes, grown children need to cut the cord. Maybe that's what she's doing. Maybe she doesn't mean it as anything against you." Not that Avenelle had much to offer in the way of advice — she didn't know a lot about children.

Over time, the rift between Bessie and Willa Jo mended, though Avenelle thought they were never as close as they'd been before Willa Jo set up shop at The Sassy Lady. Avenelle thought Willa Jo's actions were part of what drove poor Bessie to her grave. She died just five years after Willa Jo started her business, long before her time. In spite of what Willa Jo had done, Bessie left her house and beauty salon to her daughter. Bessie and Rock Bonner had split up years before, when Willa Jo was only three. So Willa Jo owned everything outright.

Within three months, Willa Jo sold her cute little building next to Belk's and moved into her mother's house, bringing the sign for the shop with her. Bessie's Beauty Parlor was transformed into the 'new' Sassy Lady, with updated everything; she even put in bright red chairs. Willa Jo and her beauty salon reigned supreme in Summerset. The shop had won the 'Best Beauty Parlor' in the *Chadwick County Chitchat*'s annual 'Best Of Chadwick County' contest for the past eight years.

Avenelle watched as a hummingbird, the first of the season, buzzed past her in search of food. She would have to get her feeder up soon. She stared at the live oak tree in the back yard, its enormous limbs stretching out to shade the entire last quarter of the area. She loved that old tree — it seemed wise and peaceful. Her sons, even The Reverend, still liked to climb onto the thick branches and gather Spanish moss for the mantle at Christmas. Avenelle's eyes shifted from the tree to The Reverend's garden, laid out with the precision of an architect, kind of like Avenelle's life — exacting and predictable.

But not anymore.

With Willa Jo dead, she could put a black mark through her hair appointment next Friday. She always had her hair done on Fridays so it would look nice for church on Sunday. Where would she go, now, to get her hair fixed? She certainly would not be going to Trudy. Avenelle would never let Trudy touch her hair unless she was dead herself.

The more she thought about it, the more Avenelle felt upset, as if Willa Jo had died on purpose. But Willa Jo hadn't died on purpose, had she? She'd been murdered. Avenelle noticed her hands still shook as she lifted her glass to her lips. She knew she should feel sorry about what had happened to Willa Jo, but she felt sorrier for herself. She'd been going to the same family for her hair for most of her life. It seemed mighty selfish of Willa Jo to up and die without telling anybody. She should have left a list of suggested beauticians for her clients — an emergency list. Any sensitive, caring soul would have done that, at least. Now, what was Avenelle going to do? The Reverend liked for her to look nice at church. As he'd told her many times, she reflected on *him,* so she better do everything by the book — the Good Book, that is.

Avenelle could feel 'the crazies' threatening. What sort of woman thinks about her hair when poor Willa Jo's lying on the cold floor, dead? It was 'the crazies.' Poor Willa Jo…dead. Murdered!

But really, who *would* do Avenelle's hair for the funeral?

Chapter Six

"A small, slim woman of around seventy wanted me to dye her eyebrows. Then she said, 'Maybe you could dye the rest of my hair, too — you know — down there! The lady in the chair next to her, a three-hundred pounder (at least!) started laughing. 'I ain't see mine for years — I don't even know what color it is!"

~The Beautician's Notebook

May

Annie Jo changed Lawson's diaper, packed his bag and fastened them both in the old Subaru her dad had given her for high school graduation. Though she barely made it through and was a year behind her class, she'd finally earned enough credits to get her diploma. The Subaru — or Frodo, as she called it — was at least a dozen years old. But the old heap still ran, though Frodo needed new tires and left oil splotches everywhere she parked him.

She sat in the car for a moment and looked around. The place was a dump. No question. But it was all she could afford on welfare, food stamps and her part-time job. And, even though she was 'on the dole' as her Grandpa Rock would say, she was proud she'd never asked her parents for a dime. Her mother offered her money right after Lawson was born. Annie Jo told her to use the money to fly to Italy — her mother had always wanted to visit 'the land that gave us lasagna and tiramisu.' Willa Jo stormed out of the hospital room in tears. Willa Jo hadn't offered any money since. And, even though Annie Jo could have used help, she refused to beg. But her mother sometimes came to the trailer with a box of Pampers and a few groceries. And she did babysit Lawson whenever Annie Jo asked.

Annie Jo never said a word about it; now, she wished she'd thanked Willa Jo.

Annie Jo felt tired just looking at her yard. So much work to fix it up. Even if she mowed the grass and picked up all Lawson's stuff, the place would still be trashy. Trailer trash. That's what she was. Annie

Jo stared at the only redeeming point on the lawn —a dogwood tree in full bloom. Pink blossoms filled the limbs and Annie Jo knew that some time, a long time ago from the size of the dogwood, somebody had loved this little trailer, loved it enough to plant a tree that would bring pleasure in each season —flowers in spring, cool green shade in summer, colorful leaves in autumn and red berries in winter. The only other trees in sight were the scrub pines at the edge of the yard.

She put the car in gear and drove to Grissettown Road. She needed to see Trudy, needed to find out what had really happened to her mom. If anybody would know what was going on, it would be Trudy.

"Ready, Lawson?" she said. She checked the rearview mirror and saw Lawson busy with his cookie. She couldn't believe how calm she was — after all, her dad had just told her that her mother was dead...maybe even murdered. If this had happened two years ago, she would have gone off the deep end, drinking and smoking dope until she couldn't remember her own name, much less her mother's death.

But this was now. And now, she had Lawson to think about. She was all the baby had in this world. She refused to upset him. She'd learned to remain calm and do nothing that would tip the delicate balance between happy baby and screaming baby.

Even though she forced herself to remain steady on the outside, she could hear her heart banging against her ribs and feel the blood pulsing down to her fingertips. She was almost light-headed...felt a little like she was high. She pushed down on the pedal, whirring past the stands of pines lining the road, the swamp dotted with water lilies. The lilies made her think of little china cups set on the table of black, brackish water. When the lilies weren't in bloom, the swamp could look menacing. She was thankful they were there, cups of comfort on this otherwise miserable day.

The drive to Trudy's house took about twenty minutes. Annie Jo knew the road by heart. She'd spent the summer of her sophomore year baby-sitting for Trudy's daughters, Tacoma and Takeena, cute little girls, always wanting her to paint their toenails and fingernails. That summer, the girls had sported every color of the rainbow. Annie Jo figured Tacoma would be in high school herself by now, with Takeena, or 'Keena' as the family called her, not far behind.

Annie Jo pulled into Trudy's driveway, a lane covered with oyster shells. The small yard was neat and tidy, as Annie Jo knew it would be. She expected the inside to be just as clean. Trudy was 'neat-freak' as her mother used to say. Her mother. Annie Jo couldn't imagine life without Willa Jo. Who would call her once a week? Who would watch Lawson when Annie Jo needed a break? Oh God — her mother — gone. Tears threatened, but they would have to wait until Lawson was asleep. She had to stay strong for her baby's sake. She was, after all, a mother now. She pushed all feeling down into her stomach. She felt nauseous.

She unbuckled Lawson, carried him on her hip up the few steps to Trudy's front door. Her van wasn't in the drive, but that didn't mean Trudy wasn't there. Sometimes, her boyfriend, Harvey, took the Chevy to go to work or in for a tune-up. Annie Jo knocked on the door.

"Come in — Oh Jesus! I'm so sorry," said Tacoma as she opened the door and realized who was there. She pulled Annie Jo in and hugged her, squeezing Lawson between them. He started to cry.

"Is your mom home?" said Annie Jo, sitting on the sofa. Tacoma handed Lawson her cell phone and he kept busy touching the screen.

"No. She still at the shop. Said the sheriff had lots of questions. She won't be back for a while," said Tacoma.

"Oh....Do you know what happened? Did she tell you anything?" said Annie Jo.

"Not really. She don't want to talk about it — you know....She in shock or something. Didn't even sound like my mama on the phone."

"Oh. You mind if I stay here a while...Lawson'll be ready for his nap soon...I ..I don't want to be alone right now."

"Sure. Want some soda?"

"Yeah...lots of ice."

Annie Jo held Lawson on her lap and she could hear Tacoma puttering around in the kitchen, fixing her coke. There was something comforting about the sound of cabinets opening and closing, the clatter of the ice from the ice-maker, the pop of the soda can. The sounds reminded her of when she lived at home and her mother would fix a snack for them to share while they watched *Third Rock From the Sun.* Again, she was afraid she was going to cry. Lawson wouldn't like that; he'd become upset. She pushed her mind to other thoughts and waited for Tacoma to bring her a tall glass of cola. She'd think about her mother later, after Lawson had gone to bed.

Her mother.

Why was I so unkind to the woman who loved me? Why did I take Willa Jo for granted?

Chapter Seven

"Willa Jo, that you? Oh, it's a damn machine. Well, I need you, Willa Jo. I need my hair done and I need to tell you what's happened about you-know-what. Oh, good-bye, you damn machine."

~The Beautician's Notebook

June

The funeral had been over for a couple of weeks. It was a nice service that filled the whole church. Rock Bonner, Willa Jo's daddy, and Annie Jo had asked Mad Dog to sit with them in the family row. He'd been real touched by that. He noticed the sheriff, Judge Luffy and Ricky Temple sat together a couple rows behind the family. Trudy and her customers crowded in towards the middle, making sort of a black dot in the sea of white faces. Reverend Young preached a good sermon, talking about Willa Jo and what a nice lady she'd been. He cautioned everybody against sin and said we should all pull together to make Summerset a safer community. His wife played the organ, but she made a few mistakes. She was crying, Mad Dog reckoned. Afterward, everybody ambled to the fellowship hall where the ladies of the church served lunch. Mad Dog had never attended Sabbath Home Baptist; neither had Willa Jo, at least not as a grown-up. But she was raised in the church and her mama'd been very active at Sabbath Home. Now, Willa Jo was to be buried in the church cemetery in a plot next to her mama. Mad Dog thought that was real nice, too.

As soon as the small lunch — cucumber sandwiches or chicken salad — was over, the crowd walked out to the grave and sat in the chairs placed beneath a big, green tent. Mad Dog tried not to cry but he could feel tears sliding down his cheeks when they lowered her into the ground. By damn, he'd get the bastard who killed her — stole her away. He'd get him or die trying.

Since the funeral, Mad Dog had thought and thought until his poor brain ached with thinking. He had to find Willa Jo's killer; he knew

Sheriff Hicks thought it was most likely Mad Dog himself who'd done it. He'd be the prime suspect unless he gave them something, or someone else to consider. But there was not one person who didn't love Willa Jo —not one. Hell, even the grocery store cashiers loved it when she shopped — sometimes, she'd buy them a dozen Krispy Kreme doughnuts to share in the break room. Other times, she'd bring them a cup of coffee. Yep, everybody loved Willa Jo.

He tried to think of any dissatisfied customers. There'd been that one lady, Avi? Avinel? Something like that — the preacher's wife. She did get upset with Willa Jo once, over the color of her toenail polish — said it was too showy for a woman in her position — but Willa Jo removed it right away and put on a light pink blush. The woman seemed fine after that — plus, that had been almost three years ago, right after he'd moved in with Willa Jo.

Mad Dog hit his head with his fist. Think! WHO would want to kill Willa Jo?

As if an angel whispered to him, Mad Dog had an idea.

Willa Jo's notebook.

That must be it! Somebody found out about her notebook and killed her for it. He immediately had doubts about his theory. Maybe he'd gone crazy, coming up with stupid shit like that. Maybe he shouldn't mention the notebook to anybody. But what if he was right? What if someone murdered Willa Jo over that notebook? Besides, telling the sheriff about the notebook might take some of the heat off *him.* Nobody *said* it, but he could tell by the way people looked at him, they thought he was guilty.

Mad Dog scrambled off the couch as fast as he could. He stumbled around, looking for the card Sheriff Hicks had given him. Oh, where the hell was it? He never thought he'd need it...where was it? Ah, there, wedged between the couch cushions. He grabbed his cell and punched in the numbers. One ring. Two.

"Sheriff, this is Tommy McGee. I think I might have an idea about Willa Jo's murder. You want me to come to the station?"

"Well, first, Mr. McGee —I never said Willa Jo'd been murdered. I'll know more when I get the coroner's report. And I know how folks around here like to gossip...everybody's talking about murder, but time will tell whether or not that's the case. Can't believe everything you hear. But sure, I'd be willing to see what you've got."

Mad Dog thought the man sounded bored. Maybe he was just tired.

"So, should I come to the station then?"

"I'm heading out for some lunch — why don't we meet at the Purple Onion?"

"Oh… okay. Be there in about ten minutes."

He hurried to the bathroom, grabbed a quick shower and put on clean clothes —jeans and a golf shirt. He wanted something a little dressier than his usual tees. He'd put away some of Willa Jo's chimes but he hadn't had the heart to get rid of all of them —just the ones he usually got tangled in. Maybe he should bring the notebook with him, but that might make him look too anxious. He'd just talk about it, and, if the sheriff thought it might be a clue, they could come back to the house and get it. That would give him more time with the sheriff, more time to make sure the sheriff knew he was a nice guy, not a murderer.

He drove to the Purple Onion where the sheriff said meet him. Good thing, too. Mad Dog was famished.

The Purple Onion was tucked into a little strip mall right on Main Street. If you weren't careful, you'd miss it altogether. Most people thought it was the best restaurant in Summerset, renowned for its cakes and other fancy pastries. Mad Dog always enjoyed their hamburgers and his mouth was watering for one right now. Funny — for the first few days after Willa Jo's death, he couldn't eat a thing. But now, his appetite had returned with a vengeance.

He pulled into the crowded parking lot and, after circling a couple of times, finally found a place after some old couple had pulled out. He saw the sheriff's car right at the front door. He pushed open the door and noticed the long case of baked goods on the left. He walked to the right side of the place and looked into the dining room itself. There was the sheriff, over in the far corner.

Mad Dog made his way carefully, dodging purses and tables and chairs. He sat quickly across from the sheriff, who had almost finished his meal.

"Fish good?" Mad Dog said.

"Always," said the sheriff. "So, what'd you come up with?"

"I…I think I m-m-might have found a m-motive," said Mad Dog, trying to stop his stutter. He feared it might make him look guilty. Or at least nervous. What did he have to be nervous about?

"Oh, really. And what might that be, besides an angry lover?" the sheriff said.

None too kindly, Mad Dog thought.

"Willa Jo's n-n-notebook," said Mad Dog, pleased with himself for settling his speech down a little.

"Notebook? What kind of notebook?"

"Well, Willa Jo always kept this n-n-notebook — it's on the n-n-nightstand by her bed. It's real thick with a fancy leather c-c-cover. Every week — well, almost every week — she'd write in it. Funny stuff, mostly. About what had happened at The Sassy Lady. She said p-p-people would tell her the funniest, craziest stories. She wanted to remember 'em, so she kept a notebook."

"I'm not quite following you, McGee. Who cares if she kept jokes?" said the sheriff, wiping his mouth carefully.

"Well, that's not *all* she kept in there." Mad Dog was warming to the subject. "She kept s-s-secrets. Big secrets. Stuff only *she* knew. Because the folks who came to The Sassy Lady would tell W-Willa Jo just about everything that was going on in their lives."

The sheriff chewed the last bite of his fried flounder. He stared hard at Mad Dog. A long, probing stare that started to make Mad Dog uneasy.

"So...did you bring it?"

"Bring w-what?" said Mad Dog, focusing on the hamburger in front of him.

"The notebook."

"Uh...no." Mad Dog took a big bite of his food.

"Why the hell not?"

Mad Dog chewed as fast as he could. He didn't like the look on the sheriff's face.

"I...well, I-I wasn't sure you'd be interested...and I thought we could just h-h-head back to my...er, Willa Jo's to get it if you *did* want it."

The sheriff gave out a big sigh and looked pissed. Mad Dog wanted to make things better.

"L-look — come back to the house with me. I'll show you. I been racking my brain, trying to figure this thing out. ...this is all I got," said Mad Dog

"Okay. Let's go."

"B-b-but I'm still eating."

"I don't have time to piss around here, watching you eat. Let's go."

Mad Dog asked them to doggy-bag his burger, paid and then followed the sheriff's car back to his house. Well, what used to be his and Willa Jo's house. Really, it was just Willa Jo's, but so far, nobody had said anything about him moving out. He pulled in beside the sheriff so Hicks could back out of the driveway with no problem. Mad Dog was nervous around the man for some reason. Maybe it was because he sensed the sheriff didn't much like him — after all, the man used to be married to Willa Jo. He still carried a torch for her. Or maybe it was because Mad Dog was, in many ways, a 'kept' man. He worked at the garage, but it wasn't full-time. Willa Jo hadn't wanted him to work all the time — said she'd had enough of workaholics. If she wanted to take a long lunch, have a little 'afternoon delight,' she'd wanted him there, available. He couldn't say no to that.

"So, where's this notebook?" said Sheriff Hicks.

"C-come on upstairs." Mad Dog entered the bedroom, the room he'd shared with Willa Jo. Sudden tears sprung to his eyes and he wiped them with the back of his hand. He strode confidently to Willa Jo's side of the bed, to her small nightstand. There was the alarm clock, one of those Zen deals that woke you oh, so gently. There was a picture of Willa Jo and Annie Jo when Annie Jo was about three years old. And right where he thought the notebook should be, he saw....nothing.

It wasn't there.

"It's usually r-right here, right on the table. M-m-maybe she put it in the drawer, or something," said Mad Dog as he opened the drawer. Nothing but the usual stuff, personal items, love toys.

"Is this where she always kept it?"

"Yeah. She n-never took it downstairs — it was what she did, sometimes, before she went to s-sleep — she wrote in that n-n-notebook."

Together, the men scoured the bedroom and the bath. There was no trace of any notebook.

"L-l-look, man — I know you think I'm m-m-making this up — but I'm telling you the truth. There *was* a notebook — I'll swear it on Willa Jo's g-g-grave."

"Calm down, calm down. Let me show you something," said the sheriff as he led Mad Dog back over to the nightstand. "It's a good thing you ain't much of a housekeeper. See that? It's an outline of a book right there in the dust. There was something there, all right. Whether or not it was that notebook you mentioned, well, I don't know."

The sheriff took Mad Dog by the elbow and led him back downstairs.

"Thank you for telling me about this, Mr. McGee. It may prove useful. So far, we got nada."

"I hope it h-helps. I want to find out who did this to Willa Jo. L-let me know if you need anything else."

"Just keep thinking — you remembered the notebook. Maybe something else will shake loose. Have a nice day," the sheriff said, tipping his hat.

Chapter Eight

"Why you have all them black people in your salon, Willa Jo? Don't you know they bad for business?"

~The Beautician's Notebook

July

Trudy Johnson puttered around her kitchen, wiping down the cabinets and reorganizing everything. She had to keep busy or she would lose her mind. No matter how hard she tried, she could not get the image of Willa Jo's body lying in that pool of blood, right in the middle of The Sassy Lady, out of her mind. Right in the middle of her workplace. How could Trudy ever go back to work? How could she ever set foot inside that house? At least, that's what she thought at first.

Trudy noticed her hands shaking again —every time she thought about what had happened, they shook. It had been well over two weeks since the funeral, but Trudy had not yet reopened the shop. She couldn't bear the thought of entering the place where Willa Jo had died. And, if she was honest, she worried about 'how' Willa Jo died. Was it a crazy accident? Or was it murder? The sheriff had not given out any information and the *Chadwick County Chitchat* only carried the obituary. But the sheriff was asking everybody in town questions. 'Had they seen Willa Jo the day before she died? Did she seem okay? Did they know anybody who was mad at Willa Jo?'

Plus, Trudy worried about what was going to happen to the business. Though the business was half hers, who knew who would end up owning the house? Most likely, Annie Jo.

Humph. That was a miscarriage of justice if ever Trudy saw one. Spoiled brat of a girl —child had bout driven Willa Jo crazy with all her shit. Oh, sure, Annie Jo had her good points; she'd been a real good sitter for Tacoma and Keena that one summer. But after that, Annie Jo Hicks hadn't been worth the clothes on her back —that girl getting Willa Jo's house? If that was the case, Trudy might as well pack her bags and move to another town. She would *not* share space with Annie Jo.

But where would she go? Back to Johnston County? All her friends had either moved away or died —plus, everybody was poor, at least *her* folks. There were a few rich neighborhoods spilling over from Raleigh, but not too many African-Americans among them. No, Summerset was where Trudy had established her business and that's where she would continue until somebody made her quit.

She knew it hadn't been such a long time since the funeral, but she was about to go crazy staying home. Willa Jo wouldn't have wanted her to starve. She'd cancelled all their appointments for the week of Willa Jo's death and funeral, but now, maybe it *was* time to open up the doors to The Sassy Lady once again. It was close to the first of July and folks would need good hair for the Fourth.

Trudy went to her desk and picked up her scheduler. She didn't like keeping things on the computer; she preferred the old-fashioned booklet with enough space to make notes. She began calling her regular customers to set appointments. Her women needed her and she was determined to be there for them. As she called each one, she accepted their condolences and avoided their fishing trips, trying to hook up some good gossip about Willa Jo's death. But no matter how discrete Trudy tried to be, all the women were convinced Willa Jo had been murdered and her boyfriend was the culprit. At least some figured it was the boyfriend. Others were convinced there was a mass murderer skulking around Summerset. Trudy had to shake her head at that idea.

She was on the last page of the appointment book when she heard someone tap at her door. Quickly, she shut the book and answered.

"Trudy? Mind if I come in for a minute?" said the sheriff.

Trudy's heart skipped. She never did trust the police and she'd taught both her daughters, Tacoma and Takeena, to be polite always, especially to cops. "Don't give them a reason," she'd said, over and over. "If they stop you, don't run. If they pull you over in a car, keep your hands on the steering wheel. 'Yessir` and 'No-sir`, that's the way to stay alive," she'd told them.

She practiced what she preached.

"Come on in, Tal...er... Sheriff Hicks. Won't you have a seat?" Trudy pushed a few decorative pillows out of his way. They both sat on the sofa.

"I know Willa Jo thought the world of you," he said.

"And you know I loved her, too, Sheriff. Loved her like a sister." Trudy's eyes teared up, much against her will. She blinked fast.

"I know you want to find out what happened as much as I do. That's why I'm here. I need to ask you a few questions."

"Of course."

"It's come to my attention that Willa Jo may have had some sort of notebook...something she kept jokes and funny stories in...."

"Oh my, yes! Let's see — I reckon Willa Jo started the notebook when we first went into business. She used to tease people about it. Say, '*You better be nice to me or I'll put something mean about you in my notebook.*' If somebody said something funny or told a wild tale, she'd say '*That is notebook material for sure, ain't it, Trudy?*' Everybody knew about Willa Jo's notebook." Trudy felt herself ready to tear up again.

"I see. Well, not *everybody* — I never heard a word about it til the other day. But that's beside the point. Was there anything in there that somebody might have regretted telling Willa Jo? Some secret that a person wouldn't want getting around town?"

Trudy folded her hands in her lap and looked at her feet.

"Tell the truth, Sheriff, I never did actually *see* the notebook. She musta kept it upstairs. I never once saw anything like a notebook in the shop — and I would have noticed. It was my job to clean up each afternoon."

"Oh. So, you *heard* about the notebook but you never really *saw* it? Is that right?"

"Yessir, that's right. But I know it was real — I mean, you know how women talk when they getting their hair done — us beauticians, we like therapists or something. People will tell you anything — who's screwing who, who's cheating the government — you would not *believe* what we hear. Well, you were married to Willa Jo — I guess you'd believe it. I know Willa Jo told you stories..."

"She did, she did." The sheriff jotted down a few more notes.

"Any idea where that notebook might be? I checked upstairs in her bedroom, but it wasn't there. Anywhere else she might have kept it?"

"I can't think of any other place ....I know she wrote in that book almost every week...just sort of recapped the events she thought were funny. Helped her calm down, she said. After her marriage to the judge — well, you know — Willa Jo was a little scared. Every noise, she'd jump. Couldn't sleep. That's one reason she took up with Mad Dog Tommy McGee. Said he made her feel safe."

Sheriff Hicks looked like he'd been gut-punched when Trudy said that, and she felt sorry to have hurt him. She knew no man wanted his woman to feel afraid. And it looked like Sheriff Hicks thought of Willa Jo as 'his.' She'd heard the sheriff still had feelings for Willa Jo, but she hadn't believed it. Maybe the gossip was true.

After the sheriff left, Trudy went back to her list of clients. She started to call, but instead, she returned to the sofa. She thought about Willa Jo, how they'd met and how far they'd come with The Sassy Lady.

Willa Jo had slipped into the desk next to Trudy on the first day of the Accounting and Business class they'd both signed up for —they'd waited until the last semester before graduation to attack MATH. Trudy was terrified she'd never pass the course. She was one of a handful of black women in the class and that, too, made her slightly uncomfortable. Willa Jo had barely passed math in high school; numbers made her brain go numb, she said.

"Where you from?" said Willa Jo. Trudy noticed the girl's dark wavy hair and her sea-green eyes. She was beautiful, even for a white woman.

"Garner. Right outside Raleigh," Trudy said.

"I'm from Summerset —it's near Temple Beach. Right smack dab in the middle of the coast between Wilmington and Myrtle. Is this your first semester?"

"I sure hope not! My last! I'll be glad to get out of here. How bout you?"

"I graduate in May, too," said Willa Jo, pulling her hair back into a ponytail as she talked. "Do you have a job lined up yet?"

"My auntie down in Charlotte said I might come in with her — start at the nail center and then move up. I'm not loving the idea but so far, that's all I got."

"I don't have anything either. My mama has a shop in Summerset, but damn, I don't want to do all the blue-hairs. Mama's shop is *so* plain....and she does hair the same old way she's always done it. I really don't want to go in with her —I know we'd fight all the time." Willa Jo let her hair fall back down, over her shoulders.

That was all they said about the future that day, but by the end of the semester, they'd become quite a team; Willa Jo was no good at bookkeeping. Surprisingly, Trudy seemed to have developed a gift for it — Trudy thought her sudden competence was the answer to prayers. But Willa Jo was the better hairdresser. No question. Based on their assessment of their strengths and weaknesses, they'd decided to go into business together. Trudy knew how to do white hair and Willa Jo learned how to do black. But they figured once they got settled in, Summerset would divide itself between them right down the color line. Willa Jo used to joke that together, they'd do all the hair in Chadwick County.

Working together had been strange at first, especially when Trudy had to explain to her auntie why she was refusing her offer. Her own mother didn't like the idea of Trudy going into business with a white woman. At the beginning, the women in her community wouldn't go to The Sassy Lady. Trudy found out from some ladies in her church that they were afraid the pricing would be too high for most of them. Trudy nipped *that* in the bud. She told Willa about it. Together, they made discount tickets — ten, twenty, even thirty dollars off. Trudy handed the tickets out after the Wednesday night covered-dish dinner. Soon, The Sassy Lady was filled to the brim and Trudy had more work than she could handle. Of course, some of the new customers were one-timers, but lots of them became long-term clients.

Trudy also remembered the talks she and Willa Jo had —about the rioting and looting in Baltimore and police brutality; about the way the black folk seemed invisible at Temple Beach, except for the few wealthy families from up North who rented in the summer — there were eleven percent African-Americans in Chadwick County, but you didn't see many of them out and about. Willa Jo wanted to know where they were.

So, Trudy invited Willa Jo to church at Brown's Chapel in nearby Southport. Willa Jo had never been to an A.M.E. church before and Trudy could tell she liked the singing and praising, the 'amens' and the clapping. A few of the older women even began to speak in tongues, dancing in place while the Spirit moved them. Trudy glanced at Willa Jo, but she couldn't tell whether Willa Jo was shocked or nonplussed. She seemed to take it all in. Afterward, they talked about the differences in worship they'd each experienced. Willa Jo hadn't been to Sabbath Home Church since her first marriage ended, she told Trudy. After that, since she had so many customers from Temple Beach, she thought she'd visit the Temple Beach House of Worship, which was right on the island. She'd been there a couple of times and was having a bite of brownie, part of the after-church snacks the House of Worship offered parishioners each Sunday. A few people had engaged her in conversation, mostly her customers. Then, just as she was ready to bite into the brownie, an older, grey-haired woman walked up to her.

Willa Jo put her brownie down on the napkin and smiled at the woman. The woman needed a more attractive, up-to-date hairdo, she thought. The woman smiled back.

"Do you live on the island?" the woman asked.

"No, I...." Willa Jo said. Then, before she could explain to the woman where she lived, the woman turned her back on Willa Jo and didn't say another word.

Willa Jo couldn't believe it, she'd told Trudy. How rude.

Trudy smiled at the memory — Willa Jo never returned to Temple Beach House of Worship. How they'd laughed about the irony of it — hell, Willa Jo had been *married* to one of the Temple's. She could have lived on the island if she'd been so inclined. But she liked Summerset, with its long Main Street, its sweet golf course, Briarwood. She'd been raised in Summerset and her insistence on staying there was one of the reasons she and Ricky Temple broke up. That, plus he couldn't match her enthusiasm in bed.

Trudy sighed and looked again at the appointment book. She wondered what would happen to The Sassy Lady now that Willa Jo was gone. Work sure wouldn't be as much fun. And she'd miss their conversations. Willa Jo was the only white woman Trudy could be honest with — they had a real partnership, respectful and balanced. Trudy just hoped whoever inherited the house would let The Sassy Lady stay open. And whoever that was, she hoped they would allow Trudy to run the shop.

Chapter Nine

"The right color can make any woman look younger and more attractive."

~The Beautician's Notebook

July

Tal Hicks didn't like questioning people who lived on the island. After all, they had their own police department, but those guys wouldn't have jurisdiction over Willa Jo's case. No, this was a matter for Chadwick County. So, he was stuck with asking a few questions to the wealthier-than-thou beach property owners. Not that they weren't cooperative and respectful. Almost always, he'd been well-received. But stepping foot on the island made him uneasy and he wasn't quite sure why. Maybe it was the majestic beauty of the ocean; or perhaps it was old-fashioned jealousy; whatever the reason, he hesitated before climbing the steps to Clarissa Myers' beach house.

Tal walked slowly, taking in everything about the house and filing it away for future reference. Who knew when a tiny detail might lead to something? Anything. Because right now, he had —zilch. A big fat zero. It was looking more and more like Willa Jo had simply suffered an accident, a terrible, tragic accident. But he needed to be sure. And, until he got the coroner's report, he would keep digging.

He noticed the vividly colored benches placed strategically on the lawn, the perfect grass, the sea shells drying on a cloth on the bottom step —sand dollars, starfish, a horseshoe crab. Someone had enjoyed a profitable morning. He knocked on the bright red door. He could hear the yap of a small dog inside. Oh no. Those little dogs *never* liked him — he was a big-dog man and they must have sensed it somehow.

Tal rapped again. This time, he could hear muffled yips from the dog and quick footsteps putting the dog away, or so he guessed. Finally, the door opened.

"I'm Sheriff Hicks. I'm investigating the death of Willa Jo Temple —I'm sure you know about it. Are you Clarissa Myers?" Tal said, his heart thumping at the beauty of the woman who had opened the door.

She nodded.

"And I know who *you* are, sheriff. Willa Jo pointed you out to me once when we were shopping at Pat's Second Chance...you were walking down the sidewalk and she said, 'There goes my first husband — the love of my life.' I suppose you're here because someone told you Willa Jo and I were best friends."

"Yeah. Someone did. I'd like to ask you some questions." Tal tried not to stare, but he couldn't help himself. He told himself he was just noting facts, facts for the case.

She had blond hair that curled under, softly framing her cheeks. Her eyebrows were dark and arched and she had very blue eyes, a light blue that reminded him of somebody somewhere. He'd seen those eyes before, but where? Oh hell, he was just getting crazy. This woman wasn't local-she didn't have any connections to anybody from around Summerset.

"Please come in," she said. "Yep, Willa Jo told me all about you — her first true love, right?"

"Yeah, something like that...first love, first husband, father of Annie Jo...that's me." Tal's collar scratched at his neckline, making him even more uncomfortable.

"How's Annie Jo taking everything? I'm sure it's difficult."

"Who knows with her...Now, about those questions?"

She led him into a tastefully decorated great room with a fake fireplace at one end and bookshelves at the other. Two couches faced each other with a coffee table in between. Behind one of the couches, he saw a doggie bed and feeding bowls. It was obvious who ran *this* show.

He was conscious of his shoes and hoped he wasn't bringing a bunch of sand into the house. Then he sort of laughed at himself — hell, these folks lived on the *beach* — a place *full* of sand. Surely, a few grains off his shoes wouldn't offend them. He sat down in the overstuffed, wicker chair she'd offered, took out his pad and pencil and looked across to where she sat on the sofa.

"Some of these questions might seem obvious and silly, but I have to ask them anyway...and I'll be writing your responses down," he said, taking pen in hand. "So, Mrs. Myers, you knew Willa Jo? Is that correct?"

"We were best friends. And please, call me Clarissa." She tilted her head just so, as if he were the most interesting man in the world. Oh shit — who was he kidding? She was just looking at him. He needed to get a grip.

"Can you tell me if she had any problems? Any enemies?"

"I can't imagine who…I think everyone just loved Willa Jo — I know I did, well, still do," she said, those clear blue eyes filling.

He was glad to see she really cared, happy Willa Jo had found such a friend.

"That's what everyone says. Tell me, did you know anything about a notebook?"

"Sure. Everybody knew about Willa Jo's famous notebook. She would put stuff in there her customers said. Funny stuff. You know, the kind of stuff to look back on later and laugh. That was Willa Jo — always ready for a good glass of wine and a good laugh."

"So, everybody knew about the notebook? I thought it was supposed to be secret, sort of."

"Secret? Oh no, no. It was an honor to be put in the 'book,' as she called it. She'd tell folks she was going to write them in there, just to make them feel good — like they were included, you know?"

"I see. Was there ever anything in there that wasn't funny? Ever anything serious?"

Clarissa put her delicate finger to her chin and tapped three times. It reminded Tal of the way Willa Jo used to think while drumming her fingers on her knees.

"I really don't know — I mean, I never read it or really even saw it. No! I take that back — I did see it one time when we were over at Willa Jo's getting ready to go out. She wanted to do something special with my hair and we were in her bedroom. There it was, sitting on the table beside her bed. It was pretty thick and had a really fancy tooled leather cover. But we didn't take time to read it then, though I wanted to. We always said when we were old and gray, we'd read that notebook and remember all the wild and crazy things we'd done," said Clarissa, twirling a curl around her finger. "I'm three years younger than Willa Jo — I used to kid her about her being old and gray WAY before I'd even found my first gray hair. She'd laugh and say as long as she had The Sassy Lady, neither one of us would ever be gray —

but when we were too ancient to shop or party, we'd read that notebook."

Tal scribbled this on his pad and sat quietly. He'd learned over the years when there is silence, most people will try to fill it. He'd discovered a lot of unexpected information that way. He looked up at Clarissa and thought what a beauty she was. No wonder Ralph Myers had snatched her up — she was a fine piece of arm candy for a wealthy, older man. Not that Myers looked old — he looked at least fifteen years younger than his seventy years. He was tall and lean, well over six two. Kept himself in shape fishing and golfing, playing tennis. Tal knew all about him because years ago, when the Myers' first moved onto the island, Myers called to report a couple of stolen items. Even though it wasn't his jurisdiction, Tal drove over. His wife hadn't arrived yet, Myers explained. She'd be coming in a couple of weeks, in from a vacation in Spain with Myer's sister, he'd said. Tal shook his head at that — he couldn't imagine just up and going to Europe — he'd have to save for a couple of years to afford such a trip.

The two men hit it off, talked about their mutual interest in fishing and boating. Tal wasn't a golfer but there was plenty they found to talk about. Myers was a friendly guy and, though Tal hadn't been able to catch who robbed the house, he was able to help the Temple Beach police find the stolen goods. That set well with Myers and if they ran into each other at the local Food Lion or down on the docks, they usually had time for a brief chat.

"Willa Jo told all her clients that someday, she was going to write a book and tell everybody's secrets. Nobody thought she would ever really do it — writing is hard work and Willa Jo would rather lounge on the beach and sip cold Chablis," said Clarissa. She trailed a long, slim finger along the edge of her chin, tapping again. Her nails were the color of the inside of a conch shell, delicate pinkish salmon. For some damn reason, Tal found himself imagining her up against him. He shook the thought from his head.

Focus, buddy. Focus.

"Do you think someone might have taken her seriously? Maybe someone who didn't know her very well? Any ideas?"

"I dunno. Would somebody kill her for that…that notebook?"

"I didn't say anyone killed her. I'm just checking things out. My job, right?" Tal smiled.

“But sheriff, everybody’s saying it was murder...do you think it was, really?”

“Who knows...?”

He took his leave of the ‘beautiful Clarissa’ as he’d just begun to think of her. Then he laughed —Willa Jo’s death had shaken him up even more than he realized. He was going nuts himself.

Chapter Ten

"*A precision cut is worth every penny — and no one can cut you like Willa Jo' — overheard.*"

~The Beautician's Notebook

July

Deputy Sheriff Samantha Stokes was getting pressure from everywhere and she was about to lose her cool. Tal, that is, Sheriff Hicks, wanted the forensic report ASAP, though it had been only seven weeks since Willa Jo's funeral. He knew better — the report usually took at least eight weeks. Only on TV did you get results right away.

On top of that, Ralph Myers was leaning on everybody he could possibly lean on to get a suspect in Willa Jo's murder. With the on-going gossip, all of Chadwick County seemed to believe there had definitely been foul play. Everyone was calling it a murder; everyone except Tal....er, Sheriff Hicks. But Deputy Stokes knew that wasn't necessarily the case, no matter what people said. Plus, the official reports weren't in. Myers was a big man over on the island and, evidently his wife was Willa Jo's best friend, or something like that. Whatever the reason, he'd been calling the Sheriff almost every day and good old Tal was passing that pressure onto Sam.

Sam had grown up in Summerset. Her dad had been a deputy for Chadwick County and she wanted to follow in his footsteps. It hadn't been easy. She'd gone up to the university in Wilmington to get her degree in criminal justice — she'd had to put herself through with part-time jobs and student loans, but she'd done it — and in three years. Now, she was working as a deputy and everything seemed to be moving in slow motion. The hours ticked by while she went over the photos of what she'd come to think of as 'the crime scene' for the hundredth time, desperate to find something —anything —that might give her a lead. She'd love to help Tal...er, Sheriff Hicks figure things out. But the pictures kept showing the same old stuff: Willa Jo sprawled on the floor on her back, scissors stuck in her chest; some hair conditioner spilled on the floor and a towel next to the body, showing somebody had tried to wipe the mess up. Whoever 'Mr. Clean' was, he'd left no footprints in the goo; and that was all the info they had, nothing else. No motive, no opportunity, no nothing. Right now, the Sheriff liked Mad Dog McGee, or so Sam liked to imagine — of course, the sheriff had not shared his thoughts with her. The only reason Sam, and maybe Tal…er, the sheriff suspected McGee was because he'd been Willa Jo's lover. Everybody knows the statistics always favor the husband or boyfriend. Plus, Mad Dog claimed he was upstairs when it happened and slept right through the murder. That part was a little sketchy, Sam thought. How could anyone sleep through a murder? Oh, you might see such stuff on TV, but in reality, sleeping through a murder was rare.

The phone rang and jogged her thoughts.

"Deputy Sheriff Samantha Stokes. Great — thanks for putting a rush on it. Four sets of prints, huh.....well, send 'em on over and we'll run 'em — see if we get any kind of hit. Thanks," said Sam. She hurried to catch the Sheriff as he was heading out the door.

"Got some prints!" she said.

"Finally! Where are they? What'd they find?"

Sam handed over the folder containing the results to the sheriff.

"Hmm. Four sets, huh? We can assume one is Willa Jo's. Go ahead and run the others…let's see if we get a hit…start with the state list, then go to the feds," Tal said as he looked at the prints, matching each set to where they'd been located on Willa Jo's plastic cape.

"Weird. Look — these prints are in a strange place — on the shoulder. Odd," said Tal.

Sam took a look, standing close enough to get a whiff of Tal…the sheriff's piney smell. She backed away quickly.

"Hey, Sam, you ever hear about Willa Jo and her notebook?"

"Sure —everybody knew about it. She used to joke with me all the time about putting me in there, doing something completely stupid like shooting somebody while I was cleaning my gun. Why?"

"You think that might have anything to do with her death? Maybe somebody wanted that notebook — to keep whatever was in there quiet." Tal rubbed his chin.

"Possible. My money's still on 'Mr. Sleeping Beauty.' Really…who could sleep while your girlfriend is get whacked right beneath you. What a piece of work he is."

"Nothing wrong with being a kept man —I always kinda liked the idea." He didn't even flicker a smile and Sam laughed. The Sheriff could be funny if you gave him a chance. Some men couldn't help being sexy as hell.

Later that afternoon, Sam ran the sets of prints against the state file. The coroner had already taken Willa Jo's prints and sent them to the office. That took care of one match. She tried the other three and waited to see what might pop. After what seemed like hours, she finally got a ping.

One set of fingerprints belonged to an Avenelle Avery, arrested around forty years ago for misdemeanor joy-riding. Avenelle Avery. That had to be Reverend Young's wife. How many Avenelle's could there be in one county?

Sam rushed into Tal's office.

"You ain't gonna believe this, sheriff," she said, almost panting with excitement.

"You got something?"

"Oh, hell yes. Take a look!" Sam pointed to the identification.

"So, who's Avenelle Avery?"

"You don't know? It's the preacher's *wife*! She's Avenelle Young now, but I know her family — she's a cousin of one of my best friends' mother's. And here's the kicker —it was her prints that were placed odd…the other three were bunched together...not her's. Hers were on the shoulder of the cape," said Sam, pleased with herself.

"Good work, deputy. Thanks," said the sheriff. "Now, go back and try to find the others."

Sam returned to her desk and started running the prints through neighboring states before she used the federal files —South Carolina, Virginia, Tennessee. She hoped she'd have another flash of good luck.

Chapter Eleven

"I never liked to read. It always made my head hurt."

~The Beautician's Notebook

July

Avenelle traced the design on the cover of the notebook. She'd never seen such beautiful leather, such intricate tooling. The design looked mystical, magical —as if the book contained stories of such elegance and heartache they could change your life. She knew those weren't the kind of stories in this book, though. This book held, well, she didn't really know, did she?

Avenelle's thoughts turned to the day she told Willa Jo everything. It was mid-October, a day full of poignant beauty —the sky that deep, clear blue she'd grown to love, the trees various shades of red, gold, purple and orange. Even the scrub pines looked lovely. Nature at her best. This final burst of glory right before the bleakness of winter was God's way of telling people that age wasn't something to be afraid of; oh no, as we humans gained in experience and did the hard work of slowly becoming who we were meant to be, we, too, grew rich in beauty. We, too, brightened up the world like sparks.

She felt like a spark, herself. She'd raised her sons and maintained herself impeccably as a preacher's wife. Not a single blot on her tally. She visited the sick right along with The Reverend; she cooked at least three dishes for all the covered-dish dinners; she started a Bible study in her own home on Monday nights; she played piano and guitar for services; and she never said a word against The Reverend, even when she heard other wives voice complaints about their husbands.

But there was something about *that* day, something about *Willa Jo,* that made her spill her guts. Maybe part of it was that she and Willa Jo already had a secret —she was teaching Willa Jo how to play guitar. Willa Jo told her once that all her life, Willa Jo'd wanted to sing and play country music. Who'd have ever suspected? Though, Willa Jo *did* have big hair, just like Dolly Parton. She asked Avenelle to give her lessons on the sly. Avenelle was happy to have a little money of her own, money she didn't have to ask The Reverend for, so she said yes. She'd been giving the lessons for about six months.

Maybe she told Willa Jo her secret because Avenelle had been best friends with Willa Jo's mother. Strange to think she and Bessie could have been friends after what happened, but there's no predicting the turns and twists of this life. That much, Avenelle knew. And, of course, Bessie already knew Avenelle's secret — but since Bessie died, Avenelle had no one to talk to about it.

Or perhaps she just needed to tell the story once again. There was something comforting in telling your story. Being heard and understood. Finding compassion and forgiveness in the listener. Maybe that had been the whole point of the confessional in the Catholic Church. Oh, that was a scary thought. The Reverend would not like that idea at all. The Reverend did NOT approve of the Catholic Church. Why, he would fall over dead if Avenelle told him she liked the idea of praying to the Virgin Mary. That she sometimes thought of God as a woman and loved to imagine herself cradled in God's arms just the way she had cradled her own babies. She knew better than to share her theology with The Reverend.

Whatever the reason, in the fullness of that amazing day, she told Willa Jo everything.

Avenelle kept listening to make sure she was truly alone. The Reverend was visiting the rest homes scattered over the county and he should be gone all afternoon. Adam was at work; he rarely dropped in. He preferred prearranged family gatherings. Who knew where Abel was? That poor boy would never come home, not after the way The Reverend banished him. Yes, she was alone. And safe.

Assured there was no one there, Avenelle opened the book. The first page was dated 1993. Wow, this book was old. Willa Jo must have started it right when she got out of school. Not much on the first page —just all about how excited Willa Jo was to be starting her own business ON HER OWN —that's how she wrote it in the book —in great big letters. Willa Jo had not one bit of fear about beginning her career in opposition to her own mama. Failure didn't enter her mind, at least that's how it seemed to Avenelle as she read on. She was beginning to relax and sink into the couch when the doorbell rang. The sound shattered the air.

Avenelle didn't know what to do. Where could she hide the notebook? She didn't have time to run back upstairs and put it under her mattress. She slipped the book into the very center of the magazine rack. No one would be able to find it there amid all the *People* and *Woman's World* magazines. She hurried to answer the door.

She was amazed to find Rock Bonner standing on her porch.

"Morning, Avie. I reckon you are surprised to see me," he said.

"Floored. What can I do for you?" she said, her voice cold.

"Mind if I come in?"

"Yes, I *do* mind. Let's sit out here on the porch. The Reverend isn't at home —it wouldn't be proper for me to invite a gentleman into my home."

"Of course."

She took a seat on the porch swing and he sat in one of the white wicker chairs. She pushed off with the tip of her toe and started going back and forth, back and forth. She didn't want to speak —she wasn't sure she could. She hadn't spoken to Rock Bonner in almost forty years.

"Reckon you're wondering why I'm here." He put his hands on his knees and pressed down.

"Yes."

He paused and then put his hand to his face. His body shook just a little.

"You okay?"

He didn't reply.

It took her a moment to realize he was crying. He didn't' make any noise; just sort of shook. She hadn't seen too many men cry, not like this.

If it had been anyone else, she would have gone over and patted him on the back, or said some comforting word. But this was Rock Bonner. He would get nothing from her.

Finally, he spoke.

"I reckon losing Willa Jo hit me hard. With Bessie gone — now Willa —I reckon I'm kinda lost."

"You were divorced from Bessie for way longer than you were married —ya'll were only together for three years," Avenelle said. Her voice was cold and her heart felt even colder.

"That's true...but they were all I had in the way of family. And, even though Willa Jo and I didn't see eye-to-eye, I loved her. Now, I truly have no one."

"You have Annie Jo, your granddaughter."

"We ain't close —I didn't like her having that colored baby and I told her. Ain't seen her since."

Avenelle wanted to tell him, well, you reap what you sow. She wanted to tell him he had no business coming to *her* for comfort, for she had none to give him.

"I'm sorry for your loss, Rock. I truly am. But there's nothing I can do for you, except give you one of my frozen casseroles."

"I don't blame you, Avie. I don't blame you one bit. I'd take one of those casseroles, though," he said, giving her a sheepish grin.

It was that grin that began to melt her. She could feel her heart give just a little, not much.

"Wait right here," she said.

After Rock Bonner left with not one, but two, of her casseroles, Avenelle hurried back to finish reading Willa Jo's notebook. But the phone rang and Adam needed to drop Kevin off while he and Pam went to the grocery. Avenelle couldn't say 'no' to an afternoon with her grandson, so she put the notebook back in the magazine rack, hidden deep in between the magazines. Then, she headed to the kitchen and started getting out the ingredients for chocolate chip cookies. Kevin loved to help her cook and chocolate chip was his favorite.

Chapter Twelve

"Whatever."

~The Beautician's Notebook

July

Clarissa sat on the front deck in one of the Adirondack chairs she and Ralph'd found at a furniture store in Summerset. She'd fallen in love with the bright yellow color and thought the chairs would look great on the deck. She was right, of course. Amazing she had any taste at all, given how she grew up. But, as things turned out, she knew how to make a house a home. Decorating was easy when you didn't have to think about money. If Clarissa saw something she liked, she bought it —no big deal. She knew the real challenge would be to make a nice place on a shoestring budget. Clarissa remembered the foster homes of her childhood, the tattered furniture, the make-shift beds on the floor. In the Johnson home, though there'd been little money, Mrs. Johnson had been able create a warm, inviting residence with stuff she got from the local thrift stores. She kept the place neat and clean and her house had been the nicest in which Clarissa had stayed. But it would never make it into House Beautiful. Yes, money made all the difference.

Clarissa sipped her wine and stared past the green water, out to the horizon. The day was perfect —the sea breeze cool and light, the sun sparkling on the water, no one else in sight. She loved this place. The birds and sea creatures delighted her and the whole scene fed her soul. No matter how sad she felt, she could come out on the deck and feel her spirits lift.

And she was sad today. She'd been sad since Willa Jo died. It had taken a few weeks after the event for her to realize Willa Jo was really gone. But now, the knowledge that Willa Jo wasn't coming back had begun to sink into Clarissa's mind. This slow realization made her arms and legs heavy, her brain almost groggy. She hadn't cooked since the funeral, hadn't done much of anything really. Ralph had been so kind, taking her out for meals, fixing breakfast and lunch at home, bringing her glass after glass of wine.

What made it even worse was that the police believed, now, Willa Jo really may have been murdered. When Clarissa thought of that, she grew even more morose. She could imagine Willa Jo, coming into work early, preparing for the day with a cup of coffee, lots of sugar and cream, the way Willa Jo liked it. Then, just as Willa Jo was going about her business, somebody entered the shop and stabbed her right in the heart. Clarissa wondered if Willa Jo'd been scared. Had they talked first? Had the killer had a little cat-like fun with his victim?

Clarissa shivered. She couldn't stand to think of any of this, yet she couldn't make herself stop. Before she knew it, she was crying again.

Clarissa was used to feeling sad. She'd spent the first eighteen years of her life that way. Until Ralph rescued her. She would be forever grateful to him for that and for all the things he'd done for her. And she loved him —she did. Who could help loving a man who did right by you?

There was an emptiness inside her, though, a hole that even Ralph and all his kind attentions couldn't fill. After she'd watched young mothers with their children, she began to understand what that emptiness was. If a baby didn't get love, real love —sacrificial love — early on — that baby didn't stand a chance at a normal life. Because no matter what happened after that baby grew up, it wouldn't be enough. Without the grounding love of a parent or caretaker, a baby didn't have a chance.

So many times, she'd wondered about her birth mother. Why did she give Clarissa away? Why did she never come looking for the baby she'd given up? After years in the foster care system, Clarissa knew better than to ask the 'why' question. Why might someone have killed Willa Jo? Why did Ralph save *her* and not some other young girl? Why? Why? Why?

She had no idea how long she sat watching the ocean. When Ralph came home, he found her shivering in the chair, goosebumps on her arms.

"Honey, what in the world is going on? You're trembling," he said.

"I guess I lost track of time," she said as he raised her to her feet and guided her inside.

"Want to go grab a burger somewhere?"

"I don't really feel very hungry."

"You need to eat, honey. If not a burger, how about a nice dinner — we can drive down to South Carolina to the Parson's Table. They have such good food — how about it?"

"Sure…whatever you want."

It was mid-July and still, not a definitive word about Willa Jo's case. Clarissa found herself sinking deeper and deeper into a funk. Ralph was beginning to lose patience with her. She felt lonely. There was no one she could call to meet for lunch — at least, no one she really wanted to call. Beside Willa Jo, everyone else seemed vapid and uninteresting.

Clarissa decided to take matters into her own hands. She asked SIRI for the sheriff's number and called.

"Sheriff Hicks, please," she said.

"He's in a meeting. May I ask who is calling?" said the secretary.

"This is Clarissa Myers. I'm calling about the Willa Jo Temple case."

"One moment — I'll see if he can be interrupted."

Clarissa waited, unsure of herself. Why had she called exactly? She didn't have any further evidence.

"Sheriff Hicks, here."

"I'm sorry to bother you, Sheriff. I was wondering if you were any further along on the Temple case." Clarissa liked his voice — just a little bit raspy.

"We're working hard on it, Mrs. Myers. Did you have more information for us?"

"No, not really. But I've been thinking about that notebook. If someone did have an important secret, that might have been a motive — and, even though I never saw the book, Willa Jo said some of the stuff in there would be enough to cause all of Summerset to go into a tizzy."

"We're studying it from all angles, rest assured. Maybe we could have coffee and discuss it further — I'm in the middle of something and really need to get off the phone."

Coffee? Was he asking her to meet him? Clarissa felt an unfamiliar tension in her chest. It was just in the line of duty, she told herself. And she wanted to solve Willa Jo's case. Well, so did he. That gave them something in common. That, plus the fact that they had both loved Willa Jo. There was no harm in coffee.

"Shall we meet tomorrow morning? Around 7?" she said, twirling a strand of hair.

"That would be great —how about over at Cappuccino By the Sea —that way, you won't have to drive very far. I've got some business on the island anyhow."

"Tomorrow then." She hung up.

She was surprised to find her heart fluttering. What in the world was going on? She was a happily married woman —why was she so excited about meeting this man for coffee? It was *only* coffee.

Clarissa felt better than she had since Willa Jo died. She was going to help Sheriff Hicks figure out what had happened, maybe even find a murderer. She would be useful to the investigation, sort of like Castle on that TV show. Castle wasn't a real cop, but he solved most of the crimes. She could do that, too. She got up off the couch and began to putter around the house. The living room was a mess —she hadn't cleaned up in several weeks. It wouldn't occur to Ralph to do so. The house was her job, so he'd told her when they got married; he'd earn the money.

She cleared dishes from the sink and spruced up the front room, the downstairs bathroom and the deck. She looked in the freezer to see what they had. Ah, ribeyes. She would toss a salad, and make those little rising biscuits Ralph's first wife used to bake —he'd shared the recipe because he loved them so. And, she could whip up some strawberries and cream for dessert. They wouldn't have to drive down to The Parson's Table, after all.

***

"I'm so glad to see you're feeling better, honey. That was a delicious meal. Thank you," Ralph said as he came to where she stood loading the dishwasher. He put his hands on her waist.

"You're welcome. I didn't feel so down today and I got a spurt of energy. Maybe I'm on the mend." Clarissa turned toward him and gave him a long kiss. He was a good man. And she loved him. But he never made her heart flutter.

Ralph kissed her again, then took her hand and led her to their bedroom. Even though it wasn't Sunday morning, their usual time for making love, they'd missed a few weeks because Clarissa hadn't been in the mood. It was only normal to think in terms of making up for lost time. She knew Ralph would be happy to get back on schedule. When they'd first married, they'd had a 'date' as Ralph called it, three times a week — Wednesday and Friday nights, Sunday afternoons. But now that Ralph was seventy, things had tapered off.

He pointed to the bed and indicated for her to lie down. He went into the bathroom, most likely to take a little blue pill —he used those for spontaneous sex. Not that they had much of that. When he returned, he was naked and obviously ready for her. He lay down beside her and began to stroke her arms, her face, her hair. He kissed her again, deep and long. Then, he lifted her blouse over her head and unhooked her bra. She knew what would happen next —he'd move on to her breasts, then her belly and finally, her woman parts. He was an expert at love-making, always taking time with her, making sure she was pleasured. But today, her heart wasn't in it. Ralph was an organized, meticulous, predictable man. Why should his skills in the bedroom be any different? One, two, three, four and now, finally, five strokes and Ralph shuddered above her. It was over. She hadn't even bothered pretending to climax.

"Sorry. I was too quick —I'll make it up to you later —promise." He kissed her lightly on her forehead. She could see him staring at her hair. She could almost hear the gears grinding.

"Now maybe you will feel like getting your hair done — those roots are over an inch. Surely, you can find a new hairdresser," he said as he cupped her breast. "For me?"

Clarissa felt all the air go out of her lungs. Yes, she knew her roots were showing. So what? She liked her dark hair; she'd always thought it was dramatic. Willa Jo had black hair and it was beautiful. Why did Ralph have to have a blond?

"I'll look into it," she said, breaking their embrace.

Chapter Thirteen

"Ponytails are for cleaning house and working in tobacco."

~The Beautician's Notebook

July

Avenelle was knee deep in The Reverend's garden, pulling weeds and plucking off Japanese beetles when the thought struck her. She would offer guitar lessons to Willa Jo's daughter — what was her name — something Jo, at least she knew that much. Bessie had told her the name Jo had been used by her family for five generations. Let's see...Amy Jo....Asa Jo...not quite right.

Annie Jo — that was it. She knew Annie Jo had been in trouble — ran wild before she had that baby. Of course, no father ever showed up, but it was evident the father had been a person of color. Avenelle knew Annie Jo's grandpa, Rock Bonner, didn't like *that* one bit. Served him right. If he had been a better father to Willa Jo, he'd have had the opportunity to step in as grandfather to Annie Jo, after Willa Jo and Tal split up. He could have guided her. The sheriff did what he could — paid his child support regular, or so she'd heard — but that's not the same as having a daddy who lives in the home. Avenelle wasn't sure what kind of trouble Annie Jo had been in — she remembered something about shoplifting. Well, she could forgive that. And having a baby without marriage? She could forgive that, too. Of course, The Reverend would never forgive such a thing.

Avenelle wished The Reverend would learn a little Christian charity. The older he got, the more rigid his beliefs. As if he had to hold them tight, or he might lose them altogether. Avenelle knew *herself* to be a sinner. If she ever felt otherwise, all she had to do was remember her past, remember what she'd been like before she met The Reverend. Then, any sense of religious pride left her and she knew she was just like everybody else — flawed and in need of redemption.

That evening, Avenelle walked into the den and glanced over at Willa Jo's notebook safe in the magazine rack. Avenelle still hadn't had a chance to read it, even though she had custody of it (that's how she liked to think of her theft). Adam needed her more often than usual to babysit for little Kevin —Pam was trying to find a part-time job and the search required lots of time to prepare her resume and comb the internet for possibilities. The Reverend was keeping her busy with typing and, of course, she had to keep up with the music for choir, which meant learning a new piece each week. She loved accompanying the choir, though she was uncomfortable playing in front of people. But if she made a mistake, the voices would cover it up. Same with the hymns. But the prelude —that gave her fits. The postlude was no problem because people were leaving, chatting among themselves, anxious to get to their Sunday lunch. They paid no attention to her. But the beginning of the service was something else. Everyone was seated, listening, waiting. Waiting to be touched by the spirit or to connect somehow with God. Avenelle positively *hated* the prelude.

At any rate, she had no time or privacy in which to read Willa Jo's precious book.

She wasn't sure how to reach Annie Jo, so she dialed The Sassy Lady. Trudy reluctantly gave her Annie Jo's number. Avenelle recognized it as Willa Jo's old number. Well, of course. Annie Jo inherited the house. Made sense for the phone to be the same. Odd for a young person to keep a land line, but maybe Annie Jo couldn't afford one of those fancy Iphones.

Avenelle took a deep breath and then called the girl.

"Yeah," a voice answered.

"I'm calling for Annie Jo Hicks. May I please speak with her?"

"I'm Annie Jo. Who is this?"

"This is Avenelle Young, The Reverend Young's wife. I, well, you might think this is crazy, but I called to see if you would like to take piano or guitar lessons with me —they'd be free, of course. You see, I was teaching your mother the guitar before she died. She wanted to keep it a secret."

"Guitar?? Why in the world would Mom be taking guitar lessons?"

"Well, I'm not sure I should say —oh, I guess it doesn't matter now. Your mother wanted to try her hand at singing country music. And she wanted to be able to accompany herself on the guitar."

Avenelle, not at all certain she should be divulging Willa Jo's secret, wanted to reach out to Annie Jo, in spite of the girl's rude phone manners.

"Well, that's news. Of course, Mother and I weren't that close, but this is the first I've heard of her desire to go on the road."

"Anyway, I hadn't done anything for you since she died — well, I do think I brought a casserole over to the house — by the way, I heard you inherited the house. Do you like it?" Avenelle's voice sounded all trembly. She took a deep breath.

"What's not to like? It's a helluva lot better than that trailer I was living in. And I don't mind having Trudy downstairs — she's still running the shop, you know. It's a little scary to be here all day with Lawson — such a big house and all."

Avenelle was glad to know Trudy would continue The Sassy Lady — she was happy The Sassy Lady lived on.

"So, what do you think about the lessons? Do you have any interest?" Avenelle said.

"I guess. I mean, I could pay you — I inherited a lot from Mom, not just the house. I have money, too."

"No, no — this is something I want to do — for you and for Willa Jo. When would you like to start?"

"Well, I'll have to find a sitter for Lawson."

"Just bring him along. I'm used to little ones — I have a grandson — he's nine now, but I still have his old toys. My house is baby-proof and I've got blocks and books and other stuff...some dinosaurs, I think."

"I don't have a guitar or a piano," Annie Jo said.

"Why don't you use your mother's?"

"I haven't seen a guitar around here."

"Oh, that's right! Your mother said she hid it in the guestroom closet — she didn't want anyone to find out she was learning to play," said Avenelle, her breathing more calm now. "If you don't find it, let me know — I have one you can borrow. How about next Friday afternoon? Say 2:00?"

"Sure. That would be fine."

Avenelle hung up but not before she heard Annie Jo mutter 'weird.'

"Avenelle, you really need to do something with your hair. Sunday is coming up and, to tell the truth, you do *not* look like a preacher's wife," The Reverend said, his mouth full of fried chicken.

"Oh, I know, dear. Since Willa Jo died, I really haven't had time to find another hairdresser."

"How much time could it take? I'll bet if old McMillan died, I'd be able to find another barber in less than a minute."

"That may be true, dear, but you are not a woman. I can't trust my hair to just anyone."

"You hear the news?" The Reverend bit into one of Avenelle's homemade rolls slathered with butter.

"What news is that?"

"That Mad Dog person — he's moved out of Willa Jo's house and into a little apartment. I think the Sheriff told him not to leave town. I think he might be our killer."

"Humph. I don't think that boy has the brains to do such a thing. When I took the car to the garage, he was the one who worked on it. I went in with a strange sound in the engine and came out with no power steering and a broken mirror."

"I remember. At least they made it right — fixed it all and didn't charge a dime." said The Reverend.

"Humph. They should have paid *me* for my trouble."

While she was clearing away the dishes, Avenelle wondered who she could call about her hair. The Reverend was right — just because Willa Jo was dead didn't mean she had to let herself go. She didn't want Trudy to have anything to do with her hair. But the more she thought about her reasons, the more she kept coming to the same ugly conclusion. *Trudy is black. That makes me a racist.*

She felt ashamed of herself. Avenelle realized the weeds of prejudice had taken root once again in her heart — if she didn't watch herself, she'd become like those ladies in the congregation who held themselves above anybody who didn't look like them. That's how Avenelle had grown up. Old Man Avery — that's how she always thought about her father — said hateful things about everybody — blacks, Mexicans, Muslims, gays — anybody who he could hate, he did. She'd promised herself, even before she came to know God, she would never be like him. Those sprouts of bigotry would have to go. This wasn't the first time Avenelle knew she'd have to have a talk with herself...and God. If you lived in this world, you couldn't help be corrupted by it — Avenelle knew that from her early years. She was as susceptible to racism as anyone. She depended on God to show her when to cleanse her heart one more time. Sadly, she knew this would not be the last occasion she'd have to go to God for help against sin.

She realized she'd assumed Trudy knew only about 'black' hair. But maybe she was wrong; maybe Trudy knew a lot more than Avenelle gave her credit for knowing. She'd give The Sassy Lady a call in the morning and talk to Trudy about getting her hair done.

Chapter Fourteen

"A glass of wine and a flat iron can fix just about anything!"

~The Beautician's Notebook

July

Mad Dog looked around at the small space he now called home. Believe it or not, he kinda liked it. Easy to keep neat, no yard work, cheap. When Annie Jo'd come to tell him about the will, Mad Dog knew his life was about to change — and not for the better.

As he'd expected, she told him Willa Jo had left the house and most of the money to Annie Jo. But, she'd also left *him* fifty thousand dollars. Him — Mad Dog McGee. Fifty thousand smacks.

Damn.

Fifty thousand was nowhere near enough to get back into racing — and now, with Willa Jo gone, he had no hope of attracting a sponsor. His racing career was done. He was pushing thirty-five, getting old for racing, old for someone to take a chance on him. He'd gone over and over what he should do now, with Willa Jo gone. Fifty thousand. It felt like such a lot of money, but it wasn't a drop in the bucket of what he'd need if he pushed the racing dream all the way to the top.

Maybe there was another way — a way he could race with no need of a sponsor. He'd have to think about it.

Part of him wanted to get shuck of Summerset, head some place new, maybe up to the mountains where it wasn't so dang hot. The July weather was about to kill him, working in the garage. And August would be so much worse.

But he couldn't go anywhere, at least not yet. Not until Sheriff Hicks was convinced he'd played no part in Willa Jo's death. Damn, but they were slow with the forensics and other evidence. He'd been told a few weeks ago that they'd found four sets of prints on the plastic wrap Willa was wearing. His was not among them, but still, the sheriff didn't want him to leave town.

At first, he'd been scared shitless that they'd try to pin Willa Jo's death on him. They called him her lover in the newspaper. Made what they had together sound tawdry. And it hadn't been. It had been real and true. And yes, he'd call it love. But, now, with Willa Jo gone, was he supposed to become a monk? He'd caught himself looking at other women, but that was natural, wasn't it? It would be unnatural if he *didn't* look.

And he did *miss* Willa Jo, though he'd started going out again. The first place he went was the Paradise Café, in her honor. He'd met a cute little bartender who worked weekends. Needless to say, he'd been back a few times. He wanted to ask the girl out, but then he was afraid it would look bad — to the sheriff. So, he just got a couple of drinks on Saturday nights and flirted with her. Name was Kayla. She was Willa Jo's daughter, Annie Jo's, best friend. Sometimes, Annie Jo would drop Kayla off at work, that little kid of hers in the back seat.

He flicked on the TV and slouched in the recliner Annie Jo had let him bring over from Willa Jo's house. Nothing on in the middle of the day and he really wasn't watching; he liked the sound of television, the human voices, the constant stream of something. Suddenly, he stared at the TV. Will Ferrel in *Talladega Nights* — he'd seen it a dozen times as a kid.

The idea hit him like a ton of bricks. Stock cars. He could race stock cars. He had enough money to get started, if he was careful and worked some overtime. Mad Dog started laughing. The dream wasn't dead! Willa Jo might be, but the dream wasn't. Hallelujah, praise the Lord! There was still hope, still a chance.

"Oh, thank you, Willa Jo. You are still looking out for me — you're my personal angel," he said into the empty air. He'd get a used Chevy Lumina and he'd name it 'My Angel,' for Willa Jo.

Chapter Fifteen

"Never go outside in curlers — even if you're just going to the mailbox, somebody you know will drive by and see you — it's a universal law!"

~The Beautician's Notebook

July

Annie Jo was surprised to discover she enjoyed playing the guitar and she liked Miss Avenelle. Miss Avenelle was a patient teacher, encouraging and funny. They laughed when Annie Jo made a mistake and Miss Avenelle was always telling her to smile, look as if she enjoyed what she was doing.

"You look like you are facing a firing squad," Miss Avenelle would say and they would both start to giggle.

But the more Annie Jo practiced, the more she realized she had a gift for this. She'd never even heard of music theory, but she picked it up like she was born to it. Before she knew it, Annie Jo was writing little songs, mostly funny animal ditties to entertain Lawson. He loved it when she sang the one about the hedgehog getting stuck in the pig pen.

Since she no longer had to worry about work and money, Annie Jo was also discovering she enjoyed being a mom. She and Lawson would start the day around 7:00, when Lawson woke up. She would make them breakfast and then take Lawson outside, sometimes to the park, sometimes to the swimming pool. They would come home for lunch and afterwards, Lawson would take his nap. That was the time Annie Jo had free. She used these precious minutes to practice her guitar and write songs.

Annie Jo liked the rhythm of their lives now. She was finished with stupid men, she decided. There was more to life than that. Miss Avenelle told her what a good future she could make for herself and Lawson. She'd told her that no matter what Annie Jo did in the past, every day was a new start.

Slowly, Annie Jo had begun to believe Miss Avenelle.

Annie Jo knocked on Miss Avenelle's door, Lawson on her hip. He was sleepy and Annie Jo wished he would take a nap in the crib Miss Avenelle kept upstairs, 'hoping for more grandchildren,' as she said. *That woman sure did like kids. Weird.*

"Whew, it's a hot one today, isn't it? Come on in," Miss Avenelle said.

Annie Jo carried Lawson inside, where the air was cool and smelled of lemons.

"Would Lawson like some lemonade? How about you?"

"Sure. It's a good day for it," said Annie Jo as she admired Miss Avenelle's tidy home. Annie Jo had given up on neatness with a toddler around. It wasn't just the uncluttered feel of Miss Avenelle's house that Annie Jo liked; the place felt welcoming and safe. The walls of the front room where the piano was located were a soft lavender. In the den, where they usually held their lessons, pale yellow brightened the day. But it was Miss Avenelle's kitchen Annie Jo liked best. It was old-fashioned and homey, though all the appliances were stainless steel and very modern. But the cabinets were white and the countertops white tile. Up to the wainscoting, there was blue and white gingham wallpaper, with shiny white above. Miss Avenelle had blue glasses and blue stuff all over the place. It was Annie Jo's idea of perfect.

Miss Avenelle said, "Here you go, my sweet Lawson. How is my boy today?" as she handed Lawson a sippy cup full of lemonade. She then handed a glass to Annie Jo. She took the cold, blue glass in her hand and sipped. Delicious. Of course, everything Miss Avenelle cooked was delicious. She'd plied Lawson with chocolate chip cookies to die for and gave Annie Jo half a pound cake to take home. Sometimes, she fixed them lunch and it was some of the best food Annie Jo ever put in her mouth. Her mom had never been one for domestic skills, had no gift of it, so she claimed. Annie Jo understood, now, that Willa Jo had been tired from work most days. It was easier to get a Happy Meal than to cook. For years, Annie Jo had held McDonald's against her mom, but now she understood. Kids could wear you out — and Annie Jo didn't have to add work to her load these days. She could imagine how hard it must have been on her mother.

Plus, Willa Jo loved her job. Annie Jo was beginning to understand that, too. She loved the hell out of playing the guitar and writing songs. A woman couldn't give everything to her child. She had to save something for herself.

Lawson's eyes were heavy-lidded, the look he got when he was really tired. He finished his drink, Annie Jo changed his diaper and Miss Avenelle put him to bed while Annie Jo tuned her guitar.

The lesson started out well; Annie Jo had mastered the chords to "Stairway to Heaven," which was one of Miss Avenelle's favorite songs. Miss Avenelle was just starting to show her the melody when Lawson cried.

"I'll go pat him a little, see if he goes back to sleep. You can work on this song until I get back," Miss Avenelle said.

Annie Jo listened as Miss Avenelle went upstairs. She did as she'd been told, practicing the music over and over. Several minutes passed. And then, several more. It was sure taking a long time up there. She wondered if she should go help Miss Avenelle. No, Miss Avenelle was a grandmother —she could handle it. Annie Jo put her guitar into its case and began to walk around the den, looking at pictures of the Young family from years gone by. She glanced at the many books in the shelves and pulled couple out to thumb through. She found one to her liking, *Wild*, by Cheryl Strayed. That name seemed perfect for an author who wrote about being wild —Annie Jo had strayed, too. She leafed through the book. She decided to ask Miss Avenelle if she might borrow it. She put the book back in its place, her eyes roving over the room. She saw a *People* magazine in a rack. She pulled it out. Even if the zine was old, she would enjoy checking it out. She loved *People*.

As she pulled the magazine out of the rack, Annie Jo spotted something. Could it *be*? It sure *looked* like her mother's notebook. Had the same fancy leather cover with all the intricate tracings. But what would her mother's notebook be doing *here*?

Annie Jo froze, listening for Miss Avenelle's footsteps on the stairs. She could hear Miss Avenelle singing to Lawson. Slowly, she pulled the book from the rack.

It *was* her mother's!

She'd recognize it anywhere. Quickly, she put the book under some papers and old music in the bottom of her guitar case. Then, she put the People back in place and made sure the rack looked just as it had before. Her heart was pounding. What in the world? What was Miss Avenelle up to? She thought she might have to call her father. She'd never liked having a sheriff for a dad; maybe that was one of the reasons she'd rebelled like she did. She wouldn't tell him everything — like she'd stolen the notebook from Miss Avenelle. Was it still stealing when Mrs. Avenelle had no business with it? She'd just tell him she might have seen it in Miss Avenelle's house. She was sorry to get Miss Avenelle in trouble, but she needed answers. She needed to know what was going on. Did Miss Avenelle have something to do with her mother's death?

***

Annie Jo put Lawson to bed for the night. Everything was quiet, except for the occasional tinkle of a wind chime. Annie Jo didn't really like her mother's chimes, but she hadn't wanted to take them down — not yet….

She picked up her cell and hit her dad's home number.

"Daddy? It's me, Annie Jo. I'm okay. Yeah, he's fine — sleeping like a little kitten, all curled up in a ball. I…I think I might have some information about Mom's murder." She wasn't sure she was doing the right thing — telling on Miss Avenelle.

"I…I think I saw Mom's notebook in Miss Avenelle's house…Young, Avenelle Young. You know, the preacher's wife. She's teaching me music and she had to leave the room and I was just looking around and….and I'm pretty sure I saw it…it was in the magazine rack. I…I thought you should know…."

Her father sounded strange, like what she said had pissed him off. But he'd thanked her and told her he wanted to take her to lunch on Sunday. She felt bad about not telling him she'd taken the notebook from Miss Avenelle's house. Maybe she should have told him she had possession of it. But she didn't want to — she wanted to keep the notebook and read her mother's thoughts. She didn't want him to take it for evidence. Maybe she would understand more about Willa Jo if she read that notebook.

Annie Jo hung up and felt confused. Why in the world would Miss Avenelle have her mother's notebook? Miss Avenelle sure didn't look like a murderer…but she'd learned from her baby-daddy looks could be deceiving. She popped open a can of beer and drank it down fast. This world was just too weird; she would never understand it.

Chapter Sixteen

"The local jail needs a good beautician — have you ever seen those poor women?"

~The Beautician's Notebook

July

It was Thursday night and The Reverend's garden was coming in fast and furious. Avenelle had fresh corn, tomatoes, beans and squash. She'd canned tomatoes all day, making her famous sauce to be used for spaghetti during the winter. She'd cut the corn off a zillion ears and cooked it with butter, then put it in freezer containers. Then, she'd called Adam and his family to invite them over for supper. She knew Pam wouldn't be able to refuse a good meal from the garden —poor Pam wasn't much of a cook

It was July 26th —Avenelle would never forget this day. For on this day, everything changed.

The Reverend had just finished saying grace when there was a knock at the door. Avenelle was going to answer, but Adam hopped up.

"Stay put, Mama —I'll get it."

She passed the vegetables around the table, along with homemade rolls and barbecued pork chops. She'd outdone herself with this meal, especially after canning and freezing all day. She was tired but happy as she looked at the faces of her family. Proud of her son and his wife, in love with her grandson, Kevin. She'd done all right for herself, in spite of everything. The Reverend could be proud of her, too. She'd overcome a little prejudice she hadn't realized she'd held in her heart. Of course, she shouldn't be too proud of herself for overcoming her bigotry. She should never have had those feelings to start with.

But, in spite of her fears, she'd let *Trudy* do her hair.

She hadn't known what to expect, but —knock her over with a feather —Trudy did a great job, almost as good as Willa Jo. The color was even a little better.

Yes, life was mighty fine. If only The Reverend would make up with Abel, things would be perfect.

When Adam came back from the door, he had the sheriff with him.

"Won't you join us, Sheriff Hicks?" The Reverend said.

"Looks mighty good — wish I could. But I'm here on official business. Miss Avenelle, I'm afraid you'll have to come with me."

"What's this all about?" The Reverend said, with all the power of his preaching voice.

"I'm sorry, Reverend Young, but I'm placing your wife under arrest for the possible murder of Willa Jo Temple."

"*What?* On what grounds?" The Reverend sprang to his feet so quickly he almost knocked over his glass of sweet iced tea. "This is madness — my wife is incapable of hurting a fly!"

"That may be true, but I have new evidence in the Temple case that places your wife at the scene of the crime," said the sheriff.

"What sort of evidence? Hearsay? Gossip?" roared The Reverend.

"Her fingerprints were on the chemical cape Willa Jo was wearing when she died. That places her at the scene of the crime," said the sheriff.

"Fingerprints? So what? She was a customer there for years....I'll bet her prints are in a lot of places. That's not enough to arrest her!"

"Actually, according to North Carolina law, it is. Plus, I have reason to believe Mrs. Young may be in possession of stolen property, which is why I have a warrant to search the place," said the sheriff. "Deputy Stokes, please read Mrs. Young her rights."

"Mom?" Adam said, his face ashen.

"Grandma?" said Kevin. The six-year-old, freckled from head to foot, looked terrified.

"This is outrageous! My wife most certainly was *not* involved in the murder of Willa Jo Temple," The Reverend shouted.

"That will be for a jury to decide, Reverend. I have to go where the evidence leads me."

Avenelle still sat glued to her chair. She knew she'd been told to go along with the deputy, but she couldn't make her legs work.

The Sheriff said, "Mrs. Young, would you please follow Deputy Stokes? We're going to the station where I will ask you some questions."

"She most certainly will *not*...." The Reverend said.

Avenelle finally was able to rise from her chair.

"Now, Rory, we have to cooperate with the police," she said as she turned to face the sheriff. "I'll be happy to go with you, Sheriff. Ya'll go ahead with your dinner. I'll be okay —No, Rory, I don't need for you to come with me. Matter of fact, I'd rather you didn't."

The Reverend was stunned into silence as he slowly sank back into his chair. He sat there immobile. Avenelle turned to follow the sheriff. She could hear Kevin and Adam calling after her, begging her to wait, to let them come. She caught a quick glimpse of Pam, her mouth slightly open, her eyes big and round. She ignored the clamor and kept her eyes on Tal Hick's head. She briefly noted a couple policemen in uniform searching the downstairs. She was in for it now. Once they found that notebook, they would have all they needed to convict her.

One of the deputies stopped Avenelle before they hit the front door.

"Ma'am, we were told you had Willa Jo Temple's notebook in your home. Won't you save us the trouble of tearing the place apart and tell us where it is?" he said.

Avenelle knew if they found that notebook, she would be doomed.

"You'll just have to go ahead and ransack my house — I don't have any notebook." She hated to lie but she had no choice.

Turning away from the man, she headed once again to the front door, following Deputy Stokes. The sheriff tapped her on the shoulder and asked her to turn around.

"I'm sorry to do this, Mrs. Young, but I'm just following procedure. Hold your arms out in front of you," he said.

"Is this really necessary?"

"I'm afraid so. Under the law, we must treat everyone the same way. Even if you were president of the United States, if I were arresting you in North Carolina, I'd have to cuff you. That way, we follow procedure. We insure everyone is treated equally under the law."

She did as he said and he put her in handcuffs. Oh, how many times had she seen this done on TV? But in real life, it was uncomfortable and irritating. Avenelle imagined she'd have very chafed wrists and she wished she'd stuck a bottle of hand lotion in her purse. Not that it would have done her any good. When she grabbed her purse off the hook next to the front door, the sheriff had gently taken it from her, telling her she wouldn't be needing it. At that moment, she felt tears threatening — the sheriff saw them and relented. He allowed her to take the purse, after searching through it quickly. What did he think she had in there? A gun? Avenelle felt a giggle about to erupt. No crazies! Not now!

The policeman opened the door to the back seat of the car and helped Avenelle inside, pushing her head down so she wouldn't bump it, just like she'd seen on TV. In a strange way, it was all very exciting. The officer got in the car and instructed the driver to get going. She could hear them talking, but the screen between the front seat and the back blurred all their words. They drove through Main Street and hit Highway 17, heading north, toward Wilmington. Avenelle watched as the setting sun splayed golden rays over everything, making the world glow. Avenelle didn't hear the siren and wondered if the blue lights were flashing. A few people on the street watched, but Avenelle was pretty sure no one could see her. She sank further down in the seat.

She began to feel odd, as if she were living in a dream. She could hear her teeth clattering together and she thought she might have to throw up. Again, she felt laughter bubble up from her throat. She couldn't stop it. Her big toe was throbbing as if she'd stubbed it hard---the crazies. She could feel them coming on — just like they did whenever she was stressed. No matter how serious the situation, 'the crazies' appeared. Avenelle did her best of keep control, but once they got started, it was almost impossible to stop them. Avenelle began to repeat the Lord's Prayer over and over in her head. Sometimes, that helped. Our Father…

The drive to the Chadwick County Government Complex seemed to take forever. Avenelle had been to the Complex before, to pay her taxes and to battle a speeding ticket. But she'd never been to the jail. She tried to put that thought out of her mind. She wondered about The Reverend and her son. What must they be thinking? Of course, they had no idea she'd stolen Willa Jo's notebook and hidden it in the magazine rack. How the sheriff found out, she'd never know.

Her poor husband. This must be the worst thing ever to have happened to The Reverend. After all, he'd led a very sheltered life — no squalid conditions in childhood, no sordid love affairs — just the worry of preaching an adequate sermon every week, keeping his flock in good order and providing for his family. He was such an innocent.

The driver turned right off the highway and drove for a few miles on a lovely, country road. An unlikely place for a prison, Avenelle thought. He pulled into the complex and Avenelle watched as he circled around the Board of Education, the Courthouse, the Department of Revenue, all the way to the back end. The driver stopped in front of a very, very tall gate. Avenelle noticed razor wire curled across the top. It glistened in the waning sunshine.

The officer opened her door and ordered her to get out. Then, he pushed a button and those gates swung open. Avenelle once again found her legs refused to work. She couldn't move. Finally, she was able to swing her legs around so her feet touched the ground. With a guard at each elbow, Avenelle was escorted to the jail entrance. The deputies paused at the door while both men took out their guns and placed them in a box to which each had a key. They locked their weapons inside, then pushed a code which allowed them to enter the jail itself.

As she entered, Avenelle noticed a cage-like space to her left. It was empty. The guards helped her up to the front counter where another deputy wrote down all her information: name, address, phone, DOB, occupation. They took her fingerprints. Then, they told her to look into a little camera on the computer screen.

"What's this?" she said.

"We just want your picture, lady. Look at the camera," said the man behind the desk.

"Do you mind if I freshen my lipstick?" said Avenelle. Oh no, how ridiculous. At first, she wondered what made her say such a stupid thing. Then she realized 'the crazies' were closing in. Hallowed be Thy name…

"Just look at the camera," he said. He pushed a button and she heard a click.

"Oh, can I see it? I'll bet it's not as good as my driver's license picture," said Avenelle. She clamped her hand over her mouth —she was clearly out of control.

"Sorry, lady, we don't have time to let the inmates see their mug shots. Whaddya think this is, a selfie we're gonna splash all over the net?"

Avenelle felt herself blush. She couldn't believe 'the crazies' were taking over. Not now; not when it was a matter of life and death. Good God, she prayed, please don't let 'the crazies' spill the beans about the notebook. If they found *that*, she'd be doomed for sure.

The deputy made her hand over her purse. Then, two guards escorted her to a small room to the right, the examination room. A nurse asked about her general health, whether she'd been out of the country in the last three weeks, whether she was HIV positive (imagine!) and if she had any allergies. When the exam was complete, a female guard directed Avenelle to another small room directly opposite the medical office.

"Strip down for a shower and put all your belongings in this bag. Even jewelry — those earrings and your watch. Here's the uniform you'll be putting on," said the woman. Her manner was clipped, businesslike.

Now, Avenelle was truly afraid. When the sheriff had arrested her, she'd been scared enough for 'the crazies' to appear. But now, she felt as if she were splitting in half — one part of her was still at home enjoying a meal with her family. This other half was play-acting in some dark fantasy come to life. Something about having to remove her clothes and wear that dreadful *orange* jumpsuit....ugh...made the jail experience it all too real. She wasn't sure what she'd do next.

"Ma'm? Ma'm? What about panties? I see there are none included —just the suit itself. Should I keep my own panties?" Avenelle said.

"Lady, this would be such a great moment for a 'don't get your panties in a wad' joke. But no, as I *said,* put *all* your belongings in the plastic bag. You'll be going commando."

"Commando?"

"No panties...just you and the suit."

Oh dear. Most uncivilized. Avenelle had never gone 'commando' in her entire life...not even when she was running wild with Rock Bonner. She sighed, then slipped her capris and panties to her ankles. When in Rome.....

She pulled off her shirt and unhooked her bra, folded everything neatly — hiding her panties and her bra inside her outerwear, of course —and stepped into the tiny shower stall. There was no curtain. And the floor was cement. Avenelle couldn't help but wonder whose feet had touched this very same concrete...some monstrous criminal....with athlete's foot, no doubt. She shuddered.

The concrete was cool, and the hot and cold spigots looked ancient, the same kind that used to be in her grandmother's house. She turned on the hot first and stepped back. It was cold...very cold. She huddled in the farthest corner, worried about getting suddenly scalded. She would give it a few minutes to warm up. She was shivering now. Still, nothing but cold water. She started singing hymns —"In the Garden,"

"Amazing Grace" — she sang very softly. She didn't want the guard to hear her — it might be illegal, for all she knew. Finally, the water made it all the way to luke-warm. Avenelle stood beneath the slow trickle and unwrapped the sliver of soap she'd been given. At least the soap was new...no hairy criminal had used it on his privates. Oh dear heavens, she felt faint.

She showered very quickly, arching her back to keep her hair from getting wet. She had no idea how long she would be in the jail, but at least her hair would look nice. She wrapped the grayish white towel around herself and tried to ignore the industrial smell emanating from it. Clorox. Lots and lots of Clorox.

She felt giddy again. And now, she thought, 'm'lady's ensemble.' She put one leg into the jumper, then pulled the suit halfway up and pushed the other leg in. The material was heavy cotton and treated with some sort of stuff that made the cloth stiff and uncomfortable. She pulled the rest of the uniform over her arms and zipped up. She felt like an astronaut.

She had about six inches of material hanging down from each leg, so she rolled the pants up to her ankles. She slipped the paper shoes on and padded around for a minute, noting the shoes didn't get wet. They must have had special chemical treatment, too. She could get some morbid illness from exposure to all these synthetics.

Avenelle tapped on the door, as the guard had instructed her. The door opened quickly and the guard took her bag full of clothes and jewelry.

"What happens next?" Avenelle said.

"I shackle you."

"Do you have to do that? I promise I'm not going anywhere. Don't I get to call a lawyer?"

"Ma'am, this is just procedure. It's the law. I'm sorry — I know it's hard to accept this kind of treatment. Out in the world, you have a life — you *are* somebody. Here, procedure rules. If we don't follow it, a murderer can literally get away with murder. So, please, step this way," said the guard, pointing to the hallway on the left. "You'll get your lawyer after the sheriff talks to you."

She led Avenelle back to the desk, where they stopped while another guard placed heavy chains around her ankles. These would certainly turn her delicate ankles into raw flesh and she wished again for her lotion. She'd always had such nice ankles. She wondered if these shackles would scar her. She discovered as she tried to follow the guard that the shackles allowed only the smallest steps. They might as well have bound her feet like the emperors did in old Japan.

"Where are we going?"

"The holding cell. You'll stay here until the sheriff calls you to come into the interrogation room. So, relax, take a nap. I'm sure it won't be too long. The magistrate has to decide your bond within 72 hours —three days. But, if they think there's enough evidence, they won't let you out at all. But most likely, unless they find that notebook, the longest you'll be in here is three days. So relax —you got nowhere to go."

Door number three. What could be behind it? Her home for the next three days —at least. All she could do was pray they wouldn't find the notebook. But how could they miss it? It was in plain view, if you knew where to look.

The room was smaller than her walk-in closet with one very narrow cot against the wall. There was an equally small sink on the opposite wall and a toilet next to the sink. No curtain or wall or anything. A person walking by could look into the one window on the door and catch her using the bathroom. Horrible. One roll of toilet paper, a very coarse variety, was attached next to the commode.

No phone. No Kindle. No books or magazines. Just a cot, a bathroom of sorts, a flat pillow and a thin set of sheets with which to make the bed. Not exactly the Ritz. Avenelle sighed. She unfolded the sheets and pulled them on the mattress. It was hard to move around with those damn shackles on, but she managed. She sat down. Hard and lumpy. Avenelle wondered if all this were necessary —after all, she'd only stolen that silly notebook. But the sheriff certainly thought she'd done much more. The sheriff thought she'd *killed* Willa Jo. But she knew she hadn't. Was all this arrest business necessary? It reminded her of the way her father made sure she paid the full price for her youthful indiscretions. To the full extent of the law....just has her father would have wanted.

Avenelle sat, then lay down, then sat again. She couldn't get comfortable in the scratchy uniform. She heard voices from outside and hopped up to the window. Just the guards laughing at something —probably *her*. She waved to them. Oh no —why did she do that? 'The crazies' again. She waved once more — it seemed uncontrollable. Either the guards didn't see her, or they refused to wave back. So, Avenelle waved more vigorously. She was determined to make them acknowledge her, realize she was a real human being, not just some ....well....*criminal.* Let them think she was crazy---what did she have to lose?

Finally, one of the men saw her and meandered to her door; she heard the lock click and there he was, an officer in her little room.

"What do you want?" said the policeman.

"Oh, I don't really want anything —I was just waving. You know, being friendly."

The officer sighed. It sounded like one of The Reverend's sighs whenever Avenelle told him she wanted to 'talk.'

"I'm sorry to disturb you — but, now that you're here, do you think I could have my purse? I'd love to dab on a little lipstick, touch up my hair. And I need to call my daughter-in-law to tell her I won't be able to keep my grandson this Thursday....Thursday's her bridge day and I usually keep little Kevin. Well, there are just a lot of calls I need to make," Avenelle said. She knew she was babbling, but her mouth kept moving —her teeth chattered again.

"Ma'am, do I look like a concierge at a hotel? You are in JAIL. You may not have your purse, your phone, your anything until you are arraigned," he said.

"Oh, I see. Well....do you think I might have some sort of curtain to put across my window —Anybody can see me if I need to ...you know."

"No, ma'am. I'm sorry but this is the way things are done here. You'll just have to suck it up."

"Do you know who I am? I am Mrs. Avenelle Young, wife of The Reverend Rory Young. I have never been in trouble with the law in my adult life, except a speeding ticket. I'm not some common criminal."

"Ma'am, the law doesn't care who you are. We have our procedure here and we must follow that protocol. If you were the President of the United States, you'd be treated just the same."

"That's what you *all* say. I wish I *were* the president —I'd change things."

The officer returned to the group and, shortly after, Avenelle heard raucous laughter. At her expense, no doubt. She lay on the cot and closed her eyes. Did the sheriff really think she killed Willa Jo? Maybe she *had* been at the Sassy Lady that morning, but she hadn't killed anyone. She would not tell them anything — she had to keep her past *in* the past. After all, keeping silent was one of her rights — the deputy had read them to her. If The Reverend discovered her secret, there would be a divorce and scandal, humiliation in front of her sons and her grandson, everybody. The whole town would know her shame — the gossips would have a field day. No, Avenelle would keep her mouth shut. They couldn't *make* her talk.

Eventually, Avenelle fell into a dreamless sleep. The opening of the door awakened her. A guard with a plate of food entered and placed her food on the edge of the cot.

"Enjoy," he said.

"Humph," said Avenelle.

On the plate was a grilled cheese sandwich that looked as if someone had been sitting on it, a cup of cottage cheese with fruit cocktail across the top, a pint carton of milk — the kind you get in elementary school cafeterias — and a dry-looking brownie. Avenelle ate the fruit and cottage cheese and left the rest.

Maybe these three days wouldn't be so bad — she might even lose five pounds. Could a person lose that much weight in three days? A person past menopause? A person whose metabolism was dead?

She thought it might help to exercise so she lay on her bed and did leg lifts, but she had to lift both legs together because of the shackles. She gave up after five. She tried pelvic tilts and the one where you bring your knees to your chest and hold for thirty seconds. Then, inspired, she got on her feet and began marching in place. Only she couldn't lift her legs very high. She sang "Onward Christian Soldiers" softly to herself, to get the rhythm right. After that, she did ten jumping jacks — which were really half-jumping jacks because of the damned shackles. She kept thinking 'damned shackles, damned shackles' with ever little hop she gave. She was right in the middle of one when she practically hit the guard in the face as he entered her cell to retrieve her tray.

"I'm so sorry," she said.

"You didn't hit me, ma'am. If you'll let me by, I'll get that tray out of here — you didn't eat much. Don't blame you — not that good, is it?"

"Not the best. You look *way* too young to be a police officer."

"I'm twenty-three but everybody tells me I don't look it."

"What's your name?" said Avenelle.

"Andrew...Andrew Carter."

"Hmmm, Carter, Carter...are you kin to Cassie Carter?"

"Yes'm. That's my granny."

"I used to play cards with her years ago — Well, how about that? You tell Cassie I said hello, won't you?" Oh, right, like Cassie would want a message from jail — where was Avenelle's *mind*?

"Will do. Good night, ma'am," he said, taking the tray as he left.

Avenelle returned to her cot. What a nice young man, she thought. He probably thought she was nuts, but she didn't care. She was completely calm. She closed her eyes and, surprisingly, fell into a good, deep sleep.

***

"Breakfast, ma'am," said another officer.

"Good heavens, what time is it?" Avenelle said, her eyes trying to adjust. It was dark inside her little room — she hated calling it a cell — and couldn't be 8 a.m.

"Six o'clock, ma'am. Time for chow," he said, setting the tray on the foot of her cot.

She very carefully got out of bed, so as not to send food flying over the floor. She'd forgotten she was in her orange jumpsuit and had a flash of embarrassment that the officer was seeing her in her nightgown. Then, she remembered — the lovely orange ensemble. And the damn shackles. How could she have forgotten *those*?

"Thank you, officer."

"The sheriff will see you around 8. Someone will take you to his office. He's just going to ask you a few questions."

She stared at the tray of food; it looked even more unappetizing than last night's meal. Mushy eggs with a hard round of sausage, a biscuit covered in something that was supposed to be gravy but looked more like sludge, a cup of coffee — no cream or sugar. Avenelle ate what she could of the eggs. She might need her strength and besides, protein was good for dieting.

After breakfast had been cleared away, Avenelle brushed her teeth with the toothbrush that had been provided. She worried about whether her teeth were getting as clean as with her electric toothbrush at home. Then, she figured it would be okay for three days. She returned to her cot and slept until there was a knock on her door.

"Mrs. Young? Time to meet with the sheriff," said the guard.

Avenelle rose to a sitting position and slowly got to her feet. Her mouth felt dry and had an unpleasant taste. She needed her TicTacs — she needed her purse. Oh, how she loved her purse — never had she realized the depth of her dependence on it — let's see, there were TicTacs, a half a pack of crackers, her make-up and comb, lotion, her phone — her whole life was in her purse.

"This way, ma'am," said the officer.

He walked next to her leading her by the elbow. She shuffled along in those damn shackles as best she could. She hoped they wouldn't have far to go. Unfortunately, the guard led her down what must have been the longest hall in the history of the world. Finally, he knocked on the door and she heard someone say, "Enter."

The guard escorted her into an office, smaller than she had expected. Behind the desk, Sheriff Hicks sat, shuffling papers.

"Thanks, Randy. I'll call for you when I need you," the sheriff said. "Good morning, Mrs. Young. Your husband called first thing this morning and has set up an appointment to see you around 10 — that is, if we're through here by then. He's very concerned, naturally."

"I expect he is," Avenelle said, determined to keep her remarks at a minimum.

"I have just a few questions for you, Mrs. Young. Were you on the premises of The Sassy Lady on May 1st of this year?"

Avenelle sat stock-still and averted her eyes.

"Ma'am, did you hear me? Were you at the Sassy Lady on May 1st? The day of Willa Jo Temple's demise…were you there?"

Avenelle continued to sit quietly, focusing her eyes on the plaque on the wall that said the sheriff had been commended for 'outstanding service. 'She noticed other certificates nearby and was glad she was in such capable hands.

"Mrs. Young, did you hear me? Look, I can't make you answer any of my questions, but it would help you if you'd respond. You're in trouble, ma'am. Your fingerprints were found at the scene of the crime. So I know you were there that morning. What were you doing there?"

Avenelle didn't move a muscle. She pretended she was the star of a movie about aliens — they had abducted her and were torturing her to get information so they could destroy the human race. She would not succumb to their methods. She would save the world with her silence.

"I know all this must be very scary for a woman such as yourself — a woman who has lived a decent life — why, you and your husband are pillars of the community here in Summerset. I'll bet you are terrified. Which is why I want to help you. If you'll just tell me what happened that day, we can move on. Maybe there's a good reason your prints were on the shoulders of Willa Jo's chemical cape. Maybe you went there to work something out. Won't you tell me?"

Avenelle had to use all the will she had not to answer the sheriff. He was so kind and understanding. Maybe she *could* tell him what had happened....No! That was the alien mind-control. She would not speak; she would keep the world safe.

"What about the notebook — Willa Jo's notebook? We know you took it — why don't you make this easy on yourself and tell us where it is."

The notebook...they hadn't found it. Thank you, God, thought Avenelle. God had answered her prayer. It would be foolish to speak now, knowing they didn't have the notebook. Avenelle might get 'the crazies' once in a while, but she was not foolish. She pressed her lips together and refused to say one word.

After what seemed like forever, with the sheriff asking, pleading with her to talk, a guard finally took Avenelle back to her cell.

Chapter Seventeen

"Fix a woman's hair, it's nice for a week. Teach a woman to fix her own hair, it will be nice for two weeks — maybe."

~The Beautician's Notebook

July

Tal drove home just as the sun was setting. The sky, so blue earlier, was now pink and orange, with deeper purple at the edge of the horizon. He always enjoyed the drive to his modest house, a three-bedroom ranch with a full, unfinished basement. He'd intended to put a game room and another bedroom downstairs, maybe a half-bath. But so far, he hadn't had the time. Besides, why did he need more space? He never expected to marry again. Annie Jo never brought Lawson over; a game room would go to waste.

Three live oaks dotted the front yard, Spanish moss hanging from several limbs. The trees were old and the limbs gnarled. They shaded the entire area and he'd hung a hammock between two of them. In the cool of the evening, he enjoyed looking up at the stars.

Trimmed in dignified black with a slate-gray roof, his brick home suited him perfectly. He liked the layout, logical and easy to maneuver. He liked the crisp line and the precise way he cut the grass, diagonally, alternating direction each week or so. He got along well with his neighbors; housewives brought him food a lot, baked goods mostly. A few had offered him....other things, which he carefully declined. All in all, a good place to live.

He pulled into the garage and hoisted his briefcase over the backseat. He intended to work on Willa Jo's case over the weekend. But first, he had three phone calls to make. He wasn't looking forward to any of them.

Since he was working Saturday, he had to cancel the date he'd set up with Wilma —that wasn't her real name; her real name was Laura. But she lived in Wilmington and that's how Tal thought of her — Wilma, Wilmington. She was a divorcee, a few years older than Tal.

She'd come on to him after he'd given a speech to the local Woman's Club about self-defense. She wasn't a beauty, but she'd plied him with drink. They'd gone to bed that night. They were 'friends with benefits,' as she called it. She knew he saw other people and frankly, he didn't care whether she dated around or not.

He also needed to give Myrtle — her location, Myrtle Beach, real name, Carolyn — a buzz to explain why he couldn't come down to see her next weekend. Carolyn was another 'friend with benefits' but she was prettier than Wilma and kinder. She was a few years younger and was looking for a husband. Tal had made certain she didn't consider him a possibility.

He wasn't quite sure how he'd ended up with his current 'friends.' As long as there was no one special in Tal's life, the system seemed to work well. And there hadn't been anybody special since Willa Jo. Though he couldn't keep his mind off Clarissa, he knew she was married and likely to remain so. He knew he'd have to make do with Wilma and Myrtle.

He hit Wilma's number. No answer, so he left a message. He knew she wouldn't call him back. He also knew she'd be expecting a call from him later in the week. He hit Myrtle's number.

"Why, hey, Tal, darlin'. What you doin'?" said Myrtle in her best Georgia peach accent. She was from Atlanta and she could really pour it on when she wanted to — she told Tal she thought her Southern accent was sexy.

"You won't like what I'm *doin'*. I have to cancel our dinner next week. I'm working a case and I'll be busy until I solve it," he said, mirroring her drawl.

"But won't you need a break? I can be very relaxing."

"I know — I know. I'll call you as soon as I get free. I'm really sorry."

He heard the click of the phone and realized she'd hung up on him. She'd get over it.

Now, for the call he'd been dreading — Annie Jo.

"Daddy?" her voice said, as if he was the last person on earth she expected to call her.

"Yep."

"What's up?"

"Well, there's a little problem, Annie Jo. I thought you might could help me with it."

"So, what's the problem?"

"You tipped me off to Avenelle Young having Willa Jo's notebook. I got a warrant to search her house when I arrested her. Guess what?"

"I don't know — what?"

"No notebook. We didn't find a thing."

"Did you look in that magazine rack in the den?" said Annie Jo, her voice carrying a slight edge.

"Yep. We didn't find it anywhere…now, Annie Jo, you didn't take that notebook, did ya? You'd be obstructing justice if you *did* take it. And that's serious." Tal didn't want to come down hard on her — after all, she'd just lost her mother. It would be understandable if she *had* taken it — to read Willa Jo's thoughts, to connect to her in some way.

"I didn't take it, Daddy. And it pisses me off you think I did. You always think the worst of me, even now. Even with Mom gone."

Tal could hear the break in her voice and a sniffle. Damn. He'd made her cry. He was a lousy excuse for a father — nothing he'd done for Annie Jo had been right. Dammit.

"Don't cry, baby-girl. I had to ask. I know you didn't take it…don't worry about it. I'm sorry," he said, rubbing the spot on his forehead right between his eyes.

"Okay, Daddy…it's just….hard with Mom gone."

"Yes, it is. Hey, I've got a great idea — why don't we go on a picnic — you know, like we used to when you were little. We'll go up to Airlie Gardens and have a big time — Lawson would have a ball." said Tal, holding his breath, waiting for her response.

"Okay…but not yet. I'm not ready for anything like that yet…but we will, Daddy — I promise."

Tal could hear Lawson crying in the background. He knew she'd have to go. He didn't want to hang up. This was the most genuine conversation they'd had in a long time. He wanted to keep talking, get to know her. He wanted to be close to his grandson.

"I gotta go — it's time for Lawson's supper and he's getting fussy…Later, gator."

"Later."

Tal sat down in a heap on the couch and picked up the remote. He turned the channel to old reruns of *The Andy Griffith Show.* Andy always knew how to handle little Opie. Tal wished he had a clue about how to deal with Annie Jo. Maybe, somehow, he could reach her. Maybe Willa Jo's death would lead them back to each other. He felt sudden tears and wiped his eyes with the back of his hand. Everything had gone wrong — first, he lost Willa Jo to another man. Now, she was dead. He'd given up on having a relationship with his daughter and now, she had a baby with no husband and Tal didn't know his grandson.

He would change things. Somehow, he'd win back his daughter.

Chapter Eighteen

"I don't know why, but big hair seems to intimidate men."

~The Beautician's Notebook

July

The Rev. Rory Young was as nervous as he'd been on his first date with Avenelle. She'd been just twenty-five to his thirty-four and she was the most beautiful woman he'd ever seen. Her laugh was like tinkling bells and her smile made him feel all filled up inside, like he had just discovered the pot of gold at the end of the rainbow. She had strawberry blond hair she wore in a cut like Farrah Fawcett on that TV show. But Avenelle was prettier than any TV star. She had purity that showed on her face — flawless skin, bright hazel eyes and that million-dollar smile.

Rory had met her at church —she started attending after the choir had given a Christmas concert —she said she loved the music, played piano herself, and decided it was time to get involved with a church again. Like a lot of college kids, she'd turned away from church, preferring late-night talks about philosophy and Eastern religions.

Rory was pushing thirty-five and it was time for him to take a wife; it was expected. And, to his mind, Avenelle was perfect.

They got married the next year —Rory didn't waste any time once he'd found out her beliefs matched his own. He'd kept himself pure, waiting for marriage, and Avenelle had told him she'd done the same. During their courtship, he maintained control over himself, limiting physical contact to kisses and hugs. But, if he was honest with himself, he could hardly wait until the wedding night.

That night had been all he could hope for. Avenelle was enthusiastic, warm, snuggly —she was everything a man could want.

He couldn't mark the exact moment when he began to take her for granted. Maybe it was after his first son had been born. It seemed she no longer sought him out after the boy came along —she was always preoccupied with diapers and baths and toys and story-time. She'd been a wonderful mother and he was thankful for that. But it changed the way they were with one another. After the birth of the second son, they were both overwhelmed and busy with the chaos of raising a family. He thought of his son, Abel. Hah! The boy was anything but *able*. Rory smiled ruefully at his little joke.

A damn musician. How would the boy ever support a family playing the guitar...Rory had been right to disown the boy — he was running wild, or so Rory had heard, living in sin with some young woman. At least, they didn't have a child — he didn't have a baby-mama to contend with. Rory could never figure out where the boy got his wild, wild ways. Certainly not from *his* family. And Avenelle's father, Old Man Avery, well, he didn't have any give in him — his way was the straight-and-narrow and had been until the day he died. No, Abel's ways must be called his own.

Rory only wished Avenelle would follow his lead where their boy was concerned. But the woman had grown stubborn over the years — he knew she still called Abel, slipped him money whenever she could. No matter how hard he tried to pull the purse-strings, Avenelle always seemed to find money to send to Abel.

Rory could feel his belly tighten, as if it weren't already tight enough with the thought of visiting his wife in jail. He forced himself to think of his first-born, Adam. Now *there* was a boy to make any father proud. A financial analyst at the NC Credit Union League — a good, solid job that paid well — not a ton of money, but enough to provide for his little family. Heck, Rory even liked Adam's mousy wife, Pam. But it was Kevin, that darling grandson, who lit Rory's world. Adam had given him a grandson and how Rory loved that boy. He'd never realized what joy children brought into this old, tired world. He didn't know why he hadn't seen it before, with his own sons. He'd been too busy earning a living to enjoy his boys. But now, as he approached retirement, he could finally understand why his wife had been crazy about their children.

Avenelle. He'd almost forgotten — he was to be at the jail at 10 am. He put on his sports jacket, tightened his tie and headed for the car.

On the drive to the jail, Rory's stomach heaved and roiled. He worried about Avenelle. He didn't imagine his wife would last long in the clink. The Big House. The Slammer. He'd visited other inmates, but never in his wildest dreams, had he imagined his very own wife would be held inside those steely gates. He drove around the complex and found a parking place. He made certain to lock his car; after all, there *could* be a jailbreak.

He walked from his car to the holding facility; he'd been told it housed about three hundred prisoners, mostly held for misdemeanor infractions, any sentence that was less than a year. He buzzed at the chain-link fence as instructed and a guard came to meet him at the gate.

The guard, Colleen Turner, was a member of his church. Oh dear Lord, why....Avenelle's arrest would be all over town. He'd have to face his congregation Sunday. He'd think about that later. Right now, he just wanted to see his wife.

Officer Turner guided Rory into the jail where he had to sign in, giving all pertinent information to the officer behind the station. Then, Officer Turner took him to a small room with a table and two chairs. Avenelle was sitting on the chair facing the door.

Rory was taken aback at how small his wife looked, the orange jumpsuit hanging on her, at least three sizes too big. He saw where she'd rolled up the legs; he started when he saw the manacles around his wife's delicate ankles. She looked pale and her hair wasn't as well-kempt as usual. She had no make-up on and her big eyes stared up at him as if he could make everything okay. The look almost undid him.

"Good morning, Avenelle," he said. His voice sounded cold and strained. He didn't want to sound that way-he wanted to sound comforting.

"Hello, Rory."

He went to her and she stood so they could embrace. The guard looked the other way.

"How you holding up, Avenelle?"

"Okay — the food is terrible. Do you know how long I'll have to be in here?"

"The sheriff said until the magistrate hears your case and decides whether or not to give you a bail bond...for murder cases, they usually don't."

"Oh, Rory, I hope they will in my case — after all, I'm a preacher's wife. A mother and a grandmother. I'm a good person — really, I am."

“I know, I know. This is just some misunderstanding — a mistake.”

He comforted her as best he could. Good thing he’d brought pen and paper as she gave him very specific instructions about how to do the laundry, what vegetables to freeze, which ones to take to the neighbors — no tomatoes to Mrs. Abernathy down the street, she was allergic. He told Avenelle he would do his best to take care of the garden. She suggested he call Abel to help out, but he just shook his head. He would NOT call that boy and he resented Avenelle even suggesting it, as if she wanted to use the occasion of her arrest to mend things between them. Besides, he had no idea what Abel’s number was — but he’d bet Avenelle knew. She probably also knew *where* the boy was.

Finally, their allotted time was over. Rory hugged his wife again, told her he would pray for her and left the jail. He drove immediately to his office at the church and prepared his remarks for Sunday. After all, he had a job to do. He pushed thoughts of Abel and Avenelle out of his mind.

Chapter Nineteen

"This salt air turns your curls to frizz and your blond to green."

~The Beautician's Notebook

July

Clarissa awoke and glanced at the clock —3 a.m. She could hear the comforting beat of the waves against the shore and that helped orient her. When she first awoke, she thought she was back in West Virginia, back in the Talbot home, where she'd been sure she would die.

The dream. Again.

At least this time, she didn't awaken Ralph. Poor Ralph. His hearing wasn't what it used to be — in earlier days, he would have heard her whimpering 'like a little lost puppy' he'd said. He would have rolled over to her side of the bed and taken her in his arms, whispering, "You're okay, honey. It's only a dream."

She decided to get up. Of course, that woke Mitzy, who was sleeping in her doggy bed at the foot of the California king.

"Shhh. Come on, girl," said Clarissa as she picked the dog up to carry her outside. She shut off the alarm system, then took Mitzy downstairs to do her thing. It was a clear, cool night. The constellations were bright against the black satin sky, a sliver of a moon hung on a hook of stars. She could see the big dipper and Orion's Belt. She could even trace the faint outline of the bear Orion was shooting. She sighed, picked Mitzy back up and climbed the porch stairs, leading to the great room.

She didn't want to wake Ralph so she lit some candles and picked up an Oprah magazine. But she couldn't focus. She tossed the magazine on the cushion next to her and began to think.

She could still see the run-down shack where she'd spent the last two of her years in foster care. She'd run away at sixteen, run from the drinking and the drugs, the dirty house and the broken people inside. She'd run all the way to Virginia, sure she could pick up work somewhere. She knew how to babysit —she had kept watch over the

Talbot's five kids, who ranged in age from two to twelve. The oldest boy got smart with her, pelted her with gum tree balls while she was in the yard playing with the other kids. She couldn't blame him; he was as starved for attention and love as she was. She grew to care for the children over time, and gave them more notice than their mother ever did. Mrs. Talbot was too busy with her job as a teacher's aide. She'd been lucky to land that position, if you asked Clarissa, but the woman treated the job as if she were president of a large corporation. The job took her away from her own children and the drudge of housekeeping. She often stayed long past the end of the school day, catching up on her 'work.' Clarissa knew better; she knew Mrs. Talbot was just avoiding the world of work that waited for her at home. At least, Mrs. Talbot cared about her *job*; at home, it was another story. Clarissa did more to raise those children than Mrs. Talbot — that's what Clarissa called her, even though she'd been invited to call her 'Miss Ginnie.' It was Clarissa who straightened the house, did laundry and packed lunches for the kids, Clarissa who cooked them breakfast. It was Clarissa who cared for their scraped knees and elbows. All Mrs. Talbot did was read her trashy magazines and romance novels. She did usually manage to prepare supper some nights — fried bologna and hash browns.

Mr. Talbot worked in the coal mines, but was often laid off. Those were the times she dreaded. He'd drink all night and sleep all day, waking up to cuss at her and the kids. He didn't bathe for a week at a time and he smelled disgusting, like dirty feet. She didn't think he ever brushed his teeth — his breath was foul and you could get a whiff of it from across the room. He would hit the children for any minor infraction. And Clarissa, well, she was nothing but a slave as far as he was concerned. He gave her even more work than Mrs. Talbot did. Plus, he looked at her funny, especially when he'd been drinking. Sometimes, he would touch her when he didn't have to, as if by accident. And, when he was really drunk, he'd insist on kissing all the children 'good-night,' including her. She thought she would never get her lips clean after one of his boozy kisses. She would take a washcloth and scrub, scrub, scrub until her lips were sore. When she finally made her get-away, the only thing she missed was the kids.

While she was living with the Talbot's, she would lie in the lumpy twin bed she'd been given when she was told to share a room with ten-year-old Carol, the only Talbot girl. Sometimes, after Mr. Talbot beat one of the boys, Carol would come over to Clarissa's bed and crawl in with her.

Clarissa could still remember gazing up at the sky, looking at the stars and wondering who her real parents were. Why had they given her away? Was she such a terrible baby? She would grow upset considering what kind of people could dump their child like so much garbage. They were trash, that's what. And maybe she was, too. After all, she was *their* baby, whoever *they* were.

The anger would begin as a slow burn, then escalate to a full-blown fire. Rage would course through her body and she would be forced to leave her bed, sneak downstairs and out the door for a long, midnight walk. She swore if she ever found her birth mother, she'd beat the shit out of her.

Clarissa smiled at the memory of her fierce, younger self. She could remember her past, now, without the anger getting the best of her. She had no hope of running across her birth mother. She never bothered trying to look for her, hoping to find some sort of warm resolution. She knew that was for the movies. No, she would be happy with her Ralph, her savior. He'd found a mess of a girl and turned her into a pretty, polished woman.

She thought of the Sheriff. He was certainly a handsome man, ruggedly handsome as she'd heard some men described. He had the softest-looking hair, a full head of it. And she liked his mustache. Ralph never had facial hair, but was still a very attractive man. He worked out every day, biked and ran and lifted weights. He was buff, no doubt about it. Willa Jo used to say she wished he had a twin —a rich twin. That was Willa Jo, always playing an angle. Clarissa smiled at the thought of her best friend. She would always have her memories, some good, some bad. Willa Jo was one of the good ones. And she decided right then and there the next time she recalled life with the Talbots, she would think of Willa Jo instead.

She blew out the candles, grabbed Mitzy and tiptoed back to bed. She curled up next to Ralph and fell asleep.

***

The next morning, a Deputy Samantha Stokes called and asked Clarissa if she'd come down to the police station. Said it had something to do with Willa Jo's case. Of course, she'd come. She'd do anything to help find out exactly what had happened to Willa Jo.

Okay, she wouldn't mind seeing the sheriff, either. If he was even there.

She freshened her make-up, hopped in the Corvette and spun out of the driveway. Ralph hated it when she did that, but Ralph was away again on business. For a retired man, he sure made a lot of business trips — but she knew he was on various boards of certain companies. She admired him for taking it all so seriously and being so dedicated to serving the companies well. Sure, he got paid, but still — he was a good man.

When she arrived at the police station, she met Deputy Stokes at the front desk. The sheriff was nowhere in sight.

"I guess you're wondering why I asked you to come down."

"Well...yes." Clarissa observed the deputy — young, plain and about thirty pounds overweight. But disciplined. Stern.

"The sheriff has asked everyone who knew Willa Jo to come in for fingerprinting — forensics found some prints on Willa Jo's cape and we're trying to figure out who they belong to. We figured we'd start with Willa Jo's friends and customers."

"Well, I was both. I'd be happy to do whatever it takes to figure out what happened." Clarissa followed the deputy to the small room where they dipped and rolled her finger into some ink and pressed her finger onto the paper.

Over in a minute. She was glad it hadn't taken long — she wanted to run a few errands.

Clarissa didn't give her early visit to the police station another thought.

Chapter Twenty

"I cannot hear a thing when I'm blowing you dry. So please don't speak."

~The Beautician's Notebook

August

Rory Young sat in one of the pews in the Sabbath Home Church sanctuary. The room was empty. He stared at the stained glass windows depicting Biblical scenes that related to the sea. After all, Summerset was only a few minutes' drive to the ocean, so the pictures were relevant.

Rory was a fifth generation preacher. As the oldest son, it was expected he would follow in the family tradition. He'd been an obedient boy, so off he went to college to study religion and philosophy. He never found the courses of much interest, but did well enough. The class he really loved was geometry. He loved the neatness of the angles, the precision of the math. He enjoyed looking at a building and seeing immediately how it had been put together. He began to read on his own about architecture, Frank Lloyd Wright, Gaudi, and others. He'd hoped to take the history of architecture as one of his electives, but the class was already full before he could sign up for it.

Now, in what little spare time he had, he designed and built doll houses and gave them away at Christmas to needy little girls. It was the closest he'd ever come to feeling he'd done something kind and gracious.

Not that he didn't try. He took his vocation seriously, studied his Bible for inspiration, visited the sick and comforted the bereaved. When his younger son, Abel, had taken up rock music, yes, Rory had disowned him, but that was to be expected. Some of the lyrics the boy sang were, well, they were reprehensible in his eyes. And, though Avenelle had tried to persuade him that is was just a case of teenage rebellion, Rory felt he had to take a stand. There was right and proper and there was just plain wrong. Rory knew the difference. He'd wanted his son to know it, too.

But now, he was lost. Avenelle, his lovely, obedient wife —being held for murder. How had this happened? He knew Avenelle wouldn't hurt a flea, much less break one of the Ten Commandments, especially such a *big* one. Murder? His Avenelle?

As he squirmed on the cushioned pew, Rory realized just how lost he was without his wife. He missed her delicious meals, hot on the table every evening when he got home. He missed the convenience of having her type up his sermons; now, he'd have to hire a part-timer. Or do it himself. And who would accompany the choir and play the hymns? Another hire he'd have to make and the church was struggling as it was. He had to admit to himself he hadn't done very well over the last thirty-odd years. The membership was down by half and there were no young people left. He didn't know why the congregation hadn't fired him long ago. He reckoned it was his family's long history with the church. After all, his great, great, great grandfather had founded it.

Oh Avenelle.

He'd arranged bail for her — thank heavens the judge ruled her unlikely to flee and had not set a high bail, even though it was a murder case. Judge Luffy had been a long-time member at Sabbath Home and he knew Avenelle. She'd taken him many a casserole over the years, once when he had a knee replacement, another time when he had the shingles. Judge Luffy had no problem allowing Avenelle to roam unencumbered in Summerset. She would be released tomorrow, but Rory couldn't imagine her picking up with her church duties. He didn't want her to, not until she'd been cleared of all suspicion. Which he was sure she would be.

Wasn't he?

The truth was, Rory didn't know what to think. For the past thirty years, since he'd married Avenelle, he'd struggled to create an image —a happy, God-fearing family; a growing and enthusiastic church; a man in charge at home and work. Now, he had to face reality: he was a failure.

He rose from his seat, his eyes streaming tears. He walked, almost stumbled to the altar table. He fell on his knees. He was not a praying man; truth be told, he really didn't believe, not in his heart of hearts.

He'd never believed because he'd never, in all his sixty-odd years, *ever* felt the presence of God.

Oh, he'd heard others talk about God speaking to them, guiding them, comforting them. Even Avenelle had told him how she'd seen God work in her life. And she *did* pray, every day during her 'morning meditation' and at night, when he'd heard her whisper prayers for Abel and Adam. Nelle even prayed for *him*, her husband.

Damn her. She'd ruined everything with this crazy murder charge and her refusal to tell the police anything. Why wouldn't she just explain herself? Everyone in Summerset would believe her. People loved her. Everywhere she went, they said 'Hey, Avenelle.' All he got was a brief nod and a formal, 'Hello, Reverend.'

He didn't blame people, though. Avenelle was a good person, a truly good person. She took complete dinners to the sick and visited shut-ins. She'd taken that trashy Willa Jo's delinquent daughter under her wing. That girl made the whole house smell like cigarettes when she came for her lessons and that little boy, well, he got into everything, including Rory's secret stash of Jordan almonds.

The more he thought about it, the more he realized he cared for Avenelle. He'd thought he'd stopped loving her years ago. Oh, he was fond of her, sort of like being fond of a dog, a faithful old hound you'd grown used to. He hadn't considered her as a *woman* for a very long time.

He realized everything was his fault —all of it. He'd been arrogant and unyielding, nothing like the merciful, gracious God he talked about.

"If only You would touch me, let me feel Your Presence —just once, I would be a better man. Please.....please," he said. He hadn't realized he was speaking out loud.

"Everything okay, Reverend?" said a voice.

Rory froze.

Was *that* the voice of God?

He shook with desire —the deepest longing of his soul —how he wanted to hear the Lord's voice, how he was desperate for help in this crisis. He held his breath.

"I clean later if you busy," the voice said.

Perfect —he'd asked for God and gotten the janitor.

"Sure, Ike. Sorry. I'd forgotten this was your day to clean the sanctuary...just having a moment of prayer.

“’s okay, Reverend. I know you got a lot on your mind…May the Good Lord bless you and that wife of yours, too. We all know she innocent.”

Rory didn’t respond. He simply walked out of the church into the hot August day.

Chapter Twenty-One

"Nobody can love you like your mama can — not nobody!"

~The Beautician's Notebook

August

Annie Jo hated lying to her father, but she had no choice. Yes, she'd stolen that silly book — Willa Jo was her mother — how could she *not* have taken it? But she had not yet read her mom's notebook, mainly because she'd been so upset about everything. And when she was upset, Lawson was upset and hard to handle. She hadn't forgotten about the book. She just hadn't found time or a quiet place in which to read it.

Plus, she'd discovered Miss Avenelle had been arrested. Miss Avenelle was in *jail.* And it was Annie Jo's fault. First, lying to her father, then discovering Miss Avenelle's arrest — Annie Jo had been filled with guilt. This wasn't the way she wanted to live her life. She was working hard to turn over a new leaf — make something of herself, now that she had Lawson, now that her mother was dead. She wanted to make Willa Jo proud, somehow. And Miss Avenelle, too.

She learned about the arrest when she showed up with Lawson in her arms for her lesson. Reverend Young answered the door, which never happened before. He was always gone when Annie Jo arrived. Miss Avenelle said he was visiting the sick or working on his next sermon. She seemed relieved he wasn't around.

But last Friday, she'd just finished knocking on the door when Reverend Young opened it.

"I'm…I'm here for my guitar lesson. I'm Annie Jo Hicks….?" She felt herself begin to heat up, as if she were ashamed of herself for some reason.

"Oh…yes. The smoker. My wife isn't here."

"Oh…well, she didn't call to cancel so I just came on over," Lawson was wiggling to be put down and was saying 'Abbie' over and over again — his word for Miss Avenelle.

"No…no, she wouldn't have called. She's, she's …..well, I'll just come out with it. My wife has been arrested."

"Arrested? Oh no." At that moment, Annie Jo realized she was probably the one who put Miss Avenelle in jail. After all, she'd told her dad about the notebook being in Miss Avenelle's house.

She quickly took Lawson to the car, fastened him into the car seat and drove away.

She felt terrible. Guilty. She'd had Miss Avenelle arrested after the woman had been so kind to her, and to Lawson, too. Yet, Annie Jo also felt sort of powerful. All it had taken to get Miss Avenelle arrested was to give some info to her dad. Talk about quick results. It showed how seriously her father took her these days — like she'd finally, finally gained a little respect.

But Annie Jo hadn't wanted Miss Avenelle to get *arrested*; she'd wanted her dad to drop by for a visit, talk and get to know Lawson. She'd wanted her dad to ask more about the notebook and what she'd been doing in Miss Avenelle's house. But no, he just jotted down the information and that was it.

What had she expected? Neither her mom nor her dad had ever given her the time of day. She was the reason they got married in the first place; her mama was only nineteen when she'd given birth to Annie Jo. The marriage must have been bad because her parents got divorced when Annie Jo was only five. After that, she rarely saw her dad, and her mom was always working at the shop. Granted, after Grandma Bessie died, when Annie Jo was about fourteen, the shop was just downstairs, but still, Annie Jo felt left out. Left out of both parents' lives.

Annie Jo had pledged she'd do better when she had kids of her own. But then, she'd gotten pregnant with Lawson. Her baby-daddy was currently living up in Wilmington, a wanabe gang-banger. After he found out about the pregnancy, he returned to the big W, moving back in with his mother. It suited Annie Jo fine that he wasn't involved in Lawson's life. But the boy would need somebody. The boy would need a father figure. He didn't have one, not really. Her dad rarely came around and her Grandpa Rock acted like she didn't exist. What a fucked-up family.

Annie Jo realized she hadn't done the parenting thing any better than her mother had, after all. Looks like good ole Willa Jo hadn't been so bad — at least she had a job, a career. People liked her and respected her skill. Annie Jo hadn't earned skills or respect. She was a loser. The bad thing was, she knew it —knew herself to be worthless down in her bones.

Only Miss Avenelle made her feel special —like she might have some talent or musical ability. Miss Avenelle used to tell her, "There is nothing in the caterpillar that tells you it's going to be a butterfly." Annie Jo loved that idea, that she was a beautiful butterfly inside, waiting in the dark of the cocoon.

Such thoughts plunged her into deeper despair. How long would she have to wait? She'd been waiting for something all of her life —her dad's attention, her mother's love —but she didn't feel like she'd ever had either one. Then, she'd fallen for her baby-daddy and had gone down yet another road, another screw-up. But Lawson was the best thing that ever happened to her. And she was glad she had him.

She could hear Lawson squirming in his sleep. She had, maybe a half hour before he would wake and want his lunch. She pulled into the drive and carefully removed him from the car seat, climbing the stairs to put him in his crib. She patted his back until he settled once again. Then, she went to her room and picked up her guitar. She starting plucking out a melody. Before she realized it, she'd created a haunting tune. She began to hum it. As she hummed, she put words to the notes. She grabbed a pencil and started writing it all down.

Three days passed before Annie Jo had time to take a look at the notebook. She'd written an entire song, not a child's song this time, but one that gave voice to all the pain she felt inside. The more she sang her song, the more she liked it. Matter of fact, she thought it was good — really good. Maybe good enough to get a band to play it. Maybe even somebody like Brandi Carlile. Man, Annie Jo loved Carlile's music — sad, raw, powerful. Maybe she'd send the new song to her, you know, just to see what happened. That sounded like the kind of idea Miss Avenelle would like. Annie Jo had heard Miss Avenelle had been released on bail. She hadn't seen her yet. She didn't know if Miss Avenelle would want to see anybody or not. Maybe Miss Avenelle had figured out it had been Annie Jo who turned her in to the sheriff. Naw, the old lady wasn't that smart.

Annie Jo took the notebook from its hiding place under her mattress and opened the heavy leather cover. The cover was thick and looked like the kind of thing you might buy at a craft show. Well, that sounded right — Willa Jo loved to go to such shows, especially the Craftsman's Classic Christmas Show down in Myrtle Beach every November. She probably picked it up there.

It was dated September, 1993. Annie Jo would have been three, her mama only twenty-two. Wow, Willa Jo was young. Oh, she'd known Willa Jo had given birth to her when she was only nineteen, but somehow, seeing that date and thinking about how old her mother had been sort of made Annie Jo see things in a different light. She began reading:

> Sept. 15, 1993
>
> I signed the lease on the building next to Belk's and I've ordered all the equipment. It was a pretty penny but old Judge Luffy gave me the money without blinking. I do believe he'd eat sugar right out of my hand. So, I'm off. Off on a new adventure. I can't wait to show Tal the place and bring Annie Jo down to the shop. How my clients will love her! What's not to love? That girl is my heart, my very heart. I would do anything for her. I would die for her.
>
> But this isn't supposed to be about my family. I bought this notebook on my own mama's advice. Bessie told me my customers would say some outrageous things and I ought to write them down. Bessie said she wished she'd done it — now, when she wanted to tell a funny story about work, she couldn't remember. So, I'm taking my mama's advice. I'm going to keep all the secrets my clients tell me right here — secrets and funny stories. And, when she's old enough, I'll give this notebook to Annie Jo. So she will know how much I love her and how hard I worked to give her a good life.

Annie Jo hadn't expected to be mentioned in the notebook. She couldn't believe how much her mother seemed to love her. But the more she thought about it, the more she remembered —picnics with the whole family, her mother singing her to sleep, staying up late on Saturday nights watching old movies —she'd forgotten those things. She hadn't shed many tears for her mother. After all, she'd known Willa Jo hadn't approved of her having a baby 'out of wedlock.' That's how Willa Jo had put it. When Annie Jo had tried to explain that nobody cared about that old stuff anymore, Willa Jo had disagreed. From that point, they had drifted. Even with Lawson, Willa Jo was somewhat cold at first —until she fell in love with him just as

Annie Jo had. Before that happened, Annie Jo had gotten really pissed at her mother. Nobody would snub her baby, Annie Jo thought. Not even her mama.

And so they drifted further apart.

Lawson called her from his crib. She closed the book, her eyes filled with tears. Her mother had loved her; loved her in the same fierce way Annie Jo loved Lawson. The tears ran down her cheeks and her nose started leaking. Soon, all the liquids comingled. When Lawson saw her, he reached his arms up to her.

"Mommy?" he said as he wiped her tears on his chubby hand.

"Mommy's okay, baby. Let's get a snack," she said, putting him on the floor. He toddled toward the kitchen while she walked behind him, grabbing a tissue on the way. She forced herself to stop crying, at least in front of Lawson.

Something about reading Willa Jo's words, written in her own hand, had touched Annie Jo. Her mother had dreamed a dream and that dream had included Annie Jo. Her mother had had the courage to follow her dreams. Annie Jo would do that, too. She vowed she would put her new song on a CD, type up the lyrics, and mail it to Brandi Carlile. She would do it that very afternoon.

Chapter Twenty-Two

"Sometimes, the meanest people in the world can be found in church."

~The Beautician's Notebook

August

Avenelle was happy to breathe the fresh air again. Not that jail had been unbearable, merely unpleasant. For a jail, it was better than most. Of course, she'd had no idea what other jails looked like, but in her mind, Chadwick County Jail was a-okay.

The Reverend picked her up right on time. Punctual —that was her husband. He didn't said a word on the ride home and neither did she. He carried her bag of items —her personal possessions, according to the police, and dumped them on her side of the bed. He then stomped down the steps, thundering like God Himself. She put her things away, then walked slowly downstairs to fix herself a glass of iced tea. She took her time, gazing fondly on all her furniture, her plants — 'I've missed you' — she called to the philodendron and the fichus. She touched the knick-knacks on the shelves and tables as she made her way to the kitchen.

Avenelle entered and looked around. Everything was tidy and in its proper place. The blue and white wallpaper always cheered her; she loved her kitchen, the bright white curtains at the window above the sink, the touches of yellow sprinkled like salt over a well-cooked meal. This was the heart of her home. This was where her family gathered to eat, do homework, talk, play board games — Avenelle always enjoyed her kitchen, but never did she love the room as much as she did at this moment. She reached for one of the deep blue glasses and filled it with ice. She poured tea from a full pitcher. Rory — he'd made tea. How very sweet. How very surprising. She was amazed at how resourceful her husband had become in her absence.

Avenelle was glad to be home, relieved to be changing into her regular outfit of shorts and a tee shirt, as opposed to those God-awful orange suits. She didn't think she'd be going anywhere any time soon, so she'd selected comfortable, casual clothing. She wasn't even sure The Reverend would allow her to go to church. He told her he'd been able to get a substitute pianist as well as a temporary secretary. She'd been relieved of her duties.

Of course, the garden would need attention — that is, unless The Reverend had hired a part-time gardener/canner. Maybe he'd hire a *very* part-time hooker to assist with his monthly needs. Avenelle was shocked at her thoughts. Maybe her four days in jail had tainted her in ways she didn't comprehend. Or maybe, just maybe, she was tired of being The Reverend's *perfect* wife. She realized while she'd been locked up that trying to be perfect was sort of like a prison in itself. She hadn't been very kind to herself, not really, since her 16th birthday. No, she'd sentenced herself to penance, doing work she didn't like for a man she didn't love.

There. She'd said it. The thought she'd stuffed down into her subconscious came roaring out. She tried to be a good wife and she *was* a good mother. But there was something freeing about going to jail, being accused of a crime. The worst had happened and she was still alive, still here, still in her own house.

Since her release on bail, a strange sense of calm had descended on Avenelle, like the white dove in the Scriptures. She wasn't sure if it was the Holy Spirit or a mild case of insanity, but she felt better than she had in years. The crazies, it seemed, had retreated from whence they'd come and Avenelle was glad. Being silly in jail would not help her case.

She was just getting ready to lie down for a little rest when The Reverend tapped at the bedroom door. The door was open; why he didn't just come on in?

"Avenelle, we have to talk." His whole body slumped and he spoke in his solemn voice, the voice he'd used with the boys to make them see the error of their ways.

"What about?" she said, reclining on the bed and kicking her shoes off.

"I think you know what about."

"If you think I'm going to tell you any more than I told the police, you're wrong, Rory. It's nobody's business what I was doing at The Sassy Lady so early in the morning. The question should be, 'What was Willa Jo doing there?' "

"It was *her* shop in *her* house. Besides, she's dead; we can't ask her."

He walked over to his side of the bed and sat down. Avenelle saw a few more gray hairs. His color wasn't good and she realized how hard this had been for him. She felt sorry for the man. He was lost without her.

"Avenelle…I know you didn't kill Willa Jo. Why, I've lived with you for thirty years — I think I know you pretty well. I just don't believe you did it."

She was touched by his faith in her. He seemed vulnerable, approachable. Not the overbearing man who had to be right with God every minute of the day. She reached up and touched his cheek.

"But!" he said.

She jumped at the high volume of his voice. She jerked her hand away from him and placed her hands on her tummy. She started twiddling her thumbs. Ah, this was the Rory she knew — The Reverend — master of the house.

"You have got to tell the police everything! The information you are withholding might give them some sort of clue as to the identity of the real killer. Avenelle, what could *you* possibly have to hide?"

At that, Avenelle smiled. He'd known her for thirty years, yes. But did he know her? Does anyone really know a spouse or a mother or a husband? Besides, The Reverend was too busy being a preacher and handing out work for her to do to really *know* her.

"My dearest Rory, I have told the police all I am going to tell them. Now, I'm tired and would love to have a nap here in my own bed — those beds in jail are not nearly as comfy as our sleep-number. Why don't you lie down with me?"

"No — we cannot be friends until you tell the truth, the whole truth and nothing but the truth."

Oh dear. When The Reverend said 'being friends.' he meant making love. So, he was going to avoid marital relations. To be honest, she didn't care. *Not much of a threat.* She smiled.

"I don't see what you have to smile about — you are going to go on trial for murder!"

Avenelle said nothing. She just closed her eyes and kept twiddling her thumbs.

Chapter Twenty-Three

"I can tell when a woman is in love — everything about her looks polished and sparkly."

~The Beautician's Notebook

August

There's nothing wrong with it, Clarissa thought as she applied her mascara. She'd been meeting Tal for several weeks, every Wednesday at the Purple Onion for lunch. They discussed Willa Jo's case; at least, that was what she told herself. After all, she wanted to solve what she thought of as Willa Jo's murder. Tal was still not completely convinced that is *was* murder. But with those fingerprints, he had to take action. Meeting him each week, she could make sure the Sheriff didn't give up on the case, just because they had arrested Avenelle Young. Neither she nor the sheriff believed Avenelle had committed the crime, even though the evidence they'd discovered pointed to her as a possibility. Fingerprints on the plastic cape Willa Jo wore over her clothes at the time of her death would have been enough to arrest Miss Avenelle. But they had more —they had an anonymous tip that Willa Jo's notebook was in Avenelle's house. Of course, the police had combed the place, but hadn't found the notebook. Still, the fingerprints had been enough for them to arrest her, Tal explained. But where was that notebook?

"I'm heading out to lunch," Clarissa called to Ralph, who was getting his boat ready for a trip they were planning to Charleston, S.C. They were going to travel the Intracoastal Waterway to participate in the "Salute From the Shore" event. Ralph was eager to test out the new boat and she was excited about eating she-crab soup at every single restaurant in Charleston. Well, maybe not *every* one, but as many as she could.

She was looking forward to their trip, but as she waved good-bye, she couldn't help the faster pace of her heartbeat as she thought about meeting Tal at the Purple Onion. She shook her head. She liked Tal —

that was all. Nothing but friendship and mutual respect. Why, she didn't think Tal even considered her as a woman.

That wasn't quite true; she'd seen his eyes light up when she approached and had felt him almost jump out of his skin if she accidently brushed her hand against his. So, if she were completely honest with herself, as much as she wanted to solve Willa Jo's murder, the primary reason she ate lunch with Tal was....well, Tal.

She backed the Corvette out of the driveway. The sun warmed her face and the wind blew through her hair. The feeling was glorious. She imagined she was a movie star skimming the highway to Summerset — glamorous and daring, kind of like the way she felt with she'd been with Willa Jo — carefree and young and beautiful forever.

By the time she'd reached the Purple Onion, her hair was a mess but she didn't care. She smoothed it as best she could with her hands, grabbed her purse and entered the place. She stopped and looked at the luscious cakes –red velvet, coconut, peppermint patty —and then, she saw Tal waving to her from a small table in the back of the room. Luckily, they were eating later than most diners — 1:30-ish. That way, they had more privacy.

"You made it!" he said as he stood and pulled her chair out for her.

"Of course. Why wouldn't I?" she said, breathless when she looked at him. He smiled at her, his eyes lingering a couple of seconds too long. He was such a handsome man and she loved the small dimple in his chin. His warm brown eyes were fringed with black lashes. His gaze was intense, at least that's how it seemed to her as he looked at her. She found his moustache 'cool,' an unexpected little rebellion against the crisply pressed uniform he wore.

"I never know for sure whether you will come or not. Basic insecurities where women are concerned, I guess," he said, his smile growing wider. He stared into her eyes. She looked away.

"You don't seem the least bit insecure to me."

His smile grew and he gave her a wink. It sent chills down to her toes.

She sat down and ordered a salad with unsweetened tea, her usual lunch. He had a double cheeseburger, fries and a coke. She shook her head —how did he stay so lean eating like that?

"So, how's the case coming?" she said.

"Well, Mrs. Young is out on bail. She refused to give us any information about what she was doing at The Sassy Lady so early in the morning. At first, she refused to admit she was there, even when we showed her the fingerprints. She very brazenly said the prints didn't prove a thing. I believe we may have underestimated Mrs. Young."

"I thought you said the judge wouldn't let her out on bail in a murder case," said Clarissa, taking a sip of tea.

"It's not much of a case yet, remember? Not until we've got more information." He dipped a French fry into the small cup of ketchup on the side of his plate.

"If we'd found that damned notebook in her house, the judge *wouldn't* have given her bail. But as things stand, there isn't enough evidence or motive *not* to allow her bail — plus, she's not really a 'run-risk.' Her husband said he'd make sure she didn't leave town."

"Well, I feel certain Willa Jo's murder has something to do with that notebook — even though you didn't find it, that doesn't mean Mrs. Young didn't take it. I mean, everybody knew Willa Jo had that notebook — and there was that crazy rumor she was going to write a tell-all book. Do you think Mrs. Young has something in her past, something she is determined to keep secret?" said Clarissa, staring into Tal's brown eyes.

"Well, we know she isn't as innocent as she seemed at first. We got a court order for her juvie records from when she was almost sixteen. Seems her father was a stickler for the law and wanted to put the fear of God into her. He insisted that the police get her fingerprints and treat her like a common criminal. That's how her prints got into our database." Tal dunked another fry and kind of slurped it into his mouth. Clarissa didn't find it offensive, though if Ralph had done such a thing, she would have had to have a talk with him. But Ralph would *never* do that. He was too precise, too cultured, too well-mannered. In Tal, she found it charming.

"So, what did she do?"

"Turns out, she and Rock Bonner — you know, the car dealer? — well, they went for a joyride in one of the cars off the lot. His dad owned Bonner Chevrolet before Rock inherited it. His dad didn't press charges and Rock got off scot free. But Avenelle, she had to do community service. Her daddy insisted on it. I guess he figured picking up the trash on the highway would tame her down some."

"Maybe it didn't — maybe something else happened. Bonner's Willa Jo's daddy, right? Maybe Mrs. Young and Bonner had something going on." Clarissa took a dainty bite of salad.

"Maybe. But she's not talking, if they did."

"I've got a good idea —why don't *I* talk to her. Maybe she'd open up to another woman."

"Wouldn't she think it was a little weird, you calling her up? I mean, it's not like you really know her." Tal gazed at her.

"I know she was teaching Willa Jo guitar lessons. I know she plays the piano for the church. Don't worry...I'll think of something. Maybe we'll get a little closer to the truth."

"I shouldn't let you do this —I mean, it's *my* job, not yours," Tal said. "But I am under the spell of those blue eyes."

He didn't smile, but held her gaze —one, two, three, four, five — seconds too long. She wanted to stare into his eyes forever —it was almost as if energy was jumping back and forth between them, some primeval language. She broke contact.

"I should be going," she said. She was afraid. She'd been telling herself the lunches meant nothing, telling herself she was one lucky woman to have Ralph, when she could have ended up waitressing forever. But at this moment, she realized everything she'd been working for, all the classes and polishing and fixing herself to become Ralph's dream woman, all of it was in danger.

Tal was dangerous.

"Don't go...we haven't solved the crime yet," he said, a half-smile on his lips. "Besides, I was going to order a piece of red velvet cake. I need somebody to help me eat it."

"I really *should* go.....but since it's *red velvet...*"

The waitress took the order and before she knew what was happening, she was sharing a piece of cake with the sheriff of Summerset. Their forks touched, clicking together as they ate. They did a little sword fight for the last piece. Clarissa laughed and then Tal joined in. Even the waitress was giggling a little at their antics.

On the ride home, Clarissa thought about what had happened at lunch. It was almost as if they'd come to some agreement, a silent acquiescence to something big, something important. She allowed herself to think of him touching her, holding her hands behind her back as he kissed her. By the time she made it home, she was in quite a state. And Ralph was out of town. So, Clarissa went into the shower and took a long time soaping herself, touching here, then here, all the while thinking of Tal. Soon, she reached a quick orgasm, then another — all the while, picturing Tal's hands roaming her body.

Whew. Hadn't done *that* in a while. She felt a little embarrassed but damn, she'd needed it after lunch with the sheriff.

When she'd finished with her shower, Clarissa considered how she might entice Mrs. Young to spill her guts. She would start with coffee. But there had to be a reason to call Mrs. Young, a reason she wanted to have coffee with her. She knew so little about the woman.

She lay on the bed and played out various scenarios in her head. Finally, she came up with an idea that just might work.

She looked up the Young's phone number —she'd been right, they still had a land line — and dialed.

"Mrs. Young? This is Clarissa Myers. I live over on Temple Beach and I heard you were giving piano lessons. I've always wanted to play and, well, I hoped we might meet for lunch to discuss it."

"I'm so sorry, Mrs.?"

"Myers, Clarissa Myers. Please, call me Clarissa."

"Mrs. Myers — Clarissa — I have a lot going on at the moment. The gardens's coming in, I have two weeks' worth of laundry to catch up on, I'm facing murder charges….I really don't see how I'd have time to give anyone lessons right now."

The woman sounded insane.

"Oh — I must say I'm dreadfully disappointed. I even begged for a piano — my birthday is in a couple of weeks. Won't you at least let me take you to lunch so we can talk about it?" Clarissa was almost holding her breath.

"Well, I suppose I have to eat lunch, no matter what's going on. Yes, let's do lunch," Avenelle said. "It might do me good to get out of the house."

That was easy. Clarissa couldn't believe her plan was working. She'd get to the bottom of this. And Tal would be so pleased. She'd meet Avenelle Young tomorrow at The Purple Onion at noon.

Chapter Twenty-Four

"The minute you walk in the door, I can tell by looking at you exactly what you need."

~The Beautician's Notebook

August

Avenelle finished ironing her pale lemon-colored blouse. She'd always looked good in pastels with her strawberry blond hair and hazel eyes. And she wanted to look especially good today. Maybe she shouldn't have agreed to meet this young woman —Avenelle could tell by her voice the woman was not yet middle-aged. Part of her wanted to hide within the safe confines of her house, but another part wanted to flaunt her recent notoriety. She knew she was the talk of the town —Preacher's Wife Commits Murder —yes, all the old biddies at the church would be discussing her, pointing out her faults and saying they'd known all along there was something *not-quite-right* about The Reverend's wife.

Besides, she had the feeling The Reverend definitely did not want her to be seen in public. She smiled. He could count this one more little rebellion.

Avenelle dressed in a light green skirt she'd picked up at TJ Maxx for a song. When she bought it, the purchase had been a whim —after all, the *preacher's* wife could never wear anything like *that*—a pencil skirt, slinky and form-fitting. Avenelle couldn't remember the last time she had enjoyed how she looked. She still had a good figure — well, good for a woman of fifty-six. All that work in the garden must have slowly defined her muscles, giving her a good structure on which to hang the few extra pounds she'd gained since her marriage. She looked in the mirror and saw a woman who could easily pass for someone in her late-forties. You know, she thought, life was just too short to hide yourself in grays and browns and blacks, tans of infinite variety, soft pinks suited for young girls. From now on, she'd wear bold red and bright yellow —teal and merlot, orange and purple. Or all of them mixed together. Oh, Avenelle was changing, all right. Morphing into one hell of a butterfly.

She left a note on the refrigerator for The Reverend, telling him she'd be back in time to pick tomatoes and corn.

When Avenelle arrived at The Purple Onion, she asked if a woman named Clarissa Myers was there yet. The waitress led her to the front part of the restaurant where Avenelle could see and be seen by every customer that came in. Great choice. The preacher's wife would not be missed by any of the gossips. The waitress indicated a small table where a blond woman studied the menu. Humph. This Clarissa woman was stunning.

Bleached hair cut in a long bob, slender and tan. Beautiful. The young woman was perfection —her hair, her make-up, her red tank top with red gingham Capri pants. She carried a Prada purse. Everything about her screamed 'money.' Avenelle approached the table, not feeling nearly as good about herself as she'd felt before seeing Clarissa Myers.

"You must be Mrs. Young —I'm Clarissa." She stood and reached out her hand to Avenelle. Her hand was soft and she had long tapered fingers, just right for playing piano. Sort of like Annie Jo's fingers, though longer and perfectly manicured.

"Glad to meet you," said Avenelle, completely entranced by her companion. Her eyes — blue and mesmerizing. And, somehow, familiar. Where had she seen eyes like that?

They ordered, each getting a grilled salmon salad with red pepper vinaigrette.

"I love that red pepper vinaigrette. Most people don't," Clarissa said, drizzling some over her salad.

"Me, too. I always ask for it, but not everyone has it. And here, I think they make it themselves."

They chatted through lunch, discovering little things about each other. Avenelle was surprised to learn the Myers had lived at Temple Beach for thirteen years. Their paths had never crossed, but then, why would they? Unless the Myers visited Sabbath Home Church. She'd have remembered this woman…but she didn't look the church-type.

Clarissa said, "So, you were born here and stayed."

"Oh yes. I married The Reverend when I was twenty-six. That's a good age to get married — you're sort of mature. Then, we had the boys. A rather dull life, I suppose."

"Until recently."

Avenelle laughed.

"Yes, recently things have picked up," Avenelle said, still laughing.

"So, do you mind if I ask you about it?" said Clarissa.

"I'm not supposed to talk about it to anyone — The Reverend hired me a lawyer and that's what he told me — 'say nothing to nobody.' So, let's change the subject. Do you have children?"

"No...Ralph has children by his first wife — two daughters. He didn't want any more. The girls come down about twice a year and we visit them — one lives in New York and the other in San Fran — so we get to travel a little. We usually see a Broadway show in New York and try to catch a ball game in San Fran. We enjoy them — neither is married yet."

"Do you have other family? Sisters, brothers?" Avenelle was glad to steer the conversation away from herself.

"No. I'm an only child. My parents are dead."

"Where did you live before you came to Temple Beach?"

"I was born in Ohio but then, we moved around a lot. Spent some time in West Virginia and Virginia before coming to North Carolina." Clarissa looked at her salad.

Avenelle could tell the young woman didn't like talking about her past. Ohio — the state from hell. At least, it would always be that to Avenelle. She shook those thoughts out of her head.

Avenelle noticed Clarissa's eyes moving away from her, toward some other object of interest. She had her back to whoever was approaching, but she could feel a shadow hovering over her.

"Mrs. Myers — how you liking that Corvette?" said a familiar voice.

Rock Bonner. Avenelle shuddered and suppressed a hiccough. Not here, not now — the crazies. If anyone could bring them on, it was Rock Bonner.

"Hello Avie," he said to her.

"Mr. Bonner," she replied.

"I'm enjoying the car very much — I'll be bringing her in for a tune-up soon. I'm following the maintenance schedule to the letter."

Instead of leaving, as any gentleman should, Bonner asked if he could join the ladies for a moment. No, no, no! But Clarissa invited him to sit right down.

Avenelle was determined not to say another word to Rock Bonner. She watched as he and Clarissa talked about cars, boats, and any other damn thing with a motor. The more Avenelle watched the two of them, the more she felt a mounting fear — those eyes. They were Rock Bonner's eyes. And the way they chatted — as if they'd been best friends forever.

It couldn't be. It was not possible. She stared at Clarissa

Every gesture the young woman made, every inflection of her voice was suddenly familiar.

"I'm sorry to break this up, but I've got so much work with the garden coming in. Clarissa, if you still want those lessons, I'd be delighted to give them to you," said Avenelle.

"It's good to see you, Avie. You look great in that dress, by the way," Bonner said.

Avenelle didn't even say good-bye to him. No reason to speak to the devil. He was dead to her and he always would be.

When Avenelle arrived back home, she changed into her gardening shorts and hurried out to the corn. She picked the ears that seemed full and ripe, plopping them, stalk-end-first, into a large bucket filled with water. The water helped keep the corn fresh until she could get around to cooking it.

She barely realized what she was doing. Before she knew it, the whole bucket was sloshing water everywhere — she'd almost picked the stalks bare. She tossed the unripe husks into the woods behind the house. At least the squirrels would have a good dinner. Her heart had not stopped fluttering since she'd left the Purple Onion.

As she inspected the tomatoes, she thought over and over.

Born in Ohio. Born in Ohio.

Ohio.

And those Bonner blue eyes.

Avenelle carried the vegetables into the kitchen and set them down on the table. She put the less-ripe tomatoes on the window sill and the ripest ones in the refrigerator. She'd shuck the corn later. For now, she began to peel tomatoes for a tomato pie. As she peeled and sliced, chopped onions and unrolled the store-bought pastry, she thought about Ohio.

Avenelle felt the tears on her cheeks, almost taking her by surprise —it had been forty years. She told herself she'd gotten over it —after all, she married The Reverend and raised her boys. All this time, though, Avenelle felt as if she were some sort of jigsaw puzzle with a missing piece. Could Clarissa Myers *be* that missing piece? She had the Bonner eyes, but that didn't mean anything. She needed to find out more about the young woman. Avenelle shook herself, trying to dislodge the disturbing memories. She looked at all the tomatoes she'd peeled — way too many for just one pie.

She unrolled another pastry from the box — she used to make pie crust from scratch, but these days, what was the point? The Pillsbury was just as good as any she'd made herself.

She thought about the notebook. The police had searched and searched for it — and, when she got home, she looked for it where she'd left it — in the magazine rack in the den. But it wasn't there. Where could it be?

Finally, it hit her...Annie Jo! She would have recognized the notebook and taken it back. Probably wondered what it was doing in Avenelle's house.

Avenelle knew what she had to do — she had to call Annie Jo. She'd missed the girl and wondered if she was still practicing her guitar. She *did* have a real talent for it. Avenelle reached for the phone in the kitchen, and called.

"Annie Jo? This is Miss Avenelle. I wondered if you were ready to begin your lessons again?"

"I would love that, actually. I've written a song I want you to hear — words and everything. When should I come?"

"How about the usual time — Friday around one? Oh, and Annie Jo, please bring the notebook with you."

Avenelle hung up, not waiting for a reply.

Chapter Twenty-Five

"Nobody gets everything they want — nobody."

~The Beautician's Notebook

August

Annie Jo flushed with shame as she entered Miss Avenelle's cool, dark house. Miss Avenelle met her at the door with a hug and a smile and a plate of cookies for her and Lawson. She didn't seem at all upset that Annie Jo had stolen the notebook. It was almost as though Miss Avenelle'd forgotten all about it.

Miss Avenelle brought child-proof gates from upstairs and closed off the den. She lugged down some blocks and pull toys, a few books and a ball from upstairs. Annie Jo put Lawson down and he immediately plopped next to the blocks and began to stack one on top of the other.

"This was a good idea — the toys and all," Annie Jo said.

"Well, I thought maybe he would like to play a little before he went down for his nap." Miss Avenelle offered Annie Jo another cookie.

Annie Jo couldn't figure out why Miss Avenelle was being so nice — it was almost as if she hadn't been arrested and charged with killing Willa Jo. Not that Annie Jo believed for one minute that Miss Avenelle had anything to do with her mother's death. She *knew* Miss Avenelle — the woman didn't have it in her to hurt anyone.

"So, tell me about this new song of yours."

"Well, I got really inspired — I reckon I was sad, thinking about things — Mom being dead and Daddy not having much time to spend with me — as usual. I just wrote it all down and before I knew it — I'd written a song. I'm calling it 'Throw-Away' and I actually sent it off! To Brandi Carlile — I want you to hear her sing — I'll let you listen later on my tablet — she's awesome," said Annie Jo, all in a rush. She was so happy to have someone pay attention to her, take her seriously.

"What an inspired idea! I never would have considered sending anything off like that — you have a good head on your shoulders, dear."

Annie Jo smiled and began strumming the guitar. She'd practiced and practiced since Miss Avenelle had been gone — she didn't want to fall behind. As she played, everything around her sort of disappeared. She was vaguely aware of Lawson building a tower beside her; she knew Miss Avenelle was sitting next to her, listening, but none of that mattered. Once she began to strum the guitar, she created a world of her own, a world where she was the queen. Damn straight.

Annie Jo sang with confidence and feeling. It wasn't something she tried to do; she couldn't help herself. When the song was over, silence filled the room. The silence continued. Miss Avenelle didn't say a word. Annie Jo began to blush and was terrified her song was awful — maybe it was stupid — maybe she'd just *thought* it was good. Now, she was even more embarrassed when she thought of having mailed her poor attempts to a *real* singer, somebody who knew what she was doing. Wasn't Miss Avenelle ever gonna speak?

"That was incredible, Annie Jo — just simply marvelous." Miss Avenelle spoke in a low and quiet voice.

"You like it?" said Annie Jo, wanting to make sure she understood correctly.

"My dear, I *love* it. I knew you had talent the first time I saw you pick up that guitar. Have you considered going to college — maybe studying music? They have a fine program for guitar at the University of North Carolina in Asheville. You could even learn how to operate a recording studio. A friend's son graduated from that program and he's in Nashville, working for Shania Twain. I'm sure your daddy would pay for you to go."

"I never thought I wanted to go to college...but maybe I just wasn't ready. Maybe now I am." *College? For real? Hard to imagine.*

Lawson's eyes looked droopy and Annie Jo took him upstairs for his nap. She and Miss Avenelle had their lesson as usual. Miss Avenelle said she was 'very pleased' that Annie Jo kept up her practicing, in spite of the circumstances.

At the end of the lesson, Miss Avenelle spoke.

"I'd like to have the notebook back, Annie Jo. I know it rightfully belongs to you, as it was your mother's, but I need to find out what's in there before I return it to you for good. Did you read the whole thing?"

"No, ma'am. I just read the first part — it was all about me back when I was little. I did find it comforting." Annie Jo held the book close to her chest.

"Well, if you don't mind, I'd like to read it all. And, if I find anything about me, anything detrimental, I'd like your permission to remove it."

"You can read it — and I don't care if you take out any part about you — just don't mess with anything about me or about Mom and me."

"Deal. I'll give it back to you as soon as I can."

Annie Jo felt terrible. It was because she'd taken the notebook that Miss Avenelle now faced murder charges. It was all her fault — surely, Miss Avenelle must know that. Why was she being so nice?

"I'm.....I'm really sorry about the way things went down. I never meant to get you in trouble." Annie Jo handed over the notebook.

"I'm sorry, too. But I don't blame you — I stole the book myself, so who am I to chastise you? As for the trouble, I'm not worried about it. Maybe I *should* be, but I'm not. I have a sense of peace about the whole business. So, what do you think? Do you think I did it?" A strange look clouded Miss Avenelle's face.

"No — I don't. You aren't the kind of person who would hurt anybody...not anybody."

"I thank you for that, dear. Oh, is that Lawson? You'd better run get him."

Chapter Twenty-Six

"If your eye color matches your hair color, that is a sign of true beauty."

~The Beautician's Notebook

August

Avenelle picked up the blocks and other toys, and carried them back upstairs. She had nothing to do that afternoon — no sermon to type, no music to practice, no garden chores — she intended to read the entire notebook from cover to cover. It didn't have more than fifty pages. She walked into the kitchen, poured herself a glass of Diet Coke over ice, and returned to the couch. She lit a candle against The Reverend's explicit command — he didn't believe in burning candles in the heat of summer. After all, they were running the air-conditioning — candles put out heat — lighting them in August did not make economic good sense, according to The Reverend. But Avenelle loved candles and decided it was about time she overruled her husband.

She opened the book to the first page. The leather cover felt like fire in her hands. She was terrified to read this tome, but she knew she must. She needed to find out if Willa Jo had recorded the confession she'd made years ago.

In a weak moment, while Willa Jo washed and massaged her scalp, Avenelle had spilled her guts. That day, January 12, was her daughter's sixth birthday. The child started school the next school year — so many changes since she'd held her baby for that brief moment. Every birthday was a tough one for Avenelle. But this one seemed especially difficult. Avenelle was twenty-two and had just graduated from Coastal Carolina University with a degree in early childhood education. She'd learned about the stages of development. With each new thing she discovered about small children and how they grew, she wondered more about her own baby. Was she getting the nurturing she needed? Were her cognitive skills being challenged? Avenelle consoled herself with what they'd told her at the Maple

Knolls Unwed Mother's Home —that each baby would be adopted by a loving family who could afford all the things a growing child would need — all the things that, at sixteen, Avenelle would have been unable to provide.

As the suds washed over Avenelle's head, the tears came. She didn't cry exactly. Her body just leaked out its sadness. Willa Jo noticed.

"What in the world is wrong, Miss Avenelle? Let me rinse you and then you and I are going to the back room where we can have a little talk. Everything will be all right. You'll see. You just come on back here and tell Willa Jo all about it."

Willa Jo seemed so understanding and kind — it was easy for Avenelle to tell her story, though she didn't mention names. Willa Jo had no idea it had been her own *father* who ruined Avenelle's life.

"Miss Avenelle — that must have been so hard...I know about loving a child —I love Annie Jo to bits. I'm so sorry. You poor, poor thing. Have you ever thought about trying to find your daughter?"

"No. She's settled in with her adoptive family, I'm sure. I wouldn't want to upset her world. This is a pain I'll just have to live with. Thank you, Willa Jo — thank you for understanding. And, I know you'll keep this just between us."

"Of course. My lips are sealed."

"Your mother was my best friend —her word was as good as gold. I know yours will be, too."

As far as Avenelle knew, Willa Jo had kept her word all these years. But Avenelle hadn't banked on Willa Jo's notebook.

***

Avenelle read the last page and closed the book. She sighed. She had enough information to mull over for the rest of her years. So much she hadn't known, could never have guessed. She could never look at the folks she knew the same way again. So many secrets....She sighed again. Even The Reverend was mentioned...but Avenelle would deal with *that* later. Every man in this sinful world must be a damn dog. She would never forget those words scribbled in the notebook:

> And then, I kissed Reverend Young right on the lips. He turned almost fuchsia! I thought he was going to die right then and there. But all he did was say in the shakiest voice, "I'm

> married." My stars and garters! He sure didn't
> kiss like a married man!

The Reverend would be home soon and she should cook supper — maybe she'd fix his favorite — fried chicken the way his mama made it, with gravy and mashed potatoes, greens cooked in fatback, sweet potato pudding and lots of biscuits with butter. Her husband worked hard and he deserved a good meal. Then, after he'd eaten, she'd confront him with what she'd learned about him and Willa Jo. Attack him when he least expected it. She placed the notebook back in the magazine rack, careful to hide it completely this time.

Chapter Twenty-Seven

"When I get old, I'll start looking like my mama — until then, I want to be as different as possible."

~The Beautician's Notebook

August

Clarissa lay on a deck chair, the hot summer sun blaring down on her, her skin slick with sunscreen. Early morning, the best time for sunning. She looked out at the ocean. Calm as milk and about as thick-looking. She wondered what made the water so cloudy. Oh well, it didn't matter. She watched as families staked out their territory with towels, those low chairs that allowed the water to rush over you, and baskets of food. Enormous umbrellas stabbed into the sand, providing shade and respite from the unforgiving sun.

She'd been reading a Diane Chamberlain book. She loved those — there was always a secret life of some sort; Clarissa enjoyed the psychology of the characters and the natural-sounding dialogue. But for some reason, this morning she couldn't focus on the book. She was too busy thinking about her upcoming piano lesson with Avenelle Young.

Of course, the lesson was just a ruse. Clarissa's real job was to look for evidence and any suspicious behavior. Clarissa couldn't imagine Miss Avenelle doing anything suspicious, though she'd only met her at lunch. She seemed a typical small-town older woman, nice enough but innocuous. Today, maybe she would find something different.

She daydreamed that she would discover some secret of Miss Avenelle's, a sordid past — maybe she'd been a hooker or a drug dealer. Clarissa laughed. If she did find something, she'd have to report it to Tal.... er, ...Sheriff Hicks. She needed to think of him as a professional lawman, not as just a regular man. But she did think of Tal as a regular man; she couldn't help herself. He was warm and funny. And he liked her just the way she was — she didn't have to behave a certain way or dress in designer clothes. He was a down-home boy and had simple tastes. And she could tell he had a taste for her. And she knew she had a taste for him, too.

Her phone alarm clock rang out "Good Morning Starshine." Rest time was over. She snatched a towel off the back of her chair and wrapped it around her torso. She needed to shower before her lesson — she had plenty of time — the lesson wasn't until afternoon.

Miss Avenelle's house was in the older part of Summerset. The live oaks along the street were mature and Spanish moss hung from their branches. It was like stepping back in time, with bungalows from the 30s and 40s set like jewels in the center of large, green lawns. In Miss Avenelle's yard a giant magnolia tree blossomed, sweetening the air. Next to the steps leading to the wrap-around porch were boxwoods and a few old-fashioned roses. As she climbed the stairs, Clarissa caught the sweet scent of the roses mixed with gardenias. At the corner of the house, an enormous bush dripped with blooms.

On one end of the porch were antique wicker chairs, a glass table with a pot of pink impatiens in the center. On the other, a swing hung from the rafters, dominating that side. Cushions covered in a pink and green flowered fabric beckoned and Clarissa could easily imagine Miss Avenelle and her husband sitting out here on sultry evenings. Everything was lovingly-cared for, neat and inviting. *Southern charm at its finest.*

She rang the doorbell and Miss Avenelle appeared so quickly, Clarissa figured she'd been waiting at the door.

"Come in, come in — welcome!" Miss Avenelle said as she hugged Clarissa. Clarissa had never been one for hugging, but Miss Avenelle's affection seemed so genuine that Clarissa found herself hugging the older woman back.

She led Clarissa into the den where an upright piano stood against one wall and a guitar leaned against the bench. Miss Avenelle sat down on a wingback chair and indicated Clarissa was to sit on its opposite.

"Tell me, have you had any musical training at all?" asked Miss Avenelle.

"No, not really. We had music class in elementary school but all I remember is singing — one time, a man came in with a bunch of bells and played them all by himself — he was amazing."

"I see. Well, we'll have to start with the basics. Let's look at the piano — I can teach you a little music theory and then, we'll try a simple tune," said Miss Avenelle. She began to explain about the various keys and the staff and other things with which Clarissa was unfamiliar.

When the lesson was over and they were having lemonade in the den, Miss Avenelle said, "So, you didn't have music in your life…what was it like, growing up in Ohio?"

"I didn't really grow up in Ohio — I was just born there. I lived most of my life in West Virginia and Virginia." She hated being asked anything about The Before. "My childhood wasn't very nice. I lived in foster care until I could escape."

"How terrible. I'm so sorry." Miss Avenelle patted Clarissa's arm. Clarissa thought the woman had tears in her eyes.

Clarissa was stunned. She *never* told people about her early life. But somehow, with Miss Avenelle, divulging her secret past seemed safe. Miss Avenelle was as comforting as an old blanket.

"I took my name from the last family I stayed with — before I met and married Ralph. He was my savior. Without him, I have no idea where I'd be…. or *what* I'd be."

"I'm glad you have him, then. Tell me, do you know anything about your real parents?"

"Not much. ….I figure my mother was some young girl who found herself in trouble and didn't know what to do, so she gave me away. At least I'm here — she could have made a different choice. I don't blame her — it was just bad luck." Liar — she resented her birth mother, sometimes hated her when she thought about all the deprivation she'd suffered.

"That's very generous of you — I think I might be angry with this so-called mother."

"Sometimes I *am* angry. I feel like I'm going to explode. You can't live the kind of life I've lived and come out without any anger. I try to talk myself out of it — you know, try to be a better person." Clarissa felt her face grow warm.

"That's very admirable — oh, won't you excuse me for a minute. Nature calls."

Clarissa thought she seemed disturbed. Clarissa looked around the den — family pictures, two little boys, then two teenaged boys, then two grown men, various puppies and cats, the whole family together at Disney World —nothing odd or sinister about any of this. Clarissa got up and walked around, studied the collection of books neatly arranged alphabetically — Bible scholars, architecture, recipes, biographies of American leaders —nothing unusual there.

Clarissa spotted a People magazine stuffed into a crowded magazine rack. Finally, something unpredictable —she never would have pegged Miss Avenelle for a pop culture fan. She began to rifle through the rack and had found a couple copies of Entertainment Weekly when she spotted something different, something that didn't seem to belong in a magazine rack at all.

She pulled it out of the jumbled pages. The cover was very fine leather with intricate markings —Celtic, most likely —on the front and back. She opened to the first page. My Notebook, property of Willa Jo Temple. Clarissa almost dropped it, as if it had been a hot potato. She closed the book, rearranged the mess of magazines to look just as they had before she'd discovered the notebook, then hid the precious evidence in her purse. She was glad she'd chosen a large bag —one Ralph called her 'suitcase.'

She knew she shouldn't have taken it, but *this* was what she and Tal had been waiting for —real documentation. Tangible proof about who might have killed Willa Jo. Finding this in Miss Avenelle's possession would convince Tal beyond a doubt. Miss Avenelle *was* guilty. This notebook would prove it.

Clarissa composed herself, returned to the couch and took a sip of lemonade. She tried to still her heartbeat. She breathed in deeply and counted —in, two, three, out, two, three —slowly, her body calmed itself. She shuddered to think she could be sitting in the home of a murderer. This woman, so easy to talk to, so kind —this woman had killed her best friend.

"Sorry I took so long —my stomach has not been right since I ate that jail food," Miss Avenelle said.

"No problem…I need to be heading home anyway. Ralph likes to eat around five." Clarissa gathering her things. She glanced at the magazine rack, the only careless thing she'd seen in the whole house. It looked just as messed up as when she'd first noticed it. Good. She'd fixed it just right.

"The Reverend eats at precisely six. No such thing as 'around' around here," said Miss Avenelle, chuckling at her little joke.

Clarissa paid for her lesson, thanked Miss Avenelle, and practically ran out of the house. She had to tell Tal. He would be *so* impressed with her police work.

But *first,* she had to read that notebook for herself. Tal could wait. Obviously, the notebook held the key to everything.

Chapter Twenty-Eight

"Men will lie, cheat, steal, and break your heart. Get a dog."

~The Beautician's Notebook

August

Clarissa lay on her sofa, staring out to sea, the notebook on the floor beside her. Oh, she'd read it all right. Read it three times and still had a hard time accepting it. Ralph — *her* Ralph — an affair with Willa Jo? How could it be? Yet, there it was. Everything she ever believed in, everything she thought she'd built with her husband was shattered, exploded by a couple of paragraphs in a scribbled hand. She thought her chest might burst, she was in such agony.

Damn him! Damn him to hell!

The affair started shortly after Clarissa and Ralph moved to Temple Beach. Humph. It seemed Ralph knew Willa Jo before Clarissa even *met* her. But then, Ralph always seemed to know everybody — it had been that way all their married lives. The man spent a lot of time away from home, at least during the day. He always had somewhere to go, something important to do. Nighttime was their time together — 'sacrosanct,' he'd called it. He must have considered 'anything goes!' as his daytime motto.

Wine. She needed more wine. She hopped up from the couch and poured an ice tea glassful, up to the brim. Yes.

Clarissa still couldn't comprehend what she'd read — Ralph and Willa Jo. No wonder he didn't want Clarissa to be friends with Willa Jo — he was afraid Willa Jo would talk. He was probably worried about Clarissa following in Willa Jo's footsteps, taking lovers as freely as she'd take an Advil for a headache. Clarissa didn't know whether to laugh or cry.

Had there been others? Oh, hell yes. If a man will cheat once, he'll cheat a thousand times — how often had she heard that from her last foster mother? After all, he got away with Willa Jo — he obviously knew how to keep a secret. He could have been having little flings throughout their marriage. Most likely had been. How could she have been so stupid?

Ralph and Willa Jo's romance had been brief, maybe six weeks, if the notebook was accurate. While Clarissa was busy organizing the house, selecting furniture and settling into her castle by the sea, Ralph was making love to Willa Jo. Clarissa shook her head slowly back and forth, back and forth. Not a pretty picture. But worse than that were Willa Jo's words about Ralph.

> The man is boring. Married and dull as dishwater.
> I don't know what kind of woman he is married to,
> but she must be a real loser. Who could live with
> a man that makes love like he's counting backwards.
> Lordy Mercy!

She thought about the other revelations in the notebook — Gertrude Talbot getting her eyelids lifted, Norita Somebody-or-other discovering her mother was a lesbian before she married her father, Jane McIver McLeod tattooing a large butterfly on her butt — one wing on each cheek, Avenelle Young giving a baby up for adoption — so many stories, so many secrets.

Avenelle Young — the preacher's wife. No wonder she stole the notebook from Willa Jo-she was desperate to keep the notebook hidden, just like her secret. This information could ruin her, especially if she'd never told her husband about having a baby. Of course, she didn't tell him; he would not have married a woman with a tarnished past. Clarissa picked up the notebook and stared at the cover. *This* was motive for murder. She immediately called the sheriff and set up a lunch date for the next day. Her fingers shook with anger as she punched in the numbers. Ralph and Willa Jo! Ralph and Willa Jo! Her husband would pay for this — she'd make sure of that. Millions. She was so glad to have something to focus on, other than Ralph and his unfaithfulness. She wanted to push thoughts of him and Willa Jo so far down, she'd never have to consider them again. And she could understand a motive for murder. If Ralph had been there, she could easily have stabbed him right in the heart. But she couldn't worry about Ralph now. She had to get ready to meet Tal, tell him all about Miss Avenelle and her baby.

***

She and Tal met at Duffer's Bar and Grill, a quiet restaurant where they could have real conversation.

"The thing is, the coroner's report didn't call it a definite homicide —they said the death fell under the 'pending investigation' category — that means we need to look into it. According to the report, the angle of the scissors came from below, as if the killer gave Willa Jo an upper cut that went straight to her heart — weird angle. See? I told you it wasn't likely a murder." Tal took the last bite of his shrimp burger.

"But you still have to keep investigating, right?"

"So says the coroner. There are definitely more questions than answers at this point." He studied the menu. "Want dessert?"

"No thanks, I have to keep my school-girl figure," Clarissa said as she smiled at him.

"Well, I wouldn't want to be the one to mess *that* up."

Flirty. He was, without a doubt, flirting with her. And pretty obviously, too. Blatant. Clarissa had to admit she liked it.

He paid the tab and they walked out to their cars. The sun blazed down, almost melting the asphalt. Clarissa hoped her cheeks weren't too flushed. Her face burned.

"You know, we really should go somewhere to cool off —I have a little time. Let me take you to Crusoe," said Tal.

"What in the world is that...some kind of 'treasure island?'" said Clarissa. He smiled at her.

"A place you'll never forget — when I was a kid, Crusoe was forbidden. Rumor had it people who went to it, never came out. I used to go there with Willa Jo when we were kids —her idea. She didn't like rules," Tal said, ushering her into his unmarked car.

"Humph, I guess she didn't. I don't think I like the sound of this place — 'those who enter, never return.' Sounds like a tag line from a bad movie." Clarissa scooted in and buckled up.

"Wait till you see it —eerie but sort of beautiful, too."

Tal started the engine and turned on the air. The coolness felt good against Clarissa's face. They were in the car together...she'd never realized how intimate a car could feel. He drove smoothly, no jerky movements, no veering over the center line. He looked as if he were one with the car. She wondered if he made love the same, unruffled way.

"It'll take about a half-hour to get there. Now's the time to tell me all about yourself."

"Not much to tell. Born in Ohio, lived a while in West Virginia. Met Ralph in Virginia twenty-two years ago. We've been at Temple Beach about thirteen years," she said, noticing the square shape of his hands, the blond hairs on his forearm bleached by the sun.

"You must have been a baby when Ralph found you —you don't look thirty-five."

"I'm forty. And some days, I feel it. But most days, I still feel eighteen —that's how old I was when I married Ralph. He was forty-eight."

Tal raised his eyebrows.

"Oh, don't you do that! It wasn't like that! I was a waitress/bartender and he was in Arlington for a meeting. We hit it off. He'd been married twice before-he said I was a breath of fresh air. I really hadn't even had a boyfriend yet —he was my first and only." Clarissa didn't like remembering.

"Didn't your daddy raise hell?"

"I was on my own —I left home when I was sixteen…they were foster parents. I never knew my real folks. Ralph saved me. He sent me to college, took me all over the world. I've been very lucky."

"If you say so."

Silence filled the car. Uneasy.

"What do you mean?" Clarissa finally said. "Is there something wrong with me marrying Ralph?"

"Naw. But you don't say anything about love."

"I *do* love Ralph —at least, I *did*." She watched as Tal turned onto a dirt road.

"Why 'did'?"

"Oh, you know, since I've been hanging out with you —it's hard to know what I think," *I can flirt, too. What the hell.*

She didn't want to tell him she had possession of the notebook yet. She worried having it might be, somehow, illegal. She certainly wasn't ready to tell him what she'd discovered about Ralph and Willa Jo. She wanted to give herself a little more time to digest the facts before she shared them with anybody.

The live oaks and long-leaf pines towered over the road, making a sort of tunnel. Spanish moss dripped low, brushing the top of the car.

There were no houses in sight, no other roads, just thick forests on both sides.

"So, what is this place, anyway? Really."

"Like I said —just a place for parents to tell their kids about, scare the crap out of them. A few folks *do* live here, though. Further down. We won't go that far." Tal turned off the dirt road onto a grassy area where some tire tracks led into who-knows-where. He stopped the car and cut the engine.

"Now what?" she said, growing just a little nervous.

"Now I make my move," he said and pulled her over to him. "This explains why these big unmarked cars have bench seats —the better to seduce damsels in distress."

She allowed him to bring her close, so close she could smell his cologne —a citrus-y odor mixed with his own scent. She couldn't say she hadn't wanted him to do exactly what he was doing.

"I'm not in distress."

"You are —you just don't know it yet." He slid his arm around her waist and brought her nearer.

The kiss wasn't like she'd expected —maybe first kisses never are. His was gentle, tender, sweet. Ralph was so different; he wasn't much of a kisser at all. And the few boys she'd been out with, casual dates really, had been sloppy and ardent, as she recalled.

This was something entirely different.

Clarissa lost all track of time. She was aware only of Tal's mouth, his face, his breath. They opened the windows and a cool breeze freshened their skin, but they didn't stop to enjoy it. She could hear his breathing become heavier, but he didn't make any move to go beyond kissing. On and on he kissed her, his tongue probing her lips, her mouth. Then, she felt a gentle pressure on her nipples as he slowly moved his hand from one to the other. She broke their embrace.

"I should probably go."

"You probably should," he said, kissing her once again. Then, after that lingering kiss, he pushed her back over to her side and started up the engine.

"That was abrupt." *What's up with this guy?*

"I'm sorry —I just realized I've got a meeting at 5:30. I think I might be a few minutes late —you made me forget everything." He glanced at her, smiling.

"Me, too. I guess Ralph will have to take me out for dinner."

They grew quiet, as if the mention of Clarissa's husband had dampened their ardor.

"Tal —I have no experience in this...area. I haven't kissed another man since I took my marriage vows. I just feel this connection to you —I can't explain it. Maybe I should feel guilty, but I don't." Hell no, she didn't. She only wished Ralph could see her now.

He pulled the car onto the hard road that led back to Summerset, looking straight ahead, his lips in a tight line.

"I don't usually do this, either. Last time I was at Crusoe was when I was married to Willa Jo. I sure don't go after married women as a matter of habit. But, like you said, there's a connection —I feel like I've known you all my life," he said, taking her hand.

"So....what do we do?"

"Beats me. What do you want to do?"

"I want to be with you. I've never, ever experienced anything like this afternoon."

"Hell, that was just making-out. Wait til we get to the good stuff." He laughed.

"Be serious. I have a lot to lose if we continue. Gossip would ruin everything. Ralph is worth millions —I had to sign a pre-nup saying that if I ever cheated, I would get nothing in the divorce settlement. I could end up a pauper."

"There are worse things."

"I can tell by *that* comment that you have never been poor, not really. Not going-to-bed-hungry poor," she said, suddenly irritated at his lack of understanding. She hadn't forgotten about finding the cupboard bare back when she was a kid in West Virginia. Not just one day, but many.

"You're right. I'm sorry —I *was* insensitive. What I meant was, if you decide to do this — *be* with me, as you put it —I'll take care of you. I can offer you an ordinary life, nothing fancy. I don't have a lot of money, but I like what I do; I'm proud of the fact I help people. I would take care of you."

She mulled over his words as he drove back to Duffer's. What was he talking about? What, exactly, were they getting into?

"You sounded very serious back there —talking about taking care of me. Is that how you usually talk to the women you kiss?" *Lighten up, Clarissa — lighten up.*

"No. I don't kiss a woman unless I mean it."

Well, that might not be quite true, but she didn't need to know everything about him just then. And he *had* been serious. She could tell.

"Look — I know this is sort of sudden, but we've been dancing around it for weeks. I know you know it. I felt it the first time I saw you. Was almost tongue-tied, I was so attracted to you. Now — you gotta decide what you want. I'm talking the whole shebang, here. The 'M" word." Tal shifted gears smoothly.

Clarissa stared at him. Marriage? So soon? Divorce Ralph? Start over? On a sheriff's salary? She shook her head. The idea of divorcing Ralph sounded pretty good about now. But she wasn't sure about the rest.

"You must think I'm crazy, talking about a long-term thing when you're married. Believe me, I don't *do* this. I've been waiting for somebody to make me feel as alive as Willa Jo did — there's been nobody all these years. And then — you came along."

Clarissa continued to study him. She found it hard to believe a man like him had lived a celibate life for very long, but she didn't care about any other women he might be involved with. Willa Jo told her, back when they were discussing Willa Jo's husbands, Tal had been a wonderful lover. Clarissa could see that would be true.

"I don't know what to say.... I need some time."

"Take all the time you want. I'm not going anywhere. But the ball's in your court. You'll have to contact me if you want to see me again." With that, he drove slowly out of the parking lot.

Clarissa walked to her Corvette, opened the door and sat in the driver's seat. After a few minutes, she drove home. She'd been so swept up in the moment, she forgot to tell Tal about the notebook. Maybe she wasn't ready, yet, to share it. Maybe she needed to hold onto it for courage — proof against her husband. She had to face Ralph, armed with the notebook. She had no idea what she was going to do.

Damn men!

Chapter Twenty-Nine

"Honey, you need to lay your burden down — tell ole Willa Jo all about it."

~The Beautician's Notebook

August

Avenelle called The Sassy Lady to see if Trudy could work her in that afternoon. Luckily, Trudy agreed. Avenelle was delighted, because after she got her hair done, she was going to turn herself in to Sheriff Hicks. She was going to confess to the murder of Willa Jo Temple and she wanted to look her best.

Yesterday, after Clarissa left her lesson, Avenelle was straightening up the den, getting ready for The Reverend to come home. She thought the magazine rack had gotten itself all jumbled up again — one of The Reverend's pet peeves. Sometimes, she left it a wreck on purpose, just to bug him. He wasn't crazy about her having a subscription to *People* Magazine anyway, but he'd finally told her to sign up — that was cheaper than picking one up from the check-out aisle every time she went to the Food Lion. She pulled out several magazines, making sure the notebook was still safely hidden — she suddenly felt stupid for hiding the notebook in the same place Annie Jo had found it. Knucklehead. At the time, she'd thought the notebook belonged with those tawdry *People* magazines — and she liked the thought of it tucked in the rack. She rifled through the magazines, looking for the familiar leather book — it *had* to be there somewhere.

It wasn't.

She pulled out every item that was stuffed into the rack — *People* (all the way back to 2014) *Entertainment, Time,* bulletins from church, a few newspapers. The notebook was nowhere to be found.

Oh no, not again! Who could have stolen that damn book this time? No one had been in the den except The Reverend. Oh dear God, do not let it be The Reverend. Avenelle could feel the panic begin to rise. She had trouble breathing and her heart raced. She felt woozy. She put her head between her knees, a technique she'd learned in ninth grade health class. If The Reverend had read the notebook, life, as she knew it, was over. He would divorce her quicker than a snap.

"Avenelle? What in the world are you doing?" said The Reverend as he entered the den.

"Oh...oh...oh...I..well, I...I was a little dizzy."

"Should I call 911? Or give Doc Willis a call? You okay?" He sat beside her and patted her back.

"No, no...don't call. I'll be okay. I think the heat must have gotten to me. What are you doing home at this hour?" Slowly, she rose to a seated position.

"Thought I might take the rest of the day off, play a little golf. Seems like it's been a year since I've been on the course. Do you mind?"

"Go ahead —I have a lot of work to do —getting my hair done at two."

"You sure you're okay?" he said, still rubbing her back.

"Of course." She was always okay.

"Tell you what...I'll take you out for supper —maybe you've been working too hard. We'll eat at Jerome's Steakhouse, how about that?"

"Fine...great." If she'd known feeling faint would get her out of the kitchen, she'd have had the vapors years ago.

The Reverend patted her back a couple more times, then ran up the steps to change into his golfing clothes. Avenelle sighed deeply.

He didn't know.

The Reverend hadn't taken the notebook. If he'd read about her past, he would have spoken to her in his low, chastising voice. He definitely would *not* have patted her back. And he sure as heck wouldn't have offered to take her to dinner.

No, someone else had taken it. Avenelle racked her brain trying to remember who had been in the house — there'd been the air-conditioning man to clean the filters, the bug-man, a couple of boy scouts asking for chores to fulfill their merit badges, Clarissa for her lesson...

Clarissa.

It must have been Clarissa.

Now, Clarissa would know all about Avenelle's past. Would she put two and two together, the way Avenelle had? No, that was silly. The woman wasn't exactly a rocket scientist and she didn't have all the facts. Avenelle exhaled a sigh of relief. She didn't want Clarissa to discover what Avenelle suspected about the two of them. No way could Clarissa figure things out from the information in the notebook. Avenelle felt her muscles relax and her breathing ease up.

Then, she remembered what *else* was in that notebook. Ralph and Willa Jo! Clarissa would read all about their squalid liaison. She would be crushed by such a betrayal. Oh, Clarissa. Even though the affair had happened many years ago, the pain would be fresh for Clarissa, a raw, gaping wound.

Or would it?

Maybe Clarissa already knew about Ralph and Willa Jo. Maybe she'd planned her revenge all these years and now, she'd killed Willa Jo, her so-called best friend. The more Avenelle thought about it, the more believable that scenario became. Clarissa, unstable from a miserable childhood, a childhood for which Avenelle was responsible, discovered her husband's affair with Willa Jo. Rather than confront him, she decided to use another tactic. She made friends with Willa Jo (you know, keep your friends close and your enemies closer!) and waited for the right moment to punish her. Poor Clarissa. Betrayed by the very man who had given her the only stability she'd ever known. Betrayed by her best friend.

Now everything made sense —the vicious stabbing of Willa Jo — in the heart, no less —exactly where Clarissa had been hurt. Willa Jo had broken Clarissa's heart; now it was Clarissa's turn. Oh, her poor baby — once again let down by people who were supposed to love her. Knowing this, Avenelle had no choice. She would be forced to give herself up to the sheriff. She had to confess to Willa Jo's murder. She had to save Clarissa.

But before Avenelle would turn herself over to the police, before she gave up her life for this young woman, she wanted to make certain Clarissa really *was* her daughter. She decided she would google Clarissa. She heard The Reverend's good-bye shout and the slam of the back door. She tiptoed to The Reverend's office. Then, she realized she didn't have to tiptoe — she was the only one at home. She caught herself before knocking at the closed door —the door was always closed — and entered The Reverend's office, his sanctum sanctorum. Avenelle never went into this room unless she had to type sermons. And she hadn't done those in months.

She sat at the desk and googled Clarissa Talbot Myers. Clarissa's Facebook page popped up and Avenelle selected it. Right there, on her page, was Clarissa's birthdate —January 12, 1975, Akron, Ohio.

It had to be! How many babies would have been born exactly on January 12, 1975? In Ohio? And how many of those babies would have been girls? And how many would have been given up for adoption? And how many would have somehow made their way to the North Carolina coast? Not many.

And only *one* with Rock Bonner's eyes.

Avenelle had no doubts now — Clarissa was her daughter. Her beautiful little girl, the one who had gripped her finger all those years ago. Her baby.

Avenelle would save her. She'd abandoned her once, but now, she would do whatever was necessary to make it up to the child. Fully convinced, Avenelle knew what she had to do.

***

The Sassy Lady's lot was packed and Avenelle had to parallel park on the street.

"Ya'll sure busy today. How are your girls? Tacoma and, oh I can never remember the little one's name," Avenelle said as she walked in for her appointment, those damn chimes ringing in her ears as she sat in the chair to get her hair washed. The hair wash felt good as Trudy massaged her head, whirling her fingers round and round — so relaxing.

"It's Takeena... Oh, they doing okay — you know, girls being girls," Trudy said as she continued to rub Avenelle's scalp.

"So, things going okay these days? I mean, with the shop?"

"Yep. Business has picked up. At first, I thought I'd have to close the doors. But slowly, folks started coming back — I think a lot of you white women didn't think I could do white hair. I learned *everything* at beauty school, not just black hair. Now, my customers are about evenly mixed. Miss Annie Jo agreed I might hire someone new in a few months — I got more than I can handle."

"I'm glad. I admit I never thought I'd be coming to you, Trudy. But I'm happy I am." Trudy was every bit as talented as Willa Jo.

"You was the first, you know. And I think you must have told other people because lots of people told me you sent them. I appreciate that."

"Well, once I had time to think about it, I realized my hesitation in coming to you was because...well, uh, because —"

"Cause I'm black?"

"Yes. Exactly. The weeds of racism grow in everybody's heart, sometimes. We got to pull those weeds."

"That's so true," said Trudy as she wrapped a towel around Avenelle's head and led her to her booth, where she would give Avenelle a new look. That's what Avenelle wanted — something different; something she could take care of by herself in jail.

"Let's try a little funky, a little wild...not too wild, though. I've worn this every-hair-in-place bob forever. Really. I can't remember when I wore my hair differently. The Reverend always liked it this way...bland. Now, I think I want a pixie cut...really jagged."

"And how about a few highlights? That would give you a little pizazz."

"Go for it." Avenelle basked in Trudy's undivided attention. She looked around the salon, over to the spot where they'd found Willa Jo. The blood stain was gone completely.

Avenelle hardly recognized herself as she paid for her new 'do.' She looked ten years younger, stylish and, believe it or not, almost pretty. She hadn't felt pretty in years. Not since she'd given birth to her baby girl, so long ago. Her baby girl —Clarissa.

She drove from The Sassy Lady directly to the Chadwick County Governmental Complex. She knew exactly where to go and she strode into the sheriff's office with confidence.

"Is Sheriff Hicks in?" she said.

"Yes, ma'm. Who may I say is asking?" said Deputy Stokes.

"Please tell him that Avenelle Young is here to confess to the murder of Willa Jo Temple," Avenelle said in a strong voice. The deputy got up very quickly, took her by the elbow and led her to Tal's small office. He was on the phone but motioned for her to come in and have a seat. She sat down delicately, feeling light as a dandelion puff-seed, floating, floating, floating.

"How can I help you today, Mrs. Young," asked the sheriff.

"Well, I know I'm out on bail waiting for my trial. I have decided to save the taxpayers some money. I've come to confess."

He didn't say a word, just stared at her. Somehow, he was making her feel guilty for confessing.

"Okay. Let me pull up your original statement —Right. You really didn't give much of a statement when you were arrested. So, I guess we'll get it now. Why don't you tell me what happened?"

"Well, I was upset. Very upset. Really, really upset. So, I went to The Sassy Lady and I killed her….that was that." Avenelle twisted her fingers together. Her big toe tingled just a little.

"I see. Um…do you think you could give me a few more details?"

"What do you mean?"

"Well, what time did you arrive at the salon? How did you get in? Why were you there?"

"Let's see. I wanted to get there before Willa Jo opened the shop…I reckon it was around 6 a.m. I've had a key to the shop for years —Bessie Jo, that's Willa Jo's mama, as you know —she gave me one back before she passed away. She was so sick —I brought her many a casserole, some meatloaf, lasagna — didn't bring her any sweets, though. The poor thing had no appetite for them." Avenelle felt a giggle bubbling in the back of her throat.

"The key? Why did you have the key?"

"Well, isn't it obvious —so I could leave the food and not disturb anyone. Willa Jo had her hands full with Bessie and Annie Jo. Annie Jo was running wild, driving her mama crazy. At the same time, Bessie Jo was dying. I knew they'd need all the sleep they could get, so I'd drop the food off in the shop in the mornings. After Bessie Jo died, I never thought about that key. Reckon I kept it to remember Bessie by."

"So, you got there around 6 in the morning, used your key to open the door —then what happened?"

"Well….I saw Willa Jo coming down the stairs into the shop, so I hid in the back room where Willa Jo kept all her hair products —dyes and stuff like that. When Willa Jo walked to her booth, I crept up behind her. She must have seen me in the mirror because she turned around. And then, I stabbed her in the chest."

The sheriff didn't say a word. His head rested on the tips of his fingers and Avenelle couldn't tell if he was thinking or praying. Finally, he looked at her.

"Mrs. Young, why did you do it? What motive could you have possibly had?"

"Isn't it obvious? That notebook of hers. I heard, well, everyone in town had heard, Willa Jo was going to write a book based on the notebook. I couldn't let her do that — it would ruin everything."

The sheriff once again grew quiet. He drummed his fingers on his desk. Avenelle didn't like the way her confession was going. She'd thought all she had to do was own up to it; she had no idea it was going to be so complicated.

"So, that notebook held incriminating stuff in it?"

"Oh yes! Why, there was something on most everybody in Chadwick County — Willa Jo had lots of customers. There's stuff about people having affairs and sex changes and eyelid lifts. You wouldn't believe all the gossip in there...but I was only worried about my own."

The sheriff looked skeptical. But why shouldn't she have a sordid past? She hadn't always been a grandmother. Once, she'd been pretty and young and full of hope.

"Do you know where this notebook is?"

Avenelle gulped. She was a terrible liar. She twiddled her thumbs.

"No, sir. I have no idea."

"What could have been so damning in this notebook, Mrs. Young? What were you afraid of?"

"I guess I can tell you, now that I'm confessing —I...well..." She fidgeted in her chair. Better to get it over with; just say the words. Say. The. Words. "I had a baby when I was sixteen. We...my parents and me...we didn't want anybody to know about it. So I went far away from here to give birth. Told everybody I was helping out a relative. Nobody knew, nobody even guessed. Eventually, I finished my education and married. I was...well, I *am*...respectable. The Reverend and my sons have no idea." Avenelle watched his face to see if he looked shocked. Nothing, not even a raised eyebrow. He didn't say anything. The silence was unbearable so Avenelle continued.

"I gave my baby away —just gave her away. I guess I thought if Willa Jo wrote a book and revealed my secret, it would ruin my life. The Reverend would divorce me, my sons would be so ashamed of me. I couldn't let that happen. How's that for motive?" Avenelle said, hiccoughing back a chuckle.

Once again, the sheriff looked off into space, as if he were weighing each word Avenelle said. She never dreamed a confession would be such hard work. She felt a rivulet of sweat trickle down her back.

"Exactly how did you stab Ms. Temple? Could you show me what you did?"

Avenelle hadn't expected that question —she never thought she'd have to demonstrate. She stood up and grabbed a pencil off the sheriff's desk. Then, with a great deal of enthusiasm, she thrust the pencil down, pretending Willa Jo was in front of her. Once she got going with the motion, she did it several times — it felt so good.

"So…you stabbed her five times?" said the sheriff.

"Well, I got a little carried away just now…I just stabbed her once in real life."

"You're sure, Mrs. Young, that you are telling the truth, the whole truth and nothing but the truth…this is very serious business. I'll have to take you over to the jail," the sheriff said.

"I'm absolutely certain that's what happened."

In one way, Avenelle was not a good liar. But then, she realized she'd been *living* a lie her whole life, acting as if she was an innocent, the perfect preacher's wife. Realizing this gave her confidence.

"Absolutely certain."

The sheriff made her write down what she'd told him. Then, he walked her from his office to the large jail where she'd been held earlier. She hated the coils of razor wire and knew that, once she walked through those gates, she would most likely never walk out again. It didn't matter. Nothing mattered except Clarissa's safety. She'd deserted her girl forty years ago; she would not abandon her now.

"What about the spilled liquid, Mrs. Young. How did that happen?" said the sheriff, as they passed the entrance.

"Liquid? Oh…..yes, the liquid. Of course. Well, as I was approaching Willa Jo, I accidentally knocked a big bottle of something over and it just went everywhere….I almost slipped before I got to Willa Jo….luckily, I didn't and was able to kill her without any further trouble." She didn't like the way that last part sounded but it was out now — she couldn't change her testimony.

"Are you sure you want to confess, Mrs. Young? Once I take your statement, that's it. You'll go to jail."

"I'm positive. Let's get this over with."

The deputies followed the same procedure they'd performed the first time she'd come to jail: they got her basic facts —name, address, phone, birthdate, etc —then, a quick medical check. Then came her least favorite part —the shower, when she turned all her belongings, clothes and all, over to the deputy who zipped them in a large plastic bag. And once again, the lovely orange suit — not her color. They shackled her at the ankles and walked her into holding cell three. The room almost felt like home. She remembered how she'd felt before, when she thought the walls would close in on her. This time, she was calmer. Now, she knew what she had to do. She had to save Clarissa, her baby girl. She hobbled over to the cot and lay down, staring at the ceiling. She knew she was doing the right thing.

She thought about The Reverend. He would be shocked. Again. And, after she explained about Clarissa, he'd be even more shocked. The poor Reverend. She felt a stab of tenderness for him; all these years and he'd never guessed anything was wrong with her. She'd fooled him; she'd fooled the whole town. They thought she was good, but she was not. She had a blight on her soul. Maybe now that the truth was out, she would be able to hold her head up again, the truth released and her burden lifted.

Chapter Thirty

"My third husband always said 'Women are God's greatest mystery' — and then, he beat the shit out of me."

~The Beautician's Notebook

August

Rory Young sat on the back deck, a deck he'd built with his own hands. He looked around — his wife had flowers and ferns everywhere, splashes of color that brought joy to him on most nights. This evening, however, joy was nothing but a distant emotion, one he was sure he'd never feel again.

The sheriff called around 5 o'clock, right as Rory was getting home from visiting the shut-ins. He'd been looking forward to a delicious dinner —Avenelle always cooked him a delicious dinner —and had barely been inside when the phone rang.

"Reverend Young?" a male voice said.

"Yes, this is he."

"This is Sheriff Hicks — I have what I think will be some surprising news for you. This afternoon, you wife, Avenelle, drove to the Chadwick County Government Complex and turned herself in — she confessed to killing Willa Jo Temple," the sheriff said, his voice a monotone. Strictly business.

"What? Confessed?"

"Yes, Reverend Young. She's back in jail."

"I don't know what's going on, but there's been some sort of mistake. I'm confident my wife did not kill anyone." Rory then proceeded to ask lots of questions, for which the sheriff patiently provided answers. Yes, he could visit his wife, but he had to set up an appointment; no, he could not bring her any clothing, books, food or make-up. Finally, after exhausting his questions, Rory hung up and walked to the back deck in a daze.

Avenelle? A confessed killer? He couldn't believe it, would never believe it. He looked out over the garden, carefully tended each year by his wife after they'd both planted and seeded the soil. All through the summer, they feasted on juicy, sweet tomatoes, bright yellow squashes, spring onions, green and red peppers, corn —oh, the corn was glorious, straight off the cob, dripping with butter.

His wife was in jail. Where, in seminary, had they covered *that* particular problem? He'd learned how to counsel grieving families, comfort the sick, and discuss marital infidelity with couples. He'd been taught how to keep his own emotions in check; after all, being a preacher was an important leadership position within a community. He had to inspire trust, even when a parishioner disagreed with him, even when there were squabbles among the various factions within the church. Oh, he knew all about conflict resolution and team-building. But where were the techniques for dealing with a wife who was a murderer?

He watched as the sun began to set —the colors were particularly beautiful, purples and oranges, pinks and golds all swirled across the sky, the light from the evening sun filtering through clouds. Rory did not feel so alone now. God was with him. In the sunset, in the garden, in the bright green leaves of the Gerber daisies on the deck, he could feel God's presence; at least, he could feel what he *thought* was God's presence. All the years of emptiness were wiped away — the jealousies he'd felt when others described their own experiences with God, and he'd had none —all gone. In one brief moment, Rory knew what it was all about —worship and connection and love. He felt it touch him right there on the back porch. He didn't hear any voices, but his heart and mind were touched, all the same. He continued to stare into the amazing sky, and was filled with a feeling of contentment. The words 'It is well/with my soul/It is well/with my soul' came into his mind, the old hymn from childhood. How kind of God to choose this particular moment in his life to come forth….how merciful and full of grace.

Rory put his face in his hands and wept. He wept with grief for his miserable self, his terrifying circumstances, the possible loss of his wife. He wept with joy, for the touch of the Holy had changed him, and he suddenly understood why Abraham and Moses and David and Jesus and all the saints in heaven lived and acted the way they had. They had tasted the Divine; and, once savored, the Divine transformed the whole world

Rory wiped his cheeks and eyes. His nose was running ceaselessly, but he didn't care. He took out his shirttail and wiped his nose on it — Avenelle would have had a fit. Oh Avenelle, his dear, sweet Nellie. He would stand by her, no matter what. He saw with great clarity now, how she'd devoted her life to him. He'd taken her for granted, forced her into helping him whether she wanted to or not. He had not been a loving husband; he'd been self-centered and arrogant. Oh, his sins ran deep, marbling his soul with qualities he no longer wanted.

He would be different, now. No matter what happened, he would love his wife the way she deserved to be loved, the way everyone deserves to be loved. He knew he would fail over and over, but he would keep trying. And God would see his effort and God would bless it.

Slowly, Rory rose. He took one more look around the garden. He'd have to weed and gather tomorrow. But for tonight, he would rest. He had a feeling he would need his strength. But somehow, deep in his soul, Rory knew all would be well.

Chapter Thirty-One

"Most men don't take the time to think...they just act and react."

~The Beautician's Notebook

August

"What in the world made her confess? I mean, after keeping quiet when you arrested her, why would she suddenly confess?" Clarissa said. She stared at Tal across the table at The Purple Onion. It was all she could do to keep from reaching out to him, touch his arm, his hand. But she didn't dare.

"I have no idea — to be honest, I don't think she's guilty. According to the autopsy report, Willa Jo was stabbed from below, as if someone had given her an upper cut that landed right in the solar plexus. When Mrs. Young demonstrated how she committed the act, she stabbed in a definite downward motion. Plus, we still don't have any real motive. She said something about a youthful indiscretion —"

"Oooh, what did she tell you?" said Clarissa, sipping her coke. Clarissa wondered if Miss Avenelle had told Tal about the baby she'd given away.

"I'm not at liberty to say...but I don't think it would be enough to warrant murdering Willa Jo. I mean, it happened so long ago...." Tal placed his crumpled napkin on the plate. He signaled for the waitress.

"Why would a law-abiding citizen, a grandmother, for heaven's sake, kill a beautician? Doesn't make sense," said Tal. He took a bite of his shrimp burger.

"I....I may have an idea." *Time for a little confession of my own.* Clarissa'd been terrified to tell him she'd stolen the notebook. But now, he needed to know for the investigation.

"Really? What?"

She took a deep breath. She wasn't sure what he would do when he found out she'd withheld evidence in a murder case...but, really, she'd *had* to read it herself first. And, boy, was she glad she did. She'd found out what a dirty, rotten scoundrel she'd married. She reached into her purse and pulled out the notebook. She handed it to Tal.

"Is this what I think it is?"

She nodded.

He was not happy. "How in the hell did *you* get it?"

"I...I told her I wanted to take music lessons —you know, as a way to get close to her, find out what I could. And I found this." She pointed at the notebook.

"So, you found it at her house, huh? Not even hidden away." Tal wiped his mouth with the corner of his napkin.

"Well, it was *sort* of hidden —in among a bunch of old magazines. She has no idea I've taken it. Should I put it back next week? What should I do? Can it count as evidence?" Clarissa poked around her grilled salmon salad for a bite of fish.

"It's evidence now that you've given it to me. It's legal for me to accept it and it will be legal in court because you aren't a cop —you stole it as a civilian." Tal clenched his jaw and she could see the vein in his neck pulsing.

"What were you thinking? Now, you could be charged with interfering in a police matter. This is *illegal,* Clarissa. Why did you wait so long to give it to me?" His voice was tight and low, very controlled, but also angry. She began to fear he might arrest her.

"I ... I wanted to read it myself first. I...I didn't mean to interfere...I didn't mean to break the law."

"Well, you did both. I should charge you right now."

She could feel tears at the back of her throat. He saw he'd upset her and relented.

"Oh hell —don't cry. I'm not going to arrest you. But why? Why didn't you tell me?"

"I don't know. I guess I wanted to read it —it made me feel closer to Willa Jo. I miss her so much. I just wanted to hold onto it for myself. I know it doesn't make any sense."

He gave her a half-smile and put her hand over hers.

"It's okay. I get it —really. So, what'd you find out?"

"I found out a lot of stuff —one thing in particular that's going to change *my* life."

"Change your life? What are you talking about?"

She wasn't sure she could say the words out loud. If she spoke them, they would become real. If she spoke them, she might cry....again.

"I discovered my dear, darling husband had an affair with Willa Jo."

"What? Are you kidding me?"

"Nope. Seems Ralph was not immune to Willa Jo's charms. I guess that's why I feel so free to hang out with you —what's good for the gander is good for the goose."

They looked at each other and smiled those tight smiles lovers sometimes share when angered. Tal's brown eyes seemed to burn into her.

"So, what happens next?" she said.

"I'll read it, of course. Is there anything about our suspect in the notebook?"

Clarissa sipped her coke. She hadn't thought too much about it while she'd been reading the notebook — she'd been too caught up with Ralph's affair with Willa Jo. But, thinking about it here, with Tal, she realized Miss Avenelle had everything to lose if the contents of the notebook got out. And those rumors about Willa Jo writing a book might have scared Miss Avenelle out of her mind.

"Actually, yes. It seems Miss Avenelle had some trouble as a young girl —not the kind of trouble you want people to know about, especially if you're married to a preacher."

"Hmmm....so, what, exactly, did the notebook say?" Tal started at her intently.

Clarissa summarized the story, explaining that Miss Avenelle had had an illegitimate child at sixteen. No one in Summerset had known about it but the father and Miss Avenelle's parents. She'd gone away for a while, an absence explained as necessary to take care of an ailing aunt in Ohio.

"She told me the same story in her confession. I'll admit, that gives her motive. If I add this to the evidence we already have...it's not looking too good for Miss Avenelle, as you call her," said Tal.

"Do you think she did it? I'm having a hard time believing it — she's such a nice woman." Clarissa thought about how kind Miss Avenelle had been to her, how easy the woman had been to talk to. Could she have murdered Willa Jo?

“Well, we have evidence. But no, my gut tells me she wouldn’t hurt a fly. Plus, her description of the event doesn’t match the facts. Who knows? People can fool you.”

“That’s the truth.” Ralph had fooled her all these years. And she was pretty sure Willa Jo wasn’t his only woman on the side. All those business trips.

“Well, I only have eight hours to verify her confession…I wouldn’t call it verified yet, but this does give her motive. As much as I would like to spend the afternoon with you, I’d better get back to work. Did the notebook say who the father of the baby was?” Tal said as he rose to pay the tab.

“No. But Miss Avenelle must have referred to him as RB, because that’s what was in the notebook…RB,” said Clarissa.

“Damn —RB. I’ll think on that for a while.” Tal walked her to her car.

Chapter Thirty-Two

"Never wait until your hair is falling out in clumps before you see a doctor. If you see a few extras in the sink, check it out right away. Better safe than sorry."

~The Beautician's Notebook

Late August

It took Tal just about an hour to read the notebook in its entirety. He'd laughed and been shocked and felt like he was talking directly to Willa Jo. He loved the part where she'd called him her 'super-hero' and she said his special power was being a 'love machine.'

Oh, Willa.

He kept running the initials RB over and over in his mind. Only one name came to him—the obvious one--Richard Bonner from the Chevrolet place. Had to be.

After he'd finished going through the notebook one more time, he realized it was way past 5 o'clock. He hurried to his car; he still had a witness to interrogate.

Tal drove to the Chevrolet dealership. The evening sun was setting, splashing gold across the sky — deep brassy gold, pale daffodil yellow gold and every shade in between. As usual, the sky caught Tal's attention and he had to force himself to focus on the job at hand. He mulled over the facts of the case.

Fact #1 — The coroner had not declared Willa Jo's death a homicide. It was categorized as 'pending investigation'. It was still possible she could have died accidently. There was some residue spilled near the body, some kind of beauty product. Could Willa Jo have slipped?

Fact #2 — The chemical cape had four sets of prints: Willa Jo's, Trudy's, Clarissa's and Avenelle Young's. The first three sets were located in logical places — around the ties. But Avenelle Young's prints had been on the back of the cape, as if she had grabbed Willa Jo from behind. Why would she have done that? Was she angry at Willa Jo? Was there bad blood between them? Sure, the notebook said Willa

Jo had kissed Rory Young, but was one kiss enough to make Avenelle Young murder Willa Jo?

Fact #3 —Avenelle Young had a sordid past, a past she wanted to keep secret. Her standing in the community, her family and her marriage depended on that secret. And rumor had it, Willa Jo was going to write about book about all secrets and confessions she'd heard over the years. Mrs. Young had possession of the notebook — she must have stolen it from Willa Jo's. Is that what happened? Avenelle Young broke into Willa Jo's to steal the notebook...Willa Jo caught her. A struggle ensued and Avenelle Young ended up stabbing Willa Jo?

Great story, but it didn't quite fit the facts. There'd been no sign of forced entry —Mrs. Young had said she had a key, so that part fit. No sign of a struggle. Several partial footprints had been found in that spill on the floor, but somebody had tried to mop it up; hence the damp towels draped across Willa Jo's chair. Whoever had done the clean-up ruined the prints...the police had been unable to get any sense of size or type of shoe. But Miss Avenelle had made no mention of mopping anything up. She'd seemed momentarily confused when he'd asked about the spilled conditioner — she seemed to be fabricating that part of the story.

Certainly, Avenelle Young was implicated, but he didn't have enough information yet to accept her confession. The way she described the events was completely off the mark. She said she stabbed Willa Jo with a downward motion while the coroner said the blow came from the ground up. Besides, Avenelle Young did not seem like the kind of person who would commit murder. His gut was telling him there was more to the story.

He pulled into the Chevrolet dealership. The dealership was still open, though Tal knew they'd be closing up soon. He hoped Rock Bonner was still on the premises. He glanced once more into the fading sky and crossed his fingers —oh, please let everything fall into place.

***

"Howdy, Sheriff. In the market for a new car?" Bonner said. He held out his hand to shake. The man's grip was still firm. "You know, every time I see you, Tal, I think to myself what a big mistake Willa

Jo made when she let you go. Whatever happened between you two anyway?" Bonner clapped Tal on the shoulder.

"Rock, I'm here to ask *you* the questions. As for me and Willa Jo....well, I guess some things were never meant to be. I miss her, though. I used to run into her every now and then — and that was enough. But now, we'll never run into her again, not this side of heaven."

"Breaks my heart...so, what can I do you for?"

"Avenelle Young has confessed to Willa Jo's murder...I'm trying to verify the confession. From her juvie records, I discovered Avenelle got into some trouble back in the day...and you were involved. Something about a stolen car, right off your daddy's lot." Tal hoped Bonner would corroborate what Tal suspected.

Rock motioned for Tal to follow him into his office. Rock closed the door and sat behind his desk.

"It's true. Avie and I, well....we had a little fling. They'd arrest me for it, these days. Hell, I was married to Bessie and Willa Jo was only three. I was not quite twenty. I damn sure wasn't ready for the marriage thing — but I did it. I worked hard under my daddy's thumb right here at the dealership."

Tal looked at Rock from across his large, imposing desk, the kind of desk that was designed to make the customer feel small. Tal stood and faced the man. Now, *he* was in the power position.

"So, is that it? You and Mrs. Young had an affair when she was underage and you stole a car together?"

"Well, there's a little more to it than that."

"Okay...."

Rock Bonner studied a paper on his desk. He reached into the top left drawer and pulled out a flask of something. He placed two shot glasses from the drawer onto the table.

"Join me?"

"Sorry. Official business"

"How can I tell you this story if you won't join me in a drink?" Rock poured a golden liquid into each glass and handed one to the sheriff.

"Reckon it won't hurt — it's way after quitting time."

Tal took the glass and swallowed the contents in one gulp. He sat back down and waited.

"We started seeing each other, Avie and me. She was on the cheerleading squad and I was assistant coach —just part-time because I'd been sort of a star on the field myself. That, plus my daddy's connections got me a job I really loved. So, we saw each other every day almost, her doing cartwheels and me running plays. We got to talking...you know how it goes."

Tal laughed to himself — oh yeah, he knew. He thought about Clarissa.

"Yeah, but you had to know she was jail-bait, Rock." Tal's voice was friendly and soothing, a technique he'd perfected over the years. It gave the suspect the feeling he could be trusted.

"Didn't think about it that way —she was a little younger than me, sure. But so was Bessie. I mean, we were all in high school together, Bessie and me-I was a senior and she was a sophomore. It didn't feel weird or like I was some sort of bad person. But Avie, hell, she was a year younger than Bessie. Reckon I didn't much care back then."

"So, what happened?"

"We got caught when I stole a car off Dad's lot. My dad let it slide, but *her* daddy —old man Avery —man, he went ballistic! Made her get processed down at the police station, fingerprints and all. But that didn't stop us. We were in love —yes, I loved Avie. Bessie was busy with Willa Jo and working all the time. She didn't have much energy left for me — you know, in the bedroom" Rock poured himself another drink. He lifted the flask to ask the sheriff if he wanted another, but Tal shook his head.

"I guess you could say I seduced Avie...she was a virgin until I came along. She didn't know anything about protection. She got pregnant. When she told me, I begged her to get an abortion. Told her I'd pay for everything. But somehow, her daddy found out. He sent her away to have her baby and give it up for adoption." Bonner tossed back the rest of his drink.

Tal leaned his hip against the desk. Could this be it? The reason Mrs. Young killed Willa Jo? Sure, the secret might have hurt Mrs. Young...but enough to murder Willa Jo? Hell, it was decades ago. Nobody cared about that stuff these days —look at Annie Jo. Sure, he and Willa Jo hadn't been happy about Annie Jo's pregnancy, but she hadn't become a pariah. Nobody blinked much of an eye, especially the young people.

"Where did she go?"

"Some unwed mother's home in Akron. When she came back in time to do her junior year, she was a different person. She wouldn't even look at me if we passed on the street. She went on to college and then, next thing I heard, she married Reverend Young. Of course, Bessie found out about the affair — I couldn't keep anything from that woman — and she divorced me. I tried to see Willa Jo when I could, but I'll admit — I was a lousy father. That's it, Sheriff. That's all I know about Avie Young. She made me swear all those years ago I'd never breathe a word of this to anyone. And you're the first person to hear it from my lips,"

"Can you think of any reason Mrs. Young would confess to Willa Jo's murder?"

"Avie's one of the sweetest people I've ever known. I remember one time she found a daddy-longlegs in the car. She wouldn't let me kill it. I had to put the damn thing in the grass. She's always been a gentle soul." Bonner poured another shot.

"She has another side, though — I used to call her my little wildcat. She's got that fierce side. I do think she would protect those she loved. She's that kind of woman. I wish I could have another chance with her — I'd marry her in a heartbeat."

Tal rose, ready to get some supper, ready to kick back on his couch.

"Thanks for your help."

"I'd appreciate it if you would keep Avie's secret — she's got enough tongues wagging with this murder thing. And I *did* promise her."

"Sure. I'll do my best to keep this between you and me."

Tal walked out to the car, sat in the driver's seat and thought. He barely was aware of what he was doing as he drove back to his office. The clock was ticking and he had not yet verified Mrs. Young's story. But he was getting closer. He could feel his brain trying to put together the pieces, but he was unable to construct anything solid and stable. Right now, all he had was conjecture and circumstantial evidence. He had no idea what to do next.

Chapter Thirty-Two

"You can't make black hair blond in one day."

~The Beautician's Notebook

Late August

Rory Young splashed his face with Old Spice and combed his hair one more time. He looked at his image in the mirror, professional, respectable, exactly the way he wanted to appear when he visited his wife in jail. Visited his wife in jail. Now those were some words he never dreamed he'd string together. His wife. In jail. Confessed murderer. He pinched himself hard to make sure he wasn't having some sort of prolonged nightmare. Nope. It hurt. This was real.

Though it was only eight a.m., the morning was already hot and muggy. The temperature might hit a hundred today. What did he expect at the end of August? He knew the rhythms of the seasons — he'd lived here all his life, except for seminary down at Bob Jones in South Carolina. He thought about the God-moment, his earlier experience. He'd tried to keep that 'all-will-be-well' feeling. But in the days after Avenelle's confession, his thoughts returned to normal — he was in this by himself, there was no supernatural help for him, he was alone and about to lose his wife, possibly his job, possibly everything.

Rory backed his car out of the driveway and glanced up to the front porch of his house. Was that....? Naw, it couldn't be. He stared hard. Was that Abel? His long lost son? The boy waved and trotted down the steps toward him. He hadn't spoken to his son in three years. What could he say now?

"I heard about Mom. I came right away," Abel said.

"Came from where?"

"Been playing at a club in Myrtle Beach-a good gig. Regular money —just a beach band for the tourists. No cussing, Dad," Abel smiled up at his father.

"Well, that's good. I'm going out to the jail to see your mother. You have to make an appointment and they only allow one person —

you can't come," Rory said. He hadn't meant to say it so harshly — what was there about his son that set him off? Just because the boy wanted to play music? So had King David. He softened his tone. "The key's under the mat. Why don't you go inside and clean up, have some breakfast? I'll be home in an hour — then we can talk."

"Great. I'm here to help, Dad. Adam is about to go crazy with this thing — he's got a big job offer in Charlotte on the table. But he doesn't want to leave you guys in the lurch. He called me and said, 'We need to pull together to get Mom out of this mess.' And I agree."

"Thanks, son. I appreciate it…but I gotta go — I only get an hour and I don't want to be late," said Rory.

He pulled away from the curb and waved good-bye. He saw Abel jog up the steps and retrieve the key from under pink welcome mat. When had his son gotten so mature? When had he become so caring, so willing to help? In Rory's memory, the boy was lazy in school, lazy in life, floating from one dead-end job to the next, couch-surfing his way up and down the coast. When had he changed?

The boy had always remained close to his mother and brother, even after Rory had disowned him. He'd been furious with his wife when he discovered she was still in contact with the boy, and, he suspected, still sending him money.

And since when had Adam been offered a job in Charlotte? Why hadn't he known about this? Would his first-born son really consider moving so far away? A four-hour drive, at least. Avenelle would be devastated; little Kevin, the one bright light in Rory's life, moving all the way to Charlotte? How could this be? When was Adam going to tell them about this new plan?

As Rory drove to the jail, he felt more discombobulated than ever. He didn't even know what was going on with his sons. He didn't understand what was going on with his wife. His whole world was spinning out of control.

He parked the car in the visitor space and pushed the buzzer to open the gates as he'd been instructed. He waited at the door for a policeman to pat him down to make sure he wasn't carrying a weapon. Then, he was escorted to the visitation room. He passed door number three, Avenelle's cell, on his way to the visitation room. He glanced in and saw her sitting on the cot, just sitting there.

Once they'd reached the visitation room, the escorting officer pointed him toward a chair. He sat down and waited for his wife.

She walked in slowly and he could see the shackles around her ankles. She'd made a sort of cuff to hold the chains so they wouldn't chaff her skin. She had such nice ankles.

He looked at her face. She wore no make-up, but that short hair made her look tough, edgy. Egad, he hated her 'new look' as she called it. She was still a handsome woman, though, even with spiky hair, even at fifty-six. He thought of all their years together, how she'd worked right beside him, a real help-mate. He was flooded with tenderness for her — she looked so small in this place, like she could be eaten up by it.

"Oh, Rory. I'm *so* happy to see you," she said as she sat across the table from him. The guard stood by the door, giving them some privacy but not enough.

Rory wanted to take her in his arms at that moment, shelter her from everything. His anger at her for disturbing their perfect lives dissipated. But he still couldn't get used to her new look — that wild hair disturbed him...but he couldn't tell her that. She had enough to worry about.

"Me, too. Oh, Nellie...Why? Why did you confess? I know you didn't do it — I'll bet everyone in Summerset knows you didn't do it — why did you confess?"

"I won't talk about the case with you, dear. It's something I've done and I'm willing to take the consequences — after all, my children are on their own, you have the church — I'm really not much use to anybody."

"Not much use? Nellie, without you, my life doesn't work. I can't find anything, I don't know what's going on in my own family — did you know Adam had a job offer in Charlotte?"

"Of course. I told him to take it — it's a terrific opportunity and a great deal of money."

"Have you lost your mind? It's a four-hour drive! We'll never see Kevin again."

"Oh Rory, don't be ridiculous. Of course, we'll see them. We'll probably see them even more — it will be a treat to come home and we'll have more quality time. Well, if you can call visiting in a jail quality time."

"You won't believe who I found on the front porch this morning, right before I drove here."

"Hmmm. One of the ladies from the alter guild?"

"Nope…our son…Abel. …just sitting on the swing. He didn't ring the bell or anything. At first, I couldn't believe my eyes."

"Oh, I can't wait to see him!" said Avenelle. "How did he look?"

"Okay. Pretty good, actually. Did you know he's playing regularly now? Some joint down in Myrtle Beach?"

"He's been doing that for about a year —he loves it and it pays the bills. He has time to work on his own music, too. I think he's happy," Avenelle took his hands in her own. "Were you kind to him?"

"I told him to get the key and go have some breakfast…he came because Adam told him about your situation. He wants to help."

"Good…good," said Avenelle.

He continued to hold his wife's hands and felt a spark of hope. He *had* been kind to Abel. Maybe the rift could be mended. And maybe, if they all pulled together, they could find out what happened to Willa Jo Temple and exonerate his wife. The rush of tenderness returned and Rory thought he might burst with it.

"There's something I want to talk to you about, Rory." Her voice sounded strained. Maybe she was going to tell him what really happened that morning at The Sassy Lady. He steeled himself.

"I'm here…listening. Go ahead."

"You know I read Willa Jo's notebook…you do *know* that, don't you?"

"I didn't realize you had that book —how in the world did you get it?"

"I stole it."

That bit of news struck Rory like a bolt from the blue. *His* Nellie *stole* the notebook? His professional training kicked in —he would listen and listen only. No judgment.

"Okay."

"When I read it, I learned a lot of things, things that would shock some of the folks in the congregation of Sabbath Home Church. Things like you, The Reverend Rory Young, kissing Willa Jo Temple!" she said, with a great deal of drama.

"What?" said Rory.

"That kiss is right in the book, Rory. It happened the same year Abel was born. That was our bad year, if you recall. I'll certainly never forget it. Adam starting kindergarten and me with a new baby —you working long hours and always coming home too tired to help with anything around the house. It was the Year from Hell!" She folded her arms and looked to the side. Rory could see she was fuming.

He'd been caught. His one indiscretion in thirty years of marriage. And now, he sat in jail with his wife, the confessed murderer, and felt as if *he* were on trial. He thought back about that kiss. He'd been feeling lousy, his wife too busy to give him the time of day. He'd gone late one afternoon to The Sassy Lady for a quick haircut. There was no one there but Willa Jo. She'd been so beautiful, her dark hair piled on top of her head. She'd cut his hair and was brushing off his neck with some powdery stuff that smelled good. All of a sudden, she reached around and kissed him right on the mouth, a long, sweet kiss that he still remembered. She said to him, "I've never slept with a man of God...want to go upstairs?"

The kiss shocked him and the proposal even more-so. It scared the bejesus out of him. On one hand, he wanted to appear sophisticated — a man of the world. On the other hand, he was terrified one of his parishioners would see him. He knew what a hotbed of gossip Summerset could be. He needed to think — he needed to get out of the situation without hurting Willa Jo's feelings.

"I would love to, Willa Jo. But we both know I can't. For lots of reasons. Thanks for the haircut." And with that, he handed her a big tip and walked out the door.

For months afterward, he'd regretted his decision. But as the years passed and his home life achieved some equilibrium, he was glad he'd had the fortitude to do the right thing. And now, all these years later, here was Avenelle, sitting across from him, fuming about a kiss that hadn't led to anything. And did he forget to mention his Nelle had confessed to *murder*? What was a little kiss compared to that?

"It was just a kiss, Nelle. Didn't mean a thing."

"Oh, I see. While I was breaking my back taking care of YOUR two sons, keeping YOUR house and playing piano at YOUR church, you just decided to have a little harmless kiss?? With a woman young enough to be your daughter?"

Rory had never seen her riled up like this — well, she was pretty riled when he disowned Abel, but that was different. That time, she was angry on Abel's behalf; *this* time, she was angry for *herself*. This passion was, he had to admit, sexy as hell.

"Avenelle —Nellie...it was nothing. I'd gone The Sassy Lady for a haircut. And, after she'd finished, Willa Jo bent down and kissed me. She invited me upstairs, but I said no. I said *no*, Nellie. And that was all there was to it. I've never cheated on you —I never would. I love you, Avenelle...I sincerely do." He reached across the table and placed his hands palm facing up, a plea for her to hold hands with him.

She refused to look at him. He rose and walked around the table to hold her.

"Sir, please remain seated. Sir, those are the rules for visitations." The guard's voice boomed across the room.

Rory returned to his chair. He kept his eyes on his wife, looking for any sign of forgiveness.

She finally looked at him and placed her arms on the table, palms up. He gently took both hands in his. They stared at each other, but didn't say a word. However, when the allotted time was over, he knew he'd been forgiven.

Chapter Thirty-Three

"I will not cut your hair in a mullet, no matter how much you pay me."

~The Beautician's Notebook

"I cannot believe you are hanging out with Mad Dog! He was my *mother's* lover, for heaven's sake. It's sick," Annie Jo said as she pushed Lawson in his stroller toward Fantasy Isle Ice Cream. She and Kayla had decided to take Lawson to Temple Beach that morning. They'd built sand castles, gathered a bag of shells, splashed in the tidal pools and eaten an early lunch. Now, it was time to head home, time for Lawson's nap.

"He's a nice guy —you just have to get to know him. He wants to get back into racing —he's doing local stuff now, but his dream is to get to the big leagues. He's *got* dreams, Annie Jo —goals. I like that in a man," Kayla said.

"Humph...it's just gross. I mean, he's way older than you," said Annie Jo.

"Just nine years. At least he's not some gangbanger," said Kayla, plopping down on the swing outside Fantasy Isle. The swing was attached to a big branch of an enormous live oak tree, with Spanish moss hanging from almost every limb.

"Thanks a lot, Kayla. Just what I wanted to hear. Hold Lawson while I get the ice cream — he loves that swing," said Annie Jo, stepping up to the counter. She ordered a cup of vanilla for Lawson and pistachio for Kayla and herself — in a waffle cone. She loved waffle cones and ever since she'd inherited from her mom, she'd allowed herself a few extras. Waffle cones included.

Annie Jo hurried to the swing and tried to lick her cone while feeding Lawson his ice cream. Just as she was about to lose the cone, a young man came to her rescue.

"Here, let me," he said as he grabbed her cone and, using Lawson's spoon, scooped the ice cream to a more tenable position. "There."

Annie Jo took the cone and gave it a long lick. "Thanks," she said. The young man stood there looking like he wanted to join them, so Annie Jo invited him to have a seat.

"I'm Abel Young...you know, Reverend Young's son," said the young man.

"You're kidding — I remember you! Didn't we both have old Choo-Choo McDaniel for chemistry?"

"And I'm Kayla Jordan," said Kayla.

"And who is this little guy?" said Abel, bending down to tickle Lawson's bare foot.

"My son, Lawson...he's two."

"You don't look old enough to have a kid."

"Well, I am. What are you doing back in these parts? I haven't seen you for, like, years," said Annie Jo.

"Well, my mom — you probably know she's in jail — I came home to help get her out."

"Here's a scene you don't see every day — boy meets girl, boy's mother kills girl's mother." That was cold, but how else could she respond to this guy. She decided to relent a little.

"I know your mom — she's a nice lady. She was giving me guitar lessons before she confessed. Honestly, I don't think she did it, either — just so you know. But if she didn't, I wonder who did?"

Abel looked at her and she almost melted — he had blond hair and aqua-colored eyes — she'd never noticed those eyes back in school. It was strange; you'd think since Willa Jo was her mother, she'd take more interest in the case. But, to tell the truth, she really didn't care who'd whacked her mom. Maybe nobody did. Maybe it *was* some kind of freak accident. She did, however, feel guilty about Miss Avenelle. Like her confession was somehow Annie Jo's fault. She should never have told her father about Miss Avenelle having the notebook.

"I'm just sorry about it...sorry for your loss," Abel said.

"Hey, let's change the subject — ya'll are getting too somber for such a beautiful day. Annie Jo and I were about to head to her place to give Lawson here his nap. Wanna come?" Kayla said.

Annie Jo could have stomped her foot into Kayla's big mouth.

"Sure — if it's cool with Annie Jo."

"Whatever."

She pushed Lawson to the car and strapped him into his car seat. She noticed out of the corner of her eye that Abel had mounted a small motorcycle. She motioned for him to follow them and off they drove, an uncomfortable silence hanging between Annie Jo and Kayla.

Lawson dozed off quickly. Annie Jo, Kayla and Abel were in the game room playing pool. Annie Jo had made lemonade and she had a few leftover brownies from the weekend, so they were snacking and shooting, with Brandi Carlile singing in the background.

"Glad to see we have similar tastes in music. I'm in a band down at Myrtle Beach but we just play the old shagging songs for the retirement crowd. I'd love to do something more like that." Abel made the five-ball in the side pocket.

"You're, like, a professional musician?" Annie Jo asked.

"Yep. Got disowned from my daddy and everything," said Abel, smiling.

"That's my dream! I would give anything to get to that point — you know, the point where you make money."

"Good luck with that. I've been at it for five years, ever since high school. I'm making a very modest living but that's about it — I sure as hell ain't getting rich."

"Did your dad really disown you?" Kayla said, lining up a shot.

"Sure did. After graduation, he wanted me to follow in my big brother's footsteps and 'make something of myself.' He didn't like the music I listened to — called it 'a tool of the devil.' When I told him that's what I wanted to do with my life, he packed my stuff in a duffel bag and, after one of my gigs, I found it on the front porch with a note — 'Never darken our door again unless you are a changed man.'"

"Oooh, that's harsh," said Kayla.

"It *is*. I thought when I got pregnant with Lawson, my mom would do the same to me. But she didn't. She just asked me what I wanted to do, what the daddy wanted to do. I told her my baby-daddy was no longer in the picture and I wanted to raise the baby by myself. She told me she would help in any way she could."

Annie Jo realized she missed her mother. She missed the way her mother fussed at her for not having any goals in life, the way her mother used to take Lawson for an afternoon so Annie Jo could rest, the way her mother *cared* about Annie Jo's life. She felt herself tearing up.

“Do you guys mind if I have some time alone? It’s been fun, but I need to rest. I’m just feeling bad right now,” Annie Jo said.

“No problem…look, I’m sorry. I mean, it’s obvious talking about your mom upset you,” Abel said.

“Yeah, Annie —go nap with Lawson and I’ll call you later, okay?” Kayla said.

Annie Jo nodded and waved them off. Then, she tiptoed up the steps so as not to awaken Lawson. She crawled into her own bed, the bed she’d had as a little girl, and fell asleep.

Chapter Thirty-Four

"The truth is, nobody ever sees it coming. You just gotta keep on going."

~The Beautician's Notebook

Late August

Clarissa walked slowly along the beach, Mitzy's paws leaving tiny prints in the sand. It was low tide and the beach looked empty, even though it was the last week in August, still tourist season. Mitzy ran ahead, sniffing every shell, piece of driftwood, any stray pieces of trash left from sunbathers. Clarissa let her off the leash because it was after five and that was the only time a dog could run free. Clarissa carried a 'poop bag' in one hand and a lovely, peach-colored whelk in the other. She was not really heading any place special. She didn't intend to stop by her neighbor's house two doors down, where she sometimes had a glass of wine. She just put one foot in front of the other, trance-like.

Her discovery of Ralph and Willa Jo had thrown their whole married lives into question, as far as Clarissa was concerned. Was Willa Jo just a mid-life crisis fling, or was Ralph a habitual cheater? Clarissa had to know. She couldn't sleep nights, wondering. Oddly, she wasn't furious at the indiscretion —her time with Tal had taught her how easily these affairs could get started. And she could certainly understand Ralph's attraction to a beautiful woman like Willa Jo; Clarissa had loved her, too —even loved her beauty and the way she moved. No, what got under Clarssa's skin was the fact that Ralph bent over backwards all these years to prove his love, his passion for her —fine dining, the best wines, cruises, diamonds —everything you can imagine, Ralph showered on Clarissa.

What if all those presents were 'guilt gifts? 'She'd read in Cosmo that if a man was having an affair, he would be super nice to his wife. Ralph had been super nice for all their marriage. Did that mean he's been cheating for twenty-two years?

Clarissa was desperate to know the truth, the whole truth. She would take a look at Ralph's laptop. She knew his password just as he knew hers. They'd made romantic passwords when they got their matching Macbooks. Hers was Ralphlove! and his was Clarissa#1. She hated to go behind his back, but she had to know.

"Come, Mitzy!" she said. The dog ran to her and leapt into her arms. She carried Mitzy back to the house and put fresh water in the dog's bowl. She poured a glass of iced tea for herself as well as a jigger of Ralph's Dewer's. She needed a cup of courage.

As usual on Thursday mornings, Ralph was golfing with his friends. He'd be gone all day. She was safe. Yet, though she knew he wasn't at home, she checked every room before opening his laptop. Satisfied she was alone, she turned on the machine.

She entered his email and saw ads for various political causes, a few messages from business associates, some familiar male names from the island….nothing incriminating. She scrolled down, but found nothing new. She was almost ready to give up, accept that Ralph's affair with Willa Jo had been a mere fling, when she noticed various folders labelled business, upcoming events, investment info, and personal. Personal. What could that be? She clicked open that file.

Every name in the personal file was female. Clarissa felt as if the top of her head had gone suddenly numb. She counted — fifteen names. Willa Jo's was among them. Clarissa did not want to read anything from Willa Jo. So, she clicked on the first name, Suzette.

"Ralph, baby, Last night was beyond wonderful —I can't believe I have to wait another week before I see you again. I'll spend every night thinking of you. Love, Suzette."

Clarissa closed that email and opened another from Louise.

"You are just the best, Ralphie. Thank you so much for the diamonds —I never dreamed life could be this wonderful —see you soon! Your baby-doll, Louise."

Clarissa opened every single email, even the one from Willa Jo. Fifteen women. From what she could gather, Ralph had been cheating on her since the first year of their marriage. She was stunned. She closed the files and shut down the laptop. Then, she curled up on the couch, Mitzy snuggled next to her. She didn't cry. She felt too sick, almost as if she was going to throw up.

Why? Why had he betrayed her? She'd done everything he wanted —gave him all the sex he asked for, just as the advice she'd read in

Cosmo suggested . She'd kept herself fit, taken aerobics and lifted weights. She trained herself to be pleasant, listen to Ralph as he told her about his business dealings, though she had zero interest in such things. Why?

She didn't't' want to see him when he returned from golf — or *was* it golf? Maybe there was a new woman — she could never be sure now. She feared if she saw him today, she might find *herself* capable of murder.

She took Mitzy, jerked the car keys off their hook and got into the Corvette. She spun out of the driveway, spewing gravel everywhere. She wasn't sure where she was going, but wherever it was, she wanted to get there fast. Before she knew it, she was at the Chadwick County Government Complex. She parked the car and picked Mitzy up. Then, dog in hand, she marching into Sheriff Tal Hick's office. She didn't knock but opened the door and found Tal writing at his desk.

"I hope it's okay to barge in," she said.

"Not really — but for you, I'll make an exception. I'll even allow Mitzy to hang around — no dogs is the policy, unless, of course, it's a service dog."

Clarissa could tell he was busy and didn't really want to see her. She didn't care. She closed the door and sat down in a plastic chair. She put Mitzy on the floor and the first thing the dog did was piddle.

"Great," Tal said as he handed a few Kleenex to Clarissa.

"Sorry."

"What brings you here?"

"Ralph. But I guess you know all the details — after all, you've read the notebook."

"Yep"

"After I discovered he and Willa Jo had been lovers, I suspected there might have been others. So I started doing a little snooping around. I found out he's been cheating on me for years...I mean, I think he took a lover even the first year we were married. I'm a mess — sad, hurt, pissed off. I can't think straight."

Tal came around from behind his desk.

"I'm really sorry — can't say I'm surprised. Even before I read the notebook, I'd heard scuttlebutt about him for a long time. But I don't usually listen to gossip — it's wrong 80 percent of the time."

"You know the percentage of incorrect gossip?? That's weird."

"You learn a lot in this business, especially about people and why they do things."

"Oh, well, then you can tell me why my husband cheated on me! I'd really like to know that!"

Tal tried to embrace her but she pushed him away.

"Sorry. I have no idea — you are so beautiful and smart and fun to be around. I can tell you this — if you were mine, I would never cheat. Hell, I don't think I'd ever look at another woman." He tried again to hold her to him. She wriggled away from him.

"I don't want to be touched right now — not comforted, not cajoled, not any-damn-thing."

"Okay-okay. I get it. Sit down — you might be interested in what I'm doing."

Clarissa calmed herself and returned to her seat.

"What — what are you doing?"

"I'm charging Miss Avenelle Young with the murder of Willa Jo Temple," he said.

"But....but I thought you didn't think she was guilty."

"I don't. But the evidence I've discovered does nothing to disprove her confession. Matter of fact, it does more to corroborate it."

"What did you find?"

"Well, I kept thinking about those initials—RB. And I took a lucky guess. It was Rock Bonner, my former father-in-law. I drove over to have a little talk with him. He told me about himself and Mrs. Young. Not anything terribly new — I mean, the notebook nailed it, but there was no name for the father in the notebook. I'm glad Mrs. Young mentioned Bonner's name during her confession. That help corroborate the story. After all, just because something's written in a notebook doesn't make it true. RB could have stood for anything." Tal looked relieved. "Mrs. Young was only sixteen when it happened."

"That's so sad. How horrible for her to have been sent away. I guess they did that a lot back in the day."

"She went all the way to Akron, Ohio — was gone part of her junior year, then came back and graduated the next year. Her family told everybody she was taking care of an elderly aunt." Tal tapped his pen against the desk. "I guess she figured her whole life would be ruined if this got out. Hers as well as her husband's. *That*, I'm afraid, is motive for murder."

"Wait a minute. Did you say Akron, Ohio?"

"I did."

"Funny — that's where *I* was born. Small world, huh?"

"Yeah...listen, I'm really sorry about ...well, you know. But I need to get this done — everything is on a schedule and if I'm late, that blows the procedure all the hell. And that would blow the whole case. Can I call you later?"

"Sure, sure. I'm okay. Do call, though," she said, standing. She leaned over the desk and kissed him on the forehead.

"I will. You can count on it."

Chapter Thirty-Five

"One woman's bob is another woman's blob."

~The Beautician's Notebook

Late August

The news was splattered all over the first page of The *Chadwick County Chitchat* — 'Preacher's Wife Confesses!' Miss Avenelle had confessed to Willa Jo's murder and had been officially charged. Now, it was up to the judge to decide her fate. Annie Jo was stunned. Was *that* why Miss Avenelle offered free lessons? Did she feel guilty for taking Annie Jo's mother away from her?

It was so unfair. First, her mom, now Miss Avenelle. It seemed like everyone who had ever cared about her was disappearing from her life. Annie Jo dipped her spoon into the rocky-road ice cream carton and shoveled another big bite into her mouth. Lawson had been impossible this morning and she hadn't had time for a proper lunch. But he was sleeping now, so Annie Jo decided ice cream would have to do.

She was going to use this Lawson-free time to work on another song. She was about to boil over with all the inspiration she'd had lately. She and Kayla had run into Abel Young a couple of nights ago at the Sputnik Club in Wilmington. Trudy and her girls had agreed to take care of Lawson for the night. Annie Jo told them she needed an evening out and they agreed. Turned out, Abel knew the band. She and Abel had a great time listening and even dancing a little. After the bar closed, they all went over to the drummer's place to make some music and to drink. She and Abel jammed with the band and they sounded really good. She didn't sing — she wasn't ready for that. But she kept up pretty well with the chords. Abel told her he'd give her a few lessons while he worked on his mother's release. He'd been almost certain she'd be out of jail by today. But he'd been wrong.

Annie Jo heard a knock at the front door.

"Abel?" she said,

"I...I just wanted you to know my mom is innocent. I know this. She just wouldn't be capable." Odd for him to come all the way to her house to tell her this —he'd already said he didn't think his mom did it. And she'd agreed. Why had he ridden over to repeat himself?

He looked rough. His curls were sticking out all over the place and his eyes were red with dark circles underneath. His tee shirt looked like the same one he'd been wearing at the Sputnik, except now, there were stains on it. He had a couple days' worth of beard, too.

"Come in...Lawson's asleep," Annie Jo said. She led him to the living room and offered him a seat.

"I know it's crazy for me to come here — after everything that's gone down. But you don't know my mom the way I do —she's gentle and kind. She wouldn't hurt anything. Hell, she even cries if she has to kill a spider."

"I'm with you —I can't see Miss Avenelle stabbing my mother. It just doesn't make any sense. But...she *did* confess."

"I've been up ever since they charged her. Her appearance before the judge will be in a week or so. If you really believe she's innocent, will you help me try to prove it?"

Annie Jo thought at that moment he was the most handsome, intense man she'd ever met. She'd have said yes to anything.

"Of course. I'm not sure what I can do — I mean, I have Lawson and everything."

"You can help me talk it out, figure how to get her to retract that stupid confession. Hell, I don't know. I just need somebody to talk to."

"You got it. So, tell me what you know," she said. "Want some lemonade before we get started?"

"Sure —maybe a sandwich? I can't remember the last time I ate. My dad has been completely freaked out...let's just say things have not been that great at home."

"PB&J okay?" Annie Jo said.

"Yeah."

Annie Jo put the sandwich on a paper plate, added a few chips and poured a glass of lemonade. He followed her into the kitchen and watched as she fixed the food.

"Why do you think my mom confessed?" he said, right before taking a big gulp of lemonade.

"I don't know…why would anybody confess to a crime they didn't commit? I mean, you don't just sit around and read *The Chitchat* and decided to confess to some random crime. It doesn't make any sense," said Annie Jo.

"Man, I know. She's not crazy — my mom. Well, maybe a little, the way all moms are. So, who leaves a decent husband and pretty cool sons to confess to murder?"

"Maybe she's trying to protect somebody. I mean, from what the paper said, her prints *were* found at the scene of the crime…maybe she saw who really did it — maybe they threatened her or something. Who knows? I know my dad wouldn't charge her if he didn't have proof."

"There must have been something in that notebook — it's being held as evidence, so nobody else can read it."

"I read it…well, at least a little bit of it. I didn't read anything about your mom — just stuff about me when I was a baby and little kid. You know, cute stuff I said….the kind of stuff only a mother cares about." Annie Jo thought she heard Lawson squirming.

"Oh…well, that's not much help," Abel said. "Is that Lawson?"

"Yep — the little booger is waking up. Want to go up with me to get him?"

"Sure. He's a cute kid…where's his daddy?"

"Up in Wilmington — probably in jail by now. He was no good — I really don't know why I hooked up with him…stupid, I guess."

"Hey, we all do stupid stuff — I'm an expert at it. I flunked out of college freshman year because I didn't want to be there. I had no idea what I wanted to study, so I didn't study at all. My dad disowned me and I started couch surfing. Bummed my way up and down the east coast, searching for the next wave to catch and the next big gig that was going to catapult me to rock star status." Abel reached for Lawson and picked him up. "Of course, that didn't happen. I know better now. If I can figure out a way to make a living doing what I love, that's enough. I don't have to be a rock star."

He tossed Lawson into the air, not high, just high enough to make the child laugh.

"Be careful."

"Don't worry — I won't let anything happen to him. He's one cool kid."

Annie Jo felt happy, seeing them together.

Later, Annie Jo and Abel talked about strategy — how to save Miss Avenelle. After looking at every imaginable angle, they came up with a plan.

Chapter Thirty-Six

"The Judge loved power — but, turns out, he didn't love me."

~The Beautician's Notebook

Late August

When Rory walked into the board of trustees meeting, he was five minutes late. He'd never been late in thirty years. But today, all he could think about was the shambles his life had become. All on account of Avenelle. He stared at the twelve trustees and could tell by the grim looks on their faces, his fate was sealed. He would have to go.

"Glad you could join us, Reverend," said John Green, the head of the board and the one man who had been gunning for Rory for the last five years. Claimed the church needed 'new blood' and a rock band to attract younger members.

"My pleasure," said Rory as he took a seat. He had dressed with great care, gotten a haircut and even had a manicure. He wanted to look as distinguished as possible when they gave him the boot.

He was not yet sixty-five years old. He had no experience in anything but preaching. He couldn't afford to retire; his church had been a small one and his salary, likewise. The little voice that had told him all would be well had gone silent. Rory was scared —scared for his job and terrified for his wife. His mind was still reeling after her confession and the subsequent news story. Everything had fallen apart.

John Green said, "Reverend Young, this is going to be a difficult meeting. The board has debated for several days about the best way to handle the current situation with your...er,... your wife. We have talked and prayed about it. And we have decided you will need to step down. It's not good for you or the church. You need to be working on behalf of your wife and adjusting to your new life. The church needs to put this unfortunate episode behind us and move into the future. You are relieved immediately. Of course, your retirement benefits will remain intact. In light of the circumstances, we are not going to hold a pot-luck dinner in your honor for all your years of service. Instead, we have decided to give you your salary for the next year, until you can sort things out. We hope this will be acceptable."

Rory stood. He looked into each face around the table. He smiled at the men gathered.

"Gentlemen, this comes as no surprise. I thank you for your generosity — I know as well as you do, the church cannot really afford it. But I will not turn it down. I don't know what the future holds. But with this continuation of my salary, I will have a year to figure out my next move. Right now, I'm talking to a lawyer —Harry Hershman from up in Raleigh — he's supposed to be one of the best criminal lawyers in the state. My hope is that he will be able to clear my dearest wife from all charges. Obviously, since she has confessed to the crime, he'll have his work cut out for him." With that, he nodded at the men, turned on his heel and walked out of the meeting.

There. It was over. The axe had fallen and he was still alive. It hadn't killed him. He almost felt relieved — no sermon to write late Saturday night, no grieving families to try to comfort when there *was* no comfort, no haggling about prices for a new air conditioner and at last, no need for him to pray. If he prayed now, it would be hidden away in his closet, as the Bible instructs. He was no longer Reverend Young. He was simply Rory, old man looking for a job.

He'd thought he'd be furious with Avenelle when this moment came. Oddly, he wasn't. He was almost ecstatic. Free, free at last — thank God Almighty, he was free at last. If Avenelle had been there, he'd have kissed her and taken her to bed. He would have ravished her with his passion. Afterward, they would have gone to Fantasy Isle for ice cream.

But Avenelle wasn't at home; she was in jail. He would go visit. He felt sure Sheriff Hicks would allow him to come if he called first.

"Sheriff? This is Rory Young. I'd like to see my wife this afternoon, if that's okay with you," he said.

"Oh, Reverend...," said the sheriff.

"Not reverend anymore, son. My church just booted me out. Call me Rory."

"Well, ...Rory, a visit would be fine. Mrs. Young has seemed a bit blue today. Wouldn't eat her breakfast or lunch. Why don't you bring her something from the outside. A lot of our prisoners like McDonald's."

"Avenelle has never enjoyed fast food. But I'll bring her something from The Purple Onion —a nice salad."

"Up to you. What time? Oh, two will be fine."

Rory took the plastic bag holding Avenelle's salad and placed it in the seat next to him. Avenelle should have been sitting beside him in the car, not a salad. He floored the car so the food would still be fresh by the time he got to the jail.

He knew the routine by heart now: get buzzed in, patted down and walk to the visiting room. And there she was, his wife. She must have lost ten pounds since her confession.

"Hello, Nelle. How you doing today?"

"Okay…wondering about my garden and who's taking care of things….Did Adam get someone else to take care of Kevin when they need a sitter?" Avenelle said as she removed the lid from the salad.

"You won't believe it —Abel is helping out. He's becoming a real family man. I think he might be interested in Annie Jo Hicks —he's been bringing her and that baby of hers to the house sometimes. I can't tell if they are courting or if they're just friends."

"I'm not the least bit surprised —Abel has always had such good heart. I never lost faith in that."

"Nelle, I need to tell you something….now don't get upset. But, well, I got sacked today — I'm no longer the minister of Sabbath Home Church."

"Oh no! It's all my fault. No, don't argue with me —I know it is. You can't be a preacher when your wife is in jail for murder…practically on death row."

"Honey, don't talk like that — I've hired a lawyer — Harry Hershman from up Raleigh —maybe he can help us figure out what's going on."

"I know what's going on —I confessed to Willa Jo's murder. In this state, that's the death penalty."

"I know you confessed, but I also know you didn't do it. Why don't you just tell me what happened —the truth! If you just tell me, maybe we can get you out of this mess."

"No one can make me say anything I don't want to say. And I'm not interested in saying a word to you, that lawyer, or any-damn-body."

"Avenelle! Such language. But I guess under the circumstances a little cussing will be all right. Why don't you want to tell me — at least me — what really happened. I'm your husband...I have a right to know. After all, this whole scandal *did* cost me my job. What am I going to do now? I'm over sixty years old. I doubt very seriously anyone will be banging on my door, begging me to come to work."

"I know, Rory. I never meant for anything I did to hurt you — or the boys. And I know how scared you are — but maybe you can look at this in a different light. Maybe now is the time to make a change — a real change. Maybe now you can figure out what you want to do, not what is expected of you. You could even go back to school — study architecture. It's not too late."

Rory held out his hands and she took them. He stared into her eyes. They were kind eyes, full of understanding, full of forgiveness. And full of love for him — Rory, The ex-Reverend Young. Failed minister and failed human being.

Maybe she was right — maybe he could figure out what God put him on this earth to do — it sure hadn't been preaching. How could this woman be guilty of murder? It simply was not possible. He had to help get her out of this terrible mess, even though she seemed determined to stay in it.

"I know you haven't allowed the boys to visit, Nelle. Why don't you see them? Their feelings are awfully hurt."

"I don't want them to see me like this — in jail. It would be too traumatic for them. They'd never recover."

"They aren't little boys anymore. They're grown men. They have responsibilities and dreams and flaws and all the stuff that makes up a grown man. You need to let them come. Abel especially. He begs me and the sheriff almost every day to let him visit, in spite of your wishes."

She didn't respond. Instead, she picked up her fork and speared a piece of grilled chicken.

Chapter Thirty-Seven

"Like Kenny Rogers says, 'You got to know when to walk away."

~The Beautician's Notebook

September

Clarissa wasn't sure of the exact moment when she decided she would divorce Ralph. Not immediately after discovering his incriminating emails and not at lunch with Sheriff Hicks. Maybe there hadn't been one instant flash of decision — all she knew was, when she woke up this morning, she resolved to have a talk with Ralph that evening when he got back from fishing.

She was finished. There wasn't any question of seeing a counselor, trying to make it work — no, things had gone too far for any resolutions, except breaking up the marriage. In Clarissa's mind, Ralph had done that a long time ago.

Surprisingly, she was not particularly moved by her decision. She didn't have any sentimental crying jags where she reviewed their history together. She didn't feel sad or sorry she would no longer be married to Ralph. She began to wonder if she'd ever really loved Ralph at all. It was hard to separate all he'd done for her from the question of love. She realized, sadly, that maybe she had never been in love with anyone. She mulled over the idea that she might be incapable of love.

But wasn't that usually the case when a child hadn't known love — how could that child ever be expected to understand what real love was all about? She'd thought Ralph had really loved her — he'd certainly spent enough money on her, fixing her. Maybe, just maybe, she hadn't been broken.

She dressed quickly in her shopping uniform — Clark's sandals because they were so comfy and she needed comfort for all the work she was about to do. White capris with a bright aqua top. Her white sun hat. There — perfect. She didn't often think about her looks; she never had to — she'd always been attractive to men, even now, at forty. As she gazed into the full-length mirror, she realized she still looked amazingly good. Not having had children helped; she'd never had to lose a baby belly, never had her body stretched beyond recognition. Her abs were still as flat as when she was a teenager. A pang of sadness hit her then —she'd given up having children so, as Ralph's wife, she would be perfect. She pushed the thought out of her mind. She had enough to deal with this day —divorcing her husband would take first dibs on all her thoughts.

First, she'd drive to Randy's Meat Market and pick up some very fine filet mignon. Then, she'd run by Ludlum's for fresh tomatoes, green peppers and organic potatoes, some local blackberries and corn on the cob. She would fix shish kabobs for dinner —Ralph's favorite. A blackberry cobbler with vanilla ice cream. She might even make homemade hot rolls. She was seized with the desire to make Ralph realize exactly what he would be missing after their divorce. She wanted to make him very, very unhappy by first making him very, very happy. She was being perverse, but she didn't care. It would serve him right.

After she'd purchased the food, she headed to Wilmington to shop for the sexiest sundress she could find with sandals to match. She was just about to enter Highway 17 when her cell rang.

"Tal...this is a surprise," she said. "A break? Really? I'm so sorry —I'd love to meet for lunch but I'm all booked up today. I'll call you soon and tell you everything that's going on here."

***

She was preparing the tossed salad when she heard Ralph on the steps outside. She knew he would kiss her, then head to the master bath for a quick shower before supper. She prepared herself so she could receive his kiss and not flinch. She didn't want him to know anything was wrong.

He did just as she'd expected. Predictable as the sun. Soon, they were enjoying steak kabobs. She would surprise him with the cobbler. She liked thinking of this as his last meal.

"Whew! What a great dinner! You've out-done yourself, honey," Ralph said, leaning back in his chair. The sun was setting and light poured down, making the water look all golden.

Clarissa didn't move to clear the table. She sat across from Ralph and watched the sunset, the pinks and purples, the rays of the failing sun pouring over the earth, honey over a biscuit. She didn't want to move, didn't want to shake up her world just yet. She wanted only to watch the ocean and the sky.

"So, what's going on? My favorite foods, you looking good enough to eat — did I miss our anniversary?" Ralph smiled his big charming smile, both dimples engaged. Did he practice that smile in front of a mirror? Most likely.

"I wanted to make tonight special. Because I have something very important to tell you," she said, not moving, not even looking at him. If she could keep her eyes on the beautiful view before her, she could do this. She could tell Ralph that she knew everything.

"Well…. what is it? You're not pregnant, are you?" he said, still jovial.

Clarissa felt like an executioner. There he was, full belly and fully anticipating a night of delicious love-making. She could tell he was already in the mood by the way he was looking at her, his eyes hungry.

"No, Ralph. What I am is furious." She made her voice stay low and calm. She fought for every ounce of control she could muster. She did *not* want a dramatic scene. She wanted this to be over and done with.

"Furious? Why on earth ….with me?" he said, his mouth open.

"I know all about them — the other women. And the worst — Willa Jo. How could you?" She still sat at the table, staring into the water.

"Has someone been filling your empty head with gossip? And you believe them without even telling me about it? What the hell….?" He stood and leaned toward her over the table.

"Don't bother to deny anything, Ralph. I found your emails."

"You went snooping in my emails? How dare you!" he said, his voice jagged.

"Well, once I read about you and Willa Jo in the notebook, it occurred to me there might have been others. So, I decided to do a little detective work —it really didn't take much, even for my 'empty head.' "

"You read that damned notebook you've been talking about for weeks? What the hell? How did you?" Ralph's eyes had grown wide.

"It doesn't matter how I got it—none of your business. What matters is what I discovered. You cheated on me. At least be honest with me." Clarissa kept her voice even and calm.

"Okay. I admit it —I've been unfaithful. So what? Haven't I given you everything you've ever wanted? Haven't I paid for your education, you expensive clothes, your nose job??? Hell, I even put this house in your name. So what if I've gotten a little on the side! So fucking what?" he said, now leaning over her, screaming at her.

"Sit down, Ralph," she said, her voice flat. She was afraid of him for the first time in their marriage. He looked capable of anything at that moment.

He sat. She was stunned her words had such an effect. They sat in silence as the last rays of the sun set the ocean glittering, as if there were stars above and below. She forced herself to breathe —in, two, three, out, two, three —. She looked at Ralph. His hands were over his face; his body shook. It took her a moment to realize he was crying.

"You've been everything to me, Clarissa. My own creation —perfectly beautiful, a perfect cook, hostess —always perfection. My wife."

"Then why, Ralph? Why did you cheat on me? Why?" She felt tears on her own face.

He looked up at her, stared in her eyes.

"Because I could."

"Because you could? That's it? You ruined our marriage because you could?" Clarissa realized how hurt she was, how angry. All those years of trying to please Ralph — of making herself as perfect as possible for him —and all the while, he was cheating. Nothing he'd ever done had been real; nothing about their marriage had been real. It was all some strange creation of Ralph's, some fantasy he'd tried to make come true.

She felt sick.

"I want you to leave my home. Now. Don't speak to me. Just get out." Her voice sounded flat in her own ears.

At first, she didn't think he heard her. Then, slowly, he rose and nodded. He went into their bedroom and she could hear drawers opening and closing. She waited, kept looking out into the darkening sky, kept herself from running to him, begging him not to go. Because part of her wanted to do just that —put everything back in place and go on as they had done. What was so bad about their lives? If she hadn't found out, wouldn't she have kept tripping along like a teenager, not a care in the world, safe under Ralph's fatherly care?

But she *had* found out and knowing changed everything; she would never respect herself again if she allowed Ralph to stay. No, it had to be this way — a clean break. He would provide for her, at least long enough for her to find work. A good lawyer might be able to get her a fair amount of money, enough to carry her into the future, now an unknown future, full of possibility and danger. She watched the full moon rise, ripe and almost yellow. The moonbeams cast a path along the water. She wanted to walk on the beach and follow that path — maybe she could even walk on water, who knew?

Ralph appeared in the bedroom doorway, suitcase in each hand.

"Are you sure this is the way you want to play it, Clarissa? Think very carefully. There's a great deal at stake." Ralph's voice was condescending, as if he would always know what was best for her.

"Yes. I refuse to live a lie — no matter how prettily you package it. Now, please leave." Her hands were shaking so she held onto the top of the couch.

"I'll leave. We'll talk again when you are a little more reasonable. I know you'll see the error of your impractical thinking. We have a good life, Clarissa — I know you don't really want to throw it all away."

And then, he walked out of the house. He hadn't even apologized. The bastard.

She poured herself a large glass of wine and went out onto the deck. The night air was cool, the breeze pleasant. Well, that had gone as well as she could have expected. She hadn't known what to expect, really. She'd never disagreed with Ralph before, never argued. She'd saved all the little irritations and hurts that accumulated over a marriage to roll into one, devastating confrontation. She laughed ruefully and sipped her wine.

She tried to gauge how she felt — so many emotions. Sadness, anger, relief, fear, excitement — all mixed up inside her. She thought of Tal — he would be surprised, to be sure. Maybe she wouldn't tell him right away; maybe she would keep him at arms' length until she could figure things out for herself. She drank the rest of her wine and poured another glass. The night was fine for dancing and Clarissa walked from the deck, out the long boardwalk to the beach. She took off her shoes and ran. She played in the surf, kicking up sand, watching the moonlight on the water. She heard music in her head, songs from the oldies station Ralph always listened to — 'and now it's Ralphie's turn to cry, Ralphie's turn to cry — y-y-y!' and she twirled and twirled until she collapsed on the sand, gazing up at the night sky.

Chapter Thirty-Eight

"Oh, mamas and their baby boys — you're so lucky to have four sons, Miss Eva. I know you just love them to death."

~The Beautician's Notebook

September

Abel and Annie Jo were waiting in a small room at the jail, waiting for the deputies to bring his mom from her cell. He was glad Annie Jo was with him — she'd begged and pleaded with her dad to allow both of them to speak with Abel's mom, breaking, just this once, the one-visitor rule. At first, Abel didn't think the sheriff would give in, but Annie Jo cried, and that was it. Funny — most men couldn't stand it when a woman cried. Abel wondered if women ever used that to their advantage. Probably.

He and Annie Jo were armed with exciting news, news that Abel hoped would break down his mother so she'd confess the truth — which would get her out of jail and back home where she belonged.

Though he'd visited a couple of times, he still couldn't get used to seeing his mother in chains and handcuffs, being led by a couple of deputies young enough to be his brothers. Seriously bizarre. He watched as his mother negotiated the chair and took a seat.

She smiled at him, the same old smile he'd seen thousands of times. When she cooked him breakfast or when she saw him unexpectedly on the street. During holiday times, when she would sneak him Thanksgiving dinner without his dad knowing about it. She'd always been in his corner, even though he knew she didn't really understand him. Now, it was his turn to save her.

"Mom, you know Annie Jo," he said, hugging his mother in an awkward way, her sitting, him towering above, bending down to reach her.

"I'm so happy to see you both — the hours just drip by in here. I used to think I wanted nothing but time on my hands, but it's terrible — I'd much rather be weeding the garden."

"We've got some news for you, Mom — First, Annie Jo and I are …well….hanging out...and…. it's….it's serious. We're gonna move in together."

His mom sat still, her smile frozen for just a moment before she said, "Are you sure that's the right thing to do? You haven't known each other very long — and there's a child involved…."

"I know, Mom. I've thought long and hard about it — it's what we both want. But there's even more news — I'll let Annie Jo tell you all about it."

"Oh, please don't tell me you're having a baby," said his mom, her face ashen.

"Mom! For God's sake!" said Abel.

"No worries on that account, Miss A. Believe it or not, I finally figured out how babies get here — I may want another kid one day, but for right now, Lawson is enough."

"Sorry — I guess I'm always looking for trouble these days." She patted Annie Jo's hand.

"Not a problem!" Annie Jo continued to hold his mom's hand. Abel thought they were sweet together.

"So, here's the news — remember that song I wrote? Well, I sent it off to Brandi Carlile — with a letter and everything. You won't believe this, but she LOVED it! She wants to meet me! She wants to introduce me to some people…you know, in the industry….just to see where that leads….She was SO cool! I told her Abel and I were playing together, so she sent us two airplane tickets! We're going to Seattle!" Annie Jo seemed to vibrate telling the happy news.

Abel watched as his mom broke into a bigger smile. He felt like the sun was shining down on him. She was proud of him and proud of Annie Jo, too. He'd never seen her look like that in reference to *him!* Adam, maybe. He felt so good inside — his mom was proud of him, he'd found the love of his life and maybe, just maybe, he was going to get his act together.

"That's the best news I've heard in quite some time! Congratulations to both of you!" His mom rose and hobbled over to hug them.

"Group hug!" said Annie Jo, wrapping her arms around Abel and Avenelle.

They returned to their seats and were silent, like a balloon with no air, deflated.

"Mom, there's just one catch —we're not leaving Summerset until you tell the Sheriff what really happened at The Sassy Lady. We know you did NOT kill Willa Jo Temple. Even the sheriff has serious doubts about your guilt —that's why he's keeping the case open. Dad knows you're innocent. So, why don't you just tell us what happened?"

"Don't be ridiculous, Abel. You must take this chance —it's the chance of a lifetime."

"I'm not being ridiculous —I'm dead serious. You've got to tell the sheriff the truth —if you don't, you'll be ruining my life along with your own."

Silence settled in the room once more. Abel watched as tears slid down his mother's face.

"Tell me, Mom. You know you can tell me anything —I love you and nothing you can say will ever change that."

His mom began to sob harder. Annie Jo pulled out a Kleenex from her purse and handed it to her. Abel patted his mother's hands and waited. He was sure she would tell him now, knowing he and Annie Jo would refuse to go to Seattle until she did. This was his big chance and he knew she wouldn't let him miss it.

"Go get Sheriff Hicks. I'm ready to tell him everything —well, almost everything."

Chapter Thirty-Nine

"You've got to nurture your hair — take lots of vitamins — everything needs tender, loving care."

~The Beautician's Notebook

September

Tal read through the last of Willa Jo's notebook for the third time. Once again, reading how he'd failed her made him sad. They'd been so young, so in love, and they thought love would be enough. But anyone over forty knows love may not be enough to see a marriage through to the end — there were other qualities to be considered — determination being the most important, he decided as he sat on his deck and watched the young cardinals come to the birdfeeder for seeds. He'd hoped reading the notebook would give him some clue, something he'd overlooked in the previous perusals, something to show him Miss Avenelle was innocent. He felt her innocence in his gut, but sometimes his gut was wrong. It couldn't be trusted; only facts could assure justice in this imperfect world.

He allowed his mind to return to thoughts of Willa Jo, how they had been in the early days of their marriage, before his ambition and her impatience soured everything. He'd been so proud to win her — he was the envy of all his high school buds — and he remembered how the guys decorated his car with all kinds of slightly vulgar sayings for their honeymoon down at Myrtle Beach. 'She got him today, but he'll get her tonight!' 'Signed, sealed and delivered — a life sentence.'

Willa Jo'd been so beautiful on their wedding day — dressed in flowing white lace, her dark hair curling along her shoulders. And that night, the wedding night — they'd made love before, but it had always been rushed. In cramped places — the backseat of his car, a picnic table at the lake, the beach — but when Willa Jo had the comfort of a bed and a ring on her finger, it must have loosened something in her. She was wild and passionate in a way he'd never seen. A record six times that night, until they were both so full of love they'd passed out in each other's arms.

He laughed at the memory — hell, he'd be lucky to do it twice these days. But that was life, wasn't it — maybe he'd traded quantity for quality. Thinking of sex brought his thoughts to Clarissa. He hadn't seen her since she'd kicked Ralph out — she'd called to tell him about the breakup and explained that she needed her space right now. Needed to figure out how to live on her own. Plus, she wanted plenty of time to meet with her lawyer to insure she got what she needed from the divorce.

He missed her — he missed bouncing around ideas about the case with her. She had a good mind and she was sensitive, noticed things. And her delight in trying to discover the truth made him enjoy the process more, too.

He tried to picture her in his mind. He could imagine her hair, blond and well-coifed. And, he could see her bronzed body, the slender arms and legs. He imagined how they would feel coiled around him. He couldn't quite bring up her features — her mouth remained a blur. But her eyes, those blue eyes — those he could remember. He imagined himself looking into those blue eyes. And the more he imagined it, the more the face began to change. Before he could quite figure out how, he found himself staring into the face of Rock Bonner. Those were Rock Bonner's blue eyes.

He jumped up! Could it be possible? Could *Clarissa* be the child of Rock Bonner and Avenelle Young?? They'd confessed to the affair, but neither knew what had happened to their daughter. Could their baby be Clarissa?

That would be one hell of a coincidence...more like a miracle. But he'd seen some weird shit in his time in office.

Avenelle Young had read the notebook. She knew Willa Jo had slept with Clarissa's husband, Ralph. Maybe Avenelle thought Clarissa might also have read the notebook somehow. Avenelle Young might have imagined Willa Jo giving Clarissa the notebook so she could see Ralph Myers for what he was. After all, the two women had been best friends. Did Avenelle think Clarissa might have killed Willa Jo in a fit of jealousy? After all this time? The affair took place so long ago. Maybe Avenelle Young figured jealousy had no statute of limitations. Could Clarissa have been *that* jealous? And would

Avenelle confess in order to protect the young woman she believed was her daughter? Did Avenelle recognize those blue eyes, too?

Tal picked up his car keys and hurried to the office. He needed to find out everything he could about Clarissa Myers.

***

Born in Akron, Ohio, the same city and state where Avenelle Young had told Willa Jo she'd had her baby. Born in the same month and year. And on the same date —January 12. Raised by a succession of foster families. Married Ralph Myers at eighteen. College and finishing school. Ralph created the perfect woman for himself. He took a child, well, practically, and molded her to his liking. She was so young. Innocent. Desperate for love, especially 'daddy' love.

Tal shook his head. Nobody could make this stuff up. How could Clarissa have ended up practically on her birth mother's doorstep? He didn't believe in anything much; no Higher Power or God. But sometimes, he imagined invisible ribbons tying people together, pulling them first one way, then another. Somehow, those ribbons brought this mother and daughter together. But who controlled the ribbons? *Stop philosophizing.*

He'd finally been able to pluck out the threads of a story that made sense to him for the first time since he'd seen Willa Jo's dead body in her shop. Clarissa may have had motive for murder. But then, so did Ralph. Tal didn't think Clarissa had it in her to kill her best friend, even if she had discovered the betrayal. It happened too long ago — but then, Tal considered the fact that, even though the event happened long ago, Clarissa's *knowledge* of it may have been fairly new. New and painful. Painful enough that, in a fit of rage, she could have killed Willa Jo. Couldn't she? People did crazy things out of jealousy and hurt.

Tal typed in Ralph Myers' name and hit search. He waited while the computer did its work. He'd plugged into the national files to see if Myers had ever been a suspect in anything, anything illegal ever. He thought about Clarissa and Ralph while he waited....and before he knew it, he could think only of Clarissa, how her body had felt up against him and how her mouth tasted. God, he needed a woman.

Something was on the screen. Ralph Myers had been arrested for solicitation in Vegas, Key West and, of all places, West Virginia. Tal looked more closely at the stats. Yep, it was Ralph all right. The dates were between fifteen and twenty years old. Nothing recent. But still, ole Ralph was a player. Poor Clarissa.

He needed to interrogate them both. Just as he was about to call Clarissa, his phone rang.

"Sheriff Hicks here."

Deputy Sam Stokes said, "We got a situation here at the jail, Tal. You need to come on over — Avenelle Young wants to *recant* her confession."

"I'll be right there," said Tal.

Chapter Forty

"Change — that's what keeps me in business."

~The Beautician's Notebook

September

When Tal arrived at the jail, Reverend Young and both sons were in the interrogation room, along with Tal's daughter, Annie Jo. Tal shot Annie Jo a quizzical look. She gave him a smile. In the middle of what looked like a small family reunion, Avenelle Young held court. Surrounded by her husband and sons, with Annie Jo grasping her hand, Mrs. Young did not seem like a suspect at all. She seemed more like the kindly grandmother she was.

So much for the one-visitor-at-a-time rule. Tal looked at Deputy Stokes and raised his eyebrows, but Stokes just shrugged her shoulders —after all, there really wasn't a rule on the books for how many people could be present when a prisoner *recanted* a confession.

"You've changed your story, Mrs. Young?" Tal said, breaking up the familial feel to the meeting.

"Yes, Sheriff. I want to explain everything."

"Deputy, bring chairs for everyone. This may take a while."

Stokes brought in cheap, folding chairs and Tal directed people where to sit. He spoke in flat tones; he wanted to sound like the voice of judgment —he wanted Mrs. Young to take this seriously.

"At first, you said you murdered Willa Jo Temple. Now, you wish to change your story?"

"That's correct. I did not murder Willa Jo."

"Then, please tell me how your fingerprints got on her cape." Tal stood over the woman, hoping to put the fear of God into her.

Mrs. Young sat up straight and fluffed what looked to Tal like punk-rock hair. She had a round, pleasant face and a soft, feminine voice. Tal could see that in her youth, she would have been considered attractive.

"I was at the shop that morning, just like I told you. You see, Bessie Jo — that's Willa Jo's mother — for the record — and I were best friends. She'd given me a key to her salon back when it was Bessie Jo's Beauty Shop. I know Willa Jo changed everything when she remodeled, but she didn't change the lock — my key still worked," said Mrs. Young. She sipped from the cup of water on her left.

Tal knew most of this, but he also knew better than to interrupt the flow of her *new* story — he waited while she took a long drink.

"So, I wanted to get there before the shop opened."

"Why?"

"Well, twenty-some years of doing everybody's hair, Willa Jo knew some secrets — secrets that should never see the light of day. And rumor had it, she kept all her secrets in a notebook. People were saying she was going to publish that book and reveal everything about everybody."

"And did you believe this, too?"

"I sure did. Willa Jo had a way about her… Like you could tell her anything and she wouldn't judge you or tell anybody. That's one reason The Sassy Lady was so popular — Willa Jo made you feel like you were her best friend." She paused.

"Go on, Mrs. Young."

"So, I wanted to get my hands on the notebook and burn it — burn it to hell. Before Willa Jo could publish it. But I got there too late."

"You mean, you didn't get the notebook?"

"No. I got the notebook just fine."

"So, what were you too late for?"

"Why, to save Willa Jo's life, of course. She was sprawled out on the floor face down. I didn't know if she was dead or fainted or what…so, I grabbed her by the shoulders and turned her over. That's when I saw the scissors stuck in her chest….and I knew she was truly dead, not just passed out." She shuddered.

"What did you do then, Mrs. Young?"

"I looked around her desk for the notebook, but I couldn't find anything. So, I tiptoed upstairs to search her bedroom — I guess I'm guilty of breaking and entering…well, just entering — I had a key, after all. There was a man snoring in her bed! I was terrified I'd wake him up, so I froze in the doorway. He must have sensed me there because he snorted and then turned over, away from me. That was my chance! I slowly sneaked over to the bedside table and there it was! The notebook! I stuffed it into my purse and drove back home."

"You didn't think to call the police or the ER? You didn't' think to report the fact that Willa Jo was dead?" Tal said in his most exasperated voice.

"Why, no. I was terrified. Unsettled. Imagine seeing Willa Jo like that —all that blood. I couldn't think straight. So, I just left. I knew Trudy would be getting to the shop soon. I knew she'd find the body and report it. I didn't want to get involved. Besides —I *was* guilty of stealing the notebook. I figured the police might think *I'd* done it. And I *am* a minister's wife. How would it *look*?"

"*Were*, Nelle —you *were* a minister's wife," Mr. Young said.

"Oh...well, yes —I *was*."

Tal took notes on his yellow legal pad. He wrote slowly, hoping the delay would jar Mrs. Young's tongue and she would explain why she had confessed in the first place. But no one said a word.

"Mrs. Young, why, then, did you confess to the crime?"

Mrs. Young squirmed in her chair. She took a deep breath.

"I will not tell you that."

"I need to know why —if I knew why, it might help me solve the case."

"I will not tell you," she said.

"Mama, you've got to tell the sheriff everything. For me and for Annie Jo and our future."

She looked him straight in the eye.

"Son, I've done as you've asked me. I've un-confessed. And I've told the truth. The rest is nobody's business."

"Nelle, I don't have any idea what's going on here" her husband said, "but you must tell the sheriff everything. Tell him. It doesn't matter anymore —I've already lost my position at the church. Please, Nelle, tell him what he wants to know. If you do, maybe we can salvage our marriage, our family. Maybe there's a chance for us."

"Do you mean it, Rory? Do you think you could forgive me for all of this mess?"

"I believe I can, Nelle. Funny, when I was still the *Reverend* Young, I couldn't have... but now....hell, why not?"

"Oh, Rory! I do believe you care...after all this, I think you do." She reached up to pat his hand, which he'd placed on her shoulder.

“I didn’t’ know it myself, Nelle. I’d grown blind to you — I’m so sorry.”

“I couldn’t tell anyone ever, Rory. I couldn’t possibly tell you…before. But maybe now is the time — maybe God is working God’s will in spite of everything.”

Tal wasn’t used to seeing so much of a marriage revealed in the interrogation room. Usually, suspects lied and acted tough. He could feel the vulnerability of this couple and it moved him.

“Adam, Abel and Annie Jo, would you please step out into the hall. I think your mom and dad need a few minutes. I’ll stay with them.”

The young people got up without a word and left the room. Tal looked at Mrs. Young.

“You can tell us now — tell us everything.”

Chapter Forty-One

"God had it right — it ain't good for a man to be alone — when mine is by himself, the house is a disaster."

~The Beautician's Notebook

September

Rory Young sat on his back deck, looking out over his garden. In many ways, the garden was his pride and joy. But, as he gazed over it, he realized without Avenelle's weeding, watering, canning and freezing, the garden would not have made it, not ever. He thought of their sons, strong, handsome boys. Adam, his successful son, the one he understood. Abel, the rebel, the artist, the one he could never understand. But Avenelle understood them both. And loved them both with a fierce and tender love he envied. Envied her for being able to give such love and envied his boys for being the recipients of it.

As he sat in the cool of the evening, he considered his whole marriage. How he'd insisted on being the 'important' one in the relationship — the way he'd dismissed Avenelle's ideas and suggestions out of hand, without ever really considering them. His father had been the same way, acting as if the woman of the house were little more than a maid and cook. Taking love for granted until it was no longer love at all. He'd seen it happen to his mother. And when his father died, there was no real grief, only relief in his mother's eyes.

He didn't want that with Avenelle, especially now that he was jobless and in the midst of a crisis of his very self. His own 'dark night of the soul.' Who was he, if he wasn't a man of God? Who was he without a respected position in the community? Who was he without a wife, a family?

He didn't have any answers; the only thing he knew was, he wanted his wife. Not in the old way —not to make him look good and keep him fed —no, he wanted to know her and treasure her and love her. And, if he did it right, maybe he could rekindle the love she once had for him.

He admitted he'd been surprised, well, shocked by Avenelle's confession. Never in his wildest dreams would he have guessed she'd been anything but a virgin on their wedding night. That was one of the reasons he'd married her. He hadn't been around a lot of women and didn't know a thing about pleasing a woman. If he married a virgin, she would never know whether he was a good lover or not. There would be no basis for comparison.

Humph. Not only had she been deeply in love before she met him — she'd had a baby. A baby girl.

Oh, the tears, the tears poor Avenelle had shed when she told him about it. How she'd sobbed and carried on. He could see a lifetime's worth of grief pouring from her body. The sheriff tried to get her to tell whether or not she'd found her child, if she knew the child's name. But on that, she was mute. She refused to divulge anything about her daughter.

Rory heard a knock on the front door, then heard the door bang shut.

"Dad? You here?" Abel called.

"Out back," Rory said.

Abel walked through the house out to the deck. He pulled up a chair beside his father. "Sure is a pretty evening."

"Yep."

"Dad," Abel said softly. "I… I know about Mom. I've known for a long time. She didn't ever tell me, but there was some gossip at school. I did a little digging and I found out. I never said anything because I didn't want anyone to get hurt. But, you can talk to me about it — if you want."

Rory grunted. Here was his boy, the boy he'd rejected and scorned and wounded, come to help him in his hour of need. Surely, God sent the boy. It made his humiliation complete.

"I see….and you are here to ….gloat?"

"No, Dad….I'm here to help. To listen. To be there for you if you need me."

"After all I've done to you, all the hurt I've caused, you expect me to believe you are here to help?"

Abel rested his chin on his fist. Rory felt as if he was looking in a mirror — the boy had his features, but on a fuller face — Avenelle's face. Maybe the boy was telling the truth, maybe he really was trying to help. If so, then Rory felt the heaviness of forgiveness on his soul. He'd been a poor father to this boy, yet here Abel was, offering love. Friendship.

Rory could not stand carrying his anger toward Abel any longer. Words tore through his throat, almost as if he were choking.

"I've been wrong, son….wrong about everything I've ever done. I'm so sorry…so sorry." He felt his son's strong arms wrap around him. Then, Rory really let go. He actually cried in his son's arms. When the shaking and weeping finally stopped, he looked up into his son's face.

"I'm so sorry, Abel. Sorry for everything. You are a better man than I am."

"Dad, you don't have to be sorry…you were doing what you thought was best. Hell, I was no easy kid to raise —I know that. But I'm finally on the road to something good — I can feel it. Annie Jo and I love each other and we're heading to Seattle —we're following our dreams. That's something you taught me."

"How the hell could I teach you anything about that? I didn't follow my dreams at all."

"I know. That's how I learned how important it was. Don't you think I saw how much love and care you put into your doll houses? Don't you think I realized a long time ago, you should have been anything but a preacher? You and Mom might have been happy… you know, as hard as this is right now, it might be the best thing that ever happened to you. You have a chance to figure out who you are, before it's too late. Not everybody gets that chance."

Rory studied his son's face. In the boy's eyes, he saw compassion and understanding. He saw love.

"How'd you get to be so smart?" he said, as he stood to return to the kitchen.

Abel rose, too. They faced each other awkwardly, each waiting for something.

Abel was right. Rory'd been offered a real opportunity to 'follow his bliss,' as the self-help books said. He'd have laughed at that 'New Age' mumbo-jumbo ten years ago. But such things didn't seem funny anymore.

He reached out and hugged his son to his chest.

Chapter Forty-Two

"Sometimes, the ones you love the most will care the least."

~The Beautician's Notebook

September

Tal drove the allotted thirty-five miles per hour down Ocean Boulevard on Temple Beach. The air felt heavy, oppressive and the sun blared down relentlessly. Had to be a hundred, even in September. About right for this time of year on the North Carolina coast. He turned the AC vents toward him; he didn't want to look wilted when he spoke to Clarissa. He hadn't seen her since she'd called to tell him she needed time and space. He'd heard she and Ralph had already separated and she'd filed for divorce. He didn't know the ins-and-outs of the break-up. He knew what he'd found out during his investigation and what he'd read in the notebook—Ralph had nailed Willa Jo years ago.

Clarissa still hadn't explained things to him. Why the divorce? They could have worked it out. Lots of people made a marriage work after one of the partners cheated. Granted, Ralph Myers might have been more of a *habitual* cheater, but still....

In any case, Tal promised not to call her or try to see her until she was ready. He wished her well.

Now, he was about to break his promise, but this time, he was coming on official business. He had to ask her about Willa Jo and where she'd been the morning Willa Jo had been killed. Stokes finally identified all the fingerprints and, much as he hated the idea, Clarissa's were on the cape. He drove the unmarked car so he wouldn't embarrass Clarissa.

He walked slowly up the steps to the front door. Clarissa had added new plants and flowers on the stairs. And there was a new chair and a small table where Ralph used to park his Porsche. Large pots containing various trees surrounded the chair and table. Tal didn't think Ralph would be coming back any time soon by the look of things.

He rang the doorbell and could hear Mitzy barking within. When Clarissa opened the door, she had on a pale blue bikini with a lacy white cover. He tried to keep his eyes away from her breasts, away from her entire body, but he knew that was a battle he wouldn't win.

"This is a surprise," Clarissa said, opening the screen to let him in.

He entered quietly, bent to pet Mitzy and then turned to face Clarissa.

"I thought we'd agreed not to see each other for a while," she said as she held open the door.

"We did. Unfortunately, I'm here on business."

"Business? What do you mean?"

"Business about Willa Jo. I need to ask you some questions. Can we sit down somewhere?" he said.

She pointed to the living area and he took a seat on the plush leather loveseat. She sat across from him on the matching sofa. He thought she looked like some dream out of an old Playboy magazine, bikini-clad, sitting on a sofa in front of a huge plate glass window that gave a full view of the beach.

"So, what? Am I a suspect these days?" Clarissa fiddled with the bottom of her cover-up, twisting the lace into strange shapes.

"A person of interest. You *did* read the notebook, didn't you?"

"You know I did. Since this is business, I assume you don't want a glass of wine."

Tal shook his head. She rose from her seat in one, graceful motion.

"Don't mind if I have one, do you?" she said, glancing back at him.

"By all means."

He watched as she walked, almost glided to the counter where she quickly opened a bottle of red wine and poured it into a long-stemmed crystal with intricate designs etched in the glass. Pricey. Like every other object in the house. Tal was resentful —how could she so easily kick out the man who had paid for all this? He remembered how Willa Jo gave him the boot when something better came along. Maybe that's all Clarissa was —a money-grubber and a user.

She returned to the sofa, glass in hand.

"So, what do you want to know?" she said, staring at him with those blue, blue eyes.

The look almost made his knees wobbly; he forgot his questions, forgot his reason for being there. All he could think about was kissing her, feeling her up against him.

He cleared his throat.

"So, after you'd read the notebook, you realized Willa Jo slept with your husband. Had you any reason to suspect this...I mean, before you read about it? Were you ever suspicious?" His pen poised was in his hand to record her responses.

"No. They had the affair —just a fling, really —soon after Ralph and I had moved to the beach. Willa Jo and I weren't friends yet —I wasn't even at the beach when the affair first started — I was in Spain. Then, I found The Sassy Lady when I got back home. Willa Jo had done my hair a couple of times and I liked the way she styled it. The truth is, I never dreamed Ralph would cheat on me —it took me completely by surprise when I read about it."

"I'm sorry I have to ask all this —I know you've already told me a lot of it before. But this time, it's official. You didn't mention Ralph's affair with the deceased when you first turned the book over to me. Why?"

"I don't know —it seemed so... personal. I didn't....I didn't want to say the words out loud. It was all I could do to digest the discovery." She rubbed her fingers across her forehead.

"I guess that makes some kind of sense. So, what did you do after you discovered the news?"

"Once I found out about Willa Jo, I did some digging on my own. I discovered emails from women —lots of women. From the beginning of our marriage twenty-two years ago until now, Ralph has been cheating."

Tal noticed her voice was now soft and gravelly. Her eyes were moist and she looked like she might start sobbing at any moment.

"I can see how that would be very disturbing...I'm sorry, Clarissa."

"Well....it's over, done. I was stupid not to have known before now —just a stupid country girl who was so happy to know she had food on the table and someone to care about her....she just forgot about anything else. I should have suspected."

"How could you? You were just a kid when he married you —he was pretty good at covering his tracks, I'd say. I'm sorry he hurt you."

"So, you want to know if I murdered Willa Jo in a jealous rage? Is that it?" She took another sip of wine.

"Pretty much."

"That answer is no. I loved Willa Jo. She was my best friend. Even if she'd told me about their affair, I don't think it would have ruined our friendship. That must say something about the marriage or about me or about something."

She stood, then, and walked over to the door.

"Let's sit outside — I need to feel the ocean breeze on my face and smell the salty air. Maybe that will clear my head."

Tal strode through the door she held for him and took a seat on the glider. Surprisingly, she sat beside him.

"So, you didn't kill her?"

"No, Tal. I don't believe I have murder in me. I did think about killing *him*, though! Instead, I kicked him out of the house and told him I never wanted to see him again."

"I'm sorry."

"He keeps calling, trying to win me back — said we should go on a nice long cruise and figure things out. I'm not having it. I got a good lawyer and I should come out of this okay. I won't be rich anymore, but I should be comfortable. I can live with that." She took a deep breath and stared at the ocean.

"I hate to ask but I have to — where were you on the morning Willa Jo died?"

"I was at Pilates from 7 until 8:30 at Temple Beach House of Worship — you're welcome to ask the teacher, Jean Byers. Before that, I had breakfast with Andrea MacInnis and Colleen Turner. We met at 6 at Main Street Grill." She looked directly at him. "I did NOT kill Willa Jo."

They slid back and forth in silence for a few minutes while Tal jotted down the names she'd given him. He felt relieved — not that he'd really considered her guilty. His gut told him there was no way she could have done it. But the facts had to be considered, too. She had motive and her fingerprints *were* on the cape. Not only that, she hadn't hesitated to steal the notebook from Mrs. Young.

"So, how do you think your fingerprints got on that cape?"

"Beats me. When Willa Jo put my highlights in, I always wore the same cape — it had a large belt that tied around the waist. Was that the cape she was wearing?"

"I don't know. To be honest, I didn't realize there were different styles…I'll have to check it out."

"If it is the same cape, maybe my fingerprints didn't get washed off. Maybe whoever does the laundry got sloppy."

"I'll look into it. And I'll check your alibi."

She started to laugh.

"I never thought I'd hear those words in my lifetime —my alibi —
I sound like some kind of two-bit hood....it just struck me funny," she said between bouts of laughter.

Tal smiled, too. It was good to see her laugh, really get silly. God, she was beautiful.

Chapter Forty-Three

"Real friends are better than chocolate."

~The Beautician's Notebook

September

Trudy pulled out box after box of hair stuff —dyes, perm solutions, rollers, papers —anything a beautician could use. Months had passed since Willa Jo's death, but Trudy'd been uneasy about cleaning her things up, putting some away, maybe using others. She might try selling some of the stuff on eBay —though business was good, she could always use extra cash.

Clearing out Willa Jo's cabinet made Trudy sad. She missed Willa Jo, missed their lunches together —Willa Jo always brought a tossed salad, but would beg Trudy for half of her Snickers bar. Trudy would laugh and tell Willa Jo she had serious mental troubles. Split personality —one side struggled to keep her school-girl figure but the other had a voracious appetite for chocolate. They'd joke about their customers, the funny things women said while under the influence of perm fumes. The Sassy Lady just wasn't the same without Willa Jo.

Finally, she'd cleared out the cabinet and the drawers, placing the items into marked boxes — For Annie Jo, Throw-away, Keep, Donate, —now, there was only Willa Jo's chime collection which she'd taped, stuck, strung and hung over the large mirror at her station, as well as throughout the salon. Some of the chimes around her mirror were only an inch high; others, up to six inches. The ones on the ends made a little noise when the hair dryers were on and Trudy remembered how Willa Jo would smile when she heard the tinkling sound. In a few of the chimes, Willa had woven strands of hair, snips from children's first haircuts. Willa Jo'd kept a sample from every child she'd ever given a first cut. Most of the hair was in labeled envelopes, but the long hair from little girls she sometimes wove into other objects.

Of course, Trudy would keep the large chime near the doorway — that had been Willa Jo's first one and Trudy knew it was special. It rang in deep, honey tones whenever anyone opened the door. When Trudy had first come to work with Willa Jo, that chime had driven her crazy. But, over time, she'd grown accustomed to it and now, she wouldn't part with it. As for the smaller ones, they'd go to Annie Jo.

The first three came off easily, clanging together, all jumbled up. After separating the strings that attached them, Trudy placed each one in a plastic bag so they wouldn't get tangled again. The one hanging right in the middle, however, did not want to come down. Trudy left it for last and carefully removed the remaining three.

She looked carefully at the middle chime. Where the others had been strung together on a strand of ribbon, the middle one seemed fastened differently, independent of the rest.

Trudy crawled onto a stool and tried to see exactly how the damn thing was hooked on. For some reason, it was attached so that the base of the bar that held the chimes 'rode' the mirror frame. Strange, but who was Trudy to judge. She carefully slid the whole contraption along the frame's edge and then, eased it right off. Something fell onto the floor. Trudy leaned over to pick it up. It looked like some sort of tiny electronic device...a camera, maybe?

Trudy's heart beat a little faster. *Was* it a camera? Could this camera have recorded Willa Jo's murder? Could this be evidence? Trudy had no idea Willa Jo had installed any kind of surveillance equipment. They never discussed it, though she remembered a couple of years ago, there'd been a break-in. The thieves didn't get much — some hair dryers and color solution, a curling iron and three flat irons plus what little bit of cash was in the register. Trudy and Willa Jo figured the thieves were a couple of teenagers, but the event frightened them. There were no suspects and that was that, as far as Trudy had been concerned. But maybe Willa Jo took precautionary action —maybe she placed a hidden camera in case there was another burglary.

Trudy knew the judge had let Miss Avenelle Young out on bail, even though she'd been arrested for the crime. Rumor had it Miss Avenelle confessed and then changed her mind. What a wacko. Luckily, the sheriff had a couple of other persons of interest —she'd read that in the *Chadwick County Chitchat.* Maybe she had the answer right in her hand. Maybe this would solve everything. She slipped the device into her back pocket. She was wearing those stretchy jeggings Tacoma had insisted she buy and she thought the camera would never be able to ease out of that skin-tight pocket. She'd give the camera to the sheriff later, after she'd finished freshening up the shop. She had a potential new partner coming on Friday to look the place over. She wanted to be ready.

***

Trudy meant to take the little bug-camera she'd found in The Sassy Lady to Sheriff Hicks that very afternoon, but when she got home, there was trouble. Tacoma, her fifteen-year-old, was crying her eyes out in the bedroom. Her twelve-year-old, Takeena, was fretting with her purse, twisting the handles around and around. She seemed very worried about her older sister.

"What it the world is all that caterwauling?" Trudy said as she headed to Tacoma's bedroom. When she reached 'the inner sanctum,' the door was locked. She knocked. "Child, you better let me in this minute!"

"Go away, Mama —just leave me alone!"

Trudy was used to scenes like this — after all, the child was a teenager, full of ranting and raving hormones.

"Mama, she say she gonna kill herself —she got a knife in there!" Keena said.

"She's not doing any such thing —you go on outside and play — I'll handle this."

She took Keena by the shoulders and pushed her towards the back door.

"Don't worry —I got this," Trudy said.

Keena obeyed and once she was out of earshot, Trudy knocked again on Tacoma's door.

"This is MY house, young lady! You will not lock me out of my own house!"

"But it's MY room!"

"You let me in right now, or I'm gonna get the shotgun out from under my bed. You know I'll use it. I'll blow this damn door open if I have to."

She could hear Tacoma moving around in the room. She waited. Finally, she heard the lock turn and Tacoma opened the door.

"What's this all about?"

"Lamarr broke up with me, Mama — what am I gonna do?"

"You'll do what every strong woman before you has done — you'll get over it." Trudy wrapped her arms around her daughter. The girl sobbed, a loud, wailing sound. Trudy thought if that noise went on much longer, she would have to slap her girl silly.

"But you don't understand…I love Lamarr…."

"I know you do, girl….I know you do." Trudy patted her daughter's back, then rubbed large circles around her shoulders, the way she used to comfort Tacoma when she was little. Soon, the wailing stopped and the girl began to breathe easier.

"I know it's hard to believe, but you find somebody else. Besides, you got college to think about — don't be needing no boys. You got a future, girl — fashion design — remember?"

For some reason, these comments started more loud sobbing and sniffling.

"You don't understand, Mama — I *gave* myself to Lamarr….and…and…and I think I might be… pregnant."

Trudy felt as if she'd been hit in the gut. Her baby girl, ruined by some no-good boy from Wilmington. But she couldn't allow Tacoma to see her pain, her disappointment. She struggled to regain control of herself.

"Well, if that's the worst of it — it's not *that* bad. Why you carrying on so? Listen, you can have your baby and I'll take care of it while you go up to UNC-Wilmington for your first two years. Then, you can transfer to Eastern Carolina — I can keep the baby here. It's not the end of the world."

"I guess...I'll bet half the girls in my class have already had a kid. I just didn't think it would happen to me — I mean, I know you told me the facts, but in my heart, I didn't believe them. I didn't think it would happen to *me*." Tacoma burst into tears again.

Trudy kept patting her daughter's back. She'd done her best to sound calm, but what in the world would she do with a baby? At *her* age? Just when she thought such days were behind her. Trudy knew how much extra work a baby would be, on top of running The Sassy Lady. Well, it wouldn't be the first time a grandma had raised a grandbaby and it wouldn't be the last. She could do it. But she wanted to make sure Tacoma understood there would be no other grandchildren to raise — not until Tacoma was married and stable.

"Are you sure…about, you know, the pregnancy?"

"I missed two months and I ain't felt too good...sick on my stomach every morning"

"Well, we'll get you to the doctor's. Now listen to me and listen good: I will help you with this baby. I will help you go to college. But I will NOT help you with any more children. Do you understand me? If there's another child before you are safely married off, I will not be taking care of that one. You'll be on your own. Are we clear?"

"Yes, ma'am. Clear," said Tacoma.

Trudy took her daughter's face in both hands and stared into her eyes.

"You better get cleaned up — we got a lot of work to do."

She smiled at Tacoma and the girl returned her smile — a little shaky at first, with tears still threatening, but then, a solid smile. Trudy kissed her cheek and hoped she was doing the right thing. She completely forgot about the tiny camera she'd put in her back pocket.

Chapter Forty-Four

"Oh, turn up that Percy Sledge — that's my song! When a ma-an loves a woman..."

~The Beautician's Notebook

Late September

Tal hadn't told Clarissa that he was pretty sure Mrs. Young was Clarissa's birth mother. He thought such news should wait while he checked into her actions on the day of the murder, made sure she was where she'd said she was. The ladies she'd had breakfast with corroborated her story. And, when he'd asked Trudy a couple of weeks ago about the cape and the fingerprints, she'd said sometimes they didn't wash them every day — it was possible to miss a cape every now and then. Which might explain Clarissa's prints.

But that left Tal with nothing — Mrs. Young wasn't the killer — of that he felt certain. He was equally sure Clarissa was innocent. So, who was left? Mad Dog? Unlikely. He just wasn't smart enough to pull off a job like this — who? Who had motive? Tal hit his hand against the side of his head. Think, man, think!

His inability to solve this puzzle explained why he was tired every morning — he spent the nights twisting and turning in his bed, trying to figure out who, if anyone, killed Willa Jo. In his mind, the accident theory was still viable. He simply couldn't turn his brain off — he'd gone to bed early tonight, figured he'd start again in the morning when he was fresh — hell, he'd never be fresh if he couldn't get any sleep.

His cell rang.

He reached over to the nightstand and answered.

"I hope it's not too late," Clarissa said.

"Naw, not at all. What's up?" said Tal.

"Guess I'm feeling lonely — it's a big house and there's a storm brewing. The wind's picking up and the house is shaking a little — it always does. But Ralph used to take my mind off it. Now, I'm a little scared."

"Do you want me to come over?" Tal wasn't sure how he felt about going to her at night. He didn't quite trust himself. He'd left things in her court; maybe this was her serve.

"Well....it would be nice — I've already opened a bottle of wine and I could fix us a little snack...."

"I'll be right there," he said and hung up.

Damn. Here he was, a man over forty, and women still confused the hell out of him.

The drive from Summerset to Temple Beach took about fifteen minutes, maybe twenty. Tal was glad the roads were clear, no cars. He didn't want the whole town to know his business, know he was going to rescue a damsel in distress. Maybe ravish a damsel in distress....no, no, he couldn't think like that — she'd told him to give her time and he would. He would. But then, why had she called? She was scared; that's why, you idiot.

As he approached the graceful arc of the bridge that led to Temple Beach Island, he saw how dark the sky was, blackening at the horizon, as dark as the ocean. He could see the whitecaps, almost florescent, chopping up the water. Sure enough, a storm was on the way.

When he got out of his truck, the wind whipped at him. It was a hot wind, the kind famous around these parts for hurricanes in September. And it was right on time, though Tal hadn't heard anything on the news about any kind of tropical storm or hurricane brewing. And he would definitely have heard something on the news — the newscasters had apoplexies of glee when bad weather threatened.

He knocked on the door and she answered quickly. He sucked in his breath when he saw her — she wore a dark blue long dress with a halter top and she was holding a glass of white wine in her hand. Her hair had grown longer since the last time he'd seen her — not much but enough to go from a conventional hairdo to something wilder, a tussled look sort of like Meg Ryan in *When Harry Met Sally.* Her eyes, so blue, reminded him of the sky on a June day. Beneath the bright porch light, he could see the iris was rimmed by a darker shade at the edge. Those eyes could command him to do anything. But damn, he better not let her know that. Around her throat hung one rather large diamond. She wore matching earrings.

"You look.....amazing," he said before he could stop himself.

"Thanks. You look pretty good yourself, considering I called you over in the middle of the night — I like the casual you," she said, pointing to his flip-flops.

"Yeah, well, I do what I can." He came inside and followed her to the couch. She gestured for him to take a seat. She then floated to the kitchen —with that long, flowing skirt, she really *did* seem to float, as if she moved by magic, he thought. She poured him a glass of wine. She returned, handed it to him and sat not exactly next to him, but not far away, either.

Close, but not too close —he could never read the signals right — did she want him to slide over next to her? Did she want to keep her distance? Damn.

"So, how are things going with the case?"

"You're off the hook, if that's what you mean."

"I'm glad to hear it —I can't believe you even thought I could hurt another person — if I weren't so upset over what Ralph did, I'd be devastated. "Her eyes clouded over and he knew his suspicions had wounded her; it couldn't be helped — it was part of his job.

"I'm sorry — my job, right?"

"Right. But what really rankles is that I'm no longer part of the investigation — I'm out of the loop." A slight smile was on her lips.

"That tends to be the case when one is a person of interest — the detective doesn't usually divulge information. But, since things have changed and you're no longer a person of interest, what do you want to know?" He grinned at her and was relieved to see her reflect his look. He knew he shouldn't be talking over the case with her, but he didn't care about the rules just then.

"Well, now you know it wasn't me and you know it wasn't Miss Avenelle — so, who's next?"

"That's the question, isn't it? I really don't know. I mean, Trudy has certainly benefitted —The Sassy Lady is doing great from what I hear. And Annie Jo inherited everything…but I really don't think my daughter would murder her mother."

"Mad Dog?"

"Maybe. But he's trying to set up his racing career and really, Willa Jo had said she'd help out —$50,000 isn't a drop in the bucket to what she might have been able to raise for him — hell, she knew everybody within fifty miles. And she could talk the Hell's Angels into serving food at the Sweet Sisters of Summerset Shelter." Stop giving away info about the case, Tal told himself. You're a professional.

"I don't know him, but from what Willa Jo told me, he was like a boy in a lot of ways —not very mature, but also, sweet and innocent. She didn't have a lot of respect for his intellect —I really don't think he could figure out how to get away with something like murder."

Silence fell between them. Tal could hear the roar of the ocean and the wail of the wind. The house shook, but then, so did every other house on the beach. They were all on stilts. What did she expect? He looked at her. In the dim light, she looked so beautiful. He knew she had a scatter of freckles across her nose but he couldn't see them now. All he wanted to do was take her in his arms and make love to her right there on the floor. He tried to dislodge that thought by standing to look out the window at the ocean. The white caps churned more than when he'd first arrived and the waves were bigger. He could see enormous clouds, pregnant with rain, skirting across the night sky. Lightening flashed over the water and thunder rumbled.

"It's amazing, isn't it?" she said, standing behind him. "I never tire of the view, even when the weather is bad...there's something mystical about looking at the ocean and that vast sky — makes me feel like God is as real as the sea. I love this place."

"It does make a person feel mighty small. Funny —you feel small but the questions in your head are pretty big. "He felt her wrap her arms around his waist and lean into him. Was this an invitation? Was he supposed to make a move? Or was this a test?

He turned to her and put his arms around her, too. They stood, holding each other, while the waves threw caution to the wind.

He kissed her, at first gently, tenderly. She responded with a soft moan so he kissed her more deeply. She put her arms around his neck and pulled him closer. He could feel her smallish breasts firm against his chest, could feel the nipples rubbing him. He was instantly aroused and couldn't keep himself from thrusting toward her, just a little.

"You said you wanted time, remember?" he said while he touched her face with his hands.

"You've given me time....the dust has settled. Ralph's gone and I'm alone —and free." She broke away from him and stared into his eyes; he thought he could gaze at her forever.

"I want you," she said.

He didn't speak — he kissed her, over and over, on and on as the sea winds blew and the waves crashed. She moved against him as if she'd known him all her life; and she seemed to sense what he wanted before he could imagine it himself. She sank to the floor while he stood trembling. Slowly, she unzipped his shorts and pulled them down with her teeth. Then, she licked his thighs with the tip of her tongue, going close to his cock, but then, veering away. He thought he would explode.

Finally, she took him into her mouth. He could feel her tongue swirling in all directions, her lips firm against him. She would bring him to the edge, then she would stop. And then, she would start all over again.

He couldn't stand it any longer — he wanted to be inside her. He knelt down and gently lowered her onto the floor. He pulled a couple of pillows from the couch and placed one under her head and the other beneath her hips, raising them to him. He began to do for her what she'd done for him.

She smelled flowery and sweet, with her own musk beneath the main odor of hyacinth or gardenia or some damn flower. She moved against his mouth and he brought her to orgasm. While she was still throbbing, he entered her and she came a second time. He couldn't stop himself — he had a brief image of the waves thrusting against the shore. Where the hell did *that* come from? And then, it was over and he collapsed onto her, holding himself up a little with his elbows.

He kissed her on the forehead, the cheeks, her nose, her chin. She giggled and locked her hands around his neck.

"You're trapped. You can never leave," she said.

"Okay." He smiled at her and kissed her again.

"You are number three — the third man I've been with."

Odd thing to say. He thought she seemed suddenly sad or depressed — something wasn't right.

"So, I can guess who the second was — Ralph, right?"

"Yes."

"Who was the first?"

She pushed him away and slipped her dress on again.

"Want some wine?" she said.

"Sure."

He watched as she carried both glasses back to the couch and set each down on a coaster shaped like a turtle. He got up, too, pulled on his shorts and joined her.

She suddenly seemed distant, as if bringing up her past had carried her back *into* that past.

"I don't know where this is going....but I know this about myself. I'm not a casual woman. When I love, I do it with my whole heart. Just wanted you to know. So you can run for the hills if you want."

"I'm not running anywhere. I'm forty-three years old — I'm not looking for casual. I'm looking for the real deal — love, and everything." Corny, but true, dammit. What was there about this woman that made him say things he didn't want to say.

"In that case, there are some things you need to know about me...."

"Okay."

She squirmed in her seat and he watched as the color came to her cheeks. She was struggling with this.

"First, I don't have any real family — I was raised in foster care until I met Ralph. I already told you that. I was just a baby really; he was middle-aged. Way too old for me, but he's always been handsome and youthful — he was much more so back then. I'd been through a very tough time," she said. She paused and leaned against Tal. He put his arm around her shoulder.

"He was tender and caring and pretty much swept me off my feet. I tried my best to make him a good wife — I studied hard when he sent me to college — even made the Dean's List a couple of times. He wanted me to color my hair, so I became a blond. He wanted me to dress in designer clothes so I did. I learned to cook and entertain — all the rules of high society. It was an alien world to me, people who wore Gucci and drove fancy cars, people who travelled all over the world and went to art museums and Broadway shows, the symphony and opera. I loved it — everything was so refined."

He traced his finger across her arm.

"Okay....go on," he said.

"I want to tell you about what happened before all that — about my growing up. But then, I don't want to tell you." A small smile creeped onto her features.

"Okay — so what am I supposed to say to that?"

"Nothing. There's just a lot of pain in this part — and I might cry. Fair warning."

"Okay — I'm warned. But don't worry — I've seen tears before. Even shed a few."

She sipped her wine and turned to him to look directly into his eyes.

"My foster care history is worst-case-imaginable. I had six different families throughout my childhood. Not one person from any of those homes cared a thing about me. Over time, I learned not to care much about myself. I quit studying and dropped out of high school. I ran wild for a time — drinking and smoking dope. When I was fourteen, I was pretty well-developed, if you know what I mean. I guess I must have looked twenty." She paused, leaning her head against him. He knew better than to interrupt.

"My foster father was a drunk who did construction. Every Saturday night, him and his buddies would drink beer and play cards at the house. My foster mother and I usually just went to bed. We didn't like those men and, to be honest, I was afraid of them."

She looked away.

"Some storm," she said.

"Yep," he said.

He waited for her to continue. He knew this story was struggling to come out and he knew he wanted to hear it all. It must have been very important because Clarissa had gone pale.

"Anyway, I was in my room asleep when I heard the doorknob jiggle. Before I knew what was happening, one of the men — Cooter, they called him — was in my bed, touching me, pulling up my nightgown. He held his hand over my mouth — I still remember how it smelled of oil and wood and something metallic. I tried to bite him but I couldn't. I almost gagged with the taste of him. He raped me and told me if I ever told anyone about it, he'd kill me. I knew he meant it, so I never told another living soul. Until Ralph. I told Ralph." She paused, took a deep breath and continued. "Soon after Cooter raped me, I got sent to yet another foster home."

She wasn't crying exactly, but tears were pouring down her cheeks. He wiped them with his hands.

"I'm so sorry. Clarissa... my love — what a terrible thing. I'm just so damn sorry." He held her for several minutes.

"When I think of all the bad stuff I went through — one set of foster parents locked me in the closet while they went to a movie — they didn't want to pay for a sitter...it makes me wonder about my real parents. I wish I knew who they were and why they 'got rid' of me. Was I so terrible? An inconvenience? Were they married? Old? Young?" She looked so sad it pierced Tal's heart.

"I guess I'll never know."

He debated whether or not to tell her what he'd discovered — or at least, what he *thought* he'd discovered. He could be wrong. Either way, he'd be stirring up a hornet's nest. But surely, she had a right to know.

"I might have found something out about all that — I don't know, Clarissa — it's detective work on my part, but it certainly seems possible, even probable."

"What are you talking about?" she said, an edge of irritation in her voice.

"It's something I discovered while I was working on Willa Jo's case…it may be all coincidence — I'm not sure. I mean, I could be all wrong."

"Now, you *have* to tell me — you've got my curiosity up. This sounds quite intriguing — and it's making me hungry. Want an egg salad sandwich?" She rose and walked to the kitchen.

"Sure. Reckon I could use a little energy." He came up behind her and put his arm around her waist. "Might need it for later." He nuzzled her neck and she relaxed against him.

"This is so nice — I mean, my life with Ralph was always very pleasant — he was a considerate lover and a generous husband. We were compatible. But with you, there's this amazing…I don't know…chemistry. I don't know how to explain it — I just feel right with you. And passionate." She turned to face him, reached up to kiss him and he pulled her to him.

"I know — I feel it, too. Animal…," he said kissing her and reaching to cup her buttocks in his hands.

She allowed him to continue for a few minutes before pushing him away.

"Oh no — not until you tell me everything." She handed him a paper plate with the sandwich and some grapes on it. And his glass of wine refilled.

"Okay, okay — let a man eat, will ya?" he said as he carried his food to the couch and sat back down. She scooted in beside him.

"This egg salad is great — does it have sweet pickles in it?"

"Just a little of the juice."

"Damn, that's how my mama used to make it — uh-oh. It's a dangerous sign for a man to find a woman who cooks like his mama did."

"It's only egg salad — wait until you sample my pot roast and squash casserole. Now, no more getting off the subject. Tell!"

He didn't want to break the light and happy mood they shared. But, he'd started — he might as well finish.

"You remember when Avenelle Young confessed to Willa Jo's murder, right?"

"Of course. But I sort of lost touch with what was going on — after discovering all Ralph had been up to. I read where she'd taken back her confession and was released. That's all I know. What did you find out? Is she guilty after all?"

"Do you know why she confessed in the first place?"

"Not really…you and I thought she might be trying to protect someone — but we never could figure out who."

"That's exactly what she was doing. And now, I think I know."

"Who?"

"You."

She jerked back, shocked at the idea…he could see the confusion on her face.

"Me? Why in the world would Miss Avenelle try to protect *me*?"

"I don't know how to say this, so I'm just gonna come out with it — I think you're her daughter."

"What??? Have you lost your mind?? What makes you think that?" she said, her voice rising in pitch.

Tal thought she was going to pass out or scream or throw up, he wasn't sure which. Her face had gone pale and her eyes were wide.

"Calm down — calm down. Like I said, I could be wrong. You read Willa Jo's notebook. You read about Miss Avenelle's baby. Her parents sent her to Ohio to a home for unwed mothers. She had a baby girl and left her in the care of the folks at the unwed mother's home, who were supposed to find parents for the child."

"Doesn't mean that baby was *me*." Her voice was small, shaky.

"No, it doesn't. The notebook didn't say anything about who the father of the baby was. So I did some checking — I was finally able to persuade the adoption service to verify that the father was — Richard Bonner. Bonner had already told me their story, but this was proof, real proof."

"That's Willa Jo's daddy, isn't it?"

"Yep. And that got me thinking — see, the Bonner family is kinda famous around these parts for their clear blue eyes — old Rock has em for sure." Tal took her hand and stared into her face. "And Clarissa, so do you."

She didn't say anything. She sat still as a sack of flour. A few minutes passed. He knew better than to speak. Finally, she seemed to wake up.

"But a lot of people have blue eyes. It's just a coincidence. That would mean Willa Jo was my half-sister...if what you're saying is true...."

He watched as she processed the information.

"Do you have any other proof? I mean, other than the *color of my eyes*?" Her voice dripped with sarcasm.

"Actually, I do. When I realized where I'd seen your blue eyes before, it gave me enough of a lead that I was able to discover more about *you.*"

"You mean, you *investigated* me?"

"I did."

Now her face changed completely. Her cheeks reddened and fury blazed in her eyes, but her voice was cold and sharp.

"You investigated me and you didn't even TELL me! And now, you're here screwing me?" Her voice was laced with anger.

"Clarissa...listen...it wasn't' like that — you were a person of interest — I had every right to investigate you."

She stood and walked over to the window, stared out at the flashes of lightning on the horizon.

"I'd like for you to leave now," she said, her eyes cast out to sea.

"Clarissa, for God's sake....okay. I'm sorry — I never meant for it to go this way. I was only trying to help... I mean, if she *is* your mother, you have a right to know." He grabbed the rest of his clothes and hurriedly dressed. She'd opened the door and was standing by the screen, holding Mitzy in one hand, propping the door with the other. The thunder and ocean roared and lightening flashed. Tal hurried out into the storm, wondering why he was so lousy with women. Especially women he loved.

Chapter Forty-Five

"I'll never forget the time old Mrs. Whittson told me my hair looked great. I changed it that very day. When an 80-year-old tells you your hair looks great, you really need a new look. But when a 20-year-old tells you you're looking good, you better keep that style."

~The Beautician's Notebook

September

Trudy was sweeping up the last bit of hair from the floor of The Sassy Lady. She'd been working harder than usual — it seemed every woman in the county needed her hair done as the school year got started. And it seemed each one wanted Trudy to do it.

She told herself that was a good thing, as she dumped the contents of the dust pan in the garbage. Between the shop and getting things ready for school, Trudy had her work cut out for her. As if *that* weren't enough, there was Tacoma to deal with. Tacoma suffered from those crazy pregnant hormones running through her system like a herd of wild horses. One minute she was crying — from joy, she said. The next, she was suicidal, swearing her life was over. *All* the time, however, she seemed pissy around Trudy. Trudy simply could not do one right thing.

Trudy had been collecting baby equipment — high chair, crib, stroller — at yard sales and thrift shops. Tacoma did not appreciate one item; not one 'thank-you' passed that girl's lips. She acted horsey all the time — like she was some kind of queen bee and Trudy, a lowly worker. That stuff was going to stop, but Trudy didn't have time or energy to address Tacoma's behavior at the moment. She was too busy.

She took a quick look around to be sure The Sassy Lady was spic-and-span, ready for the next long day. Satisfied, she closed the door and locked it. She double-checked the lock. Since Willa Jo's death, Trudy was nervous about leaving The Sassy Lady unattended. The Lady was vulnerable to break-ins. On the edge of town tucked behind a patch of trees, the location was isolated and somewhat desolate. Trudy thought she should re-attach that camera she'd found.

Oh no! She'd forgotten to give that little camera to Sheriff Hicks. And it might hold the identity of Willa Jo's murderer. How could she be so stupid? She hit herself upside her head, racking her brain. Where had she put that damn camera? Just a little button of a camera, small enough to lose without even knowing you'd lost it. Oh dear Lord, please help her remember.

Trudy got in her Chevy van and sat still. She prayed for God to help her recall what she'd done with that camera. *Lord, I know you can help me find it. I'm going to sit right here, praying, until You do.*

On and on the words echoed in her brain — *Help me, Lord, help me.* She continued to sit, willed herself to relax. She'd done this before, a technique she'd learned from her preacher…he called it the be-still-and-know meditation. Practicing this method, she'd found lost school books for Tacoma and Keena, a lost wristwatch and a misplaced bra-and-panties set. She had faith she'd find the little camera, too.

As she relaxed, she remembered the last time she'd seen the camera, just days ago. She'd stuck it in her the pocket of her black jeans, the skinny jeans Tacoma talked her into buying. That was the same day she'd found out about Tacoma's pregnancy. As far as she could remember, the camera was still in the pocket of those jeans.

Trudy put the car into gear and drove down the dusky road. It was already close to dark, the night coming earlier these days. Trudy loved this time of year with its shades of gray —the dove gray of dawn, the slate gray clouds before a cold rain, the charcoal gray of the tree limbs, soon to be bare against the pearly sky. She knew most people didn't enjoy this season, everybody waiting for spring and summer. But Trudy knew the fallow months after the harvest were rich in time for reflection, for withdrawing from the world into the safe warmth of home. But she didn't have time to cogitate on philosophy now. She had to find that camera.

Trudy was knee-deep in laundry when she heard Tacoma fumbling with the kitchen door.

"I'm in the laundry room — there's leftover pizza in the oven. Keena's at band practice. You got homework?" she called.

"Finished it..." Tacoma said, her voice dull.

"Come on in here, then." Trudy checked the pockets of various jeans and slacks. She'd found her skinny jeans right away, in the middle of the dirty clothes basket, but the camera was no longer in the back pocket. She figured it must have fallen out, so she was sorting through the entire laundry basket in an effort to find it.

"Mama, you gone crazy?"

"Maybe. I'm looking for a little tiny camera...it's real important. I'd love some help."

"Why you looking for it?"

"I think it might solve Willa Jo's murder."

"What?? Seriously?" Tacoma reached for a shirt on top of a small pile of clothing.

"No, I been through those already. Start over here."

Tacoma picked up a pair of Keena's shorts and rummaged through the pockets. Nothing.

"You think you gonna find Willa Jo's killer? What makes you think that?"

"Well, when I was clearing out Willa Jo's booth, I found this camera stuck on one of the wind chimes that hung across the top of her mirror. I thought it might have caught whoever killed Willa Jo. I was gonna take it to the sheriff right away, but that was a couple of days ago, the day you told me about....well, you know." Trudy pointed to Tacoma's belly. "Now, I lost the camera."

"So it's *my* fault..."

"I didn't say that...it just happened. Sometimes, stuff just happens —ain't nobody's fault."

Trudy continued searching —gym clothes, underwear, jeans, tee shirts, hoodies — but no luck. With Tacoma's help, the search pile grew smaller and smaller until there were no garments left.

"Well, that's it. Reckon it's gone." Trudy slouched in defeat.

"Wait a minute —let me look around on the floor," said Tacoma, bending down and sweeping her hands across the tiles. "What's this?"

Trudy hurried to look at the small, round object held in Tacoma's hand.

"Praise the Lord! You done found it, girl! Oh, my stars and garters! You found it!" Trudy hugged her daughter and before she knew it, they were both dancing and laughing, swinging each other around.

"Be careful, Mama, you lose it again!"

"I got *you* to find it if I do." Trudy smiled, holding onto her daughter.

"You do, Mama — you got me." Then Tacoma hugged Trudy, a nice warm hug, the kind she'd given when she was just a little girl.

Trudy felt herself tear up.

"Let's go get that pizza — don't forget — you eating for two these days." She linked her arm with Tacoma's and they walked, arm in arm, to the kitchen.

***

Early the next morning, Trudy headed to the governmental plaza. The camera was secured in a zip lock baggie; she was not taking any chances with it. Last night, she and Tacoma shared a pleasant evening, the first since Tacoma announced her condition. They watched TV and Keena joined them, laughing at the antics of the 'swamp people.' Right then, things looked like they were going to work out just fine. She'd do everything she could to make that happen.

She pulled into the parking lot. She hoped her efforts to bring the camera to Sheriff Hicks would pay off. She hated to think she'd spent all that time searching for the camera, only to discover there was nothing on it. She walked down the sidewalk and entered the sheriff's department.

"May I help you?" said a large white woman at the desk. Her manner was not particularly friendly.

"Yes. I'd like to see Sheriff Hicks."

"State your business," said the woman.

"I'd like to see Sheriff Hicks," said Trudy, drumming her fingers against the desktop.

"For what, ma'am," said the woman.

"I think I might have some evidence in the Willa Jo Temple case." Trudy didn't want to tell the rude bitch one more thing.

"I see. Have a seat while I buzz the sheriff." The woman indicated the nearby vinyl-covered couch. It was orange-to match the inmates, Trudy surmised. She couldn't help but smile at the thought.

She sat down and the couch made an unpleasant noise. She hoped she wouldn't have to wait long. A couple of *Sports Illustrated* magazines from 2012 and 2013 were scattered across a small round table. Trudy pulled out her phone and sent a text to Tacoma. In a few minutes, her phone buzzed and she checked it.

"hang n there see u later"

Humph. At least Tacoma had responded. Progress.

Finally, she heard the door of the sheriff's office open. Out walked Tal Hicks. Whew, he was still one good-looking man. Willa Jo had been crazy to let that one go.

"Mrs. Johnson? Oh, *Trudy*! Good to see you," he said, giving her a brief hug. Trudy watched as the unfriendly woman at the desk sucked in her breath in surprise.

"You, too, sheriff," she said, following him into his office.

He sat across the desk from her and folded his hands to that his fingertips were touching, making a tent.

"What can I do for you, Miss Trudy?" he said, addressing her the way he had when he and Willa Jo were married.

"I think maybe *I* can do something for *you*, Tal. You won't believe this...but I found a camera. When I was clearing out Willa Jo's booth — you know how she had all those little chimes hanging around — well, I found this stuck up amongst them," she said, handing the baggy to the sheriff.

"Damn. Sure looks like a camera. Did Willa Jo ever say she was setting up security?"

"No. I was shocked to find it. I have no idea how it works or whether or not you can get the stuff off of it. But I thought you should have it---I'm sorry I didn't get it to you earlier — but I had a little family issue."

"Whew, I'm sorry, too. Well, hell, that time's lost now. Thanks for bringing it in — it may be just the break we need. I won't get too excited yet — I'll have to send it to the Computer Forensics Department in Raleigh. Most likely, they'll take a couple of months to get back to me — they're slow as Christmas — damn bureaucracy. I'll let you know if there's anything on there. You doing okay?"

"So far, so good. At first, business took a nose-dive. But now, folks are coming back. Avenelle Young has been great — telling everybody how I've done her hair and what a good job I'm doing. Matter of fact, things are so good, I'm hiring somebody new...which is why I was clearing out Willa Jo's stuff. I tried to make myself go through everything sooner, but I just couldn't bring myself to do it."

"Yeah. Hard to believe she's gone."

"Reckon I better hit the road — I got some blue-hairs coming at 9 a.m. sharp. I dare not be late."

“Thanks again for the camera.”

“I hope it’s some help.”

Trudy returned to her van and headed for The Sassy Lady. She felt like she always felt on Election Day — proud and happy that she’d done her civic duty. Even if she’d done it a few days late.

Chapter Forty-Six

"A full heart is like a good head of hair."

~The Beautician's Notebook

October

Avenelle sat at the kitchen table, thumbing through recipe books. Thanksgiving was still a month and a half away, but she wanted this year to be special. Because this year, she had so very much for which to give thanks.

She was out of jail.

That was a huge reason to celebrate. Plus, Abel and Annie Jo were doing very well in Seattle —that big star had set them up with gigs and Abel was playing backup for several bands in the area —what was it he called himself? A studio musician. He told Avenelle he wanted to get Annie Jo a ring at Thanksgiving — another one of Avenelle's many reasons to give thanks. She was so happy he'd found someone to love. Abel said he wanted *her*--- Avenelle---to help him pick out the diamond when the time came. She thought that was the sweetest thing.

Surely, her cup did runneth over. Rory, that dear, sweet man, heard all there was to hear about her sordid past and he forgave her. Well, he said there was no reason for forgiveness —he just wanted to love her and be with her. He told her he realized, while she was incarcerated, just how much he cared and how much he needed her. He also accepted blame for taking her for granted and not giving her the respect she deserved. They'd made love after he said that, the first time in over a year. Oh, that dear, dear man. He was after her at least once a week, sometimes twice. *Thank you, Jesus!*

Now that he was no longer a preacher, Rory was like a new man. A man she didn't know very well —and that, in itself, was exciting. He was only sixty-four; he believed he could start a new career — the second half of life, he'd called it. A do-over, he said. He'd already enrolled in at Cape Fear Community College to take classes in architectural technology. He figured after a couple of years there, he could transfer to UNC-Charlotte for his full architectural degree. Avenelle had never seen him so happy.

Yes, the more she thought about her life, the more she found for which to be grateful. The past did not hold power over her any more. She felt cleansed.

She'd just located her recipe for sweet potato casserole —Mamie Eisenhower's recipe, too— when she heard the doorbell.

"Oh, who could that be?" she mumbled as she made her way toward the door.

"Sheriff? I must say, this is a surprise." She didn't want to invite him in —not if she didn't have to.

"Morning, Mrs. Young. May I come in?"

She hesitated just a half-second.

"Of course...please," she said as she opened the door.

She showed him into the living room where he sat on a straight-backed chair; she took a seat on the couch.

"I hope you're not here to arrest me again," she said, smiling.

"No, ma'am. I'm here to give you some information which, when you hear it, I hope you'll be persuaded to help me."

"Why, Sheriff Hicks, you know I'd be happy to help you with anything you need. After all, you were very kind not to charge me with obstruction of justice, after I confessed to Willa Jo's murder. You were even nice when I un-confessed."

She offered him some hot tea —pumpkin spice, her favorite for the fall —but he refused. He made a little joke about drinking 'on-duty.' She then excused herself to go into the kitchen to bring out a plate of her homemade chocolate chip cookies. She knew he wouldn't be able to refuse those; she also poured them each a glass of milk. Nothing goes better with chocolate chip cookies that good old milk. She carried the plate, balancing both glasses with her fingers, until she could set the whole shebang on the coffee table.

"Now I know you want a bite of my special, secret recipe chocolate chips."

"Well, how can I resist....but only if you tell me your secret." He smiled. "After all, I *am* a detective —I want to know everybody's secrets."

Avenelle returned his grin. She wondered what in the world he wanted from her. And what could he possibly have to tell her.

"Mrs. Young, in the course of our investigation, you admitted you'd had a daughter forty years ago in Ohio. You did not name the father of the child, but we could only imagine he would have been local, given your youth. Upon further investigation, we realized the father was Rock Bonner." Tal watched the surprise register on her face when he mentioned Bonner's name. "As I continued to look into Willa Jo's untimely death, I discovered something I think you might find interesting."

Good grief. Why was he bringing all that stuff up now? Just when she'd been feeling so good. What was he getting at?

"Mrs. Young, I believe I know who your daughter is. I don't know if you want to know her identity or not...but I thought it was only right to share with you what I found out."

She was still smiling at him, that polite Southern half-smile that really meant, why-don't-you- mind-your-own-business. But she was far too genteel to utter such words. So, she sat there on her sofa, her mind reeling, that smile frozen on her face.

Finally, she was able to speak.

"Who? ...ahem, who do you believe to be my daughter?" she said in a whisper.

"I think you already know. Matter of fact, I believe you were trying to protect your daughter when you confessed. When you recanted your confession, you said the reason you'd confessed in the first place was because you didn't think you mattered to anyone — and you wanted to grab everyone's attention. But I think you'd discovered your daughter's identity and you thought she might have had a motive for killing Willa Jo. I believe your daughter is Clarissa Myers, from over on Temple Beach."

Avenelle felt her heart beating fast and her face flushing. How could he have guessed? How?

"What makes you think Mrs. Myers is my daughter, Sheriff? I mean, she's a beautiful, wealthy woman — married to a millionaire. How could she possibly be mine?" The look in his eye told her he knew. Not only that, he knew she knew.

"I've spoken with the folks at The Maple Knolls Unwed Mother's Home. They confirmed the birth — same day Clarissa was born — and they explained they had never been able to place the child in an adoptive family. She grew up in a series of foster homes — none of which could give her the love and nurturing she needed." He spoke softly, gently.

"Stop! I will hear no more of this! I can't stand it!"

Avenelle felt as if she'd been stabbed in the heart. She could not bear to think of that tiny baby girl, the one she'd held in her arms, suffering through foster care, feeling unloved. Not when Avenelle had been right here, loving her so deeply, all those years. She felt tears threatening. Old tears, sour with age. They flowed down her cheeks and dripped onto her blouse. Her nose began to run, too. She couldn't stop any of it.

"Mrs. Young, I'm so sorry to cause you more pain. I understand the regret and guilt you must feel. I wouldn't tell you any of this if I didn't think there was a chance for reconciliation — some kind of redemption. You see, I'm deeply in love with your Clarissa. And I think she loves me, too. But when I told her I'd investigated her life, she felt betrayed yet again. She hasn't spoken to me since. Can you help me? Will you?"

Avenelle stared at him. She realized he was miserable. His eyes were full of sadness, brimming with it.

"I think I can make Clarissa happy —I want to do all I can to give her a good life, an honest life."

"But she's already married," Avenelle said, wiping her nose on a Kleenex — she was glad she'd just replenished the supply in the living room.

"They're getting a divorce."

"Because of you??? She's letting a millionaire go because of YOU?" Her voice took on the sound of banshee. Oh, she hated it when she sounded that way — so unrefined.

"No —I suspect you know why she's letting him go. You read the notebook."

"If you are referring to that small indiscretion with Willa Jo — well, I hate to speak ill of the dead, but Willa Jo was a bit of a floozy." Avenelle thought about all the times Willa Jo had broken Bessie's heart — oh yes, she and Bessie had known all about Willa Jo's wicked, wicked ways.

"Turns out, it wasn't just one little indiscretion — the man had been having affairs for years. Clarissa began digging and she dug up an ugly mess —he didn't even try to deny it. She called an end to it, so he moved out. He'd put the house in Clarissa's name — another one of his generous guilt gifts. He's left the state. Now, they're just waiting for the year to pass so they can divorce."

Avenelle was surprised and dismayed by this news. She'd thought her girl was all set; thought life had turned out well for the child in spite of everything. Her poor girl. Probably still felt completely unloved. And rejected and humiliated.

"I'm so sorry to hear that," said Avenelle, now calm. "You know, I would do anything to help her —make it up to her. Anything."

"I've been thinking —why don't you meet with her —just go see her. Talk to her. Tell her your story. Maybe, if you two can work things out, maybe she'll forgive me. If you put in a good word...."

Avenelle thought, humph, just like a man — always thinking of himself. He had no idea the agony she'd gone through over the years. And the terror that filled her heart now, when she thought of facing the daughter she'd abandoned all those years ago.

"I'll think on it. I promise you that much —nothing more."

And she showed him the door.

Chapter Forty-Seven

"My Annie Jo is the best little baton twirler in the class. Nothing like a daughter to bring you joy."

~The Beautician's Notebook

November

All Saints Day. Time to remember those who had passed, those you had lost. Avenelle sat at the kitchen table, peeling sweet potatoes. She was going to make sweet potato pudding, a difficult task involving grating the raw potato so fine, it could be mixed with eggs and milk and a little flour so that the meat of the potato didn't clump, but blended smooth as custard. Not her favorite dish to prepare, but she wasn't making it for herself. The pudding was for Clarissa Myers. Her daughter. Clarissa.

Avenelle would have chosen a different name for her daughter. She wondered who selected that fancy name. Maybe one of the people from the adoption agency. Certainly, no one asked *her* what the baby's name should be. She would have selected something simple, something good — like Grace or Beth. A one-syllable name. Who needed three syllables? Her own name---AVENELLE —had plagued her all her life. No one could pronounce such a name, and it sounded like Avenelle had delusions of grandeur carrying such a heavy nomenclature.

Of course, Rory often called her Nelle, especially when they were in bed together. And Rock Bonner always called her Avie. She wondered if Clarissa had a nickname, used only by her best friends. She thought about whether or not Clarissa liked her own name. She wanted to know what Clarissa thought about *everything*! She'd missed so much of the girl's life that now, knowing what she knew, she was desperate to investigate her daughter. But first, she had to tell Clarissa everything. She had to beg for forgiveness. And she needed to make as much restitution as she could.

She pulled the old grater from the cabinet, the one with the loose handle. Though Rory had bought her a new one years ago, for some reason, she preferred the old one. She turned the grater to the smallest side and began to rub the potato down and down and down against the rough metal. She was so busy thinking about Clarissa, she quickly cut her middle knuckle. She grabbed a paper towel to stop the blood, but one little drop spilled into the bowl. She dabbed at it, getting most of it. Oh well, she told herself. It seemed appropriate for the sweet potato pudding have a little of her blood in it — because she would give every ounce of blood she had to make things right with Clarissa. Her daughter.

***

Later that afternoon, Avenelle, along with her best casserole dish filled with sweet potato pudding, drove from Summerset to Temple Beach. As she crossed the large, concrete bridge, she had to force her eyes on the road. She wanted more than anything to look at the water — it called to her, diverting her attention. But the bridge was curved and with only two lanes, she knew she'd better focus or she'd have a head-on collision and fall to her death before she got to talk to her daughter.

At the stop sign at the bottom of the bridge, she turned right, as the sheriff had told her. She drove past the pier and counted one, two, three, four houses down. There it was — Clarissa's house. The place looked peaceful and elegant and it reminded Avenelle of her childhood, when her father took them down to South Carolina to an island. They'd stayed in a cottage for a whole week and Avenelle had never felt that relaxed and ready for fun since.

She pulled into the driveway, turned off the engine and rolled down the windows. Now that she was here, right here in front of Clarissa's house, she wasn't sure she had the courage to go through with her plan. Clarissa may not even be home, she told herself, though the yellow Corvette was parked in the carport. Avenelle went through all the possible responses Clarissa might make to her — slam the door in her face, curse her, throw something at her, hug her, forgive her, love her, hate her — she'd been over and over these reactions in her mind until she'd felt certain she could take whatever came her way. Now, she wasn't so sure. Now, she really, really hoped there would be no violence.

Slowly, she got out of the car and balanced the casserole dish in one hand as she slammed the car door. She wasn't sure which way to go as there seemed to be two entrances — one staircase was on the outside and led up a story to a large porch facing the ocean. The other steps led directly to the interior of the house. Avenelle decided she would take the outer stairs. Maybe a glimpse of the ocean would give her strength; besides, it seemed the longer route and she was happy to have a delay.

She couldn't believe she was doing this — confronting the baby she'd left behind years ago — another lifetime, before she'd married Rory and birthed her sons. Who had that wild young girl been any way? What had her dreams for the future included? Did she realize any of those youthful aspirations? Avenelle didn't know. She could barely remember that terrified girl of sixteen.

Avenelle rang the doorbell and waited, the casserole growing heavier by the minute. A little dog ran to the glass door, jumping up and down in excitement. *Well, at least somebody is glad to see me.* Soon after, Clarissa followed. She watched as Clarissa seemed to take a step backward when she realized who was waiting. Then, she bravely marched onward to the door. *Good girl — courageous.* Clarissa opened the door.

"How can I help you?" she said, her voice like a drone.

Avenelle decided not to let a lack of enthusiasm stop her.

"I…I made this sweet potato casserole...it's one of my specialties — my whole family just loves it…I thought maybe you would like it, too. So….I brought some for you…it's for you."

"How…lovely…."

They stood, staring, sizing each other up. Avenelle felt like they were play-acting a shoot-out in the Old West. Finally, Clarissa spoke.

"Won't you come in?"

Avenelle carried the casserole into the living room, saw the kitchen counter and hurried to put the sweet potatoes down before she dropped them smack on the floor. She suddenly felt weak-kneed.

She sat down on one of the chairs at the table.

"Must be the heat — I got a little swimmy-headed." She could feel her heart beating so fast, so fast.

"Would you like a glass of ice water?"

"Yes…yes," Avenelle said. She could see spots before her eyes and things were quickly getting dark. *Put your head between your knees.* Avenelle did just that.

"Are you all right?" Avenelle could hear real concern in Clarissa's voice. She tried to nod her head to signify that yes, she was fine, just give her a minute....but she couldn't really make her head move the right way. She grunted 'uh-huh.'

"Would you like to lie on the couch?" Clarissa said, now sounding worried and exasperated.

Avenelle sat up quickly, then stood. She headed toward the couch, but before she could reach it, she went down; the blackness overcame her.

When she came to, she was lying on the couch and Clarissa was holding something under her nose. It was Vick's VapoRub. She'd recognize that sharp smell anywhere. She looked up at Clarissa and stared into those Bonner blue eyes. Those were the eyes that had gotten her into trouble in the first place — how odd to see them on this young woman. Her daughter. Her daughter and yet, a stranger.

"Feeling better?"

"I think so."

"Should I call a doctor?"

"No...I...I'm sure it's just the heat."

Slowly, after she'd regained her balance and the dots no longer danced before her eyes, she pulled herself to a sitting position. She didn't move, wanted to make sure she wasn't going to pass out again. All seemed well. Avenelle remained upright.

They sat together without speaking while Avenelle returned to herself. It was pleasant to sit there, looking out the big window onto the ocean, which was an emerald green today. Avenelle couldn't believe she lived so close to this special place, a place that reminded her of the majesty of the Creator, yet she rarely drove the few miles to get here. She'd have to change that. Life was too short to miss even one moment of the serenity she felt looking at the sea. Avenelle could have stayed like that forever, sitting on Clarissa's couch, staring at the unfathomable ocean. With her daughter.

Her daughter.

She needed to tell Clarissa everything.

She tore her gaze from the water and looked at Clarissa. The young woman was beautiful, her blond hair a little longer than when she'd taken music lessons from Avenelle. She'd swept her hair up in a French twist. Today, she wore no make-up and Avenelle thought she was even prettier without it. And there was no mistaking those blue Bonner eyes.

"I guess you're wondering why I'm here."

"Not really. I had a feeling you'd show up one day," Clarissa said, her arms folded in front of her, her mouth a thin line.

"So....Sheriff Hicks came to me a few weeks ago with some pretty startling news...said you were my daughter. He had proof; he'd contacted the unwed mother's home where I gave birth to you and followed the trail of your life...of course, he wasn't telling me anything I didn't already know. I knew you were mine from the moment I saw you with Rock Bonner at the restaurant — do you remember? It was the eyes and the familiar way you moved — much the way my mother used to move. And you had her smile, too. Yes, once I saw you, really *saw* you — I knew."

"Don't you think all of this supposed *news* is unlikely at best? I mean, it's just a happy coincidence I ended up here? At Temple Beach?" Clarissa seemed to hug herself even tighter.

"It *does* seem....miraculous. But I believe there are forces at work in our lives we can never understand...call it what you will — fate, God, the universe — I can't explain how the world works...but I do believe there is *something*...."

Neither woman spoke for what seemed to Avenelle like hours. Finally, Clarissa looked out at the beach and said, "And...what am I supposed to do with this information? Am I supposed to hug you gleefully and call you 'Mama'? Or would you rather I cry with joy?"

Avenelle was taken aback at the anger she heard in the other woman's voice, the hatred.

"I'm not sure you're supposed to do anything with it...but I had hoped we might become....friends...maybe more...I really don't know."

Silence again.

Avenelle watched as Clarissa's body grew more tense.

"You know, I had a shitty childhood...no one loved me — ever. I was whipped with a leather strap, locked in a closet — I never got enough to eat. My foster parents, however, ate very well. Let's see, how many different ones did I have???? Oh yes, SIX! And not one ever loved me. Not one gave a fat rat's ass about me. Last but certainly not least — I was raped when I was fourteen. So, you can see why I might be a little perturbed by your coming here...claiming to be my mother, the mother who deserted me, the one who left me to enjoy such a *beautiful* life," she said in a low, controlled voice. Sarcasm dripped from her words.

Avenelle didn't know what to say. What *could* she say? She had failed her first-born and bequeathed her a horrible existence for the first eighteen years of her life. She began to feel water trickled down her face.

"I'm sorry… so very sorry," she whispered.

The two women sat on the couch and didn't speak.

Finally, Avenelle thought the time had come to return home. She rose.

"I cannot ever tell you how sorry I am for all of this. I'm deeply grieved to learn what happened to you," she said as she walked toward the door. She turned once again to face Clarissa. "But I do know this…all those years when you thought nobody loved you, I was loving you. I was missing you and thinking about you and sending my prayers to you. And I will love you for the rest of my life — my love will always be here," Avenelle said, pointing to her chest, "— whether you want it or not."

Avenelle walked out without another word, leaving her daughter once again.

Chapter Forty-Eight

"Blondes don't always have more fun."

~The Beautician's Notebook

November

Clarissa watched as Miss Avenelle —her mother —walked right out of her life. Again. Ever since Tal told her of his discovery, she'd been thinking about Avenelle Young. What did she know about her, really? She was a preacher's wife, she had two sons, she taught music. She seemed kind enough. But that was the outside life — what was she really like? And why, oh why, had she given Clarissa away?

Clarissa slipped on her tennis shoes and a light jacket, put Mitzy on her leash and headed out towards the beach. The wind was cold and constant, but she didn't care. Sometimes, she simply had to walk, fast and hard, pulling Mitzy along so that her little paws barely touched the ground.

The sea, still pale green, but choppy, lapped at the shore in short, angry waves. Clarissa's eyes were drawn to the horizon. She loved to imagine she was sailing away, across the great water to wherever the winds would blow her. She had no attachments any more — Ralph now lived in an apartment in near D.C., the penthouse of one of those tall, tall buildings in Arlington. He called her once a week 'to check on her.' Every now and then, he begged her to reconsider. She didn't need checking and his pleading got on her nerves. Lately, when the phone rang, she didn't pick up.

Maybe she would travel —she could afford it. Why not? Why not see the parts of the world *she* wanted to see — Africa, China, the South Pole. Ralph had taken her to Europe, trips that had broadened her view of the world. But he'd never had any interest in places that might be a little more dangerous, a little more exotic.

The longer she walked, the better she felt. She moved past the long pier where a few lonely-looking fishermen had cast their lines. She kept going. Hell, at this rate, she felt like she could cover the whole island — all eleven miles of it.

Walking on the beach helped her clear her mind. Maybe it was all that blood moving around in her head. Maybe it was the salt air. Whatever the reason, walking seemed to fix just about everything, most days. But not today. Even a dose of sea and salt air wasn't enough to lift her mood.

The farther she walked, the sadder Clarissa felt. It seemed everything in her life was a shambles — her marriage over, her love affair with Tal kaput — and now, her mother had left her, too. She cried, the wind drying her tears almost instantly.

All her life, Clarissa dreamed of finding her mother; sure, she'd wanted to find her to slap the shit out of her — at least, that's what she always told herself. But deep down, she knew she wanted to discover whether or not her mother ever loved her, or even gave her a second thought. Somewhere deeper than she could understand, she wanted to find her mother and find the love she'd longed for all her life.

She scanned the beach, focusing on the shells scattered along the shore. She bent down to pluck up a sand dollar, amazingly all in one piece. She stuffed it into her jacket pocket. Should she try to establish a relationship with Miss Avenelle? No, it was too late for all of that. Her childhood was over and she was a grown woman. She didn't need a mother in her life now. To hell with her.

Mitzy stopped to pee and Clarissa waited.

Miss Avenelle said something about loving her all those years ago. Was that true? Had her mother longed for her, worried about her? There was some comfort in the thought, anyway. And maybe it *was* true. Maybe Avenelle could still love her. Maybe that old saying, 'Better late than never,' was true, too. The idea surprised Clarissa. Late better than *never.*

Clarissa picked Mitzy up and carried her back home.

Chapter Forty-Nine

"Some people get exactly what they deserve. But I try not to gloat when it happens."

~The Beautician's Notebook

November

Almost six months since Willa Jo's death, and Tal Hicks didn't have a clue as to who might be responsible, if anyone. He was still waiting on Raleigh to get the video from the camera Trudy had given him — damn, they were so slow. Avenelle Young had been his best suspect, but he knew she hadn't done it; Clarissa had been, ever so briefly, under suspicion, but her alibi checked out — plus, he didn't believe for a minute Clarissa was capable of the deed. Trudy's fingerprints were on the chemical cape, but that was likely, since Trudy worked there. Plus, Trudy was the one who found the body and called the police-hardly, the actions of a murderer. So, that left him with nada. A big, fat zero.

That is, until this morning when he'd walked into the Purple Onion and discovered a couple of good ole boys talking about what great luck Mad Dog McGee was having at the local racetrack. He'd got himself a Chevy Lumina frame with an engine he'd built himself and man, that baby could go. He'd taken it up to Jacksonville and had won a couple of thousand bucks. He hoped to take it to Dunn and win five thousand. Tal started thinking again about Mad Dog. He'd done all right since Willa Jo's death. Had a new girlfriend — Tal's daughter's friend, Kayla — he had that race car...yep, old Mad Dog was doing just fine.

Tal thought maybe, since Mad Dog had come out of all this smelling like a rose, he should pay him another visit, see what he might stir up. He revved up the police car and headed to the automotive shop where Mad Dog worked.

The unexpected appearance of the sheriff just might shake Mad Dog into revealing something he wouldn't want to reveal. Tal knew the element of surprise to be effective. He hoped it would work with this one. He couldn't stand the sense of failure he felt about not being able to figure out, once and for all, what happened to Willa Jo. Just like years ago, when he'd failed her as a husband, working too many long hours, not taking time with her the way he did before they were married. The divorce was as much his fault as hers; he could see that now.

Tal pulled into the parking lot next to the garage and cut his engine. He could see a couple of mechanics inside, grease streaking their coveralls and their faces. His eyes lit on Mad Dog, who was bent over an engine. Tal walked into the garage, right past the sign that said 'Employees Only.'

"Afternoon, Mr. McGee. You look busy," Tal said.

"Sheriff. D-didn't expect to see you here — you got a engine problem?"

"Naw, naw. I just come by to ask you a few more questions...you know, about Willa Jo." Tal kept his gaze eyes on the man. There was no flinch, no giveaway.

"Sure — let me t-tighten this and then we can go into the office — set a spell." Tal watched as he finished the job, dipped his hands into a can of GoJo hand cleaner, wiped them, dripping, onto a towel and motioned for Tal to follow him.

"Have a s-seat, Sheriff. You want a cuppa coffee? Co-cola?"

"No thanks — I'm on-duty." Tal smiled, friendly-like, at his old joke. He never tired of it.

"Mind if I do?"

Tal shook his head and observed Mad Dog's steady hand as he poured the coffee.

"So, w-what can I do for you?" Mad Dog said, sitting behind the desk.

"Well, I still don't have a suspect and I was hoping you could tell me a little about Willa Jo's life, you know, things we might have missed before...Just trying to find a way to close this case."

"I done told you all I know — I was sleeping upstairs. I never h-heard any kind of noise or nothing. I know that sounds kinda strange, but it's the truth. The first thing I remember is when you woke me up that morning. Somebody banged on the bedroom door at the crack of dawn, but I just ignored em and went back to sleep. Then, after you came with the p-p-police marking off the crime scene, Trudy explained it was her who tried to wake me up earlier. She'd done called the law after she come in to work and found Willa Jo. I always thought she shoulda come upstairs and told m-me first…I reckon she tried. Hell, she coulda tried harder, but then, Trudy never did like me all that much. Willa Jo and I used to party a lot and Trudy didn't like anybody who drank liquor. Reckon you could say I was a might hung-over that morning…."

Tal heard it all before —the details were the same, all except the part about Trudy not liking Mad Dog.

"You know, Mr. McGee, I used to be married to Willa Jo — I know how she could be. Sometimes, she'd make me so damn mad I wanted to slap some sense into her. You know?"

"Willa Jo and me never did f-fight that much. She must of mellowed out, getting older and all. We got along g-g-great. I woulda married her in a heartbeat, but she told me she would never get hitched again."

Tal smiled and shook his head.

"Well, she didn't have much luck with husbands, I reckon. Do you know if she had any enemies at all? Maybe somebody who didn't like their hair or something…anything?" Tal was desperate for a clue. Or even the hint of a clue.

"Naw…can't think of anyone."

"I see you doing a lot of racing these days…much money in it?"

"Naw. Mainly, it's the exposure I'm looking for. If I start w-winning all the time and the right person sees me, I could move on up."

"Reckon that's your dream, then…and Willa Jo leaving you a little money didn't hurt, did it?"

"I had no idea she was g-gonna do that….she'd already p-p-promised to get me some money from a few of her rich friends to back my racing career…I think she c-coulda raised more than $50,000."

"I'd like you to come on down to the police department with me, Mr. McGee. I'd like to get all this in a formal statement."

"You arresting m-m-me?"

"Not yet. Let's just say you are a person of interest." Tal figured he could place Mad Dog under arrest once he got to the jail —that way, he'd have back-up, in case Mad Dog gave any trouble. Plus, he wanted to obtain a warrant from Judge Luffy to search Mad Dog's apartment. Maybe something would turn up.

"I n-never lifted a finger to Willa Jo."

"That may be true. But I did a little checking up on you...from South Carolina. You had a few drunk and disorderlies, a couple of assault charges. And one domestic altercation — with a girlfriend. Plus, the fact is, your story about sleeping through whatever happened to Willa Jo is more than a little fishy —you don't really have an alibi. That's enough to get me started. And if I keep digging...who knows what'll turn up."

Mad Dog shrugged.

"You w-won't dig up a d-d-damn thing cause I ain't done nothing. I'll c-come with you, peaceful-like, just to show you I'm cooperating. You go ahead and d-d-dig. You won't find nothing on me."

Tal stood and so did Mad Dog. They walked to the car and Tal placed cuffs on Mad Dog, lowered his head and helped him into the back seat. He wasn't sure he was doing the right thing, but he had to do something. If he shook Mad Dog up a little, who knew what might fall out. He had to try —he owed that much to Willa Jo. He knew the statistics...it was almost always the husband or boyfriend who did it. Besides, arresting Mad Dog made it easier for him to watch everyone else involved. Whoever committed the murder might begin to feel safe, make a mistake, something that would lead Tal to him. Or her.

Tal started the engine and drove carefully to the jail. He didn't much care if Mad Dog was guilty or not —he most likely deserved to be locked up a day or so for *something* before his lawyer would get him out. By then, Tal would have searched his place real good. A little jail time wouldn't hurt Mad Dog one bit.

Chapter Fifty

"Even mother's milk can go sour."

~The Beautician's Notebook

November

Clarissa had not been able to sleep since the visit from Miss Avenelle. That's how she thought of the woman who, supposedly, was her mother. Miss Avenelle —the nice preacher's wife who had given her a music lesson. A stranger, really. She couldn't imagine this was the woman who'd brought her into the world....and then left her, abandoned her to a life of depravation and despair. Clarissa looked out onto the slate-colored ocean and the low-hanging pewter clouds. Everything was gray. She sat on the sofa with a cup of green tea and watched the sky roil. Another storm must be coming. She felt sort of like those clouds —her belly rolling and rumbling. No matter how many times she promised herself she wouldn't think of Miss Avenelle, the woman came to her mind. Funny —since Ralph left home, she hadn't thought of him nearly as often as she'd thought of Miss Avenelle. Matter of fact, she was obsessed with Miss Avenelle. She was hungry for the woman's story — the whole story. Miss Avenelle's story was a missing piece of Clarissa's own life; maybe, if she learned it, she would feel whole somehow.

She stroked Mitzy absent-mindedly. She loved the silky feel of Mitzy's fur, the softness. Petting her dog comforted Clarissa and she remembered a time when she was around six years old, in her third foster family by then. The mother had a loud voice, even when she spoke about everyday matters. When she was angry, her voice made Clarissa's head ring. She recalled one of the other foster children getting in trouble for taking a chocolate chip cookie without asking. The mother screamed so sharply at the child, Clarissa ran to her room and curled up in an old blanket she'd had with her since she could remember —her 'binky', as she called it, was the one steady thing in her otherwise wobbly life. And the 'binky' had a very soft outer edge that brought Clarissa the same kind of comfort Mitzy did. All of a sudden, Clarissa started crying. She wept for that little forlorn six-year-old, for all the hurts and aches in her heart, pain she didn't imagine would ever stop, not really.

Miss Avenelle said she'd loved Clarissa all along — how could that be true? Abandonment wasn't love. It was dismissal — an act of complete disregard. Clarissa shook with sobs, almost feral-sounding. The moans and grunts didn't seem to come from her body, but from some other place, some place she wasn't aware of, a part of her she, too, had denied.

She didn't know how long she cried. Mitzy never moved at all, just curled up beside her and sat very still.

Finally, Clarissa quit shaking and her tears stopped. Those guttural sounds she'd made seemed to have been healing in some strange way. She opened the door to what had become a bright November day. She loved that about the beach — how quickly clouds could give way to blue sky. She watched as a V of pelicans skimmed the shore, looking for fish.

"Come on, Mitzy — let's take a walk," she said. It was the off-season, so Mitzy wasn't required to wear a leash. She really didn't need one because even in a crowd, the dog stayed at Clarissa's ankles, padding along as fast as her short legs could go.

The now cloudless sky seemed brighter than usual and the sun, the pale yellow of home-churned butter. The breeze was brisk but Clarissa found it refreshing after her long crying jag — bracing. She walked past the pier, past the water tower, past the cute little peach-colored house from the 50s, an anomaly against all the newer homes. She loved that house with its green shutters and the neat yard, always well-manicured. Such an unassuming house was much more her style than the one Ralph had bought for her. Maybe she should sell. After all, the house was hers. And so was the Corvette.

Funny. Ralph still called every week. They'd discussed the pre-nup and the divorce agreements. He was very generous — told her he'd support her the rest of her life, unless she remarried. And he offered 200K a year to keep her 'in the manner to which she'd grown accustomed,' he said. He didn't seem angry or even sad about the split. Clarissa figured he already had a replacement. And she thought he sounded like he felt sorry for her. Because now, she had no one.

Clarissa kept walking, a little faster now.

No one.

But that wasn't true. She did have someone — she had her mother. If only she could get past all the anger and hurt, maybe she could have the family she'd always wanted. Maybe there was still time to right the wrong her mother committed against her. Maybe, if she went to see Miss Avenelle — her mother — she could at least hear her story. She could, perhaps, in the fullness of time, learn to forgive.

***

Clarissa changed her clothes at least five times. She wanted to look just right when she showed up on Miss Avenelle's front porch. She wanted to look perfect. Finally, she decided on a deep blue short-sleeved sweater with a crew neck and beige slacks. She wore beige sandals and carried a matching purse. She put her hair into a high ponytail and secured it with a blue head-band. Just as she was reaching for her make-up, she stopped. No make-up. She wanted to be her truest self with Miss Avenelle. No barriers — not even lipstick.

She put Mitzy in her dog crate, ran down the steps and hopped into the Corvette. She revved the engine, happy to hear it purr — she'd never dreamed she could love such simple things — the sound of the engine, the feel of Mitzy's fur, the thrill of doing something she was terrified to do. Now cleansed from her tears, she was filled with euphoria. She was going to see her mother. Her mother. Mother. She whispered the word over and over as she drove the fifteen miles to Summerset. Her mother.

The Young home, a charming bungalow with a big front porch, was filled with rockers and a swing, small chrysanthemums and various squashes arranged artfully on a small table near the front door. On each step sat fat pumpkins. On the window of the front door were some scribbles obviously made by a child with the words 'I'm Thankful For' at the top and strangely shaped blobs beneath the words. Clarissa could make out a stick family at the very top of the list.

Family. What did that feel like?

She worried she might catch Miss Avenelle — that is, her mother — at a bad time. Maybe she should have called first. Yes, definitely — she should have called. It was rude to show up uninvited. Clarissa had been about to ring the doorbell when she was overcome with fear. She turned on one heel to walk away.

"Clarissa? Oh, yes, it *is* you! Come in, oh please do come in," Miss Avenelle said, hurrying to put her arm around Clarissa's shoulders and lead her inside. "I was just in the kitchen making a pound cake for Thanksgiving. I thought I heard somebody and I'm so happy it's you."

Clarissa could smell cinnamon and nutmeg, the sweet scent of homemade baking, and the welcoming odor of coffee simmering. There was something so comforting about the house— she'd felt it when she took her one piano lesson, before her world split apart. The front room was gently cluttered with multi-colored afghans and throw pillows, jackets and hats hanging on a hook near the door, stacks of magazines and papers on the coffee table and on the floor next to the couch. A neat mess. And, though Clarissa never allowed her own home to appear anything less than perfect, she felt immediately at ease here.

"Have a seat — I've just baked some pumpkin and molasses cookies —would you like one? And how about coffee? Tea? Water?"

"No, thank you. Well…maybe a cookie?" Clarissa felt shy and knew her face was reddening, but she also felt comfortable, but scared. And not. Oh, dear, she was a mess. What was she doing here?

She watched Miss Avenelle retreat into the kitchen and return with a generous plate of cookies and a cup of coffee, already sweetened and with lots of cream.

"How did you know I like my coffee like that?" Clarissa said.

"I didn't know for sure, but it's how I like mine, so I took a chance." She set the items down on the coffee table and sat next to Clarissa. Their thighs touched and Clarissa pulled away.

"I…I'm not sure why I came…" Clarissa said.

"I hope you came because you want to know more — about me and about yourself. Your people. Your family."

"Yes. I guess more than anything, I want to know why…why you left me in Ohio." Clarissa took a tiny bite of a cookie.

It seemed as if that one sentence had sucked all the air, all the comfort, out of the whole house. Miss Avenelle didn't speak for a long time. Clarissa sat, nibbling her cookie, or at least pretending to do so. Finally, Miss Avenelle spoke.

"So long ago — forty years. A lot can happen in forty years….I was only sixteen. I could say an older man seduced me, but that wouldn't be the truth. And I want to be as honest as I know how to be with you, Clarissa. I've waited most of my life for you and I want to start out on the right foot. The truth is, I couldn't wait —for life to begin, to get away from my stuffy parents, to go to college...get the heck out of Summerset."

"But why did you abandon me? Why didn't you keep me?" Saying that made Clarissa's throat hurt.

"You want the whole story, don't you?"

"Everything."

Miss Avenelle folded her hands in her lap and twiddled her thumbs. Silence descended for a few moments.

"Before I begin, I want to set a few ground rules. First, please do not interrupt me. It's going to be hard enough sharing my story with you. An interruption might mess me up completely. And second, I beg you not to judge me too harshly."

"I promise not to interrupt...but I can't make any other promises."

And so, Miss Avenelle began.

She was sixteen. An innocent. But she thought she was tough. When Rock Bonner, older by four years, began to flirt with her during cheerleading practice, she blushed with pride. He was a volunteer assistant football coach —he'd played quarterback in high school, so the official coach allowed him to assist. He'd been everybody's heartthrob. But Bessie Jo caught him, caught him with a baby, and that baby turned out to be Willa Jo.

Willa Jo was just three years old; prettiest child in the world with those dark curls and green eyes. She was a pistol, even then, according to Miss Avenelle. Bessie Jo didn't seem to know quite what to do with the child. Neither did Rock.

At first, the teasing had been just fun. She flirted back with him, sure of herself. She was pretty and had a good figure —plus, she was a cheerleader and good student. She had a bright future ahead of her. She could play games and lead him on —after all, he was married and older. Yes, her own future looked bright. Until Rock Bonner stopped it in its tracks.

He dared her to go drag racing with him. Said he had the fastest car in town. She jumped at the idea, told her daddy she was going to a friend's house to study; instead, she hopped into a fire-engine red Camaro, taken right off Rock's daddy's car lot.

Speeding down the highway with a handsome boy in a 'stolen' car had thrilled her and 'the crazies' came out in full force; she screamed and laughed like a wild tiger. The faster Rock drove, the more frightened she became and the laughter and screaming grew louder and louder. She felt out of control, but Rock seemed to like her that way.

What happened next was as predictable as rain. His daddy thought the car had been stolen, so he called the police. Just as they were dragging with a green Mustang, Avenelle heard the sirens. She figured they were for the racing, but they were for a lot more than breaking the speed limit.

Avenelle and Rock were arrested. Of course, once Rock's father figured out it was his *son* who had 'borrowed' one of his cars, he dropped all charges. But Avenelle's dad wanted to teach her a lesson — she'd lied, been racing with a married man and had been running wild in general; at least, that's what her father thought. Let her get finger-printed, let her see how serious the police took infringements on the law. That would settle her little butt down.

But it hadn't. Her father's strategy had the opposite effect. She saw Rock every day after school —they had a bond. They'd been arrested together. Before she knew what was happening, they were kissing behind the stadium, then sneaking off to Cherry Hill, a local cemetery where all the couples parked on Saturday nights. Rock Bonner had seen the effect of 'the crazies' and he liked it. He liked her, Avenelle. He called her his little 'wildcat.'

Soon, Avenelle found herself pregnant.

She told her mother, swearing her to secrecy. But her mother didn't keep the secret and her father found out about the pregnancy. She would never forget their one conversation about it.

"I suppose you are thinking about an abortion. Well, young lady, not so fast. You will have to live with the consequences of your actions. You will have this baby. I've already made arrangements. You leave tomorrow on the train to Akron, Ohio, for the Maple Knoll Unwed Mother's Home. I've arranged for everything." Her father's face had looked hard as stone and she knew there'd be no arguing with him.

She was filled with shame and too cowed to fight against his plan for her. Just as he'd said, the very next day she was on the train to Akron, her small suitcase packed with gowns and two pairs of maternity pants, a couple of big blouses and a one hundred dollar bill hidden in the side pocket. She figured her mother had stashed her egg money there, just in case. Avenelle thought about taking that money and heading west. But she was too scared. Her parents knew best...after all, they hadn't messed up---she had.

Her father explained what would happen when Avenelle got to Ohio: when she went into labor, they would knock her out with some kind of drug. When she woke up, it would all be over. She would never lay eyes on her baby, hold it or touch it. She would recover and come home as if nothing had ever happened. The baby would be put up for adoption.

But Avenelle wasn't sure she wanted to give her baby away. She wasn't sure of anything. And she knew her life would never be the way it was. She'd never come home as if all of this hadn't happened. She'd never forget.

Avenelle became pregnant in the spring. Rock brought her bouquets of daffodils and dogwood blooms. They'd made out on Cherry Hill with the trees in blossom. However, her baby would be born in deepest winter.

The head mistress at Maple Knoll was Miss Ivy, a middle-aged, heavy-set woman who meant business. Miss Ivy was no-nonsense herself, and would put up with no nonsense from the dozen or so girls in her charge. She discouraged friendships, giggling, chatting about boyfriends, singing — anything that might resemble joy or life or happiness. She wanted these wayward girls to be miserable, right until the moment they were released from her care.

Miss Ivy spent a great deal of time explaining the home's rules and procedures. When a girl's time came, when the pains were about five minutes apart, she was to get her bag and walk to the bus stop on the corner. From there, she rode the eleven blocks to the hospital. There were no transfers, just a direct and simple route. No one was to accompany the girl. This was to be a journey she took alone.

Miss Ivy kept a special 'waiting' room used by the girls in labor. No one else could enter the room, only the girl who was about to deliver, only the girl in pain. An old iron twin bed had been transformed into a day bed — someone had painted the frame bright yellow and had covered the mattress with a green and yellow sheet. Huge pillows matching the vibrant design covered the back wall, making the bed into a sort of couch. The delivering girl was allowed to lie on this special bed — the brightest, most cheerful item in the whole house — before she made her trip to the hospital. Avenelle saw many a girl enter that room, never to be seen again.

Breakfast was served promptly at seven a.m. Any girl who was more than two minutes late would have to wait for mid-morning snack — a boiled egg with some fruit. Lunch was at noon, then afternoon snack and dinner at six sharp. During the day, the girls cleaned the house, learned to sew and knit, read Biblical texts and prepared meals. In nice weather, they tended the garden and the yard. Avenelle discovered she had a talent for growing things and she loved working in the garden when she could. She obeyed every rule and promised herself she would do so for the rest of her life.

Late one January night, Avenelle felt the first pangs of labor. She informed Miss Ivy, who suggested that she wait in the special room until things were farther along. So, Avenelle reclined on the daybed and traced the green and yellow flower design with her finger. She was alone and scared to death. She could hear rain on the roof, or sleet or hail — something pelted down for most of the night. When her pains were coming more quickly, she left the 'waiting' room and moved as quietly as possible to Miss Ivy's room.

"Miss Ivy? It's Avenelle again. Sorry to bother you, but I think it's time to go."

"So, run catch the bus. And don't forget your bag."

Avenelle wrapped up in her coat and hat, pulled on her gloves and picked up her suitcase. The bus stop was a block away. When she opened the front door, she gasped. Ice almost an inch thick covered the stoop, the sidewalk. The trees drooped with the weight of it, and a few limbs had fallen. She went back inside.

Once again, she tiptoed to Miss Ivy's room.

"Miss Ivy? I'm really sorry to bother you again, but the ground is covered in ice. I don't think I should walk to the bus stop. I might fall."

"Oh, by all the saints! Wait a minute — I'm coming."

Miss Ivy lumbered from her room wrapped in a fuzzy red robe with fuzzy red slippers. She opened the front door, took one look and turned to Avenelle.

"You'd better call a cab," she said as she went back to her room. She returned quickly with a twenty-dollar bill which she handed to Avenelle. "The fare will be charged to your father, missy."

Avenelle took off her coat and stood very still. Another labor pain was coming. It felt like menstrual cramps only much, much worse. Avenelle waited as her belly hardened, the pain increasing and increasing. Finally, the spasm let up. She dialed the number to the Yellow Cab Company and was told to wait, the cab would be there as soon as possible.

She waited two and a half hours as the sleet piled up, pelting the house, the sidewalks and the streets.

Finally, the cab arrived and the driver had to help her into the car. He drove as quickly as he could, but the roads were in terrible shape. Then, suddenly, boom! The car veered to one side. Avenelle screamed.

The cabby cursed and stopped the car. He turned around to yell to her — 'Flat — will take just a minute.' Avenelle felt another contraction coming. She tried to breathe the way Miss Ivy had told them to breathe, but she couldn't control her breath. All she could do was bear the pain and hope they would get to the hospital in time — she did *not* want to give birth in this taxi! She prayed for protection while the cabbie changed the tire. Finally, he hopped back inside and off he drove, but slowly, carefully. Avenelle could feel the car sliding as the driver rounded a curve. She felt a gush of warm water down her legs.

"Can you hurry, sir?" she said to the driver.

"One more block, ma'am. Hold on."

Once they arrived, there was no time to lose. Avenelle was in terrible pain and she felt her bones break open, actually felt her pelvis widen and the baby's head pushing its way between her legs. The ER nurses took her straight back to the delivery room. The doctor got her on the table and suddenly, she was giving birth. Grunting and screaming, she brought her baby into the world.

The nurses cleaned the baby while the doctor stitched her up. One of the nurses must have been new or perhaps didn't know Avenelle was a girl from Maple Knoll. Whatever the reason, the nurse placed the wrapped bundle into Avenelle's arms.

"It's a little girl. Beautiful, too," the nurse said.

Avenelle took her daughter and stared at what her body had produced — a perfect baby with dark, thick hair and big blue eyes. Unlike many newborns, this baby was not all wrinkled and ugly. This baby was truly beautiful. Avenelle touched the baby's face, her hands. The baby grabbed Avenelle's finger and held on tightly. Avenelle had never loved anything so much in all her life. The love came to her like a huge wave, washed over her and transformed her. She was a mother and she knew she would do anything, everything, to make sure her baby survived and was happy. She would die for this little bundle. How strange. She'd thought she'd been in love with Rock, thought she loved her parents. But those connections were nothing compared to this new feeling, this fierce love she felt for her baby.

Avenelle held her baby for twenty-three minutes. She watched the time tick by as the doctor finished up. When he looked up and saw that Avenelle had her baby in her arms, he abruptly told one of the nurses to take the baby away, telling Avenelle it was time for the baby's feeding, as Avenelle would not be feeding the baby herself. The nurse took the baby from Avenelle's reluctant arms.

Avenelle never saw her daughter again.

Clarissa watched Miss Avenelle's face as she told her story. Her eyes were sad and full of disdain. Clarissa could hear the self-hatred in her voice. Telling the story was not easy for Miss Avenelle. Any words Clarissa might say were stuck in her throat.

"In those short minutes with you, I memorized everything about you that I could — your soft tuft of brown hair, your curious blue eyes...I touched each finger and toe. I kissed your eyelids and your nose and your pursed-up mouth. You were a miracle to me. I came alive when I held you. And then, the nurse took you away." Miss Avenelle's shoulders trembled ever so gently.

Clarissa suddenly felt sorry for the woman —she'd been so young, so vulnerable. She reached over to touch her on the shoulder, to pat her in sympathy. Miss Avenelle leaned into Clarissa and, without warning, Clarissa began to cry softly. Miss Avenelle held her and patted her back. Then, Miss Avenelle reached for Clarissa's hands and folded her own over them.

"I have loved you for all these years. I know things were not good for you and I'm so sorry. If I could go back and change it all, I would. I would never have left you —no matter what my parents or anyone else said." Miss Avenelle stared hard at Clarissa. Clarissa noticed the hazel color of her eyes —the color seemed to change as she spoke.

"But I can't go back. I can only offer you my love *now*...and beg your forgiveness."

Clarissa continued to stare into her mother's face, almost the way she imagined she might have done as a newborn. As she gazed, the features seemed to rearrange themselves and Miss Avenelle looked sixteen — young and beautiful and everything Clarissa had ever imagined her mother to be.

"I do forgive you — at least, in this moment. It surprises me to say so — I've hated you for so long — not you, but the image of you I had in my mind. But you're nothing like that woman. Maybe…maybe we can become to be friends."

"More than friends. You're my daughter and I've found you at last. You may never come to feel any sort of daughterly affection for me…wouldn't blame you. But I do love you and I want to welcome you into your family. Will you come for Thanksgiving? My husband, Rory, is ready to welcome you, too. He's a changed man since I got arrested. My oldest son, Adam, and his family will be here — they all know about you. Adam said he always wanted a sister….Abel, my youngest, is in Seattle, so he won't be here, but he knows about you, too. We're all ready to welcome you with open arms. Oh, please come." Miss Avenelle rubbed her thumbs over the back of Clarissa's hand

Clarissa thought the woman's voice was a blanket, so soft and gentle Clarissa wanted to curl up in it. Could she face this new family of hers? Was she ready?

"I'll think about it …."

"I hope you'll decide to give me — all of us — a chance."

Clarissa nodded. But she had one more question — one more thing she needed to know.

"What about….what about my father?" Clarissa said, her voice choking.

"Well…of course. He doesn't know about you — not yet."

"It's the man who sold me the Corvette, right? That's what the sheriff told me."

"The very same."

"Oh hell! He should have given me a better deal!" Clarissa said. Why on earth had she said such a thing? A joke, now?

The women fell together, sharing a strained laugh. Clarissa rose to leave and Miss Avenelle walked her to the door. She hugged Clarissa, a long, close embrace that lasted and lasted. At first, Clarissa was uncomfortable with so much affection….she was stiff in Miss Avenelle's arms. Her mother's arms. But her mother didn't release her, just kept holding on. Finally, Clarissa felt herself relax and felt her body molding itself into her mother's body, as if she belonged there. All the tension melted away and she could hear her mother's heartbeat.

Finally, Miss Avenelle broke away.

"You are such a fine woman — I'm so proud of you. I hope we'll see you on Thanksgiving Day. One o'clock. Sharp!"

"Okay," Clarissa said, surprising herself. Yes. The word slipped out involuntarily.

***

As Clarissa drove home, she thought about all she'd experienced — the gentle touch of Miss Avenelle — really, she needed to get in the habit of thinking of Miss Avenelle as 'mother.' Her "mother's" touch, the family who seemed ready to welcome her — she couldn't believe her good fortune. Of course, she'd been hurt too many times to tear down all her protective walls, but here, in this moment, she felt better than ever. She smiled thinking of Rock Bonner as her father — that meant she and Willa Jo really had been half-sisters….no wonder they made such a quick and strong connection.

Willa Jo — humph, just when Clarissa discovered she had a sister, that sister gets herself killed. Not fair. Not fair at all. Yet, the times they'd spent together had been such a delight — and she'd never guessed about Ralph's little fling with Willa Jo. Willa Jo never let on one iota. Why had Willa Jo slept with Ralph anyway? She had more men lined up than anyone Clarissa'd ever known. In her notebook, Willa Jo said Ralph was just a short fling. After a few weeks, when he called to see her again, she turned him down in no uncertain terms. She and Willa Jo weren't friends yet — Willa Jo had only done her hair a couple of times. Maybe she felt guilty about it — not likely — Willa Jo always said guilt was a wasted emotion; it doesn't do anything but make a person feel bad and who needs that? She wrote that Ralph bored her. That would be enough to turn Willa Jo off, no matter how much money a man had. And Ralph could come across as arrogant and condescending. He was even that way to Clarissa sometimes. Willa Jo'd been between husbands — who knows why anybody does anything? Willa Jo was unfathomable, a force of nature. Like the waves, she was never still, always restless, always wanting something.

Clarissa decided to stop at Bonner's Chevrolet on her way home. She wanted to take a good long look at her father. And she wanted to talk about trading cars. But she wouldn't tell him anything. She'd let her 'mother' handle that.

Chapter Fifty-One

"Honestly, the longer I have to wait for something, the longer it takes."

~The Beautician's Notebook

Late November

Two days before Thanksgiving and still no information about that damn camera. Tal hoped against hope the device would catch the killer red-handed. He also realized the camera might not be of any help at all. But he wanted to know, one way or the other. He was getting antsy waiting. He'd sent it to the computer forensic lab up in Raleigh, but sometimes they took six months or more. Luckily, he knew the assistant —one Ms. Louise Callison with whom he'd had dinner several times when duty called him to the capital. And he'd begged Ms. Callison to rush his order. He'd promised her lobster next time and hinted at more. Ms. Callison was eager to oblige.

Only a couple of months had passed since he'd sent the camera, but he'd been hopeful for quick results. He owed it to Willa Jo to solve this case. He'd loved her with his whole heart. No one had claimed that much of him since. All he could think about was how Willa Jo died. And how he'd failed to find the exact circumstance of her death. Hell, maybe he was destined to fail Willa Jo —he must have been a really bad husband because she cut him loose fairly quickly —five years. That's all they had.

His mind returned to the present and to the night he'd spent with Clarissa. Clarissa might be the only other woman he'd met who had the potential to capture all of him. Two women, both of them beautiful, both driving him crazy. Sisters. Never in his wildest dreams....

He drummed his fingers on his desk. Nothing much going on right before Thanksgiving. The real action would start afterwards, when people without enough money for food or heat would try to provide Christmas for their families. There'd be a spate of robberies, pursesnatchings and burglaries — he'd have to attend to them all. But for now, things were quiet.

And quiet gave him time to think.

That night with Clarissa was …well, it was fucking awesome — the way they fit together, the way she made him feel. He felt himself getting hard just remembering her. He should call her, just to check in. Make sure she was okay.

He thought about how angry she'd been with him. Did all men fear a woman's anger or was it just him? Naw. Every man he knew would do almost anything to keep his woman happy. That anger, hell, it could unman even the baddest ass in town.

She might have simmered down some by now, though. She was out on the beach all alone. Maybe she'd welcome a call. He needed a reason.

Hell. Why didn't he think of it before now? She'd want to know about the camera…the possible evidence. Of course.

He didn't have to look up her number — he'd memorized it after his first phone call. Plus, he'd added it to the contact list on his cell. He pushed the button and waited.

"Hello," she said.

"It's Tal. Just wanted to see how you're doing…I…I've been thinking about you…."

"Thinking about me as a woman or as a suspect."

Hell. Still pissed off.

"As a woman. But, speaking of the case, I have what might be a case-breaker." He knew if he steered the conversation toward Willa Jo's death, she'd stay on the phone. She had that curious turn of mind, much like his own.

"Oh? So, tell."

"I'm not that cheap. But I'd be happy to explain everything over dinner tonight," he said, taking charge. What was he anyhow — a mouse or a man? A man, by God.

"Hmmm. Where?"

"Duffer's?"

"I'm not that cheap," she said.

He could hear the smile in her voice. Where, where, where to go? Some place nice, really nice — impressive nice.

"How about steaks at The Brentwood?" Sure, he'd blow a week's pay, but to get her back into his life would be worth it.

"Oh, you really *are* serious about seeing me, aren't you? But I can't go tonight."

Shit. He'd give it another try.

"How about tomorrow?" He kept his voice light and playful. There was a long pause.

"Okay. But I'm only accepting because I want to hear all about the new info…I want to be clear…."

"Understood. I'll make reservations. ?" he said.

"Fine. In the meantime, you can tell me about the case," she said.

"No can do. I want to be there to see your face when I reveal all. Actually, there's nothing to reveal yet, but it's only a matter of time. So, have you talked to Mrs. Young yet?"

"You mean, my *mother.* Yes, matter of fact, I have. She's invited me over for Thanksgiving with her family. I'm to meet my half-brother Adam, and his family. And Miss Avenelle's *husband.* Talk about weird. But, she seemed very happy when I agreed to come."

"Are *you* happy?"

"I've got a thousand different emotions going on — I wouldn't say happy was one of them. I'm curious. Scared. Maybe a little hopeful — that's about it."

"You know, she's a very nice person. This could work out really well for you….if you give it a chance."

"You should come with me," she said.

"Naw, I wouldn't want to intrude," he said.

Damn. She asked him to Thanksgiving — meet the folks. She hadn't even met them herself. Poor thing — she really was terrified. Maybe he should go — for moral support, in case things went south.

"You wouldn't be…I mean, *I'm* the intruder. The unwanted child come home to roost. They won't even notice you are there — all eyes will be on *me.*"

"I'll come on one condition — you call Mrs. Young and make sure it's okay. If she says yes, count me in. Hey, gotta run. Just got a call about a robbery case I'm running down. See you tomorrow night."

The call hadn't gone half bad. He'd see her soon. Maybe he was right — maybe this would work out well for him, too.

Chapter Fifty-Two

"My stars-and-garters, there's nothing to make you pull your hair out like family."

~The Beautician's Notebook

Late November

Clarissa walked onto her porch and gazed at the ocean, which was calm, glass-like. There was no wind and she watch as a couple of dolphins arced out of the water, their gray bodies flashing silver in the sun. The day was warm for November, very different from West Virginia, where she would have needed a heavy winter jacket this close to Christmas. Another thing to love about the North Carolina coast — those mild winters when every morning brought a new gift from the sea —whelks, sand dollars, starfish — Clarissa loved them all.

Tomorrow, she would have dinner with Tal and then, the next day, she would celebrate Thanksgiving with her new-found family. She was terrified and she knew she wanted Tal with her, just in case. Just in case everyone hated her, everyone, that is, except Miss Avenelle...what *was* she supposed to call the woman, anyway?

She pulled out her cell and punched in the numbers she'd written on a slip of paper. She didn't know what she was going to say if Miss Avenelle picked up. She hoped she'd get the answering machine.

"Young's residence," a female voice said.

"May I speak with Mrs. Young, please?"

"Speaking."

"Oh...Mrs. Young, this is Clarissa...your daughter."

"Oh my dear, how are you? I'm so happy you called," said Mrs. Young. "And please, call me Avenelle or Nelle or ....Mom — — whatever suits you."

"Oh...yes, well....I really haven't quite come up with a name for you — I mean, something I'd feel comfortable saying." Clarissa pinched her elbow as she tried to find the right words.

"It doesn't matter what you call me, dear. I'm just thrilled you are coming to dinner ...happy you are willing to allow me into your life...I'll take what I can get." Miss Avenelle's voice sounded like honey.

"How about if I call you Avie?"

"Oh, that's so strange —that's what your father always called me. No one else ever used that nickname. Of course. You most certainly may call me Avie."

"I wanted to ask a favor. I was hoping I might invite a guest for Thanksgiving — Sheriff Hicks. He and I have become friends and...well, to be honest, I think I'll need a friend that day." Clarissa hoped she didn't' sound ungrateful or suspicious or stand-offish.

"The more, the merrier, I always say! Sheriff Hicks is more than welcome —he was very kind to me when I was incarcerated. And I hope you won't mind —I invited your father."

"What?"

"Your father —you know, Rock Bonner. I've invited him, too. I figured you might as well get to know your entire family."

"So...you must have given Mr. Bonner the news...about me."

"Yes...he's thrilled! You know, losing Willa Jo hit him hard. What a blessing to discover his *other* daughter will be in his life now."

"But...but what about your husband? And your son? I mean, what will *they* think if Mr. Bonner is there?"

"My dear, we are a family of miracles. Since he left the church, my husband —Rory —has become a saint. He is perfectly fine sharing Thanksgiving with Mr. Bonner — after all, he's purchased every single car we've ever had from the man. They've talked business many a time," said Avie and laughed.

"That's...that's very nice of him...but what about your son, the one with a family?"

"Adam has always been the kind of young man who does the right thing. Funny, he follows his dad's lead in everything —he always has. If Rory is okay with it, then so is Adam. You're going to like him, I think —and his wife, Pam. And of course, the baby...well, he's not a baby any more —little Kevin."

"Why did you tell Mr. Bonner about me so soon? I thought it would be a while before I had to deal with an actual 'father.' "

"The minute I confessed everything to Rory, we agreed I should tell Rock that you were his beautiful, talented daughter. He's so proud."

"I…I wasn't expecting to have so much of my…er…my..."

"Your family. We're your family — like it or not — we're all you've got. That's what I used to tell the boys when they were teenagers. It's going to be okay, Clarissa dear. Really."

And if it's not, Tal can take me home.

"Well, then, the sheriff and I will see you day after tomorrow. Thanks for allowing me to bring him along," Clarissa said, her finishing school manners kicking in automatically. She set the cell phone on the yellow table next to her Adirondack chair and continued to watch the ocean. The sun beamed down on everything, everyone. She was a part of that everything and she felt the connection. It moved her, this feeling that she belonged…finally belonged… somewhere on this old earth.

***

The night was clear. By six thirty, it was already dark. Clarissa put Mitzy in her kennel and dabbed on a bit of Chanel. That perfume seemed the perfect choice for dinner at The Brentwood —formal and elegant, not a bit sultry or seductive. It went perfectly with the black slacks and demure pink sweater she'd selected. She didn't want to give Tal any encouragement —after all, he poked into her past behind her back. He was not a man she could trust.

Oh, but he was a man she could love, a little voice in her head whispered. No! She was going to find out about Willa Jo —that's *all.*

The little voice answered back —you can't fool me.

"Shut up. I don't even like the man," Clarissa said aloud.

Yes, you do, replied the little voice.

"Well, maybe I like him…but not much." Mitzy whined as if confused about Clarissa's conversation with the air.

"No, I'm not going crazy, girl — just talking to myself…and answering — maybe I *am* going crazy after all." Clarissa, laughed nervously.

She definitely was on edge. She was afraid she'd get within two feet of Tal and rip his clothes off. Alternate scenario, she'd get close and claw his eyes out. Either way, she would be in trouble.

She heard him tapping at the front door. She gave herself one quick look, fluffed her hair a little, and forced herself to walk slowly to answer. She didn't want to seem anxious.

"You look amazing. But then, you always do," he said as he handed her a dozen yellow roses.

"Thanks — and thank you for the flowers — how did you know I loved yellow roses?"

"Lucky guess."

He escorted her to his car, opened the door for her and quickly backed out of her driveway. He turned the music up. Obviously, he didn't want to talk. She sat quietly. She'd let him break the silence.

The Brentwood was a good twenty-minute drive. And, Tal seemed determined not to say a word the entire way. Finally, she couldn't stand it any longer.

"So, what's the news about the case?"

He turned down the radio and cocked his head to her.

"What?"

"The case — what's up with the case?"

"I'm saving that for the main course. So, tell me all about tomorrow. How in the hell did you get invited to the Young's for Thanksgiving."

"She brought me a sweet potato pudding...we talked. She begged my forgiveness and, in a moment of complete insanity, I said I'd come."

"Hmmm, you like people to beg?"

"Absolutely."

He smiled at that. And his smile broke the awkwardness between them. Not that she wasn't still angry with him, but he sure could be irresistible. He told her all about his week, what had been going on at work. She watched the way he handled the steering wheel, with confidence and slow, steady control. Hmm. Even that was sexy. She shook her head. Those thoughts had to stop.

They arrived at The Brentwood. Clarissa loved the look of the old home which had been turned into a fine French restaurant. Inside, the wood paneling around the bar made the place seem warm and vaguely European. Tal had reserved a table in the private dining room. He looked handsome in his suit and tie, his dark hair slicked back. She could smell a sharp tang of lime and something spicy as he pulled out her chair. She couldn't help but think of their night together, what a wonderful lover he'd been, how right they seemed to be for each other. Before he *investigated* her. She felt her anger rise, then fall.

"You know, I'm dying of curiosity." Clarissa ran her fingers through her hair.

"I'm afraid you'll be disappointed—I really don't have anything yet."

"So, this was all a ruse to get me to have dinner?"

"No…I'm not that devious. What I have is a camera…Trudy found it while she was cleaning out Willa Jo's station. A tiny little camera which I hope will reveal everything."

"You mean, you don't have what's on there, yet?"

"Hell, no. I sent it to Raleigh —I don't have the expertise to get the data off it. They take forever…I'm just waiting." He sighed deeply.

"So...this information could blow the lid off —you think it will show what really happened to Willa Jo?"

"I think it's a distinct possibility."

The waiter approached their table, bringing a bottle of wine. Tal took his glass, raised it to her and made a toast.

"To partnership and solving the case."

"Here, here."

The rest of the evening passed pleasantly, Tal making her laugh and telling her about his life, his family, his feelings about Annie Jo and Lawson. Finally, they'd arrived back at her door. She wanted more than anything to ask him inside, but she didn't. He hadn't brought up the fact that he'd investigated her; neither had she. But the subject simmered beneath their conversation, waiting to boil over at any moment.

"Clarissa," he said.

Her name coming from his mouth sounded soft, sexy. The way he said it made her feel as if she belonged to him already. She forced herself to remain aloof.

"Yes?"

"I'm sorry for any pain I caused you…by my investigation. That was never my intent. I hope we can put it behind us. I still think we could have something really special together…"

"Maybe…too early to tell. And you know what they say about good intentions…but no more about it tonight —give me time."

He moved toward her, kissed her on the forehead, whispered 'Okay' and left. She felt the place where he'd touched her had been sealed with a lump of burning coal.

Chapter Fifty-Three

"I thank God for everything — and I do mean everything — in my life. Even the bad stuff makes us think."

~The Beautician's Notebook

Thanksgiving Day

Clarissa paced back and forth, waiting for Tal to pick her up to go to Avie's house for what promised to be the weirdest Thanksgiving ever. She'd changed clothes three times, trying to strike the right balance between cool and confident/hot and nervous/excited and terrified. No matter what she put on, however, she was still as fidgety as a rooster on Saturday night. No outfit could calm her nerves. So, she settled for a royal blue light sweater with black slacks and Mary Jane's. She could only hope her ensemble would send the right message. What *was* the right message? That she was a grown woman. That she'd grown up in spite of her parental lack and she wanted explanations and apologies and love and acceptance. Oh, Tal needed to hurry before she lost her nerve all together.

The ocean was calm, with small waves rippling to shore. Earlier, she and Mitzy'd taken their morning walk and Clarissa plucked a beautiful whelk from the sand. It was large and heavy, its pinkish insides in whorls, she imagined, curling tighter and tighter. She wanted to be at the very center of the shell, safe and cozy, where no human beings could bother her. Her insides were anything but calm or cozy, yet, as always, walking on the beach gave her a temporary peace.

She picked up the shell again as she waited for Tal. She rubbed her thumbs over it. The interior was smooth and cool to the touch. She heard a car door slam shut and knew Tal had arrived. She put the whelk back on the table and hurried down the steps to greet him.

Their date the night before had been chaste and tentative. She tried to hold on to her anger, but somehow, as they talked and laughed, all the rage dissipated, rising into the air like the morning fog. She told him she'd think about the possibilities of their relationship. But there was no thinking to it, really. She was already half in-love with him. With Ralph, she felt secure and treasured, at least, until she found out about his affairs. With Tal, she felt on equal ground, as if she had a real say-so in things and her say-so meant something. They'd argued. So what? For the first time, she realized it was okay to disagree, okay to fight. Okay to be herself.

"Ready?" he said, offering her his hand.

"As I'll ever be, I guess," she said, giving him a weak smile.

He ushered her to the passenger seat and tucked her in. Slowly, he pulled out of the driveway.

"You know it'll be okay, right?" he said, taking her hand.

"No. I don't know any such thing. I'm going to eat my first meal with the family I've always wanted, and I have no idea what to say or how to act. Everyone will be uncomfortable. It might be just awful."

"It won't be. I've come to know the Youngs — what with the investigation and all. They're nice folks. You'll see," he said.

"Humph...I guess...like you say, we'll see." Clarissa didn't want to talk any more. Her stomach was already cartwheeling. She squeezed his hand and they rode in silence.

The front porch of Miss Avenelle's...er, Avie's... house looked festive — yellow and orange mums, even more than the last time Clarissa visited, more pumpkins and squash arrangements, a big wreath on the door with little Pilgrim men and women intermingled with little Native American people. A big turkey fluffed its feathers at the top.

Clarissa reached to ring the bell, but before she could touch it, Avie opened the door.

"Welcome, welcome... let me take your jackets. Go on into the kitchen — everybody always gathers in the kitchen, it seems. Beautiful day, isn't it? Oh, it's just going to be the best day ever."

Clarissa felt Tal's hand on her waist, steady and strong. She was happy he was with her. She couldn't have done this alone. As they walked toward the kitchen, Clarissa could hear talking and laughing — it sounded to her like a slightly rowdy party.

When they entered the kitchen, wonderful smells wafted in the air — spiced cider, onion and garlic, pumpkin pie, turkey — all mingled together in a rich blend. Clarissa wanted to inhale those odors — if you could bottle all that, you could make a million. Avie was taking her by the arm and leading her to an older man standing next to the sliding door which seemed to lead to a large deck.

"Clarissa, this is my husband, Rory. Rory, my beautiful daughter."

"Welcome to the family, Clarissa. Any daughter of Nelle's is a daughter of mine." He held a glass of red wine. It seemed an odd thing to say and Clarissa couldn't tell if he was being serious or if he was having difficulty accepting his wife's long, lost daughter. He was somewhat portly; his face inscrutable. Clarissa quickly shifted his attention from her to Tal.

"And I'm sure you know my friend," she said, turning to Tal.

"Good to see you again, Sheriff...better circumstances than last time, eh?" Both men laughed in a way that showed neither thought the comment was funny. Clarissa glanced around and it seemed everyone was staring at her, everybody waiting their turn.

Clarissa felt surrounded. Avie pulled her toward another older man. She recognized him immediately. Her father.

"Of course, you know Rock Bonner — I know he sold your that fancy Corvette. Here she is, Rock — our girl."

Everyone was smiling. Clarissa's cheeks hurt.

Clarissa didn't know what to say. Before she could get anything out, Rock Bonner wrapped her in a big bear hug. And Avie's eyes had taken on a glassy sheen. Were they all drunk? Crazy?

Clarissa was happy to escape her father's enthusiastic hug as Avie led her to a couple engaged in keeping their young child from destroying the centerpiece on the dining room table.

"This is my oldest son, Adam and his wife, Pam. And that little monkey is Kevin — get off there, sweetheart. I've already promised you can play with it after we have our lunch."

Clarissa held out her hand to her half-brother, who gave it a limp shake. His wife just smiled. Obviously, the woman couldn't think of anything to say to this interloper, this intruder. Never had Clarissa felt more alone, more unmoored, than in that kitchen, with people who were her blood relatives.

Tal was right behind her and immediately began engaging Adam in talk of the Kiwanis Club baseball team. Evidently, Adam was a great pitcher and Tal knew all about it. While the men talked, Clarissa moved toward the boy.

"Would you like for me to tell you a story?" she said. "About a bear and a lion?"

The little boy smiled at her and before she knew it, he was sitting on her lap at the dining room table, laughing as she made funny faces and told the tale. His mother, Pam, sat nearby. When the bear and the lion became friends in the end, the young woman finally spoke.

"You seem to have a way with children."

"I had to babysit a lot growing up."

"You must have come from a big family." Then Pam's face turned bright red as she realized what she'd said. "I'm... I'm sorry. I guess it's hard to know what to say..."

"Don't worry about it. I grew up in foster care. Most of the families I stayed with had other children. Relax...it's okay."

Pam reached out and gave Clarissa's hand a squeeze, looking into her eyes. "You know, finding you has changed this family. For the better. Someday, when we're friends, I'll tell you all about it."

Just then, Avie called everyone to the table. They each had a name tag and it took a few minutes for everyone to find the assigned seat. Avie was at the end of the table nearest the kitchen and Mr. Young — Rory, as he'd told Clarissa to call him — sat at the other end. Clarissa was seated on Avie's right and on Clarissa's other side was her father. Right in the middle. She felt a lump rising. She glanced around for Tal who had settled in directly across from Clarissa with Avie's son, Adam, on his right. Next to Adam, Pam and Kevin.

"Attention! Attention! As you all know, this is a very special Thanksgiving for our family. I'd like to ask my husband to bless the food." Avie's cheeks were bright red and her voice sounded a little forced.

All heads bowed in unison except Clarissa, who was the last one to do so. She could feel Tal's foot against her leg, giving her courage. She had no idea what this former minister might say about her, his wife's love child.

"Dear Father, we are gathered today to give You Thanks for everything. Most importantly we thank You for our family. And we thank You so much for bringing Clarissa home to us. I won't lie. Some of us have struggled to accept secrets that have surprised us. I know I have. But seeing how much joy Nelle has in her heart since finding Clarissa, I cannot, nor will I, stand in the way of their possible happiness. As a younger man, I would not have entertained Rock Bonner at my table after learning about his treatment of my beloved wife. But today, I *do* embrace him. Thankfully, even I have 'matured.'

Rock, too, is part of our family. Indeed, Lord, we are *all* part of Your family. And we thank You for that. Amen."

When Clarissa looked up, she saw Avie mouth 'Thank you' to her husband. He gave her a wink. He didn't seem like the winking kind, but who knew? Anything could happen.

As they were eating and talking and eating and talking, Abel, Annie Jo and little Lawson burst into the kitchen, their cheeks red and their hair going in all directions.

"Surprise!" shouted the young man as he made his way to Avie and enveloped her in his arms.

"Abel! I don't believe it!" she said as she half-rose in her chair to hug him. She looked at the young woman behind him and held out her arms to her, too. "Annie Jo! I'm so glad to see you!"

Lawson was holding Annie Jo's hand but when he saw Avie, he put his chubby arms in the air, reaching for her. "Up! Up!" he said. Avie bent over and picked him up, covering his cheeks with kisses.

"I've missed you, Lawson — I've missed you all."

As the young folks made their way around the table, hugging and glad-handing each person, Clarissa thought how lovely it was, this family of hers. This new, strange, scary yet glorious family. Her throat tightened and she thought she might break into sobs of something like joy.

"Don't want your dinner to get cold so please, go ahead and eat. Annie Jo and I will get our plates in a minute — but first, I want to make an announcement," said Abel as he tapped a spoon against a glass of iced tea.

Everyone grew quiet. Clarissa could see a look of consternation pass over Mr. Young's— Rory's— features and noticed Avie's face grow pale. She wondered briefly what sort of announcement Abel would make — surely, it could not be any more surprising than his mother's announcement about Clarissa herself.

"Mom — Dad — all of you. I'd like to introduce you to my wife and my new son!" Abel said, holding hands with Annie Jo, Lawson in her arms.

Clarissa turned to look at Tal. She knew he hadn't expected *this.* He had on his professional face, the one he used when he interrogated people. Absolutely no emotion. She squeezed his hand, but his fingers felt like a dead fish in her hand.

"You got married?" Avie said. "Well, come here, child! Welcome! Welcome to our family!"

She pulled Annie Jo in and Clarissa could see tears in Avie's eyes as she hugged the three of them. Clarissa glanced over to Mr. Young. His face was hard as stone. His eyes turned coldly to Abel.

"This is some stunt — waltzing in here married and with a child! Haven't you broken your mother's heart enough?" roared Mr. Young. Clarissa could see he was gearing up for a rant and she also saw the hurt in Abel's face. And the anger. Annie Jo looked like she wanted to melt into the wall. Clarissa felt Tal stiffen beside her and noticed red splotches on his neck. Annie Jo was his daughter, even though they weren't all that close. Clarissa was afraid Tal might ask Mr. Young to step outside if he said one more word. Tal didn't move, but she knew he was coiled for action. A quick, deadly strike.

Lawson began to whimper, burying his head in Annie Jo's neck.

Avie stood up, glaring directly at her husband.

"Our son has brought us wonderful news, Rory. He's found a soulmate, someone who will make him happy. He has a son to love, to raise. They've taken the vows of commitment to each other, the same vows you and I took so many years ago. This is Thanksgiving — a time to be grateful for all our blessings. Abel has blessed our lives since the day he was born." She pausing, looking into her son's eyes. Then, she stared a hole into her husband and whispered, "Please don't make me start calling you 'the reverend' again."

Clarissa had no idea what she was talking about, but evidently, Mr. Young got the message. He seemed to deflate, relax. And then, he smiled.

"I'm sorry. Abel, my son, you have a lovely bride and a fine-looking boy — Annie Jo, I'm sorry. Welcome."

Clarissa watched as Abel's face registered surprise, hesitation and then happiness. He hugged his father and brought Annie Jo into their embrace. Lawson continued to cry until Mr. Young lifted him from his mother's arms and held him high in the air. Then, he did the strangest thing. He blew right onto the child's belly. Clarissa held her breath. She was certain the little boy would burst into tears. But he didn't. Instead, he started to laugh, a deep belly laugh that made them all chuckle. Avie moved toward the new family and joined them.

"Group hug! Group hug!" Kevin shouted. Before she knew what was happening, Clarissa and Tal were huddled together with everyone else in the room. Clarissa was next to her father and he awkwardly brought her into the mass of bodies circling the newlyweds. Tal stood behind her make a shell of his body over her. She felt protected and odd and confused. She'd never be able to swallow one more bite of the delicious-looking food. Her whole body seemed electric; even her bones buzzed.

Tal quietly worked his way to his daughter and Clarissa heard him whisper, "Congratulations, honey. I wish you all the happiness there is."

Annie Jo smiled at him.

"I wish Mom could have been there with us…and you, too, Dad. It's just…well, we wanted to do it on our own. I don't know how to explain it…" Annie Jo said.

"Baby, you don't have to explain anything. I know your mom is happy for you, wherever she is. And I'm happy for you, too."

The group began to sway back and forth, talking and laughing and hugging. Annie Jo started to sing — "Amazing Grace." Soon everyone joined in and they kept moving back and forth and singing. Avie was laughing and so was her husband. Clarissa moved over and hugged her, singing softly as they rocked back and forth, back and forth. Clarissa didn't want the song to end, didn't want to let go of her mother. She felt all the anger and hurt and sadness begin to evaporate, like steam from the asphalt in August. She drifted on the voices, drifted beyond all bitterness and resentment, on and on, moored only by the arms around her — her father's arms, her mother's arms, her niece's arms, even Mr. Young's arms, tenuous as they were, all lifting her, lifting her. Annie Jo moved next to Clarissa.

"So, I guess you're my aunt now?"

"I guess so…are you okay with that?"

"Hell, yeah…" Annie Jo said. They both rejoined the singing.

"I don't know about ya'll but I'm damn hungry! Let's eat!" Abel shouted from the center of the crowd.

"Yes!" echoed his father.

And, just as quickly as the family had gathered, they dispersed and returned to their seats. Clarissa watched as Adam made room for his brother and his new sister-in-law. Lawson sat on his mother's lap and ate from her plate. Already, Lawson and Kevin were eyeing one another, getting acquainted the way children do. Soon, all Clarissa could hear was the clinking of silverware and a constant chatter that rose and fell like crickets singing on a spring night. She said very little, except to talk to her father about her car's wonderful performance, which seemed to please him.

But something had shifted within her, something had been sung into being. She felt happier than she could remember, yet sad at the same time. Full of longing and yet satisfied. Sorry for the past, yet hopeful for the future. She couldn't name this new feeling, but she wanted to treasure it forever, keep it buried in her heart. For this moment, she felt loved, completely loved.

Later, the women were in the kitchen clearing away leftovers and loading up the dishwasher. Annie Jo and Clarissa found themselves in the dining room together, gathering stray glasses and knives and forks.

"So, tell me about the wedding," Clarissa said.

"It was awesome. We got married on a boat — the "Skansonia"...so romantic. All our friends from the studio came and Brandi sang. She made me cry, it was so beautiful."

"A boat, huh...I never heard of that. But I'll bet it really was wonderful."

"You could see the Needle and the skyline of Seattle from the front bow. The wedding was at 6 so we got the day and night views. Lawson was our ring-bearer and he did a great job. Marched straight down the aisle, just like I told him. Look," Annie Jo said, holding up her phone and scrolling to find the pictures.

Clarissa could see the sparkling lights of the city, the candles on the tables of the boat and the people sitting in various arrangements. Annie Jo, Lawson and Abel stood at the front of the bow beneath a canopy of flowers. She wore a sort of pale pink peasant dress and he was in jeans with a white button-down collar. Lawson was dressed like Abel, except his shirt was pale pink to match his mother's dress. They made a perfect family.

"You look so beautiful — everything is. I love it."

Annie Jo showed her a few other pictures, telling her about Brandi and the other members of the studio band. She gushed on and on about how wonderful Abel was, how kind, how thoughtful.

"He's great in bed, too."

"Oh. Well. I guess that's good to know."

They looked at each other and burst out laughing.

Annie Jo said, "Too much information, huh?"

"WAY too much!" They laughed until Clarissa thought she couldn't laugh anymore. Her stomach hurt. Annie Jo had tears rolling down her face. Suddenly, Annie Jo stopped.

"It's amazing that you and my mom were best friends and, now, it turns out, you're sisters —I mean, how cool is that?"

"I know…I've been thinking a lot about your mom. How I wish she were here with us —I wonder what she'd say about all this?"

"You know what she'd say — 'my stars and garters, 'Rissa, we're sisters!' "

They laughed again and Clarissa thought it was true — Willa Jo wouldn't have resented her, wouldn't have hated her for being the cause of Rock and Bessie's divorce. Willa Jo loved everybody. She often said she loved too many people, too easily. Especially men. But she couldn't' help herself. Clarissa always thought Willa Jo had been made for love…for sex, too, but her spirit was made for love. She felt close to Annie Jo, closer than she'd felt while Willa Jo was alive. All she knew of Annie Jo then was the troubles she'd caused Willa Jo. She'd never said more than 'hello' to the girl, as Annie Jo borrowed the car or dropped off Lawson for Willa Jo to babysit. Clarissa thought the girl had been taking advantage of her mother; now, however, she began to understand — Willa Jo *wanted* to be with her grandson, and *wanted* to help her daughter.

"It would be cool with me if you and Dad, well, you know…got together. I think even Mom would be okay with it — after all, she loved you both. Dad's never really gotten over her. Maybe you can change that."

"I don't know — it's a little early to think about any kind of relationship…I just recently filed for divorce."

"Man, that sucks. I'm sorry."

"What about you? What are your plans?" Clarissa was uncomfortable talking about Tal with his *daughter.*

"We're heading back to Seattle after the holidays. I'm writing songs for Brandi— she really digs my stuff. I'm learning so much! Abel loves studio work. He says he's finally found the life he was meant to live —with me and Lawson. I never dreamed my dreary old life could turn out so awesome."

Clarissa smiled and gave Annie Jo a quick hug. It was nice to see the girl becoming a woman. No matter what was ahead for the little family, right now things were good. They walked back into the kitchen and loaded the glasses and silverware in the dishwasher, barely squeezing it all in.

"Girls, y'all are gonna have to do another load," Avie said.

Clarissa smiled. Avie sounded just like a mother, giving orders and marshalling the kitchen. She watched as Avie cut pecan and pumpkin pies into wide slices. Annie Jo scooped vanilla ice cream onto each piece and Avie admonished her to be careful carrying them into the dining room. Clarissa picked up two plates and followed Annie Jo. She carefully set each plate down and then placed the dessert forks and spoons at the appropriate places. Avie had told her exactly how it was done, here, in Summerset, North Carolina.

Here, in Clarissa's new home.

***

"I'd say that was one helluva Thanksgiving," Tal said as he drove Clarissa home.

She hadn't said much on the ride to Temple Beach. She was too busy trying to tame the wild beating of her heart. So fast, so fast. As they topped the bridge leading onto the island, she caught sight of a couple dolphins slicing the air, the sun flashing on them. They looked joyous and Clarissa felt just that way —leaping in the sunlight, free of anything but light. She knew the euphoria wouldn't last. Family squabbles, hurt feelings, misunderstandings —these things would be part of her life, too, if she embraced the strangers who were her kin.

"It was wonderful. A little crazy, but wonderful." She'd almost forgotten that he'd had quite a shock that day, too. A big shock. "Are you okay? I mean, about Annie Jo?"

He looked straight ahead. At first, he didn't say a word, but she could see the thin line of his lips pressed together.

"You know — she's my only child. I'd always thought I'd walk her down the aisle…you know, give her away. All that. Now, I guess I never will."

"I'm sorry, Tal. I know it must be hard. What do you think of Abel?"

"Hell, I don't know. He's not exactly perfect… Even his own father seemed put out with him. I really don't know the boy."

"*Man.* He's a man and he's your daughter's husband. I know they're young but it might just work out —she's crazy about him and he seems the same about her. You know, not just any young man would take on the responsibility of a new wife *and* a child."

Tal remained quiet for a few minutes.

"I reckon you're right about that. I'm not sure I would. Okay, so maybe the kid's okay."

"Man!"

"Right…man."

He pulled into the gravel driveway and cut the ignition.

"Thanks for going with me — I know it must have been a little awkward…your ex-father-in-law, your daughter showing up *married.* Dinner with a jailbird." Clarissa caressed his hand, which had dropped to his side.

"We survived. I thought Mr. Young was going to blow a gasket at first. I was ready to cold-cock him if he said one more word about Annie Jo — he's a piece of work."

"Avie reined him right in, though. Did you see it?"

"Avie?"

"Yeah. That's what I've decided to call her — Miss Avenelle seemed too …I don't know…formal. But I don't feel like calling her mother…I don't' think I ever will. Avie seems just right to me…plus, it's what my father called her, all those years ago. I think he still calls her that."

"Whatever works. But please don't start calling me 'Tallie,' " he said, smiling.

"No worries." She paused, not knowing what to say. She really wanted to digest all that had happened that day, sit by the fireplace and have a glass of wine and think. "You know, as much as I'd like to invite you in, I really need some time alone. I need to chill. So, call me later. Okay?"

"Absolutely. I know how you feel. I got a lot of stuff to work out, too. I'll call you soon."

He kissed her lightly. She stepped out of the car and waved as he drove away. She was glad to be returning to her empty house. *Her* house. Though only a few months had passed since Ralph moved out, she hardly noticed his absence. Instead, she embraced the hours alone. She had only one person to please — herself. After twenty-two years of creating a woman Ralph wanted and admired, it felt good to be herself. She climbed the steps but rather than go into the house, she headed out the wooden walkway to the beach.

As always, the view of the ocean meeting the sky lifted her heart. She scanned the water for the dolphins in the gloaming. A few gulls called overhead and the wind carried their cries out over the waves. She walked onto the beach, removed her shoes and felt the cool sand. She wiggled her toes, digging them a little deeper. She began to walk, slowly, without purpose. She wasn't looking for shells or picking up tourist trash. She just strolled beneath the setting sun, the sound of the water washing over her.

She bent over, picked up a handful of water and poured it over her head. She was, indeed, a new creature.

Chapter Fifty-four

"Things have a way of working out — that's what my mama always told me."

~The Beautician's Notebook

Early December

Two weeks after Thanksgiving, Tal sat at his desk, fiddling with some paperwork. He'd gotten lucky with his search of Mad Dog's apartment. One of Mad Dog's boots had some of that hair stuff on the heel, the same stuff spilled on the floor when Willa Jo died. Tal was pretty sure Mad Dog had something to do with it. The new evidence was enough to charge him, though it was pretty thin. His lawyer would have him out soon.

Tal still hadn't received the results of the video from Raleigh. The Monday after Thanksgiving, he'd put in a call to Louise Callison, but she had no results yet. She'd promised to expedite matters, but Tal had doubts about whether she could. He'd just about given up any hopes of ever getting that video. Without it, he'd have a hard time putting Mad Dog away.

The phone rang.

"Sheriff Hicks, here," Tal said.

"Good morning, Tal —you owe me a dinner —I got your camera footage," said Louise Callison.

"Did it show anything? Do we have evidence?"

"I'm emailing you the clip…You'll see for yourself. I'll send the official version later today. So, when are you taking me out?" Her voice dropped low, sort of purring.

"Next time I'm in Raleigh — some place special, okay — The Angus Barn."

"I happen to know you're scheduled for a meeting with the Sheriff's Association in two months. I'll see you then," she said.

"Thanks, Louise —thanks for all your help. See you then."

Tal quickly opened his email, searching for the message.

There it was. He clicked and read Louise's brief note.

"Shocking I know. See u soon xoxo Louise."

What the hell?

He hit the attachment and then the play arrow.

Willa Jo.

The pain of seeing her alive, captured forever on this tape, made him gasp. He watched and it made him feel like he was right there with her.

She picks up her shears and a bottle of something. Oh, she drops it. The liquid is spilled everywhere — her station, the chair, the floor. She grabs a towel from the back of the chair and wipes it up. She squats to rub what is still on the floor. The towel is too wet — she wrings it over the sink. Then, she walks over to the cabinet to get another towel. She is carrying her scissors. She starts back to continue cleaning, when her left foot slips. She tries to grab the chair, but she misses. She falls, landing on the shears. She doesn't breathe. She doesn't move. She dies. Soon after, Avenelle Young walks through the front door of the shop. She sees Willa Jo, turns her over to check whether or not she's alive. She backs away from the body, her face ashen and looking terrified. She searches Willa Jo's station, then leaves the range of the camera.

The feed cut off.

Tal sat in his chair, stunned. An accident, just like he'd thought. He'd known it in his gut from the beginning, but, of course, he'd had to investigate, follow protocol. He felt relief. But he also felt a vague sense of disappointment. Let's face it---he liked solving puzzles and this one felt like a sort of trick. But then, at least there was no one to blame, no one to arrest. He sat there a moment, trying to clear his head. Seeing Willa Jo alive for a moment hit him hard. With a quick snap, he stood and hurried to the jail next door.

Mad Dog.

Luckily, he'd only been locked up a few weeks but still, Tal hoped he didn't have a lawsuit on his hands.

He placed his weapon in the locked box outside the jail, pushed the combination to get in and entered.

"Morning, Sheriff," said Deputy Colleen Turner.

"Morning — listen, I want you to start the paperwork to release Mr. McGee. He's innocent. I'm going to speak with him now."

"Yessir. You'll have it by noon."

"Thanks, Colleen," he said.

He entered Mad Dog's cell.

"Well...m-morning, sheriff. I hope you come to let me outta here, since I ain't g-g-guilty of nothing."

"I'm here for just that, Mr. McGee. Once the paperwork's finished, you'll be free to go. That should be around noon — I've put a rush order on it."

Tal watched as Mad Dog's face lit in a grin. His curly red hair didn't look like it had been combed for weeks and he'd grown a scruffy-looking beard, also carrot-red.

"It's about d-damn time. I told you I would never have hurt my Willa." Mad Dog's face was bright with the thought of freedom. Tal could almost see the gears working in his brain.

"So, who done it?"

"I guess you could say Willa Jo did it."

"What? What the hell does *that* mean?"

"Willa Jo had a security camera installed —you didn't know about it?"

"Naw. She never told me m-much about work or what she was up to."

"Well, Trudy recovered it. We just got the results from Raleigh — Willa Jo's death was an accident — she spilt some stuff and slipped. Fell. Landed on the scissors."

Mad Dog was quiet. He hung his head for a few moments. Then, he glared at Tal.

"I ought to sue your ass."

"Reckon you have a right."

Again, the wheels turned in Mad Dog's head and he seemed to reach some sort of decision. Tal sure hoped Mad Dog wouldn't be so pissed he'd force them to trial. He was surprised when Mad Dog gave him a small grin and offered his hand.

"Reckon I ain't the suing kind, sheriff. You was just doing your d-duty. I can respect that. I got to get back to my cars...I've missed at least two races. But that's okay. They say sometimes it's good to take a b-break — you come back stronger than ever."

"I hope that will be the case. I'll have the deputy bring your clothes so you can go ahead and get ready." The two men shook hands.

"No hard feelings," Mad Dog said.

"Thanks."

Tal turned to go.

"Say, sheriff, you know them scissors? She kept em razor sharp. When she was new on the job, she cut off the tip of her finger with them scissors."

"Yeah. That was back when we were first married — I'll never forget it — her bleeding all over everywhere, screaming and crying. Ironic, isn't it?"

"Yeah."

Tal could tell he didn't have a clue what 'ironic' meant. He'd be glad to get rid of Mad Dog, once and for all, he hoped.

"By the way, sheriff, if you ever have any extra c-cash, you know, a little investment money, I sure hope you'll c-onsider me and my racing c-career. I mean, since you locked me up and all."

"I'll keep that in mind, Mr. McGee. I surely will." Tal walked out of the cell, closing the door.

Chapter Fifty-five

"At the end of the day, I just want a nice glass of wine and the sweet song of the earth."

~The Beautician's Notebook

Early Spring

Avenelle packed a red-checked tablecloth, two bottles of good, French champagne — and not the cheap stuff, either — some homemade chocolate éclairs, a tin filled with melted brie covered in honey and shaved almonds, a box of fancy crackers and four fluted glasses, her best crystal. She placed four wrapped boxes on top of the other items, each with a different colored bow-white for herself, red for Clarissa, pink for Annie Jo and green for Trudy. She threw in some beach towels and a couple of blankets, just in case.

In the months since Thanksgiving, the four of them had grown closer than Avenelle could ever have imagined. Reclaiming Clarissa had changed Avenelle's life, bringing a sense of completion she never would have known otherwise. Her heart was whole again, just as it had been back when she was sixteen, before she got pregnant, before everything went to hell. Each morning, she said a prayer of thanks, bowing to the tree in her back yard. That tree had come to symbolize all the good she knew in the world. The tree was a beautiful part of God's creation and, on her best days, Avenelle recognized that she, too, was part of the vast web of life.

Tonight—the spring equinox—night and day would be in perfect balance —a time of resurrection, new life. And, tonight, the four of them would celebrate Willa Jo Temple's life the way Willa Jo wanted it done. They knew Willa Jo's wishes because they'd all read her notebook and the desires were scribbled right there, written in Willa Jo's own, loopy hand. Maybe it was strange for a person to put her 'ideal funeral plans' in a notebook, but that's just what Willa Jo had done.

Annie Jo had flown in from Seattle earlier, so she could participate in the celebration, leaving Lawson with Abel. Avenelle was so proud because Annie Jo was going to be featured on Brandi's new CD. She'd been singing as well as playing in the band. Avenelle thought of Annie Jo as her protégé. The girl was almost like a daughter to her already.

When Clarissa first approached Avenelle in January about them following Willa Jo's final instructions, Avenelle had been reluctant.

"I know it's what she wanted, but really, what if somebody sees us?" Avenelle said, sitting in front of the fireplace, poking the embers to stoke the flames. It was the day after New Year's and Clarissa was spending a few nights with Avenelle, so they could continue their explorations of one another.

"We'll do it at the east end —nobody's ever there until May. It's completely desolate, I promise," Clarissa said.

Avenelle looked at her daughter and thought she was the most beautiful woman in the world. Her hair had grown to shoulder-length and was a sort of mahogany color. Deep, deep brown with a reddish undertone. Clarissa let all the blond go and often wore her hair swept up in either a sophisticated French twist or a loose ponytail. She didn't' wear as much make-up as when she was 'Mrs. Ralph Myers.' She told Avenelle she liked her face, so why cover it up with gobs of powder and eye shadow. Now, she wore a red lipstick and a little blush —that was it. She looked younger.

"But we'll be *naked*! Naked out in public!"

"That's the plan. Look, it's a little weird for me, too. But it's what Willa Jo wanted. She wanted to do it herself, with her friends. But she can't. She's gone. We've got to do it for her."

Avenelle couldn't imagine stripping down to her birthday suit under the light of the full moon and dancing in the sand. What had Willa Jo been thinking? Avenelle felt glad she no longer had to preserve her reputation as a preacher's wife. She would never have considered such a thing if Rory was still 'The Reverend.'

"Annie Jo said she'd fly in for it, if you'll do it, too," Clarissa said. "Please...won't you do it for me and Willa Jo? Please?"

Avenelle was completely taken aback by Clarissa's begging. Neither of her sons ever begged for things. They might have asked and hinted and left notes but they'd never begged like this —this was a woman-thing. And Avenelle had no defense against it.

"Oh...all right. When are we going to get ourselves arrested for indecent exposure?" Just what she needed— another jail sentence. The Summerset gossips would have a field day.

"No worries —I have a special 'in' with the sheriff's office. There will be no patrol cars at midnight on March 19, I promise."

"You know you're the only person in the world who could talk me into this, right?"

"Yep, I know." Clarissa gave her a quick peck on the cheek.

That was two and a half months ago. As the time passed and the equinox approached, Avenelle found herself getting more and more excited about their escapade. She started planning to make this truly a night they would remember. That's when she decided on the champagne and all the rest.

She did not tell Rory what they'd be doing — she explained, instead, that they were going to watch a movie Even though Rory was a changed man since leaving the ministry, she didn't think he'd changed *that* much — not enough to okay his middle-aged wife frolicking naked on the beach in the moonlight. No, better for Rory not to know *everything* she was up to.

She glanced at her watch. Annie Jo was picking her up at eight. She tried to lift the picnic basket but with the champagne bottles, the basket was too heavy. She called Rory to help her.

"Why do you need all this stuff just to watch a movie? What are you gonna do —make camp?" he said as he struggled with the basket out the front door. He put it on the nearby table. "You need help getting it into the car?"

"No. I think Annie Jo and I can handle it —thank you, sweetie."

"You and that Annie Jo are getting along pretty good, huh?"

"*That* Annie Jo is your daughter-in-law, Rory. I think it's time you started treating her like family."

"I do. I paid for her airfare."

"You did? I didn't know —oh Rory!" she said, flinging her arms around him.

"Not out here on the front porch, Avenelle —oh hell, what am I saying — why not?" He swung her around and kissed her, a long, romantic kiss.

"You'd better stop that —I'll be tempted to stay home"

Just then, Annie Jo pulled in front of the house. She'd borrowed their car to go shopping and to see her friend, Kayla, who'd just broken up with Mad Dog Tommy McGee. According to Annie Jo, Kayla said all Mad Dog wanted to do was work on his car. He got pretty boring after a few months.

Annie Jo ran up the steps and hugged Avenelle and Rory, too. "Ready?" she said.

"As I'll ever be." Avenelle gave her a secret smile.

"Let's do it then."

Annie Jo picked up one end of the picnic basket and Avenelle got the other. They shouted their good-bye's to Rory and off they drove, the March air brisk and breezy.

"We're going to freeze —probably catch our deaths out there. Are you sure you still want to do this, Annie Jo? We don't have to...I'm sure Willa Jo wouldn't care if we just forgot all about it."

"You getting cold feet?"

"They'll get cold for sure out on the beach."

"Ha-ha. It'll be fun — an adventure. And I'll think you're the coolest mother-in-law *ever.*"

"Well, in that case...."

Annie Jo turned up the radio to the 'golden oldies' channel. "Just for you," she said to Avenelle.

Together, they sang along with Three Dog Night — 'Jeremiah was a bullfrog" —at the top of their lungs. The night sky was clear, except for the creamy color of the moon, which was fat and full and bathing the trees with cool light. Avenelle loved to watch the shapes of the bare trees against the night sky, the limbs like shadows. She'd grown so attached to trees over the past year —the live oak outside her deck, the loblolly pine along the back edge of her yard, the cypress trees in the Greens Swamp as she drove on Hwy 211 —all these had become special to her. In every season, the trees seemed to sing to her. Spring's song, the pale green whisper of 'I'm coming, I'm coming.' Summer's playful melody of crickets and frogs. Fall's sad, sweet song — 'good-bye, good-bye.' And the deep silent song of winter...'rest, rest, rest.'

Annie Jo rolled down her window and sang into the night. Avenelle did the same. They crossed the bridge onto Temple Beach and Avenelle was surprised at how dark the island was — very few houses were lit, only the homes of those who lived on the beach year-round. They drove to Clarissa's familiar house and got out of the car.

They decided to leave the basket where it was; no sense in dragging it all the way up to the house. Trudy's car was already in the driveway.

"Come in, come in!" said Clarissa, meeting them at the door. As always, her house was spotless, but not in an antiseptic way. Mitzy's bed and a few dog toys cluttered the otherwise perfect rooms. Trudy was lying on one of the couches with her feet propped up, reading a paperback. Avenelle caught the scent of something delicious.

"What's cooking? It smells wonderful," she said, sitting on one of the couches. Annie Jo sat next to her.

"I made some stuffed pepper soup — I thought we might need sustenance for our adventure," Clarissa said, stirring a large pot. Avenelle noticed a tossed salad on the table, which had been set formally, with linen napkins, sterling silver and delicate stemware. The china looked antique and valuable.

"Yes, Avie, I pulled out all the stops. After all, it isn't every night you say good-bye to your friend....naked."

"Don't remind me," Avenelle said. "I still can't believe I'm doing this."

"Oh, you love it, Avie — don't pretend." said Annie Jo.

"I must. Here I am."

"Don't you worry, Miss Avenelle. I ain't too crazy bout this naked dancing-on-the-beach mumbo-jumbo myself," Trudy said. "You ain't alone."

"But here you are, Trudy!" Avenelle said, laughing.

They ate with gusto, each telling a story about Willa Jo, something they liked about her and something about how she drove them crazy. Avenelle didn't have as many tales as the others did, but she thought it was good for Clarissa and, especially, Annie Jo to remember Willa Jo. It was healing. Most of the stories were funny and the time passed quickly and pleasantly.

After dinner, they watched *Steel Magnolias.* Though it was an old movie and Clarissa, Trudy and Avenelle had seen it, Annie Jo had not. They all cried when the Julia Roberts character dies and by then, the time had come to head for the beach.

Avenelle, Trudy and Clarissa struggled with the picnic basket, finally managing to hoist it over the dunes and onto the hard-packed sand. Annie Jo carried her mother's ashes in a beautiful blue urn. It was low tide and the moon made a silver trail along the water.

Avenelle felt relaxed and unafraid. They'd had a couple of glasses of wine during the movie, along with buttered popcorn. Plus wine with dinner. Lots of wine for Avenelle, more than she usually imbibed. Clarissa drank water, pouring it into a wine glass, saying she was not sure her stomach felt like it could take alcohol this night. Trudy limited herself to one glass, but she seemed a little tipsy.

Avenelle opened the picnic basket and pulled out the blankets. Annie Jo and Clarissa spread them on the ground. A gentle breeze blew constantly, but they secured the blankets with the champagne bottles and other paraphernalia Avenelle pulled from the basket.

"A feast! Again!" Clarissa shouted. "I'm going to gain ten pounds from this one night!"

"See if you can find some driftwood," said Avenelle.

The younger women set out to scour the beach while Avenelle and Trudy arranged the glasses, the cheese and crackers and the champagne. She'd brought some kindling and matches. Annie Jo put Willa Jo's urn in the middle of the blanket. Funny, Willa Jo seemed to be at the center of everything.

Avenelle lost sight of the younger women. Trudy decided to walk in the opposite direction, saying she needed to be alone. She wanted to think about Willa Jo and this final good-bye.

Avenelle sat on the blanket and looked out at the ocean. The sea was a shade darker than the sky and deep, so deep. The water made her think of all the mystery in the world. How her daughter had been dropped almost on her doorstep. How her husband had become a better man after suffering public humiliation and losing his job. How her black-sheep son garnered success and happiness, almost overnight. All miracles. All mysteries.

Avenelle heard 'the girls,' as she'd come to think of them, before she saw them approaching with a large piece of driftwood and a couple of smaller logs. They laughed as they half-walked, half-ran to the blanket. Avenelle arose and motioned for them to drop the wood a good distance away from where they'd be sitting. Trudy headed toward them.

"Over here — not too close to our stuff. This wind might carry a spark — we sure don't want the fire department out here tonight!" she yelled over the noise of the wind and the surf. They piled the wood they'd gathered and then Avenelle scattered the small bundle of kindling across the top, building the fire the way her father taught her, back when she'd been a kid and they'd camped every other weekend. Once she was finished with the construction, Avenelle struck a match and cupped the flame in her hands. She protected the tiny spark while she held it to the kindling. Soon, the wood caught, and, before Clarissa could open the champagne, a fairly decent blaze burned.

"Okay, ladies —this is it. Almost midnight," Clarissa said, pouring the bubbly into flutes. She handed one to Avenelle first, Trudy next, then Annie Jo, pouring from a bottle of sparkling water for herself. Where had that come from? Avenelle shrugged her shoulders and gazed at the other women as they huddled in a circle, standing on the blanket —her daughters.

"To Willa Jo," Avenelle said.

The others echoed her words and they touched their glasses together. After they'd gulped it down, Annie Jo began to remove her clothes. Clarissa soon followed. Avenelle watched them, their bodies glowing from the moonlight, their limbs moving like liquid silver in the cold night air. Trudy glanced at Avenelle, gave her a what-the-hell look and slipped out of her dress.

"Are you freezing?" Avenelle said.

"Yes!!" they all yelled at once.

"Come on —" Clarissa said, hugging her arms across her breasts as she moved toward Avenelle. "Come on, Avie —you promised." The rest followed Clarissa. They surrounded Avenelle.

Avenelle allowed them to pull her to her feet and help her off with her clothes. She felt like a queen with her ladies- in-waiting pulling and pushing the jeans and sweatshirt off her body. When she was down to her bra and panties, she shooed them away.

"I think I can manage the rest."

When she was completely in the buff, all the women held hands and began to circle the blanket. They sang "Kum-Ba-Yah" and then "Bridge Over Troubled Water," just as Willa Jo had instructed. They continued singing and dancing, breaking apart to move freely, then coming back together.

Avenelle couldn't explain how she felt, bare beneath the stars. Their bodies looked almost alien —glowing and strange, much like the phosphorescent fish she sometimes caught glimpses of in the ocean. Everything was in sync —the waves, their bodies dancing, the flickering of the fire. Avenelle felt time drop away. Everything dropped away, except the four of them and Willa Jo. Avenelle sensed

Willa Jo's presence, though she'd never been one to believe in apparitions. But on this night, at this sacred place, anything seemed possible.

Annie Jo said, "I feel her — she's here."

"Uh-huh. She here all right," Trudy said.

"Yes…I feel her, too," Clarissa said.

"I was just about to say the same thing — she's here," said Avenelle.

They continued to sing and dance. Avenelle watched the younger women moving slowly and gracefully. She watched Clarissa's body, lean and trim, her small breasts swaying with the rest of her body. The moon shone on Clarissa's belly, which looked round and full. Avenelle didn't remember Clarissa having an ounce of extra fat on her body. What was that little pouch? Was history repeating itself?

"You're pregnant, aren't you?" she said to Clarissa.

Everything grew silent in that moment, except for the constant sound of the surf.

"How did you know?"

"I don't know — I just knew. Are you okay?"

"Yes…I'm only a couple months along—it's taken me by surprise, that's for sure. I never thought I'd be lucky enough to have a child. I'm so very happy."

Avenelle walked deliberately to her daughter and stood directly in front of her.

"Does Tal know?"

"Yes. He wants to get married…I'm not sure…"

"I'm so happy for you, my dearest daughter. I…I can barely contain it." Avenelle hugged Clarissa, their bodies touching, as if Clarissa were a baby and they were bathing together. The feel of her daughter's flesh was delicious — soft and sweet-smelling.

"It feels quite overwhelming…bringing a new life into the world. I can imagine how you must have felt, pregnant at sixteen. How frightened, how completely unprepared. I mean, I'm terrified and I'm a grown woman. But at sixteen? I would have freaked out completely."

Avenelle felt Clarissa's eyes taking her in, measuring her yet again.

"I think I'm beginning to understand you a little bit….Avie," said Clarissa, so tenderly it seemed to Avenelle she'd actually said 'mother'. Of course, that wasn't what Clarissa said — but the word didn't matter. Avenelle could feel the love as Clarissa whispered it — her name, fitting into Clarissa's mouth, fluttering on the wind, going straight to her heart.

Avenelle couldn't speak. She held onto Clarissa, an embrace both fierce and tender. Annie Jo and Trudy joined them, chanting 'group hug' in a loud, excited voice.

Before she realized what was happening, Avenelle began to cry. Soon, Clarissa was crying, too. Even Annie Jo teared up.

"What the hell? Ya'll just feeling Willa Jo — ain't nothing sad here," Trudy said. "Those tears — they the price of love."

The cold wind blew, raising goose bumps on their bodies, but still, they didn't get dressed. Instead, Annie Jo took her mother's ashes and walked to the edge of the water.

The others followed.

She opened the urn and took a handful of the ashes and threw them into the water.

"Thank you, Mom...thank you," Annie Jo said softly

Each woman took handfuls of the ashes and scattered them, returning what was left of Willa Jo to the sea, from whence all life came. When the urn was empty, the women walked back to the blanket and dried themselves on towels. Then, they put their clothes on and sat around, eating the food Avenelle had prepared. As they ate, Avenelle took each of the boxes from the picnic basket and distributed them.

"I think we should go ahead and open them."

She watched as they opened their gifts. Annie Jo tore into hers, crumpling the paper and bow together as she lifted the lid of the small box, while Clarissa meticulously undid the wrapping and slipped off the bow. Trudy ripped off the ends and slipped the box out, like a snake sheds its skin. Avenelle waited until the others finished, then she opened her own gift.

Inside each package was a gold necklace with a filigreed butterfly on the chain. Two small opals graced the wings and a tiny diamond was set into the center of the body.

"Damn," Trudy said.

"It's ...it's beautiful ....so beautiful," Clarissa said, staring into the box.

"It is! Oh, Miss A— thank you, thank you so much," said Annie Jo.

“Each one is identical — so when we wear them, we’ll think of each other and Willa Jo… and this night. I’m so glad you talked me into this …there are no words.”

They fastened the necklaces on each other, packed up their things and slowly walked toward Clarissa’s house. Avenelle turned once more at the top of the walkway to look at the beach, where Willa Jo’s ashes had already melted into the sea. She heard the others calling her into the house for coffee. She turned away from the water, but the ocean wouldn’t release her just yet. She looked out over the waves one more time.

Water. Sand. Stars. Moon.

Everything…..

Afterword

This book began as a story about Willa Jo and her crazy ways, but quickly evolved into a story about mothers and daughters and secrets. I don't have a daughter, but I am lucky enough to have two lovely granddaughters. I can see how tricky, yet strong the mother/daughter bond is. I'm very fortunate to have my own mother still with me; she's ninety-three. My fondest days are the ones where we go shopping and out for lunch — rare, but special days that remind me of all the times we've shared. I'm not sure she has always understood me, but I have no doubt that she's always loved me. What more could a daughter ask?c

CPSIA information can be obtained
at www.ICGtesting.com
Printed in the USA
BVHW030555140720
583602BV00005B/678

9 781945 181115